Praise for Katherine Reay

"*The Printed Letter Bookshop* is both a powerful story and a dazzling experience. Katherine Reay has the rare ability to delve into her characters' private worlds with such clarity that they come alive on the page. Truths are slowly revealed as Reay peels back the layers of her characters and of our hearts. This novel skillfully knits together family, forgiveness, and redemption with the understanding that books can change our lives and mend our souls. As three women come together in a charming bookstore that needs saving, they discover that they might just save each other with the power of friendship and community. I want to give this book to every woman I know—I adored falling into Reay's world, words, and bookstore. Powerful, enchanting, and spirited, this novel will delight!"

—Patti Callahan, bestselling author of *Becoming Mrs. Lewis*

"*The Printed Letter Bookshop* is a softly elegant and invitingly intricate ode to books and the power of their communal solace. With the charm and insight of Nina George and the sheer reckless book love of Jenny Colgan, *The Printed Letter Bookshop* enfolds the reader in a welcome literary embrace. Reay's natural talent of putting the reader at ease in her fictional world is evident from the first page. But the story is also deceptively accessible, for the moment you fall into its continued spell, you are confronted by a mature narrative that allows three remarkably different women to become the unlikely heroines of their own stories."

—Rachel McMillan, author of *Murder in the City of Liberty*

"Dripping with period detail but fundamentally a modern story, *The Austen Escape* is a clever, warmhearted homage to Austen and her fans."

—*Shelf Awareness*

"[*The Austen Escape*] is a charming romp full of dancing, misunderstandings, and romance."

—*BookPage*

"Reay's exquisite phrasing will resonate with readers and provide much fodder for pondering . . . Overall, this is a beautifully written novel and one to be savored and enjoyed."

—*RT Book Reviews*, 4 stars, on *The Austen Escape*

"Reay handles . . . scenes with tenderness and a light touch, allowing the drama to come as much from internal conflict as external, rom-com–type misunderstandings . . . Thoughtful escapism."

—*Kirkus* on *The Austen Escape*

"A romp among contemporary Austen fanatics. Readers eager for anything Austen-related will enjoy this clean romance that explores the concept of escapism and what it may reveal about our real lives."

—*Publishers Weekly* on *The Austen Escape*

"[*The Austen Escape*] seamlessly blends modern-day characters into a backdrop of Regency-era England. Readers who like Tamera Alexander and Jane Austen will enjoy this book."

—*CBA Christian Market*

"Katherine Reay's writing shines in this modern tale that's sure to please fans of regency fiction. Admirers of Jane Austen, especially, will delight in the delicious descriptions and elegant prose as the protagonist is transported to the English countryside, taking readers along for the ride. Both cleverly written and nicely layered, Reay's latest proves to be a charming escape!"

—Denise Hunter, bestselling author of *Sweetbriar Cottage* and *Blue Ridge Sunrise*, on *The Austen Escape*

"At once sophisticated and smart . . . Clever and classy . . . Whether for the first-time *Pride and Prejudice* reader or the devotee with an ardent affection for all things Austen . . . *The Austen Escape* is an equally satisfying retreat into the wilds of Jane's beloved Regency world . . . As amiable as an Austen novelist could be—but with a pen just as witty—Katherine Reay proves she's ready to become Jane to a whole new generation of women."

—Kristy Cambron, bestselling author of *The Lost Castle* and the Hidden Masterpiece series

"Wildly imaginative and deeply moving, *The Austen Escape* is Katherine Reay at her very best."

—Billy Coffey, author of *Steal Away Home*

"*The Austen Escape* has the remarkable ability to be both lighthearted and gripping. The dramatic elements are first rate, the characters even finer. Wonderful writing. Highly recommended."

—Davis Bunn, bestselling author

"Reay's sensually evocative descriptions of Italian food and scenery make this a delight for fans of Frances Mayes's *Under the Tuscan Sun*."

—*Library Journal*, starred review, on *A Portrait of Emily Price*

"Another rich, multilayered story from Katherine Reay. This is a lovely tale that will nest in the reader's heart and won't let go."

—*RT Book Reviews*, 4 1/2 stars, TOP PICK!
on *A Portrait of Emily Price*

"Romance novelist Reay (*Dear Mr. Knightley*) crafts another engaging and sprightly page-turning bildungsroman. The American-goes-to-Europe plot is a real chestnut, familiar but nicely revived by Reay, who hits a sweet spot between adventure romance and artistic rumination; the novel finds a fantastic groove where chick lit meets Henry James."

—*Publishers Weekly*, starred review, on *A Portrait of Emily Price*

"*A Portrait of Emily Price* is a portrait of grace and love. Reay expertly weaves a story rich in taste and sight, wrapping it all with sigh-worthy romance. Reay is carving her name among the literary greats."

—Rachel Hauck, *New York Times* and *USA TODAY*
bestselling author of *The Wedding Dress*

"Katherine Reay is a remarkable author who has created her own subgenre, wrapping classic fiction around contemporary stories. Her writing is flawless and smooth, her storytelling meaningful and poignant. You're going to love *The Brontë Plot*."

—Debbie Macomber, #1 *New York Times* bestselling author

"Book lovers will savor the literary references as well as the story's lessons on choices, friendship, and redemption."

—BOOKLIST ON *THE BRONTË PLOT*

"Quotations and allusions flow freely in Reay's third tribute to the female giants of English literature. Fans may find themselves unearthing their classic novels after savoring this skillfully written homage."

—*PUBLISHERS WEEKLY*, STARRED REVIEW, ON *THE BRONTË PLOT*

"Reay treats readers to a banquet of flavors, aromas, and textures that foodies will appreciate, and clever references to literature add nuances sure to delight bibliophiles. The relatable, very real characters, however, are what will keep readers clamoring for more from this talented author."

—*PUBLISHERS WEEKLY*, STARRED REVIEW, ON *LIZZY & JANE*

"Katherine Reay's *Dear Mr. Knightley* kept me up until 2:00 a.m.; I simply couldn't put it down . . . If you've read Jean Webster's charming epistolary novel, *Daddy Long Legs*, you'll know where this is going. Webster wrote her book in 1919; *Dear Mr. Knightley* is a brilliant update. I absolutely loved the story of a rigidly bookish young woman who comes to know herself—not to mention the real Mr. Knightley."

—ELOISA JAMES, *NEW YORK TIMES* BESTSELLING AUTHOR OF *ONCE UPON A TOWER*

"[*Dear Mr. Knightley*] is an intriguing story told through letters the heroine writes to her benefactor. It is enjoyable to watch her learn about life, gain maturity, and, in the end, find love. A lesson readers will learn from this engaging novel is that it's not so much where you come from but where you're going that matters."

—*RT BOOK REVIEWS*, 4 1/2 STARS, TOP PICK!

"Book nerds, rejoice! *Dear Mr. Knightley* is a stunning debut—a first-water gem with humor and heart. I can hardly wait to get my hands on the next novel by this gifted new author!"

—SERENA CHASE, *USA TODAY*'S HAPPY EVER AFTER BLOG

The Printed Letter Bookshop

Other Novels by Katherine Reay

Dear Mr. Knightley

Lizzy & Jane

The Brontë Plot

A Portrait of Emily Price

The Austen Escape

The Printed Letter Bookshop

Katherine Reay

Thomas Nelson
Since 1798

The Printed Letter Bookshop

Published in Nashville, Tennessee, by Thomas Nelson. Thomas Nelson is a registered trademark of HarperCollins Christian Publishing, Inc.

Interior design by Lori Lynch

Thomas Nelson titles may be purchased in bulk for educational, business, fund-raising, or sales promotional use. For information, please email SpecialMarkets@ThomasNelson.com.

Publisher's Note: This novel is a work of fiction. Names, characters, places, and incidents are either products of the author's imagination or used fictitiously. All characters are fictional, and any similarity to people living or dead is purely coincidental.

Library of Congress Cataloging-in-Publication Data

Names: Reay, Katherine, 1970- author.
Title: The printed letter bookshop / Katherine Reay.
Description: Nashville, Tennessee : Thomas Nelson, [2019]
Identifiers: LCCN 2018055368 | ISBN 9780785222002 (softcover)
Subjects: | GSAFD: Christian fiction.
Classification: LCC PS3618.E23 P75 2019 | DDC 813/.6--dc23 LC record available at https://lccn.loc.gov/2018055368

Printed in the United States of America

19 20 21 22 23 LSC 5 4 3 2 1

For all my dear friends—

Thank you!

For the present is the point at which time touches eternity.

—C. S. Lewis, *The Screwtape Letters*

Chapter 1

Madeline

People parted around us in the courtyard. No one stopped to say anything—why would they? No one had ever seen us before. I paused, hearing something about champagne and a celebration. I was sure I was mistaken. Two women slid around me into the sea of black. From behind they appeared an unlikely pair. One stiff, as if held up by a single rod, while the other walked with the grace of a yogini. Black pants swirled around her ankles.

At the close of the service, we had walked back down the aisle, heads straight, following Dad's lead. But once we spilled out into the stone entryway, the crowd separated us. I looked around for Mom and found her several feet away, talking to a group of women. One reached out and held her arm, as if Mom needed consolation. Perhaps she did. She was the only one in our family who had kept in touch with Aunt Maddie over the years.

The icy rain had stopped, but the clouds felt no less foreboding. The sleet or snow would soon return. Dad watched the sky for a long time. So long, I tipped my head back as well.

"Almost twenty years." He dropped his gaze and stared at me. "That's how long since I spoke to my sister before last month, but she didn't tell me. She said she was calling to say she loved me." He gripped the back of his neck. It wrinkled white under the pressure. "I wouldn't have answered if I'd recognized the number."

His eyes held a rare hint of vulnerability, so I pressed the advantage. "Well, it was about time. It wasn't your fault. None of it."

He cast me an odd, questioning look. Dad, who never questioned. Who held all the answers. "It *was* my fault. Every bit of it. I had never seen her so angry. But I was angry too, and . . . ashamed . . ." Dad breathed in. And out. "I hated that she judged me, but I don't think she did. I don't think she ever held it against me."

"What? What are you talking about?"

His gaze flickered in alarm or pain before it drifted above and beyond me. He shook his head and walked toward the church's circular drive.

Bits of conversation snagged me as we passed.

"Isn't there a reception?"

"What about her house?"

"Her brother should host one. Didn't she have a brother?"

"No . . . That was Pete's brother in the front row. Maddie didn't have any family."

I looked to Dad and wondered if he'd heard. If those women had done the same, looked at my dad, they would have seen he never could have been Uncle Pete's brother. He and his sister shared the same deep-set eyes, eyebrows, and nose. Her "Irish twins," Granny Caoimhe called them. They looked alike, walked alike, laughed alike. Both bit the side of their cheek when deep in thought, narrowed their eyes when something didn't sound right, and laughed loudest at their own jokes.

Though, if I remembered correctly, Aunt Maddie's laugh was more of a contagious giggle that held strong until you caught on and joined her. Dad's, I knew from experience, held a slight condescension—you simply hadn't caught the brilliance of his humor.

Mom reached us as their driver pulled to the curb. "Maddie was certainly adored. So many people. Shouldn't we go by her house to make sure it's okay? Houses don't like to be left alone."

Dad opened the car's door. "I haven't heard from her lawyers. Who knows who owns it now? We could be trespassing . . . Madeline?"

I shook my head. "I have no idea. No one has contacted me."

"That's it then. Until told, it's not our concern." He dropped inside.

Mom pulled me into a hug. "I hate leaving you like this. We hardly saw you this trip." She glanced into the dark car.

"It's okay, Mom. You both are busy. I'm busy."

"It's not okay, but I'll be back in four days."

I nodded.

"I land on the seventh, as I'm sure the firm will host something extravagant on the sixth. I'll get myself to your apartment." She gestured to the parking lot. "How are you getting back downtown?"

"I took the Metra up."

"In the rain? Let us take you back before it starts again." She leaned into the car. "Do we have time to take—"

"Don't worry about it." I tugged at her shoulder. They didn't have time before their flight back to New York. And Dad rarely veered from his predetermined schedules.

"Charlotte?" he called as if cued.

She waved her hand into the car. "As I said, I'll be here on the seventh." She curled a finger around my ear the way she used to do when I was young and drew a loose strand of hair forward. She often chided me for being too severe. The gesture made me smile and I leaned into her touch.

"My daughter is about to make partner, the youngest partner I might add, at one of Chicago's top law firms. That's worth celebrating." She pulled me close and kissed my cheek. "It's important to celebrate, to mark occasions, dear. Don't forget that."

"Thanks, Mom."

One more squeeze and she, too, dropped into the car. I was left standing alone, with a sea of black behind me all consoling one another over their loss, and an empty street in front of me. No one knew me. I knew no one. And I wasn't sure what I'd lost.

Rather than turn into the crowd, I let memories of Aunt Maddie wash over me as I stepped across the church's driveway and headed toward the train station. Past the small village square. Past the gas station that had served soft swirls so long ago. I tripped over a shift in the sidewalk and found myself at the edge of the small park I had sat in before the service. I swiped at the bench and dropped onto it again. There was time before the train.

Madeline Cullen Carter. Same name as me, minus the Carter. I'd been named after her and, until that summer, my dad had only spoken of her in glowing terms. He worshiped her. Only thirteen months older, his "crazy" brilliant sister was everything he wasn't. And *crazy* was his highest compliment. I could hear it in his voice. *My crazy sister went skydiving. Skydiving at forty-five . . . She and Pete are headed to Haiti next month to help with relief efforts from Hurricane Gordon . . . She's up to more craziness; she and Pete want to open a bookstore . . .*

Crazy meant bold, daring, fearless. It was a radiant word, endowed with virtue and supernatural strength. For years, I wanted to be called crazy too. But after my last trip, nineteen years ago, the same word, previously laden with excitement, adoration, and a hint of envy, emerged with snarled derision and disgust.

Their retirement savings caused the rift and divided us all. She and Uncle Pete had invested in Dad's Millennium Tech Fund and—like practically every other tech fund in the spring and summer of 2000—it vanished.

But shouldn't she have been more understanding? More forgiving? Shouldn't family have meant more than money? Everyone was hurt when the tech bubble burst. Everyone lost money. Yes, some more than others, but it wasn't the managers' fault. That was like blaming Hurricane Gordon on the meteorologists.

But anger can be as irrational as it is visceral. I felt it at school as my best friends avoided, then shunned me, sure my dad had caused all their parents' troubles. And after we returned from Aunt Maddie's house that summer, the apartment felt as silent and somber as school. Mom and Dad retreated to separate corners to heal. They never laughed, never went out to parties or dinners; they hardly spoke. In my most honest moments, I admit I chose Northwestern Law School in an attempt to push reconciliation. Maybe I was trying to rewrite history and prove people could be forgiving and kind. Maybe I wanted assurance that money, gained or lost, didn't rule the world. New York had taught me otherwise, but Chicago? Maybe . . .

It never happened.

Aunt Maddie occasionally called and invited me to Winsome for dinner, or volunteered to come visit me downtown, but she never mentioned my father, never said it was all okay, never let him off the hook, and never forgave him. And I never pushed it—I shouldn't have had to.

I leaned back against the bench. *It was my fault. Every bit of it . . .* Dad said those very words. How was that true? Aunt Maddie had spent years blaming him for something out of his control.

"Are you okay?"

I bolted upright. Somehow I had missed a bright-red Patagonia fleece standing feet from my face. "I— How long have you been standing there?"

The face above the fleece flashed straight white teeth. The straight teeth led to a slightly bumped nose and remarkable green eyes. His whole face lit with a smile.

"The length of that question. I just came from there." He pointed across the street to the Catholic church's rectory. "The church maintains the park and I was working earlier, but needed to take a break." He used the same hand to sweep behind him. I noted a pile of burlap and a wheelbarrow. As he turned back, he pulled his other hand from his jeans pocket and offered a white handkerchief.

I then felt what he must have noticed—my eyes were sticky and most likely red. He jiggled the handkerchief in front of me until I reached for it.

"I haven't seen one of these since my grandfather died."

"My granddad left me all his. They feel old-fashioned, but I find comfort in that."

"Me too."

"And damsels in distress love them." His eyes were an extraordinary color. They danced with laughter. His voice dripped with innuendo.

"Damsels?" I gave a barkish laugh before I could choke it back and felt myself grow red. I waved toward the rectory. "You're a priest. How is that appropriate?"

His eyes followed my hand, and his smiling face blanched. It had held a hint of tan that I only noticed as it washed away. "Where'd you get that? I'm—I'm the yardman."

He stumbled over his job title as if surprised—or lying.

"Are you?" The lawyer in me awoke.

He leveled his gaze on me, and the eyes glittered again as if he knew exactly what I was doing and found it amusing. But people don't deal straight unless pushed.

"Yes. My brother lives there. Father Luke, he's the priest. You can go ask him who stole half his roast beef on rye if you'd like."

"I believe you." I remembered why I was holding the handkerchief and dried my eyes. I then forgot it was a handkerchief and blew my nose.

He caught my shocked expression and smiled again.

"I think I should keep it now. I can wash it and get it back to you."

He flapped his hand. "That's what you were supposed to do with it. I have plenty."

I scanned the park. We were the only ones out.

"It's not a nice day for yard work." I gestured to the burlap.

He twisted to follow my gaze. "It's not, but it's my job. And if I don't get all these covered today, we might lose some. We weren't supposed to get really cold weather for another week, but we're dipping to the single digits tonight and snow is coming. Shows what the meteorologists know."

"I didn't know it would be so bad when I left downtown. I came for a funeral." I waved my hand in the general direction of the Episcopal church.

"Madeline Carter?" At my nod, he added, "I was there too."

"I'm not surprised. It was packed. She was well known, wasn't she?"

I heard the lift in my question even if he didn't. *Who was she? Really?* After seeing Dad, hearing him, feeling his shame—for that's what had layered him like a thick coat this morning—I wondered if I knew her, or him, at all.

"Well loved, that's for sure." The man pulled pruning shears from his other back pocket and tipped them across the street. "She met me at Luke's about a year ago. She brought me soup, and books. Always books. You?"

"She was my aunt."

His brow furrowed. Years of watching clients had taught me well. My comment either confused or bothered him. Before I could ask, he cleared the emotion from his face. "You sit and I'll leave you be."

Irritation tempered by disappointment.

I shook my head and stood. "I can't." I found myself eye to chin, thinking his was a nice chin. Clean-shaven with a good, firm jaw and straight lines. I liked straight lines. Clear facts. Strong foundations. My gaze drifted north again and, despite his obvious displeasure in me, I found kind eyes—and ears that stuck out a little. That made me smile. Dumbo's ears stuck out too.

I noted that he caught the change in my smile. His eyes flickered a question.

"The train," I blurted. "I have to catch the 12:11 back downtown."

"I'm sorry for your loss." He turned and walked away.

I hesitated, not long enough to get his attention, but long enough to feel silly staring at his back.

Then I did the same; I turned on my heel and walked away, booking it double-time to the train station.

Janet

Ten forty and the church is packed. It should make me happy that everyone feels about Maddie as I do, that everyone loves her and will miss her, but it only ticks me off. I spent every day for the past two years with the woman, and now I can't find a seat from which to send her off. Who are all these people? Where were they these past months? Or these past weeks when hospice came and her house grew quiet with that warm, sticky scent of death?

I can't blame them. I want to, believe me I do. But I can't. Maddie never let anyone know how bad it was. I only found out because I trampled on her privacy, for my own purposes. I had nowhere else to go, so I forced her to let me in.

Each night as we closed up the bookshop I'd ask her, "What are you up to tonight?" She was my employer, and more than ten years my senior, but I secretly hoped that one night she might hear my loneliness and maybe suggest we go out to dinner.

Despite being a widow, Maddie was never alone. "It's bridge night at Suzie's house . . . My prayer group is meeting for dinner at Valley Landing . . . My book club, the former squash players, not the library group, is meeting to discuss *In the Midst of Winter* . . . I'm volunteering at the soup kitchen on Waukegan . . . I'm . . ."

There was always something or someone filling her days—and her evenings.

Until one day I couldn't take it any longer. "Can I come?"

She stared at me, a long smile building until it burst out. It made all the wrinkles in her face dig deep. Maddie's wrinkles were born of a million smiles. She was all horizontal lines, stairstepping into her salt-and-pepper crown.

"That wasn't so hard, was it? I wondered when you were going to ask to join."

"You could've invited me," I fired back.

"And you could stop playing the victim." The words shot out staccato and seemed to startle her as much as they did me. She followed with a quick, "Let me grab my keys," and fled the room.

By the time she returned, her bright smile was back in place and the moment had passed. And though my surprise and anger lingered, to revisit her sharp reply felt petty and beyond pathetic. I kept my mouth shut.

I only remember that exchange because it was one of the rare times I did keep my mouth shut. Maddie used to tease me about "living in the present tense"—allowing no time for reflection or a heartbeat of pause to separate my will and my actions.

She was right. I do live in the present. But I don't see how it's wrong. The past only brings regret, and the future holds nothing bright.

I survey the church. There are two pews in the front draped with red velvet Reserved signs. For family, I assume. They are empty. Figures. When Pete died ten years ago, I didn't hear much about family. I didn't know Maddie back then, but I still attended the funeral. Half of Winsome showed up, and all those groups of women came in hordes to help her. Every book club, volunteer organization, church group, and the town's business association banded together to make sure all her needs were met—well, not all her needs; her husband *had* just died.

But they brought enough food that Maddie didn't cook for almost a year. My husband—my ex-husband—Seth was close to Pete, and to her. It was his idea to give her a trunk-style freezer for her garage. At the time, I balked—I balked at most things in those days. But over the past few months, that freezer came in very handy.

Back then, no family came to honor Pete. And it looks like no family has come today. Not that Maddie didn't call us all family. I can't name a single person in Winsome who didn't love her. The letters framed all over the shop attest to that. They're from kids Maddie taught and tutored, and from friends who were excited about the new bookshop. They are letters of love, which Pete framed and hung when they opened their doors. She could recite each by heart.

But it's not the same—I know. Family means more. You can miss your family so much you have to look down to see your chest rise and fall, to confirm that it hasn't been cut open and you're not bleeding out and you're still breathing. Friends can't hurt you like that, nor can they fill that fissure.

There's a questioning hum around me. People aren't just missing her or whispering about her. They're wondering. I sense it more than hear it.

Did you know? How long was she sick?

No one knew, people. No one knew she got the diagnosis in late July. It's only December! She'd commented about headaches, backaches, stomachaches for the past couple years, then brushed them aside each and every time. *I'm getting old, girls.*

No one knew.

I'd barged in on her in September. The shop's restroom door was ajar and I needed a tissue. I banged it open and landed right on her, slumped over the toilet bowl.

"Maddie, Maddie, Maddie . . . You naughty girl . . . Late night?"

"I wish. My head . . . Everything hurts. How can everything hurt so much? How bad can this get?" She pushed back from the toilet and leaned against the wall.

"How bad can what get?" I whispered and slid down the wall next to her. Her tone warned me Advil could not fix this, whatever *this* was.

"Dying." Her eyes widened as if she'd said "Voldemort."

It felt as hideous and evil as Harry Potter's dark wizard.

She then shook her head—not in an *I can't believe I said that* gesture, but in a *Please don't tell anyone* gesture.

I rubbed her back and I kept her secret.

I LOOK AROUND THE church more slowly this time, corner to corner, and across the nave. I begin to recognize people. Margo from the bank. Veronica Beven and her husband from one of Maddie's book clubs. Lisa Generis . . . Jasper from the gas station. Maddie left her mark on the hearts of everyone here.

For the past couple years, she did more than that for me. She was Seth's friend first. Then, as everyone else in my life drew away, she pulled me close. I felt the press of her every day. She kept me from flying about like ash scattered in the wind. Now she is gone, and I fear blowing away.

Claire, the Printed Letter's only other full-time employee, plucks at my sleeve. "We're too late. There's nowhere to sit."

I gesture toward the first two rows. "Let's sit up there. We have as much right as anyone."

"We will not," she hisses. "It's reserved for family."

Always doing the right thing. If Claire weren't so nice and perfectly polite, you'd want to hit her, constantly. Instead I cast her a glance, head to toe. She wears a wool crepe A-line dress—*Who is she, Kate Middleton?*—pumps, not boots, despite the icy mess outside, and stockings. Real silk black panty hose, not tights. Only the red-rimmed eyes and a few flyaway gray hairs escaping the neat brown bob let me know she's human. I run a hand down my black pants to smooth the wrinkles. I don't dare look at my boots. I couldn't find the slim Ferragamos Seth bought me years ago, so I wore cowboy boots. They're black so it's okay. It's not okay, but it's the best I can do right now.

"They're probably not coming anyway. Remember Pete's service?"

"I didn't live here then." Claire glances across the church. "Besides, she has a brother and a niece. Remember? The one who lives downtown. They'll come."

I scoff at that. "The niece didn't bother coming to the house these past months. What makes you think she'll show up now? And if any of them do show up, they don't deserve those seats." I take a step down the aisle.

Claire tugs me.

"Fine." I step back and loop a finger into my blouse's neckline. I rarely wear more than one layer, but even this thin silk feels warm. I pluck again; it's sticking to me. "It's too crowded and it's hot. We'll never find seats . . . Why don't they have the air on?"

"It's thirty degrees outside. They probably have the heat on." Claire levels a measured look at me. "And we will find seats."

A man steps into the aisle in front of us. He extends his hand into the sixth row. "Please."

I want to object. Not because I don't appreciate his gesture or because I don't want the seat, but because I simply want to protest. I want to stamp my feet and yell.

"Thank you." Claire speaks for both of us. She slides in first and widens her eyes at me when I don't move.

"Thank you." It takes me that moment to focus and recognize him. Though twenty years younger, Chris McCullough has become a good friend. I squeeze his hand, and a wave of calm washes through me. It's his green eyes. Green eyes are wondrous things and will always make my heart jolt. Seth had green eyes, has green eyes. I simply don't look into them anymore.

Seth . . . He must be here. I settle into the pew and scan the nave—and land smack on him. On his eyes, looking at me. Moss in the fall when he pulls out his dark-green sweaters. Pale grass-green, citron almost, with flecks of gold, on a hot summer day or when he's really tired. Electric emerald, hard and unyielding, in anger . . .

I'm used to emerald. I have endured over two years of Seth's emerald eyes.

Yet today . . . moss. Seth, standing against a side wall, acknowledges me with a nod. I feel as if he's been waiting for me to find him. Not because he's reaching out, but because it's a duty. Politely acknowledge the ex-wife. Check. Seth always performs his duty. He's kind of like Claire in that way, which is probably why I never bop her. There's something comfortable and secure about people who color within the lines.

He looks good, really good, in a dark-blue suit, blue shirt, and a dark tie with flecks of gray. Not flecks . . . tiny dolphins. He's wearing the tie I gave him for our twenty-fifth anniversary. We swam with the dolphins in Hawaii for our trip that year. It'd be our thirty-second anniversary in eight months . . . It'll never be our thirty-second anniversary.

"Where's Brian?" I shift my focus from my ex-husband to Claire.

"He couldn't miss some meetings in New York," she whispers without turning her head.

Couldn't or wouldn't? The question floats unspoken between us. I nudge her again. "Seth is here."

Claire leans around me and waves before I can stop her. "Of course he is. He adored Maddie."

She smells of gardenias. I open my mouth to snap at her. *It's December! Change your perfume!* I clamp my lips tight before the words escape. Not to save her feelings, but because it's a beautiful spring smell—a green-blossoming, hope-filled smell, full of fresh new beginnings.

I'm in the fall of life and I hate it.

I close my eyes and breathe deeper. Spring fills me, and I almost believe . . .

"But she was my friend," slips out instead.

The hard silence opens my eyes to Claire's raised brow. Not for the first time, I wonder how much money or time she spends to get them that way. She has the darkest brows, not a hair out of place and contoured into perfect arcs. They're her best feature really, quite remarkable. She holds the brow up so long it becomes insulting.

"Don't." I raise a single finger.

She uses that look on her kids, or on me when I behave like one. But I'm too close to tears right now. Too close to becoming a puddle in public, again. That's all anyone thinks of me anymore—not the woman I used to be or imagined I could be—just a lying-cheating-emotional puddle. I keep the single finger pointed stiff and straight. It was my signature move, years ago, on my own kids. It divides the space between us.

We stay frozen for a moment, eyes clashing, but not in anger. That's not the emotion coursing through me, and I know Claire well enough to know she's not mad either. We're adrift. As stable as Claire is, Maddie was our anchor. Without her, we are each other's lifelines, whether we like it or not, whether we can handle it or not.

I sense the panic in her eyes, and I'm certain she's getting flooded as it pours from mine. Bottom line, we're sinking.

I face forward and press my shoulder into her. "I don't feel well. Maybe I'm dying too."

"That is not funny." She grinds out the words with perfect diction, but still reaches for my hand. I enjoy her comfort until she squeezes one shade too tight.

I butt-scoot a few inches away. "I'll be quiet."

I can't resist looking back to Seth. He's gone. I shift to find him, and the pew creaks with each twist. Now the entire congregation knows I'm searching for my ex-husband. He's nowhere in sight. Movement draws my eyes forward again. The family is filing into the first row. They don't fill it. There are only three of them.

"Told you," I whisper in Claire's ear. When she doesn't turn or reply, I continue, "That must be her brother. And the one on the end is probably that niece she always talked about but who never came to visit. She lives forty miles away, in some Chicago high-rise, but still couldn't make it here once to see her dying aunt."

Claire

Claire kept one eye on Janet and one ear on the service. It was traditionally beautiful in many respects. The minister read a passage from Corinthians and one from the gospel of John. *Do not let your hearts be troubled.* The words felt like a warm spear, entering and stabbing, making her aware of how fragile she felt. But they didn't wound. They consoled. Hers was not the first heart to be troubled—and that meant she wasn't alone.

She shifted in her seat. Janet squirmed beside her as the service took an unconventional turn. It ended. The family didn't make any comments or remarks. Songs, Scripture, sermon. There were no childish anecdotes, no expressions of thanks for support, no kind words about a sister or an aunt who would be missed. No scheduled time for friends to say good-bye. Claire peeked at her watch. A life wrapped up neat and tidy in nineteen minutes. Maddie had been an approachable, warm, and true friend with remarkable depth. She spent more time on the birthday cards she gave.

Claire looked at Janet. During the service she'd plucked at her blouse and pulled her highlighted blond mass of curls into a loose bun. She'd stopped short of fanning herself. Now she was swiping her eyes with another tissue. In the year Claire had known her, all Janet's emotions came out in one form: anger. The tears were unexpected. *Be patient with her* was the first advice Maddie gave Claire with regard to Janet, the day she began working at the shop. She had intimated to her that Janet was deep in a valley and it had washed out all her color, resilience, and grace.

As the notes of "Lift High the Cross" swelled around her, Claire cast back to the first day she'd met Maddie and Janet. Lost and alone in a new town, she had wandered into the Printed Letter Bookshop in hopes of escaping. Brian had started work, the kids were settling into their new school, and the cable company hadn't arrived yet, so she couldn't find some over-the-top romantic movie to hide within. And the coffee shop down the street terrified her. The Daily Brew was packed with groupings of people, almost like a town meeting of sorts, with friends calling *Hello* and *How are you?* across the tables, fireplaces (there were two), and lattes. She'd taken three steps in, patted the top of her head as if looking for her sunglasses, and backed right out.

Blocks of aimless walking landed her only a few storefronts from the coffee shop and outside the Printed Letter. A peek inside confirmed it was welcoming. She headed straight to her safe harbor, the classics. *Anna Karenina*? Too depressing—and that made it too dangerous. *War and Peace*. Too trying. Too fraught.

They were the solid novels that had anchored Claire with deep roots and generational solidity through ten corporate moves, but that day they'd felt heavy and constricting, and she feared if she lingered in them she'd never break free and feel the sun again. After all, Dr. Zhivago and Lara lingered in gray, and look how it ended for them. She ran her finger across the spines . . . Alcott, Austen, Brontë, Cather, Chesterton, Dickens, Dostoyevsky . . . Didn't anyone write from Italy? Greece? Didn't anyone bask in sunshine and joy?

Then came that shuddering exhale, as if her last breath of hope and expectation was leaving her for good. It was embarrassing to have someone else hear it, and the two women working in the shop had definitely heard it. The older one, with the gray hair and laughing eyes, smiled at her. The highlighted blond one gave a quick glance and moved on to help another customer.

The gray-haired one focused on Claire. She lifted her head in a disconcerting way to look through her reading glasses rather than push them up on her nose—as if she saw beyond the surface.

"What do you like to read?" She stepped from behind the counter and narrowed her eyes as if daring Claire to lie.

Claire remembered how she'd waved a hand at the hand-printed New Fiction placard standing sentinel at the center table. She started the gesture in confidence, ended it in defeat. "Nothing there. I stick to the classics. I guess I'm old-fashioned. Or boring." Claire shrugged—it was that or cry.

"Classics are never boring." The woman's voice arched as if the classics were the hottest thing off the press. Yet she led Claire away from them, leaving behind all those paperback Penguin copies with their slightly Baroque oil painting covers.

Claire wondered where they were headed until they arrived right back where they started, the classics. But this time, the stories were adorned in bright cloth covers and lined six shelves. "This is Penguin's Project Drop Caps. All these fresh faces for some of the best works. But that's not what I want you to see. Have you read *The Secret Garden*?"

"Too long ago to remember it. My children are older than that now, but even when they were young I couldn't get them to read it."

"I meant for you." She slid a book from the shelf below the rainbow of color. This, too, was bright and fresh—striking and bold, with yellows, greens, and reds. She laid her palm on the cover as if offering a delicacy. "It appeals to the young or the young at heart, or to those who need to believe in dead things growing again."

She offered Claire the book; rather, she laid it in her hands. "Mary Lennox begins her journey in a new and unfamiliar land, but makes her mark on it. She transforms it, and renews the people around her as well as herself. She blossoms . . . And when you're finished, come back and we'll talk some more . . . I'm Maddie."

The hymn ended as Claire let the memory settle over her, as bright and clear as if it had happened that morning. She had pulled the book to her chest with one hand, knowing she had to buy it without understanding why, and reached for Maddie's outstretched hand with the other. "I'm Claire Durand. We moved here a couple months ago."

Maddie's hand was weathered and her knuckles enlarged. Claire had felt every joint. She didn't squeeze, and Maddie didn't pull away.

As they walked to the counter, Maddie had rubbed one hand against the other. "They're a little swollen from too much work in the garden yesterday. I'm planting some fall flowers to make the next few months more colorful. Do you garden?"

"Can anything last the winter here? It gets so cold."

Maddie laughed. "Pick hardy plants and they'll survive."

Now, over a year later, in a church devoid of mirth, the memory of that laugh filled Claire with the same sense of wonder it had that first afternoon. It was a laugh without subtext—genuine, soulful, and rich. It filled her with a sense of awe and terror—both then and now. Awe that someone could feel such genuine pleasure at the mundane; terror that she might never again feel it herself.

Janet ended Claire's memory with a poke in her back. "Go . . . It's our turn."

The pews were filing out. Janet tucked close behind her. "Can you believe that? That's all she gets? My hot flashes last longer than that service."

Claire reached behind for Janet's hand, unsure what message to send—commiseration or reprimand. She willed herself to commiserate. To always reprimand was hard, unbecoming, not who she wanted to be. She wanted to be Mary Lennox and enliven those around her.

She glanced back. Janet was a beautiful woman, with her long, loose curls and blond highlights, a spark plug most days, who carried herself with all the sophisticated armor she'd acquired in her youth. Even distraught, the woman had style and the hair to make twentysomethings envious. The tie at the neck of her silk blouse had come undone, revealing a chunky black and silver necklace, and her pants swirled around intricately detailed black boots.

But when Claire looked past the armor, the truth was evident in the deep lines around Janet's lips and the dark, hollowed skin beneath her eyes: Maddie's death had dealt a severe blow.

Claire withdrew her hand and pulled at the sleeve of her own wool dress. It had inched past her wrist again. "I'm sorry," she whispered over her shoulder.

"For what?"

"You carried too much these past weeks."

Janet's curls bounced as she shook her head. "Don't say that. You did your share at the shop. It would've gutted Maddie to close the doors, and you couldn't have stayed nights with her. You have a family."

"And . . ." Claire waited to catch Janet's eye. "It's your birthday. I almost forgot."

"Fifty-four is not a memorable number. You're welcome to forget. Everyone else will."

She gave Janet's hand another squeeze as, like water through a funnel, they followed the widening flow from the nave into the church's lobby and spilled out into the stone courtyard.

"Let's go have lunch and a glass of champagne. We'll celebrate the spectacular life of one dear friend and the birthday of another. My treat."

Chapter 2

Madeline

I walked toward the train station, the number settling within me. *Twenty years.* Nineteen, actually, since we visited, the summer after eighth grade—the worst spring of my life.

The original plan that summer was a weekend visit on our way to California—just Dad and me. Spring had been hard on both of us—all New York was reeling. The tech bubble had burst in April, and my school turned into a war zone: those whose parents still had jobs and money versus those who were moving out of the city, broke and humiliated. The sharpest knives were hurled at those whose parents had been "responsible" for the catastrophic losses—the financial advisors, the hedge fund managers. The people like my dad.

But rather than the great father-daughter escape I anticipated, because the crash hadn't hit bottom, Dad left me with Aunt Maddie while he headed alone to Silicon Valley to "see what could be done." Clearly nothing, for when he returned a full three weeks later, he packed my bags, red and furious and looking on the verge of a heart attack, and shoved me out the door before I had time to dry off from the beach. Aunt Maddie stood there, she, too, in a red-faced silent fury. And I knew: blood might be thicker than water, but both were thinner than money. After all, she and Uncle Pete had invested in Dad's fund too.

Memories from those three weeks flooded back. Rather than push them away as I usually did, I chose to dwell within them. Aunt Maddie and Uncle Pete never had kids, so they hadn't treated me like one. We laughed hard, watched movies late, took long walks, and worked together at their new bookshop. That's what they called it, a bookshop, not a bookstore.

"It's more intimate, more friendly and communal," Aunt Maddie said.

They had purchased it only the month before I arrived, and they were so excited. Uncle Pete insisted on calling it the Printed Letter Bookshop because, he said, "We'll include all the letters!"

Aunt Maddie glowed every morning as we pushed open the alley's sticky door, and she asked us the same question a hundred different ways. Each boiled down to something like *Aren't books pure joy?*

Uncle Pete and I came up with new and different answers daily. He offered that Stephen King and Aldous Huxley did not feel like joy. One day I chirped about that story where the brother and sister got locked in an attic and—

That was my last answer, as I got a lecture about the "inappropriateness" of V. C. Andrews for middle schoolers. Aunt Maddie then handed me *The Giver* and an Advance Reader Copy of its soon-to-be-released sequel, *Gathering Blue*.

For the first few days, between helping customers and taking reading breaks, I took charge of clearing out the shop's two back offices. Uncle Pete repaired the plumbing in the tiny restroom and Aunt Maddie worked the store front. In addition, having retired after twenty-five years teaching high school English, she tutored out of the storage room. It was big enough for one desk and two chairs—and the chairs filled instantly. I was flummoxed at how happy kids seemed to be entering the shop, despite the fact that it was summer and their parents had forced them into tutoring.

At the end of a kid's first session, Aunt Maddie assigned a summer reading list. She then walked the student out and helped them locate a book in the shop. Uncle Pete teased her every day that the shop wouldn't stay afloat if she gave away the books rather than sold them. But there was no need to worry. From the moment she flipped the hand-painted sign, *Welcome—Please come in*, the shop was packed.

It was only the day before I left that I learned what Uncle Pete had meant by "We'll include all the letters!" I had assumed it was because all the books included all the letters of the alphabet—and they do. But he meant something more.

As a surprise, he had framed years of letters from students and parents thanking Aunt Maddie for her work, for passing on her love of books and learning, and for her gifts to the community. He also had a few new letters from friends excited about the shop and Aunt Maddie's next "adventure." Uncle Pete had also framed a few treasured letters Aunt Maddie had been given over the years, including a letter from F. Scott Fitzgerald to a Lake Forest resident thanking his family for an "enlivening" visit and a note from Ernest Hemingway to a friend about fishing.

Aunt Maddie stood in tears as Uncle Pete and I measured the space around the ceiling molding and hung each letter, almost forty, precisely twenty inches apart in their matching black wood frames. We hung the Fitzgerald and Hemingway letters at eye level behind the counter so everyone could see and enjoy them as well.

I also learned how long Aunt Maddie had planned for her shop and how hard she had been working behind the scenes. As we straightened and shelved books after closing, she told me the margins they needed, the composition of the stock, what genres were trending, how far out she could rely on sales forecasts, how she had contacted all the publisher reps months before and had registered with the local business bureau, and how, each night while I slept, she peppered her website designer with changes to make the shop's website perfect. She'd already taken the Printed Letter's first online orders.

On my final day, before heading to the beach with a couple new friends, I cleaned the kids' section, freshened the window displays, and colored in the black-and-white placards they'd ordered to delineate each genre. I painted Fiction with a red and purple floral border; Nonfiction with blue on top like sky and green across the bottom; and my favorite, Gardening, with a little grass border and tulips in all the colors the palette of acrylic paints offered. I drew good tulips back then.

It was a perfect morning. The last perfect morning.

The train's cadence pulled me from the distant past to the recent.

"I'd love to see you. It's been too long, darling . . . Can we have lunch or dinner this week? Can you come up here?"

Her call last month wasn't unusual. She had called many times since I started law school with invitations and anticipation-filled pauses, as if nervous I would put her off. Most of the time I did—a paper, a test, a trial, a brief. Something always commanded my time.

"Oh . . . Aunt Maddie . . . I'm swamped. Maybe next week?"

The fact was I didn't want an invitation. I wanted an apology. And I replied with eleven years full of *next weeks* with only a smattering of *yeses*—because I was a coward. If I had confronted her, made her talk to my dad, maybe then I wouldn't have felt caught in the middle like a traitor. Instead, I occasionally went to dinner, again felt the stab of injustice at how she'd treated my father, and left our time together confused and angry all over again. Every encounter left me racked with disappointment in myself. As a lawyer, I was well versed in the vagaries of human nature, but that didn't stop it from hurting when it bit or from recognizing it within myself.

Gather the facts, make an assessment, and deal with the reality presented—and never wish for something that doesn't exist, in a client, in a case, in a relationship, and especially in a life. Professionally, I'd have taken her apart. Personally, I never stepped up to the plate.

Nevertheless, I should have picked up on her hesitation in that final call, the hitch in her breath before she accepted my excuse. Something was wrong. And that's my job—to understand when a client is lying or telling the truth, to know what to ask and what not to ask, to press when necessary and to shore up defenses when required. But last month I was too busy to notice anything. Today in my memory I heard her pause—that slight hiccup—loud and clear, and condemning.

I did check my calendar. Sometimes I pretended, but that day I had scanned it, and I hadn't lied. There was no space. No time.

"I'm underwater, Aunt Maddie. It's the final push for partnership and I'm the youngest associate ever considered. How about I call next week?"

Again, the pause stretched long in memory.

"Thank you, dear . . ." Her second hitch bled into a shaky breath. I felt her rummage for a new topic. "I had a nice talk with your dad today."

That lengthened my neck and stilled my hands over my keyboard. "You did?"

She could not have said anything more shocking.

Then someone rapped my doorjamb. I rushed out a hasty "Excellent. I have to go, Aunt Maddie. I'll call next week."

So many red flags. Yet I clicked off my phone, answered someone's trivial question, and returned to my case du jour—a client sued, in violation of township ordinances, for keeping backyard chickens in Evanston and creating a nuisance, mainly a large colony of rats.

One week later . . . I forgot to call her.

One month later . . . the coroner called me.

Janet

Claire pushes open the door to Bistro North, and warm air hits me heavy with the scent of sourdough rolls. I love those rolls. It's still early, only noon, so there's plenty of seating in the bar area. If I have my choice, I always sit up here. The back of the restaurant wasn't redone in the recent remodeling, and it still carries that cluttered eighties feel. The bar, on the other hand, makes me feel the way I'm certain the Modernists felt once they escaped Victorianism—they could breathe. Rather than overstuffed red velvet booths and heavy hangings, it gleams with white Calcutta marble countertops swirled with rich brown striations. High tables with high-backed stools covered in a buttery brown leather, brass fixtures, and little lamps with black shades radiate all the light and kick the warmth up a notch. It's sleek and modern, with a timeless sensibility that makes me feel hip and relevant—even if I'm not either anymore. I watch Claire's shoulders rise and drop down in a more relaxed mode, and I suspect that's why she likes it here too. On some level, it reminds us of the women we were and would like to be again.

In many ways, it's the complete opposite of the Printed Letter. Money has been lavished upon this space. Like the bookshop, the atmosphere is warm and inviting, but details here are perfection. The heat is set at an ideal temperature, a light sweater will suffice in winter, and the windows are double-paned. We're only a few blocks from the shop and yet a world away. We can't hear the street traffic, don't feel the breeze through the window frames, won't lose a light-bulb every time someone flips the switch too quickly, and needn't yell over a heating system that knocks like Jacob Marley climbing Scrooge's steps whenever it clicks on. Not to mention floors that creak every time you pass from Self-Help to Cooking, reminding you that you should probably head back whence you came.

"Is this okay?" Claire pulls off her coat and hands it with a quick thanks to the hostess.

I do the same, giving Claire a shrug for a reply. I still don't trust myself with words.

She leads me to the far high table, where there is a little more space and a lot more privacy.

"Champagne?"

I press my lips tight and shake my head. Maddie loved champagne. She said every occasion was worthy of "a little bubbly."

"Right." Claire nods, probably with the memory of our last glass in her mind as well.

Maddie had raised a tall, full flute to both of us the night she determined no chemotherapy, no treatment of any kind. "I've lived a wonderful life, my friends, and . . ." She paused, then lifted her chin with that look we both knew. "It's too advanced for the kind of fight required, and even then the odds are not in my favor." She winked at her own literary humor and continued. "I'm at peace with what's ahead."

She raised her glass with joy-filled eyes and drank deep. I hoisted mine in wobbly fingers and choked down a few sips. I'm not sure what Claire did.

"A glass of red then." Claire lifts her gaze to the approaching waiter. "Two glasses of your Syrah, please."

I smile at her, wan and worn, but grateful. A good Syrah is my favorite wine—so deep and bold you can chew it. "Thank you."

"We'll be okay . . . You'll be okay."

"Oh, Claire, I haven't been okay in a very long time, and now I feel like the ground's fallen out beneath me. It all shifted too fast, too far."

She lays down her menu. "You've got me."

"Not once the store closes."

Claire's face falls, and with it all her color. I reach out and clutch her hand.

"I don't mean to be harsh, but it will close and you'll move on. I have to work, and there aren't many jobs in Winsome. And if I found one, no one will pay me what Maddie did. I can barely keep the house as it is, but to move means I'll never see my kids. If it's more effort than a couple miles' drive from Seth's apartment when they come to town, they won't do it. It'll be one more reason . . ."

I close my eyes to stop the speed of this scenario. I've been over it a thousand times in the past few weeks, and the crash at the end is devastating. "I need to find a job locally, but no one's clamoring for fifty-four-year-old snarky employees. Besides, you have your family and you don't need to work."

Claire drops her eyes to the table. She can't deny the truth in my words, but with them, I've also dismissed the Printed Letter's importance in her life. It isn't fair, but I don't have the bandwidth for fair right now.

"Claire?" I squeeze her fingers, then pull my hand back. "All that is for another day. Not today."

"No . . . You're right." Rather than calling me out for being a jerk, she agrees, then shifts the conversation. As usual, she keeps the peace. "What are your plans?" She blanches again and self-corrects. "For tonight, not for tomorrow or next week. For your birthday."

I lean against the stool's leather back, stalling. Then it comes to me. "Nothing big. I'm heading to the city for dinner with a couple friends, and I've already heard from Chase. He sent a text this morning and added that Laura is due soon. I'll be a grandmother. I still can't get over that."

"That's so wonderful. And how's Alyssa?"

I shift again. Talking about my son is hard enough. To talk about my daughter, to lie about her, is brutal. "She's great. I expect I'll hear from her later. West Coast time and all."

"See? This is a good day. Maddie would have loved all this."

"Yes . . . A good day."

Claire scans her menu and I look blindly at mine. *Liar, liar, pants on fire.*

Through that whole conversation I willed myself not to blink, and certainly not to let my gaze drift up and away. It was a perfectly delivered lie, and held that casual flippancy that really sells it. *I'm heading to the city for dinner with a couple friends.*

I have no dinner plans. I have no friends. Practically every friend I had—we had—sided with Seth in the divorce, and I can't blame them. Even my closest friend let me have it on her way out the door. And while, yes, I hope Alyssa will call, I also hope for world peace. Neither is likely to happen soon.

No. Never give up hope—world peace is still a possibility.

And Chase might call. I'm sure I'll get more than a mere text on my birthday. Maybe. Then again . . .

What if Alyssa texted him or has already talked to him today? He always yields to his older sister. And who wouldn't? So confident in her judgments and abilities—my golden girl. How many times had her dad and I joked about that one? Our golden girl who did so much right. We missed that judgmental streak, that stubborn unforgiveness within her.

Maybe we hadn't missed it—I was once that girl. But now I'm on the other side, outside the sunshine, and it's cold. Yet again, I can't blame her. She's right not to forgive me and I'm not saying she should—I'm just saying . . .

Nothing. I'm not saying anything. One text is enough. It has to be. And Claire is right . . . This is a good day. Maddie would narrow her eyes and cluck her tongue if I said otherwise. *Every day is a gift and a blessing.* She said that constantly, and the way she walked the talk proved her out. Death itself never scared her. How can I argue with that?

I asked her once, "How are you not scared?"

"Of what? I'll see Pete. I'll see God."

Those thoughts brought her peace. They terrify me. Like in that kids' book when the beaver mentions a lion and three kids feel different iterations of joy, but one feels absolute terror. I'm the kid in terror.

I replied flippantly, "It might not be as pleasant as you think. There's a lot of fire, brimstone, and judgment, besides all that love you talk about."

Maddie smiled at me then. She was depleted of energy, but she was peaceful. So peace-filled I felt breathless for her advice. "You're misunderstanding God and grace, and mercy too. Promise you'll keep at it."

I laughed off her concern and care, for it wasn't the magic pill I thought it would be. "Sure I will, but with my limited understanding, I've got him pegged close to Gandalf and I fall right beside him into the abyss. The Balrog gets us both."

She shook her head. That slight motion looked painful. "I never would have recommended Tolkien if that's all you got from him."

"I'm kidding."

"I'm not," she whispered. Her hand was ice. "Our understanding is so limited, Janet. Be careful not to assume God's role or presume you understand his ways or the depth of his love. Promise me."

I gave a quick promise as something switched our attention. We were soon laughing together, but that stayed with me. *Don't assume God's role or presume you understand his ways . . .*

Knowing Maddie, she probably thought I was being too hard

on myself, that all could be forgiven, that good can come from pain, and that all this will have meaning on some level, someday.

But sometimes—not often, but sometimes—Maddie was wrong.

Claire

Lunch was a quiet affair. Claire tried to engage Janet in conversation, but every attempt sputtered out. Soon she, too, became lost in memory. So lost that after lunch, she pulled into Maddie's driveway rather than her own. She turned off the ignition and sat. The house was dark, and dead leaves dotted the front steps. It felt empty, lonely. Oddly, it evoked the same feeling she often got from her own house when Brian and the kids were out.

She walked up the front steps, making a mental list. She needed to sweep the porch and buy timers for the lights. The sun would set in a couple hours, by four thirty, and that was much too long a night for the place to be dark. Maddie's house shouldn't look abandoned—no matter what happened to it or who might own it next. At present it was still Maddie's and deserved to be cared for.

Claire stood on the porch. Something about the uneven floorboards or the smell brought her first house to mind, and that first summer after she and Brian married. They both worked full days, then sanded, painted, and caulked every inch of that house most nights, falling into each other's arms, tangled and speckled with paint, in the early hours of each morning.

"I've never been so tired," he often whined as he pulled her close.

"Too tired?" she'd ask with feigned innocence.

"Never . . ."

Claire bent down to pull the key from under the mat and added *Find new hiding spot for key* to her list.

She opened the front door and walked through the living room toward the kitchen. It had dropped well below freezing through the morning, so she wanted to check the thermostat. She pushed at the kitchen's swinging door while registering a bright light. Her own panic and another's scream hit her simultaneously.

She clamped her hand over her mouth. After two breaths, she spoke through her fingers. "What are you doing here? I didn't see your car."

Janet held one hand pressed to her chest and used the other to point out the back door. "I came to check the thermostat . . . Now I'm making tea. What are you doing here?"

"Same thing."

"We shouldn't be here. It's the new owner's problem now. Unless Maddie didn't have a will, and then it goes to probate. Did she have one?" Janet pulled down two mugs.

"I have no idea."

"If she didn't it'll go to her brother in the end, as her only living relative, and that means we're trespassing and, considering her sweet family, we'll end up in jail. Last cup of tea before we go?"

Claire tried to bank her smile. Janet often made reality sound droll. "Sure. How do you know all that legal stuff?" She pulled out a chair and sat down.

"You learn a lot in a divorce." Janet poured out two cups and grabbed a box of chocolates from the refrigerator. "These are only a week old. Some neighbor sent them. Ridiculous. Who sends chocolate to a dying woman? And she'd stopped eating a full week before that." Janet's buoyancy fell. "But the neighbor couldn't have known that."

Claire kept her face blank. She hadn't known that either. "Will the shop go to her brother too?"

Janet nodded. "If there's no will, everything is his. Without kids, all the property goes to siblings and parents. She only had the one brother left."

"Then, if you're right, we're both out of jobs. He'll sell it."

"Do you think if we offered to run it, he'd keep it as an investment?"

Claire shifted her gaze from Janet's now hopeful one. She shook her head. "The shop has been deep in the red the past eight months. We've been dipping heavily into the store's savings account and Maddie's personal accounts too."

"Why didn't you say anything?"

"I did." Claire pulled back at Janet's tone. "Who do you think gave me permission to do that?"

Janet stopped. She dragged her top lip through her teeth. "I thought that was the one thing doing well."

"No, at least not in the year I've been there . . . Do you really want to discuss this now?"

Janet nodded again.

Claire sighed. "Maddie paid us a lot. She ran promotions. She gave away books. But none of that is as important as the fact that the mortgage rate is high and we haven't kept up with customer service like we should."

"We have parties and signings all the time."

"Not in the past couple years. I trolled through the calendars and the accounts for the last five years to make sense of it. While indies are experiencing a renaissance, it's because of hard work. Maddie was probably slowing down long before without realizing it. You came on board as things really dipped, so you wouldn't have known. Did you realize that in 2017 the shop hosted *fifty* events, with an average of forty-one customers and 63 percent of them buying? That's all well above industry average. In 2018, the shop only hosted sixteen events."

"I get the point."

"Break it down more, and those thirty-four fewer events last year also averaged twenty-seven people per event and twenty-three dollars in average sales for purchasers, but only 18 percent made purchases. If those people still bought books, then we sent about five hundred people and over fifty thousand dollars elsewhere. And the events we've held this year have only averaged—"

"Stop already." Janet clamped her hands over her ears. "Stop with the numbers."

"I'm sorry . . . You asked."

"So we deserve this."

"That's not what I meant." Claire put down her cup and stood. "I should go. This isn't helping, and I've got to get home and figure out dinner." She looked around the kitchen. It was perfectly tidy and she briefly wondered who had handled that, who had handled all the details of Maddie's last days and after. Then her gaze landed on Janet again and she knew. "I'm sorry, Janet. Are you going to be okay?"

Janet looked at her watch and in the process sloshed tea over the side of her mug. She grabbed for a rag. In one deft motion she wiped the table and deposited the mug in the empty dishwasher. "I need to go too. I'm running late to get downtown for dinner." She turned at the sink. "You go and I'll lock up."

Claire laid Maddie's house key on the table. "This was under the front mat. It probably shouldn't be now. It's too predictable."

"I'll put it with the others. I've got one and there's another hidden under the flowerpot in the back garden, if you ever need it."

"Happy birthday, again." Claire stepped away. "Have fun tonight."

As she drove the few miles home, she realized what else was missing at Maddie's home, and her own. Christmas lights.

They usually came out, along with everything else, the day after Thanksgiving—and it was her favorite day of the year. This year it had passed unnoticed. Brittany played in a field hockey tournament Thanksgiving weekend and Brian worked most of it too, and Matt was only concerned with basketball, Xbox, and food. No one, including Claire, had noticed the oversight.

Her phone rang through her car as she pulled into the garage. *Brian.*

"Hi, hon. Are you on your way home? We forgot to decorate for Christmas last week. Can you believe that? Want to do it tonight?"

"I wish. My flight got delayed, and I won't land until midnight."

"I'll wait up."

"Don't do that. It could be almost two by the time I get there. Was today okay?"

Claire closed her eyes, thankful he'd remembered, disappointed he wasn't beside her. But those wishes, or discussions, were not for garages and airports. "It was okay. Hard, but okay. But about the Christmas decorations?"

Nasal-toned boarding announcements overpowered Brian's reply.

"I didn't hear you."

"We'll get it done this weekend. I promise. I have to go. Love you."

"Love you too." She clicked off and rushed through the back door. "Hey, kids . . . I'm home. Sorry I'm so late."

The house felt quiet. Too quiet. It was already dark, and the absence of glasses and dishes in the sink meant the kids hadn't come home after school for a snack.

She pulled her phone out of her handbag and found two text messages.

Matt's was to the point: Eating at Ryan's after practice today.

Brittany's was much the same: Dinner at Chipotle for team fundraiser then studying at Sara's. Home by 10.

"Welcome home and Merry Christmas." Claire leaned against the counter. Everyone was busy, involved with plans, life, work, friends. In a little over a year and a half, they'd made Winsome their home and found their places within it. Everyone was happy. Thriving. That should make any mom happy.

Claire pulled a single chicken breast out of the freezer.

Chapter 3

Madeline

A tap on my doorjamb preceded the shadow to my right. "I thought you had a funeral today."

I shrugged. "Do you ever want more than this?"

Kayla spread her hands across the back of the chair facing my desk and stretched her back. "More than working eighty-hour weeks and being so tired you can barely eat, much less do anything else? No. This is Nirvana."

"I'm serious." My tone caught her attention.

"Once I pay off all my loans and help my sister through school, I'll lift my head and let you know. Right now I can't afford that question. I take it you do want more?"

"Rarely. Sometimes. Not often." I smirked. "Maybe only today."

"Funerals can do that."

I rocked back in my chair. It bounced on the downswing. "My aunt was more a mystery than I thought. I mean . . . everyone loved her. She owned a bookstore, volunteered a lot, had tons of friends, and was really involved in everything around her. That's what I remember from spending time with her. But other things, other memories don't reconcile with that . . . I don't know. I'm thinking too much."

"Occupational hazard."

I bounced upright. "The church was packed today. Standing room only. That says something, right? You can't fool a whole town."

"What are you saying, Madeline?"

"I'm not sure. Maybe it was merely a case of irreconcilable differences."

"I'm up to my ears in those. Duncan has me working the Pencer divorce."

A noise outside my office redirected our attention.

Kayla turned back to me with a lowered voice. "By the way, Schwartz was looking for you this morning about the Cunningham brief."

I tapped my calendar. "I have another week. It goes to court on the fifteenth."

She raised a brow. "It got moved up."

"Are you kidding me? What'd you tell him?" I reached for the file.

"That you were at a funeral. It may buy you through tomorrow if you play up the emotional angle."

"I will not."

"Then tell him you simply didn't get it done." She stretched her arms above her head. Her eyebrows stretched up too.

"I can't do that, not now. Drew's gunning for that partnership . . . He didn't used to put in the hours I've noted lately."

"True, but one can overdo it. Balls get dropped." She cast her eye to the file clutched in my hand.

"Thanks for the heads-up." I tilted my head to the door. "Is Schwartz in?"

"Left for court at noon. I don't think he's coming back today."

"I'll have it done by tomorrow then. What's another late night?"

"Nothing new." She waved a hand at me as she walked out. "See you later."

THE OFFICE WAS QUIET. Those of us who worked late did it alone and hoped no one called us out. Duncan, Schwartz and Baring's expectations as a firm required late hours, but as individuals, Duncan, Schwartz, and Baring frowned upon them. Anything past a sixty-hour week evidenced a lack of "work-life balance"—regardless that the workload obliterated any hope for one.

Six hours and three Kind bars later, I closed the file, flipped the lights, and headed to the elevator. Drew's lights were still on. I walked carefully, willing my heels not to make a sound against the marble. I failed.

"Madeline?" he called from his office the instant I thought I was clear. I backtracked and peered in.

"Wasn't your aunt's funeral today?"

"This morning. My parents flew back to New York, so I came in this afternoon." He stared at me. While we dated, that look had always made me uncomfortable. It was assessing—there was no other word for it. Now it unnerved me. I shrugged, unsure what to say or do. "I didn't know her well."

My words sounded flippant, almost callous. I didn't want to be that, never that. Besides, they weren't true—not really. On some level I did know Aunt Maddie, and despite my confusion, I'd always hoped she was what she had appeared that summer—that there was integrity and coherence within her, kindness and truth too. All those people this morning confirmed it. And Dad . . . *It was my fault.* Had he confirmed it too?

"You must be exhausted." Drew's soft words stopped my internal whirling.

"You too. You used to not believe in such long hours." I meant to lighten the tone and change the subject. His eyes clouded.

"Yes . . . Survival of the fittest and all that." His mouth curved. He had this sardonic expression that hovered at the edge of insulting. The partners were never sure about him—neither was I.

I pressed in an attempt to be sure. "A partnership on the line does bring out one's true colors."

He opened his mouth to reply when my phone rang. I raised a finger to him while I dug in my bag.

He waved me away. "You go. I need to get back to work."

I spun myself from his doorway and tapped to answer the call. "Madeline Cullen."

"Madeline, Greg Frankel here. I don't know if you remember me, but we talked a couple months ago."

"I remember." I headed to the elevators. I was not likely to forget one of the strangest calls I ever received—a lawyer, Aunt Maddie's lawyer, calling to introduce himself. *That's it. We haven't met and I wanted to say hi.*

I squeezed the bridge of my nose, willing this day to end. "Are you calling to say hi again? Because it's not a good day. Were you at the funeral? And it's past eleven o'clock."

"No—is it? Wow, I lost track of time, but yes, I was there this morning. I saw you and hoped to catch you, but the church was packed . . . I had no idea so many people would be there. I should have—your aunt was a wonderful lady, a first-class act. But of course you know that. She deserved that send-off, despite the fact no one spoke and I couldn't get a seat. I was in the back left corner, and by the time I—"

"Is there something we need to discuss?" I cut into his meandering.

"Your aunt's will. I'm the executor of her estate."

"It can't be too complex. Have someone in your firm check it over, if you're unsure, then file it. I guarantee no one will contest it. Her only surviving family is my father, and he's already flown back to New York. You can email him the details." I lowered my phone to disconnect the call as I tapped the elevator button with my free hand.

"There's nothing wrong with the will. It's perfectly sound, filed, and your father is not mentioned." Greg's voice turned abrupt, and I sensed that I had mis-assessed him. Something deep, authoritative, and surprising came across the line. "I'm referring to the terms within the will, not the document itself. She left you . . . Well, she left you everything."

"What? What does that mean?"

"Madeline Cullen Carter left you her house, her bookshop, her car, a storage unit in Waukegan, and four thousand in cash and investments, as well as all her jewelry and personal effects."

"I don't want it." I pulled my phone from my ear again as if distance could make it disappear.

"You don't want what?" His voice sounded small and far away. I pushed the phone into my ear.

"Anything. Everything. Give it all to someone else."

Frankel chuckled.

I'd thought he was young, straight out of law school, when he first called. Now I wondered. "I don't find this funny."

He stopped. "Excuse me. I thought you were kidding . . . You of all people know it doesn't work like that."

"She must have other beneficiaries, other stipulations. There have to be options."

"None."

"How is that possible?"

If one could hear a smile, I heard a grin. "It's very simple. You see—"

"I don't mean how a document like that was drafted. I mean why did she do it? How could you let her?" As soon as my final question flew, I cringed. He had no say in the matter, and I sounded young and naive acting as though he did. I hated sounding young and naive.

"You have no idea how much you meant to her, do you?" His voice was soft and full of a second, unspoken question. *How could you not know that?*

I slumped against the elevator wall. "What do you need from me?"

"I'd like to meet. Sure, I can send you all the paperwork, but your aunt liked face-to-face meetings and so do I. While there are no other beneficiaries or stipulations, there are several notes she left. It's an unusual file. We could meet at her house, your house now, in Winsome."

"No . . . Things are too busy for that right now. Can you come here?"

"I'd be happy to . . . Tomorrow? Eight o'clock?"

"No . . . I . . ." My days were packed. Three days until the partnership announcement, and every hour mattered. But this distraction needed to be dealt with too. It needed to disappear.

"Eight a.m. is fine. I'll be here."

JANET

I am tempted to stay at Maddie's house after Claire leaves. It feels more like home than my own house does these days. We lived there twenty-nine years as a family, but now . . . it's too empty. After all, in all those twenty-nine years I never lived there alone.

I tap my phone again—to feel the connection.

> Happy Birthday, Mom! Five weeks till the baby. It's busy here.

Five weeks until my first grandchild . . . I hadn't been sure. Chase isn't very good with the details, and Laura and I don't speak anymore. They never got a landline after their marriage, so I call his cell phone. I suppose I could call hers and get updates, but the prospect of hearing those stiff, cutting tones in yet another family member is too much. It's easier to pretend her voice might still fill with laughter and love when I call.

I leave my car at Maddie's and walk the couple miles back to the shop. It's a miserable day and a miserable walk—exactly right for how I feel. I let myself in through the back door. I'm only delaying the inevitable, but I can't go home yet. Home is overstuffed with memories, and I'm not strong enough to withstand them today. It's also too large a house for one person. I rattle around in it. I need to sell it, but I loathe giving the kids yet another reason to despise me. Selling their childhood home might be the last straw—if I haven't broken that camel's back already. But there's no worry at present; real estate isn't moving well in Winsome, and I refuse to lower the price. I suppose I'm playing both sides of the fence. My Realtor suggested we pull it off the market and list it fresh in the spring. Maybe she's right. A new beginning in spring.

My hand hovers over the shop's light switch. You can't flip it too quickly or you blow a fuse. I opt not to flip it at all. At night the Printed Letter feels like a fishbowl. Dark outside. Light inside. Everyone can see you through the large bay windows, and you can see no one. It's advantageous during an author event or an evening party; all the lights, books, food, wine, and chatter draw people in. Tonight I want to slip between the cracks in the floorboards and vanish.

It's a Thursday, however, and that means people are out and about. A couple years ago, the local business association voted to keep stores open late on Thursdays to encourage people to stroll around town after work or dinner and shop. In the summer, there's music in the square. In winter, there are carolers, Santa, and lights twinkling on every tree lining Main Street. It all makes this little, almost-forgotten town feel like home.

A group of shoppers walk by and glance in. I'm tempted to flip on the lights and unlock the door. Apparently we could use a sale or two. It wouldn't help. Maddie's brother will sell the shop without a second thought, as anyone would a bad investment. A bookshop. It's not glamorous, not original, and apparently it's no longer profitable. And I thought we were partaking in the Indie Renaissance—shows what I know.

The shop will sell, and Claire and I will have the privilege of unloading stock and shutting it down. We will lose one more link to Maddie and the life I've come to accept, if not enjoy. And along with everything else that has slipped away, there is no turning back to grasp it again, nor any chance to make it better. The past holds no hope.

A copy of *The Girl on the Train* sits nearby—out of place. I hurl it across the store. Everyone loved that book except me. That girl spent most of the story ruining her life—drinking, lashing out, lying, spinning out of control . . . How is she a heroine? What does that term mean anymore? Just because one is a main character, does that make her a heroine? Not her. Never her. She was weak, reactive, pathetic, lost—

The paperback thwacks the front bay window.

Two women walking by yelp, and I drop to the floor, my heart in my throat. *One, two, three* . . . I peer above the Holiday New Releases table. The women have pressed their hands to the glass, straining to see inside. I sink lower. What if they see me? Worse, what if I shattered the window?

I count to ten this time and inch up to look across the store again. The women have moved on. I slump with relief. In the glow of the streetlights, I note gum pressed underneath the display table. And not only one disgusting person has done that, but three. A blob of bright pink—a kid with bubblegum? A nondescript beige—most likely mint, maybe Trident? And a red one—cinnamon . . .

Oops. That one is mine. I pick at the gum with my finger until it pops off and falls to the floor. I stuck it there as Seth walked in one day almost two years ago. It was the last time he came to the shop, formerly a favorite stop for him.

The ink wasn't dry on our divorce papers yet, and I thought *maybe* . . . So I spit out my gum so as not to chew like a cow, fluffed my hair, and smiled sweetly. But I was wrong. That ship had sailed—or rather, I had set it ablaze like a Viking funeral pyre. Seth simply handed me his house key and said he had gone back to remove the last of his belongings. Anything more I found, I was to discard. He didn't want it.

I lean back against the table leg and feel the pain of that afternoon stab me anew. I had raced home wondering what he had left. I felt certain that I would know his heart, and our chances for reconciliation, by what he had taken. There had to be some things, some memories, he would still cherish. Would he have wanted that small painting we bought for our seventh anniversary? The one we deemed too expensive and then, after sharing a bottle of wine over lunch, purchased because it really was priced right? He would have taken that—and then I would know.

I feel now as I did then, unlocking our front door, heart in throat. But that time the sensation was riddled with hope, not fear and shame.

I'd stood in the front hall, able to survey the living room, the dining room, and the short passageway into the kitchen, and I felt myself fall . . . He had left behind every picture, note, knickknack, and memento of our lives together. His sketch of Wrigley Field drawn in commemoration of the 2016 Cubs win still hung above his desk. I could glimpse it through his study's glass door past the living room. Every single item remained. After all, I was part of all of it.

I push myself to standing. There's a bottle of wine in the office refrigerator left over from our last Conversation with an Author.

What was her name? That perky twentysomething who wrote the memoir about finding love in San Francisco over a cat, a dog, and a rainy afternoon? Considering how much said twentysomething drank, wine should have been featured in her story as well. All through her talk, I suspected there was more fiction than fact to her story, and wine was her primary source of inspiration. But who am I to judge?

"Happy Birthday to me."

I grab the bottle and the opener, skip the clear plastic cup, and return to my spot on the floor. Somehow it feels appropriate. If no one can see me, if I'm not where a proper human ought to be, then none of this counts. I'm not drinking alone and I'm not living this pathetic life. I'm outside it all, toasting my birthday and Maddie's life from afar.

The cloud cover shifts and moonlight floods the store. I watch as the moon provides the yellow high note to the glittery white drops dappling the books. I glance outside. The trees are lit with thousands of tiny lights . . . Winter . . . It's almost Christmas! I had forgotten how close we were, only weeks away.

The cynic in me whispers, *Time to shop*. The romantic in me gasps. Sure, I make the displays for the store and set up the Holiday New Releases table, but that's my job. I compartmentalize with the best of them. But the trees are now lit. Seth and I used to walk into town, hand in hand, to see them lit for the first time on the night after Thanksgiving each year. Last year I walked into town alone. This year I forgot.

The tears surprise me. They shouldn't. It's more surprising that, after the past two years, there are any left.

I raise the bottle of an indifferent Sauvignon Blanc and toast the trees. "Here's to you, Maddie, and to me. I wish you were here."

And I drink.

Chapter 4

Claire

Claire pushed open the shop's alley door with another mental note—*Oil door hinges*—and examined the alarm. It was off—it was never off. She was always, or at least every morning for the past six months, the first to arrive. And she wasn't late this morning. In fact, probably early . . .

Brittany had left in a blaze of teenage indignation, bullying Matt out the door fifteen minutes early. She could still feel her daughter's contempt and her son's defeat. He'd learned his lesson well. Keep your head down and your mouth shut in hopes the Brittany-storm would blow past you. Not this morning. Brittany had been angry about the laundry. The darks, meaning her leggings, weren't dry yet.

"They'll be dry by this afternoon. I can't put them in the dryer or they'll pill and fade."

"I need them today." Arms crossed, the girl had ground out each word.

"Find something else. You have plenty of clothes." Claire had worked to sound nonchalant, as nonchalant often quelled the rising storm.

"You don't get it. You never do. This is what the team is wearing today, and when you're new, you don't want to stand out, Mom." She spat the last word.

"Lucky you're not new this year," Claire quipped back.

The look on Brittany's face stripped her comment of any humor. "I'll always be new."

She had stormed out of the room as Claire sank onto a kitchen stool. She knew her daughter was right to some degree. Moving as a junior in high school to a new town where most kids had lived their whole lives had put Brittany in a tough spot. And, as they now applied to colleges, she faced "new" again, as she called it. It was an adjective, a verb, and a noun packed into three little letters.

"You never get it." Brittany blew back through the kitchen and threw open the back door. "Matt, get down here. I'm leaving in one minute with or without you."

"You can wait for him."

"Not today." She stomped out the door.

Claire had stepped to the window, thankful for the previous night's ice. The need to scrape off the windshield would give Matt extra time. He raced through the kitchen.

"Grab your lunch off the counter."

"Bye, Mom."

"You don't have to rush."

"If I want a ride I do." Then he, too, was out the door.

Claire dwelt on Brittany during her drive to work—not that anything could be solved in three miles. She asked herself if it was a phase. Some experts would say yes. Others stood firm that there was no such thing as a phase, but that theory worried Claire more. Had she been too lenient when they moved? Given in to too many demands to try to make up for the loss of their Ohio home? Had her daughter intrinsically changed, never to return? Whatever it was, somehow the fine threads between them had been severed. There was no communication or respect, only recrimination and disdain all wrapped up in an angry, blond, seventeen-year-old girl.

Now Claire made her way through the back office, dropped

her bag and coat, and rounded the corner into the shop—and met chaos.

"What are you doing here so early? And what . . . What are you doing? We open in a couple hours."

Books lined the center aisle. Paper, lights, and boxes were scattered everywhere. She could barely find the floor. And was that a model train?

"This won't be done by then," Janet commented over her shoulder.

"I figured that." Claire stared, unsure what to say.

Janet spared her a quick glance. "I'm changing the windows. I remembered Chase's model trains last night and got this wonderful idea of running them through the window display and into the store across these two tables. It'll be spectacular. We can load the little coal cars with small gifts and stack the books in the center like a mountain range."

Claire picked up the engine. It was heavy, impressive, with its real screws and soldered pieces. "These were Chase's? They're antiques."

Janet paused. "Seth owned them first. I think they were his father's, but he gave the whole set to Chase for his tenth birthday." She pointed to the engine. "The engine is actually built from Ephraim Shay's original geared locomotive designs, scaled down."

"Are you sure it's okay with Seth to use them?"

Janet's hands worked double-time pinning a garland to the upper corner of the window. "He left them behind. Chase did too. I'm sure he'll want them someday, but it's not like I'm going to ruin them. I'm helping them. The gears will freeze if they don't get used and stay lubricated."

Claire shook her head. "Any idea how long this will take?"

"Does it matter if it takes all day?"

"This close to Christmas, foot traffic is usually high. This season we need it to be high."

Janet threw her a look.

"I guess not."

Hours later, Janet was still deep into the window, leaving Claire alone to unpack the daily book boxes and handle the foot traffic. The shop burst with customers as if everyone needed a dose of their beloved friend's shop.

"Maddie always picked out my gifts for my great-grandchildren. Are you still holding the Holiday Bazaar?" Dottie Neuland asked, then purchased a variety of gifts, books, and another pair of plus-five readers.

"You won't change anything in here, will you? We love this store."

Claire smiled as two young moms gathered their collective five kids after a full hour of play. They'd sneaked off to the armchairs in the shop's back corner to chat while the kids pored through dozens of books and scattered the toys.

"*The Further Adventures of Ebenezer Scrooge* is this year's book club holiday selection. We need thirty copies by next Wednesday." Doug Benson never smiled, but he always placed a large monthly order.

Camille Johnson, one of Maddie's closest friends, simply stood in the center aisle and breathed deeply. "I still feel her here, don't you?"

"Yes, but the Holiday Bazaar is a little later this year. On the twenty-first, at six o'clock."

"We wouldn't change a thing . . ."

"We can have thirty copies here by Tuesday afternoon . . ."

"Yes, and I hope she always stays close by."

Claire fielded the questions, rang the sales, consoled the friends, and placed the orders—all while Janet finished her masterpiece.

The store quieted after the lunch rush, and Janet joined her at the counter.

"Welcome to the fourth quarter." Claire dropped to a stool and rubbed lotion into her hands.

"We need help." Janet arched her back. "You should ask Brittany to come after school and help with all that unpacking."

"I asked last week. She's not interested. She said we couldn't pay her enough."

"She and a friend used to do it last fall for free."

"That was before I worked here."

"Is that a problem?" Janet reached for the lotion.

"Apparently."

"That's too bad, but we need someone." Janet opened her mouth as if to pursue Brittany again.

Claire felt a wave of relief when nothing came. She knew Brittany had once enjoyed working after school at the Printed Letter. She'd enjoyed Janet and Maddie. And somehow Claire had ruined that, along with everything else in Brittany's life.

Janet opened her mouth again. "Latte?"

"Sure. Let me—"

"My turn. I'll be back in ten." Janet was out the alley door, without a coat, and without shutting it behind her.

Claire closed it, then headed to the front door, stepping over a few decorating elements still in the center aisle and straightening books as she went. She walked outside to look back at the window and into the shop. Janet was right—it was going to be spectacular. She had covered the table in green velvet and tied huge red grosgrain bows along the skirt. On top she'd set the tracks around the perimeter, then displayed books in the center, green covers, spines out, with a sprinkling of white books thrown in, growing whiter near the top like snowcapped mountaintops. In the second bay she had created a display full of red-, brown-, and orange-covered books that gave Claire the feeling of a lodge's roaring fire and the sense that if she walked into the store, behind this display of green and cold to the left, she could find that warm place depicted to the right. She laughed aloud. Janet was a challenge most days, but she was brilliant, and when she created, you could see her heart—and it was beautiful.

She felt a presence beside her and turned. "Seth?"

"Are those . . . That's my train set, isn't it?"

"Janet brought them in this morning. She thought they would make a welcoming display for the store. She ran to get coffee if you want to wait."

"No." His reply was quick, but it held no anger. Claire heard notes of surprise, even panic in the simple word. She tried to read his expression, but he kept his eyes trained on the tracks and the one car Janet had set on them. It was a coal car, and she'd placed a small gold-wrapped, red-ribboned box inside. "Don't tell her I saw this. Don't mention that I walked by."

"Why not?"

"Please. Don't." Seth glanced toward the coffee shop. "She looks thinner. I saw her at Maddie's funeral yesterday . . . Is she eating? She's a wonderful cook, but she tends not to prepare food or eat much when she's alone. When I used to travel . . . Never mind." He cut himself off and studied the train tracks.

"Honestly, I don't know."

Without another glance or word, Janet's ex-husband walked away.

Claire watched him until he was out of sight, then turned back to the window. She had met Janet after her divorce. She knew little of Seth, other than Maddie had adored him.

A paper cup materialized before her face. "Almond-milk latte."

"Thank you."

"What's wrong? You don't like it?" Janet stepped closer. Their shoulders touched as they both gazed at the window.

"I love it. Looking at it makes me happy."

"Same here. It's the closest I've felt to home in a long time."

Madeline

A light rap on my door preceded "Mr. Frankel is here for you."

"Thanks, Patricia." I tapped my screen black and slid the case file aside before looking up. Liam Duncan, of Duncan, Schwartz and Baring, taught me that. *Put your work away, physically, as the client enters. It not only shows you're giving them your attention, but it makes them reticent to waste your time.* Maybe that meant less drama and hand-holding for a divorce lawyer like Duncan, but it rarely made a difference in contracts. Nevertheless, I followed his edict.

I looked up, action ended, and no one entered. I leaned back, waiting and preparing myself for small-rimmed glasses, young, and sloppy. Still no one. Ten more seconds passed before I found myself faced with tall, dark, massive, and a dusting of gray hair.

I stood immediately. "Mr. Frankel?"

"Miss Cullen." He boomed like James Earl Jones—the Darth Vader version, not *The Sandlot*'s. "Call me Greg."

"Please come in and have a seat."

My eyes must have appeared huge, because he grinned a full set of bright white teeth. His eyes almost folded shut with the smile.

"I'm not what you expected, I see."

"I expected you to be young, and your voice is different . . . I . . . I know I sounded so patronizing."

He did not refute my statement as his smile grew broader. "People say I sound different on the phone. I'm not sure what that's about. And I found you refreshing. Not many people coach me so readily. But then again, I don't work in wills and estates often. Perhaps a little coaching was warranted."

"What is your specialty?"

"I work mainly in the prison system and a little with the Bluhm Legal Clinic when I can, mostly in children and family justice."

"At Northwestern?"

"Yes."

"I went to law school there." Pride straightened my posture.

"Yale man myself."

I swallowed. Hard. I felt my throat lift up and lodge and it didn't settle back in place. I swallowed again, and again, working out my embarrassment, and something that tasted worse.

"Now I'm the one who's sorry." He leaned forward, eyes still crinkled.

"For what?"

"I'm enjoying this a little too much."

My face flashed hot. I waved to his chair and lowered myself into mine. And while his chair was a few inches lower than mine, he still sat taller. "You deserve the moment."

Again he didn't contradict me. Instead he pulled a file from his messenger bag and laid it across his lap. "I'm sorry, as well, that we meet under these circumstances. Maddie was a good friend; I can't imagine the honor of calling her family."

My face stayed warm.

He dropped his eyes to the file as if giving me a private moment—it only added guilt to my emotional mix.

"It's very straightforward. She left you everything. The will's been filed, and you mentioned no one is likely to contest. I suspect it will clear within a couple months, partly because she left her property directly to you rather than requiring her estate to dispose of it. If she had done that, we'd be talking . . . There's a backlog; who knows how long?"

"She left me her house?"

"And the bookshop."

"You mean the inventory, not the actual store. She and Pete rented the space."

"She bought it outright with Pete's life insurance."

I sank back. Selling a house was straightforward. Heck, closing out the inventory could be outsourced. But the entire store? Somehow it no longer felt cut-and-dried. This was more than books and stuff; this was Aunt Maddie's life's passion, and her legacy.

He slid a piece of paper, a summary of the estate's assets, across my desk. I scanned it top to bottom. "I don't understand why she did this."

"She loved you."

I kept my eyes trained on the page. "How did you know my aunt?"

He slouched, getting comfortable, and his breath felt expansive; he was inviting me into a memory. "Almost twenty years ago, when she and Pete first opened their store, they provided a book cart for the Juvenile Temporary Detention Center on South Hamilton and another for the one up in Lake County. There were a few titles I thought should be there, so I reached out to Maddie and Pete. We became friends."

"What titles?"

"The missing books?" My question surprised him. He smiled, eyes drifting up in memory, as he cast back. "The usual suspects: *The Catcher in the Rye*, *The Outsiders*, *Lord of the Flies*, *Fahrenheit 451*, *The Brothers Karamazov* . . ."

"Those are the 'usual suspects' for teenagers in juvie?"

"If you want them to learn something about life, decisions, anger, angst, survival, and human nature they are." Greg chuckled. "That's where we started at least. Maddie had her own ideas. Now I can't keep the kids from Green, Rowling, and that dystopian fairy-tale author . . . What's her name?"

I shrugged.

"Anyway, that's how we started. I met Pete first, but they always were more of a pair than stand-alones."

He was spot-on. I remembered that about Uncle Pete and Aunt Maddie too—and after only spending a few weeks with them. They were the personification of synergy—more whole, more joyful, and more fun together.

I always wondered about that. The day we left, only Aunt Maddie stood by, beet red and scowling. Uncle Pete was nowhere to be found.

"He was a quiet, gentle man. I spent a few weeks with them, summer of 2000, and almost every evening he walked with me to the ice cream shop on Third Avenue while Aunt Maddie puttered around and locked up the shop."

Greg chuckled again. "Pete was a good and steady friend. I miss his counsel."

I dropped my eyes back to the page and hit a point at the bottom. "How was she still in business? Her expenses are higher than her income. She was broke."

"Your aunt wasn't the shrewdest businesswoman. No head, or care, for money. She was all about people. You have your work cut out for you if you want to make a go of it."

"What?" My sharp tone surprised us both.

"What what?" Greg sounded as confused as I felt.

I shook my head, clearing away the past to focus on what lay ahead. *Irreconcilable differences.* I didn't have time for them today.

Greg shifted his gaze to survey my office. I followed his sweep and could almost hear the gears in his head turning.

Mahogany walls to the chair rail; a wool Berber rug revealing exactly fourteen inches of flooring around the room's perimeter; my Northwestern Law School degree prominently framed above my head, with gold edging on two mats rather than one to make it appear even larger. All associates were required to frame their diplomas and any honors at a shop on North Clybourn. The firm determined the specifications, and the new hire paid the $1,200 bill. After all, as we were reminded almost daily that first year, the signing bonus *was* generous. My office was big-law opulence at its finest.

Greg said nothing as his eyes recaptured mine.

I slid the page across the desk. "Didn't she have a financial advisor?" On second thought, I didn't want an answer to that, so I pushed out more questions to cover it. "Didn't you find it odd there wasn't one allocation, one bequest, to anyone else? Favorite charities? Organizations? Her church? I don't know her interests or her intentions."

"They are all listed in here. She hoped you would help each as you saw fit." He patted the file on his lap. "And that you'd run the bookshop."

"What?" Now my tone wasn't sharp, it was incredulous.

"That was her wish . . . Look, your aunt was a unique woman, I'll give her that, but she was also wise. Get to know her shop and her life and you'll figure it out. She had to have good reasons for what she did."

"Do you have any idea how busy—" I stopped. My whine scraped my own ears.

His eyes darted above my head again.

Darn that gold trim.

"I can imagine all this takes quite a bit of upkeep. But . . ." He dropped his focus. It was laser sharp, and I sensed how formidable an adversary or ally he might be. "Maddie trusted you with her legacy. That should not be taken lightly."

He tucked the paper I'd handed him back into the folder, then laid it on my desk. "She built this file over years. You'll find all the contact information you'll need, along with lots of little notes and lists. That woman loved herself some lists."

I pulled it to me.

"Careful."

I opened it slowly and understood. The file was packed with small notes. A few lifted with the release of pressure. I pulled off the top sheet. There were several napkins covered with Aunt Maddie's scrolling hand.

"There are dates on some of these. 2005?"

"I noticed that too. I'm not sure if the file was always meant for you or those were once reminders to herself. You'll have fun either way. It's all Maddie in there."

"Who are Claire and Janet?" I picked up two thick cream-colored linen envelopes.

"They work at the Printed Letter."

The envelopes were sealed. I was intrigued at what Aunt Maddie left for them in my care.

Unbidden, a line from a long-ago book came to mind. *No one is told any story but their own.* I couldn't recall the book or the time or the context, but I understood the message. I placed the envelopes back within the folder and noted an identical one with my own name. I lifted it in question.

Greg stood. "You were important to her, Madeline."

We stared at each other. On any other day, I suspected, he would have shared his opinion of me with me—and I wasn't sure it was positive.

"Thank you." My words were a fifty-fifty split between *Thanks for bringing the file* and *Thanks for holding your tongue.*

"You're welcome." His words sounded evenly split too.

As he walked out, I called, "Is your contact information on one of these little notes, if I have questions?"

"It's across the binding on the will and at the top of my cover letter."

He chuckled again. I warmed again.

Of course it was—and I should've known that.

Janet

I leave the shop at five. It's my first full working week since October. That's when I took over Maddie and Claire took over the Printed Letter. I appreciate that we didn't talk about it. I simply didn't come in one day, and she picked up the slack—all of it. She acts like I did all the heavy lifting, but Maddie was never heavy. She never took, she gave, all the way to the end. I was and am the one kicking my heels, dragging my feet, and every other cliché about small kids who don't get their way.

It's amazing what your body does when your mind is elsewhere. I pull into Maddie's driveway with no memory of steering my car this direction. No memory of one stoplight, two stop signs, and the twists and turns of her curvy street. Someday I'll make this drive and find kids playing in the yard and new owners staring at me with suspicion. I'll be the strange lady with the crazy hair who had a friend here once and can't let go.

I could sell my house and buy hers. It's the perfect size for me. Mine is too large and packed with the ghosts of Christmases past. And who am I kidding? Keeping my house is not the thread that will pull Chase and Alyssa back to me. If anything, it does the opposite. Chase might say to his baby someday soon, "It's too painful to visit Grandma. She still lives where I grew up, as if everything is okay and she didn't destroy our family."

I let myself in Maddie's back door and fill the kettle as I've done a thousand times before, as I did yesterday and as I'll probably do tomorrow. I stop myself from calling out to the day nurse, "I've got tea going. Come pick your flavor." They were good women, the hospice nurses who came at the end—stretched too thin, often too tired, but filled with hearts of gold. Either they were naturally like that or Maddie brought it out of them, because each one who entered this house was kind and good and willing to wait. It felt as if it was a privilege, being here with Maddie, and no one wanted to see her go. Then she did go, and the nurses stopped coming, and . . . Here I still am.

My rounds are quickly done: water the plants, run a rag across every flat surface I pass (my version of dusting), and grab the mail from the front hall—all while the water heats. This close to Christmas the mail is mostly catalogs. The postman dumps them through the slot in the door, although he knows Maddie is gone. I wonder who will officially stop the mail and how one does that for the deceased. I carry the pile back to the kitchen, pour a cup of chamomile citrus tea, and sort through it. Catalog. Catalog. Christmas card. Bill. Bill. Bill. Catalog. Christmas card. I toss the cards into the recycling bin right along with the catalogs. After all, how close to Maddie can you be if you're sending a card this Christmas? I add the bills to the growing stack on the counter. Someone will need to take care of those soon too.

A knock at the back door startles me, and tea spills across my lap. I leap up with a cry as the door flies open.

"Are you hurt?"

"What are you doing? You scared me."

"I saw you and thought you'd look rather than jump. You okay?"

Chris grabs two clean towels from the second drawer by the dishwasher and tosses one to me. He uses the other to mop the table and dry the last of the mail. "I saw your car. I noticed it yesterday too. Do you come by every day?"

The way he says *every day* makes him sound like a therapist.

"Thanks for your seat at the service, by the way." I sit back down. "It's weird I'm still here, isn't it?"

He leans back against the counter and crosses his arms. He is studying me. He can't help himself. "Not at all. Clearly I'm checking too, or I wouldn't have seen your car."

"I'm not sleeping well. Will you prescribe something for me?"

A slow smile spreads across his face. We both know the answer, but enjoy the little ritual. I asked it every day that he came to visit Maddie, and he came to visit Maddie every day. I like to think we sound like a nagging older sister to her know-it-all little brother, but that's stretching it, as he's only four years older than Alyssa.

"I can't, won't, and wouldn't if I could. Keep up the chamomile tea and, as I've said, try 400 milligrams of magnesium glycinate."

"Fine." I push out of the chair and head to Maddie's liquor cabinet. "Want something stronger?"

"Not tonight. I'm on snowplow duty." He looks out the window. "I hoped it would hold off a few more days since I have more yards to winterize, but tonight's the night. Are you ready?"

"I've got salt for the walk, but I forgot to call the plow company." I reach for my phone.

"Don't." He lays a hand over mine. "I'll take care of it for you."

"Thank you." I press my lips together. Calling the plow company had always been Seth's job. Last year I hadn't called, didn't know whom to call, and when the snow came I simply sat on my front steps and cried. Lucky for me, it never got above four inches at any one time all winter, so I never had to solve the problem. But the prognosticators say this year will be different. Snow, and lots of it, is coming our way.

Chris withdraws his hand and his gaze from me and focuses on the window. I suspect he knows when I slip away in memory and shifts his focus to be polite. We've been through a lot in our short friendship, and on some level we understand each other better than most.

"Have you thought about what Maddie told you?" I ask.

There was a "last conversation" between the two of them. I was supposed to leave, but I'd hovered behind the door, and he knew it.

Chris quirks a sideways smile. "I'm not sure she was right. I don't feel ready."

"You may never feel ready until you begin. Apply for a position, go to work, and see how it goes."

"Sonia would like that."

I snort, a horrible piggy-truffly noise. "I'm sorry, that was rude, but you can't do it for her and she shouldn't want you to. That's not how healing or love works."

"Listen to you." Chris smiles, and rather than feeling pleased with how evolved and reasonable I sound, I feel like a hypocrite. He continues, "Maddie only said what Luke's been saying for months. They're right, I need to move forward."

"Luke better not be making you feel guilty," I snap back. I've had enough of priests and ministers making you feel bad—a whole childhood and divorce full of them.

Chris holds up his hand like he's calming a jumpy puppy. "He's not. I promise. But he does say there's a fine line between healing and hiding and that I'm flirting with it."

"Wonder what he'd say to me?" The words come out in a slightly less offensive snort and I mean them rhetorically, as I have no intention of ever asking Chris's brother, the priest, his thoughts.

"He'd say you're loved and then would probably ask if he could hug you. He's as big on hugs as you are."

He says it so quietly and with such deliberation I want that hug. I can almost feel it.

"I have to go." Chris pushes off the counter. "I told Luke I'd salt the walks of some of his parish's elderly."

"Does your boss pay you for that?"

"This is on me. I used last month's paycheck to buy a front plow for my truck. That way, after taking care of company work, I can get the parish houses and you plowed too. I'll salt walks now, but they're calling for over ten inches."

Chris opens the door and is backlit by a new world. In the few minutes we've been talking, huge fluffy flakes have dusted everything like powdered sugar and the sky reflects the pinky-purple of Chicago's lights, over forty miles away, bouncing across the low clouds and the now white ground.

"Thank you." I follow him out the door and lift my head. Flakes fall on my nose and lashes. They're so big I see them resting there. "It's beautiful. Snow makes everything feel new."

Chris speaks from across the drive. He doesn't yell. In this soft, silent world, he doesn't need to. "Maybe if we believe it, it will be."

Chapter 5

Madeline

How ya doin'?"

"I'm going to throw up." I dropped my head to my keyboard. It hit too hard, and a soft whirl of letters filled the office. I straightened and started the one-finger deletion of a million *g*s.

In my periphery, Kayla lowered herself into the chair across from me. There was no flopping, flouncing, or plopping. The woman billed almost as many hours in a week as I did, yet nothing she did was hurried—it was like she floated through the crucible, and none of the heat, pressure, or grind burned her up or broke her down.

"You're not going to throw up, because you've got this—and you're a woman." Her voice remained steady, flat.

"Meaning?"

"That all blind scales are even—race, gender, you pick—in theory at least, and in that sense, Drew Setaro is formidable and on an equal footing with you. But let's be honest enough to recognize we don't live gender blind, or any form of blind, and with an all-male partnership, your being a woman will help."

"That's sexist."

"You don't say?" Her voice arched, and I was reminded again; Kayla moved smoothly through the water because she was more shark than seal. Growing up where she did, she had to be—she measured the lay of the land and never shied away from spelling out the truth, to me or to her clients.

"I want to be valued for my work. I've earned this."

"We all want that—the other may be an added bonus today." She leaned back and crossed her legs. One short block heel bobbed in a regular beat. Another thing I admired. Women around here wore three-inch-plus heels—including me. They made us feel tall, with all the power height carried. Kayla's heels never went above an inch. She frequently pointed at my shoes with a *Why do you do that to your back?* expression.

"Celebratory lunch? One p.m." She flicked a finger to my computer.

I tapped the keyboard to retrieve my calendar.

"I've got half an hour at two."

"I'll be ready. Meet me in the south conference room. I've ordered from Jay's Lobster and have a half bottle of champagne chilling. How's that for planning?" She winked and rose from the chair.

Without another word she left, and I smiled. Her confidence quelled my fear. Then I heard a soft "Liam" as she rounded the corner, and it roared to life again.

Liam Duncan.

He tapped on my doorjamb upon entering. His "Cullen, a moment?" was rhetorical.

As was my "Of course. Please come in and have a seat."

I gestured to the suede chair opposite my desk. My arm stalled halfway, as it always did.

Our office manager let it slip one day that, at the three managing partners' request, the seats across from our desks were custom-ordered to sit inches lower than standard. They were designed to put clients, opposition, and everyone else at a subconscious disadvantage.

Knowing this, I never sat in anyone's office except Kayla's, and

I felt I embodied every horrid lawyer cliché when I offered the seat to someone else, especially to one of the named partners.

Liam considered the chair. "I'll stand. This will take only a minute." He shifted as if prepping to launch that minute. "We've issued a press release. Drew Setaro has been named partner." He lifted his watch, a sleek silver Patek Philippe. "There will be a celebration dinner at Shanghai Terrace tonight at seven . . . I didn't want this to surprise you."

The words slid out so smooth and swift, and the glance to the watch gave them an extra-casual air.

I had to break down each word and digest it before I could breathe. Even then I wasn't sure I'd heard correctly. "You. Chose. Drew."

"We did."

Nothing worked. At least not my head. It felt stuffed with cotton. I stood, and the heels helped—at least I was now a couple inches above him. "May I ask why?"

"He's ready. It was a tough decision—" Something in my eyes stalled him. "But it was a unanimous one."

"I see." I shook my head. "No. To be honest, Liam, I don't see. Please explain this to me."

He dipped his head as if my request was unexpected, or rude, but he was willing to indulge me. "Setaro's work is clear, authoritative, concise, and effective. We studied case by case and—"

"And I've worked more cases, winning cases too."

"True." Liam's eyes hardened. "But when you look deeper, Setaro is covering innovative ground with his arguments."

My mind drifted back to a conversation between Drew and me a couple years ago—back when we had only two things on our minds, the first being the law. His eyes lit with his latest case.

"I love my argument for the Briony case."

"How can you love an argument? You cite precedent, again and again, and hope you win." I pulled the sofa cushion between us. I remembered that. It felt as if I needed comfort, as if I was about to discover something I had missed out on.

While I curled away, Drew shot forward. "Not at all. The goal is to find something new and stretch the law. It's not a closed loop, and if you know the tenor of the court, any court, you can win new ground, set precedent, and create change. Take any Supreme Court decision you want and you can trace how culture, the justices' personalities, and the times in general appropriate it and change it, as does each subsequent allusion. It's alive, Madeline."

The scene closed and Liam materialized again before me. "I see."

It was something I never saw coming. It wasn't quantifiable or billable. I did my job. Drew followed his passion.

"What's your advice? For me?" My voice broke on the last word. I cleared my throat.

Liam wasn't fooled. He took a deep, slow breath to either consider my question or savor the relief. Last year's losing Millennial, as Schwartz called us all, screamed so loudly the entire office heard her. My stupor surprised me as well—in the midst of it.

Liam smiled.

I felt my breath release. Then his smile shifted a fraction and I felt it. Condescension. Maybe it happened between every generation, but mine never got the respect of actually having grown up.

"Keep doing what you're doing. You do excellent work and your time will come."

"Good to know."

He forced out a half laugh and a "We'll see you tonight" as he walked out. Mission accomplished.

"Okay then." I dropped into my chair, tapped on my computer, and opened a blank document.

ONE HOUR LATER, A paper in hand, I walked the hall. The top of 333 West Wacker was a swanky place with a view of the city overlooking the river and glass, glass, and more glass. Then there was the marble, the art, and the antiques.

Each named partner had his own style and commanded a third of the effect. Liam Duncan's was Modernist Intimidation. Schwartz leaned toward Old Boys Club with his cozy-cigar-law-tomes and deep leather chairs. Baring reached for 1930s Art Deco, mobster-meets-the-law in Old Chicago.

"Is he in?" I threw the question to Liam's ancient assistant and kept walking.

"Madeline— You can't— M—" Mrs. Walker chirped after me, chair scraping, drawers slamming in her haste to rise.

But laughter through the open door told me Liam was in, and I was still riding my wave of courage and indignation, supported by a healthy dose of humiliation.

I crossed the threshold and waited. He was on the phone. I scanned the room and absorbed the two massive paintings on the interior walls, oils by Japanese artist Takashi Murakami. Late at night, we associates often scoffed at the hubris of displaying such extraordinarily pricey pieces to clients.

My eyes dropped to the gray and red hand-woven Persian rug. I'd had my eye on one just like it. I thought to use my partnership bonus to buy it. I gripped the sheet of paper in my hand tighter. It crinkled in protest.

Liam locked eyes on me and continued his conversation. "We'll discuss this at our meeting next week. They don't have grounds for an injunction. They won't risk the exposure, and if they do, we'll handle it . . . Good . . . Yes, I'll see you there. Give Donna my best." He put down the phone. "This must be important." He pointed a couple fingers to the set of Arne Jacobsen Swan chairs in the corner.

I stretched out my hand.

He eyed the paper before reaching for it. "You can't be serious. If you don't get a trophy, you quit?"

"That's insulting."

"So is this." He gave it a cursory glance, then thrust it my direction. "It's impetuous. I expected more from you."

I noticed his eyes drop to my sides. He fully expected me to take the paper back, to slink away, maybe to apologize. I didn't move my hands, but I did sense the light fist each created.

"This is carefully considered. I've been here long enough to know it wasn't merely the partnership at stake. It's the partnership's faith in my work. It was judged and found wanting."

I heard an old movie, *The Knight's Tale*, play in my head. My best friend Mandy and I used to chant the line to each other ad nauseam when we were teenagers. *You've been weighed. You've been measured. And you've been found wanting.* I looked it up once and found it originally came from the Bible's book of Daniel, but it was still the movie voice that played in my head.

I nodded to the paper. "Associates don't get two shots at partner."

"Making it one's first time is like shooting par your first time on a golf course—very tough to accomplish. If associates get sensitive and display a lack of tenacity, it is not the firm's fault they leave and miss another shot."

"Perhaps not. But the vote never comes back around for an individual. Everyone knows that. And that doesn't make it tough to accomplish; it makes it impossible."

Liam dipped his chin. I wasn't sure if he was surprised by my statement or that the associates had discovered this truth.

He stood, and I pulled myself a bit taller with each slow breath. *One . . . two . . . three . . .*

He slid the paper into his black leather inbox. "I'll start the process this afternoon. I'm sorry to see you go, Cullen. You've been an asset to this firm."

I pressed my lips shut against the many comments poised to fly. My brain generated them at lightning speed. Yet none sounded right. They needed anger to sell them, and I wasn't angry. I was sad.

I managed a dry-eyed nod as I turned to leave.

"Madeline?" Mrs. Walker's sturdy heels clicked after me across the marble hallway. Her voice had morphed from indignant matron upon my breezing past her to concerned grandmother. I kept walking. If I stopped or turned, the dam would break.

At the elevator doors I made a mental note to apologize to her.

Kayla met me five minutes later in the lobby. "It's all around the office."

"How? It just happened."

"Mrs. Walker heard you . . . How could you?"

We stepped outside. Kayla waved down her Uber and we hopped inside.

"How could I not? You know my chances now. Nada."

"Not—" She wavered a split second before truth won over diplomacy. "Fine. You're done . . . But who knows? Maybe it's for the best. Duncan is a misogynist. Schwartz is a misanthrope. And Baring? Something's wrong with him too, but I'm not sure what."

"Baring is a good man." I swiped at my eyes. "That's why he seems odd."

"That must be it." She wiggled into the Prius's seat belt. "What's the plan now?"

"As I said, this was moments ago. I don't have a plan." My stomach bottomed out as I noticed the traffic surrounding us. "Where are we going, by the way?"

"When Mrs. Walker told me, I called Imani. No lobster and champagne for you. We've got a corner table at the Purple Pig. We need well-cured fatty meats and better wine."

"Not during—"

"What? They gonna fire you?"

I shrugged. Kayla was right. This did call for wine—but not champagne. It needed a hearty red to ward off the season's chill and the frost of my future. And her old roommate was a chef there—we always got a good table and the royal treatment. Right now I needed the TLC.

Within minutes we were surrounded by octopus with green beans and fingerling potatoes, house-made meatballs with a green garlic ricotta puree, and the turkey leg confit with crisp lentils and cabbage. I swirled a glass of Montepulciano Cabernet while Kayla sipped club soda.

"You're not joining me?"

"Sorry. I've got work to do and this isn't a celebration. What might help your afternoon won't help mine."

"True." I raised my glass. "Cheers. To new beginnings."

We each took a sip, lowered our glasses, and stared at each other.

"Madeline . . . Part of me congratulates you. This is no way to live, and as soon as I can manage it, I'm out too." She sat back. "But if you want big law, you need to move fast. Word will get out why you left, and how. Finding a new job may not be so easy soon."

"They should all know I deserved the partnership." I cracked down on a wedge of French bread.

"And quit when you didn't get it. To other firms, it's a little cliché and a liability."

I stopped chewing.

"You didn't need to hear that." Kayla had the grace to backpedal, a little bit. "I'm sorry. What can I do?"

"Join me for lunch. Nothing more."

We ate in silence as my vision narrowed. She was right—my options were limited and becoming fewer with each passing minute.

It was a quiet lunch. Kayla didn't know what to say and there was nothing I wanted to hear regardless. The walk through the office's hallways was no better. Everyone had heard and pretended they hadn't as they swiftly walked out of sight.

I heel-kicked my office door shut for some relief, then pulled it back open at the last second. Firm culture kept our doors open, and I refused to hide now.

"Picking up your ball and going home?"

The question sounded too familiar. *If you don't a get a trophy, you quit?*

Drew stood in my doorway. Eyes that were once soft and inviting were sharp, almost accusing. He'd broken up with me, yet I always got the impression I'd somehow wronged him. He didn't step into my office. He filled the doorway, arms crossed and his face equally strident. He had this expression that flattened his eyebrows and made him look somewhat like a vulture.

"What were you thinking?"

Rather than reply, I began to clear my desk. It was time for this day to end, even if it was obscenely early.

"Madeline?"

"Don't snap at me. I made a choice, and as you well know it was the right one. You're the one who worked up the data."

He cringed. "I'm sorry."

In those two words, I sensed the Drew I once knew—the one who sneaked kisses in high-backed booths, the one who always reserved a conference room so when we worked late, we worked late together, and the one who had called it all off with three little words: *I need more.*

I hadn't seen or heard from that man in over a year and a half. Instead I found a stranger, a competitor, in the office on a daily basis, and learned the hard truth that iron sharpening iron only makes for very lethal weapons.

Again, I refused to cry. I widened my eyes to air dry them and I noticed something, many things, little things. Changes within

Drew that I now recognized had been there for some time; I simply hadn't paid attention. "Your hair is shorter."

He reached up and brushed his hand against his short brush cut. I remembered running my fingers through that hair. It had been soft with a touch of curl at the ends.

"Has been for almost a year."

There was more. His suit was more tailored, perhaps custom-made. He was always loose limbed and loose suited when we dated. He lived too distracted by the law and all the possibilities before him to worry about the mundane. As part of a couple, that was my job.

I cast back to his cases. Liam was right, Drew had pushed in the last year. I had cleared a few, but he'd cleared almost as many. So much of what never appeared to matter to him before seemed to have morphed into his being. I wondered who stood before me.

"Congratulations are in order."

"Thank you." He stalled, unsure of me. "I appreciate that."

Words burst forth before I could stop. It felt like the hourglass was running out, for my career and my answers. "Was this why you called it off between us? This was your 'more'? The partnership?"

His half smile twisted with the last question.

"It was never about the partnership. That's not what I'm about even now . . . but that's not helpful for this discussion. We wanted different things, Madeline. I was honest from the start. You didn't want to hear." He swept my office with a single glance. When the silence stretched beyond comfort, he waved his hand at my desk. "Are you already packing?"

I looked down. Without thinking, I had stacked three picture frames, including one photo he'd taken of Kayla and me after we ran the 2015 Chicago Marathon. "I'm clearing some stuff out. Who knows when they'll set security on me."

"Not until you summarize your work." There was that semi-smile again.

"True."

"Want to walk me out?" Kayla rounded the corner full steam. "Excuse me— Drew!" She stopped so fast her momentum tipped her forward. He turned to catch her, but she caught herself. "I . . . I'll come back later."

"No." I stood. "Drew's leaving." I gestured to him and tried with my expression to convey I was happy for him and maybe sorry for anything I'd done. It was a lot for a look, but I didn't trust myself to offer anything more.

"Yes. I'm leaving." He pulled his gaze from mine and nodded to Kayla before walking away.

I straightened my desk, hoisted my bag over my shoulder, and led the way to the elevators.

We walked to the Peninsula Hotel in relative silence. Kayla had a wonderful gift of knowing when to speak into silence and when to let it lie. She asked few questions, demanded no details—until we hit Michigan Avenue's bridge over the river.

"Will you move?"

"Not if I find something fast. If I don't, well . . ."

The disparity between my income and expenses hadn't hit me until that step. It was no secret between us I lived paycheck to paycheck. While Kayla had saved for the past seven years, to pay off her loans and help a couple siblings, I had furnished my condo and taken a few extravagant, albeit short, trips. After all, I was young, single, and worked endless hours.

My signing bonus had been the down payment on an outrageous condominium, and every dollar in had practically meant a dollar ten out—with interest rates so low, credit was deemed a form of "portfolio diversification." But now, with no income, credit was a liability.

Panic churned low in my stomach. "I won't lose my condo. I—"

"Even if it takes time to land somewhere, that won't happen.

You could part with some of your beloved treasures to tide you over. That *is* why you buy them."

"I'm not sure I can. It's bad when investments become family."

"It's stuff, girl, not family." Kayla sighed. She'd never shared my definition of safety.

"Fine. If it comes to that, you decide who gets orphaned out."

"You could go home. Join a firm in Manhattan."

"I'm not sure I want that, and Manhattan's not for me."

My reply about work took me by surprise, but my comment about New York didn't. Ever since middle school, I'd only ever wanted out. Coming west to Chicago for law school was the best decision I'd made. It was my city now—the home of "broad shoulders," good neighbors, deep-dish pizza, and classic hot dogs. We weren't too stuffy, too fancy, or prideful. We braved the wind off the lake, tolerated our corrupt politicians, helped our neighbors, and rooted every season for all our teams, regardless of the outcomes. We had a flag—one I liked so much I carried a small needlepoint replica as my keychain.

"I'm staying here."

"Good. I'd miss you."

At the Peninsula Hotel, Kayla paused.

I lifted my head as if expecting to see the partners toasting Drew within the Shanghai Terrace, perched on its fourth floor. "What have I done?"

Kayla one-arm-hugged me. "Don't question it now. It's done, and I say it was right. They've never revisited an associate, and if you're after a partnership there's no reason to linger." She dropped her eyes to mine. "Unless you want to take a one-eighty? You can come up with me and pull Liam aside. He'll take you back. They're not idiots."

I shook my head. "I can't . . . I won't do that."

"Then go home and think about it tomorrow."

She pulled open the Peninsula's glass door, and I headed down Michigan to East Pearson and home. The word beat a steady refrain as I crossed Michigan Avenue. *Tomorrow . . . Tomorrow . . .*

Tomorrow!

I stopped in the center of the sidewalk. A man, with a groan and a glare, two-stepped around me. "Sorry." I dodged out of the way and pressed my back against a building. The cold stone felt bracing and necessary. I tapped my phone. "Mom?"

"I didn't expect to hear from you tonight. I thought you'd be out celebrating."

"Don't come tomorrow."

A beat fell between us.

"Why?"

The question was soft and inviting, covering two syllables at least. It invited the full story. It invited confession. I felt like a kid, as though if I crawled into her lap she could make this right. I slumped against the building and opened my mouth to talk. I then swallowed any words that might escape. I couldn't tell her. I couldn't say it out loud.

"Do you want to talk to your father?"

"No." The word barked out involuntarily. I took a deep breath. "I mean . . . He's home? Why is he home so early?" Eight o'clock Eastern Standard Time was early for Dad.

"He had a doctor's appointment this afternoon and decided not to go back to the office."

"His ulcers are back?"

"Most likely. He won't talk about it."

I smiled. I gave my mom credit. No one could ever accuse her of nagging. She fought her battles in different and highly effective ways. Rather than hound my dad to open up, talk to her, or change his habits to alleviate said ulcers, she simply stripped the house of anything that could do him harm—many of the spices, most of the hard liquor, and all the processed snacks. We hadn't heard about his ulcers in years.

"When did they start up?"

"I have my own theories on that one, but let's discuss the ulcers later. Tell me why I shouldn't come." When I didn't supply the answer, she filled in the blank. "Ah . . . I'm so sorry, dear. That must have been a shock. What are you going to do?"

I squeezed my eyes shut. Thirty-three and I still didn't want to disappoint my mom. I couldn't face my dad. "I quit."

"I see . . ." She let the words trail. She would not ask if I wanted to speak to my dad again. Cullens never quit.

We said little else. It wasn't her style to press or to offer meaningless assurances. My decision was my own, and I would bear the consequences. If anything, she was thinking up ways to break it to my dad with a positive spin.

She landed the same place Kayla had. "You've had a good salary for a long time, dear."

I rubbed my eyes. "You're right."

"Then don't worry about dipping into your savings to pay your mortgage—that's what it's there for."

Mom and I had secrets.

"Ten percent each paycheck." I mimicked Dad and hoped Mom didn't catch the derision in my voice. I hadn't saved one percent, much less ten each paycheck.

"That'll carry you through . . . I can still come; we can spend some time together."

I begged off and we soon hung up. Kayla's concerns, and my mom's assumptions, filled my head as I took the elevator to my apartment. After I opened the door, they overwhelmed me.

I lived on the thirty-third floor, overlooking the lake, in a corner apartment with full north and east views. I lived in the clouds and caught the curving expanse of Lake Shore Drive as it dipped around

Oak Street Beach, and a few old and interesting buildings before the lake captured everything to the east. I even spied bits of Navy Pier to the southeast with its Ferris wheel and tentlike rooftops. The views were breathtaking—day and night. It was my sanctuary—and I paid dearly for it.

I let my eyes drop from the view and focus on what was directly before me. If Duncan had his power play aesthetic, Schwartz his Old Boys Club, and Baring his vintage Chicago gangster vibe, I had Multigenerational Stability. It felt safe and secure. I often wondered if I was trying to reimagine my childhood, with brighter notes to make it happier and lighter. The sturdy eighteenth-century English antiques gave it that feel, but the art—sleek, bright, modern, almost minimalist—kept it and me from getting too serious too soon.

A friend at Sotheby's always tipped his hand to me when something came along undervalued and interesting. The living room rug from Iraq, George III end tables, and the George V file cabinet I'd found at Sid McKenna Interiors and Antiques. Also my latest acquisition, the French breakfront I'd filled with my collection of British law books. And right in the center of it all, my favorite piece of furniture: a brilliant green velvet sofa with brush trim that made the whole place look jaunty and alive. It was my home—one I'd created and felt comfortable within. I felt in control here. There was nothing to surprise or harm me. I could breathe.

I dropped my keys in the early twentieth-century Chinese bowl I'd placed on the hall side table. They had made a few chips over the years—it was probably not the best spot for my keys—but I wanted to use everything. Enjoy everything. So often valuable items were placed beyond reach growing up—*Don't touch that. Don't sit there. Take your shoes off.* What was the point of owning anything if it had no use? If you didn't interact with it?

I walked to the windows and gazed out across the lower buildings to the east and to the lake. Kayla was right. Decisions would need to be made, quickly.

My eyes drifted north. The Hancock Building had added new lights for Christmas. Each week more red and green adorned the top. The additions cast a glow so bright it hit the small bronze statue tucked into the corner. The little Henry Moore radiated red.

"Of course you're in the red—you and me both now."

It had cost me last year's entire bonus, plus a little more.

Claire

Lisa Generis pivoted to the right and walked down the bookshop's side aisle, trailing her finger along the spine of each and every book at shoulder level. Claire let her be. She understood. It was like walking through a European emporium and embracing the merchandise—touching the colorful silks of adventure; pricking the cool, sharp metals of self-help, DIY, and politics; tasting the sweet and spicy flavors of fiction, nonfiction narrative, and biography; catching your breath from the electric shocks of romance and the heady scents of gardening.

She glanced over to Janet, who sat cross-legged in the children's section like an elementary school kid. Though eight years younger, Claire cringed at Janet's coil; she could never get her knees to fold so tight. The left one ached while standing behind the counter on cold days. And in winter, the Printed Letter was always cold with its drafty windows, loose floorboards, and a heating system Maddie should have replaced a decade ago.

Janet leaned forward, bending into a semi child's pose. Her brown skirt puddled around her. The dark made a sharp, beautiful contrast to her hair and the whitewashed wood floor. Corkscrew curls flowed down her back. Fifty-four years old, and she moved with the energy and agility of a kid—had all the highs and lows of one too.

"If you kill any of those stuffed animals, I'm taking it out of your salary," Claire whispered to her.

"Lucky buggers. They're unbreakable." Janet flicked her hair back with one hand and shoved a giraffe into a cubby with the other. It now resembled a baby duck, yellow and folded impossibly tight. She then moved on to the books, pulling out a handful of the colorful Puffin Classics for Young Readers a few inches before knocking them into alignment. They presented a strange cross between soldiers and Easter eggs.

Claire watched her move through the shelves and on to the picture books displayed on the freestanding tables. The whole cleaning ritual took only minutes. The children's section was always a mess.

But not today . . .

Claire wondered if Maddie's welcoming nature had been a boon or a curse. On rainy cold days, the Printed Letter was often more daycare than bookshop—as some of the framed handwritten letters circling the ceiling molding attested. Kids loved the bookshop. Kids had loved Maddie.

Today—although it was miserable out—there were no kids about. No adults either. An early snowfall kept everyone away, and the usually bustling and welcoming shop was empty except for Lisa. And it felt sad, as if the shop itself had just realized that what lay ahead could never be better than what lay behind.

Claire twisted toward the front and took a deep breath. Lisa had migrated to the end of an aisle and stalled in Nonfiction. She knew Janet would not come forward. In fact, once Janet registered Lisa's presence, Claire wouldn't be able to find her at all.

"Good morning, Lisa. May I help you find something?" she called as she circled the counter and wove between the tables. Lisa smiled as Claire drew beside her. "You're the first customer we've seen today. I doubt anyone expected so much snow."

"It's all supposed to melt by the end of the week. Welcome to winter." Lisa peered around the store. "I had to stop by my office, but thought it was a better afternoon to curl by the fire with a book than be the only one working."

"I agree . . . And you've landed on some perennial bestsellers." They stood before the *Hs*. Claire tapped the spines of *Unbroken* and *Seabiscuit.* "I always wondered what it'd be like to write . . . but to write like Laura Hillenbrand?"

"I've read those, but . . ." Lisa crouched on the balls of her feet, bringing her eyes down to the later letters of the alphabet.

Claire noted supple black leather boots, highly polished with only a slight scuff on one toe, and the black cashmere coat that spread across the floor behind her. She opened her mouth to say *I like your boots*, then warmed at how silly the comment sounded in her own head. Yet the *I* had already escaped. She turned it with a slight stutter. "I . . . I can try to help you find something if you tell me some of your favorites."

It was a bold request, and Claire wondered if she could fulfill it. Maddie had been the expert at that. She always knew the right book, for the right person, at the right moment. That was one reason for the town's extreme loyalty—one among many. But now that she was gone . . .

Claire shook her head to banish the thought as Lisa stood with a book in hand, and she drew her eyes from the boots to the book.

"People were talking about this at work, and the reviews look good." Lisa held out *The Extrovert Dilemma*.

"Already? It released Tuesday. Copies shouldn't be here though, but on the front table." Claire scooped up the other two copies and pointed to the narrow draped table in the center aisle. And what a table it was. Janet had created a masterpiece; a patriotic extravaganza meets Cleveland Cavaliers meets culinary wonderland, with draped cloths and decorative signage that complemented the bay windows.

Two former presidents, a celebrity chef, and an NBA All-Star had released memoirs in the same month. Those four, along with *The Extrovert Dilemma*, commanded the entire table, as well as an e-newsletter and a special promotion.

Many customers bought the books based on Janet's display alone. Yesterday, in fact, Dottie Neuland, ninety-three, who hated politics and never followed sports, had purchased both presidents' books and started in on the NBA memoir while standing at the display table. She had grabbed the store's only pair of plus-five readers off the display rack in order to do it. Claire had doubled the store's reorder for the books only yesterday.

Lisa's eyes, then feet followed Claire to the table. The transition allowed Claire to study her more fully. All black clothing from her scarf to her coat to her dress or skirt peeking from beneath, down to her boots. She had a quieter style than Janet, but no less commanding. Claire had learned in snippets of conversation, tidbits gleaned, that she and Janet had been best friends, but words had been said, or something done, and now they never spoke. Yet Lisa still came into the store. She purchased books and always looked around, as if searching for something lost.

"She is talented." Lisa fingered a long, loose ribbon draping down the table skirt. "Is Janet here today?"

"Somewhere. Shall I find her for you?"

"No. I'll get this." Yet rather than hand Claire the book, Lisa surveyed the shop again.

Claire felt the opening and searched her mind for what she knew about Lisa. *Law.* She could do this . . . "I can make another suggestion you might like."

She crossed to Fiction and pulled down *The Life of Pi.* "The author, Martel, has a unique voice, and this novel is based on an 1884 British legal case involving cannibalism. Though in this story, the sailor, Richard Parker, is a tiger rather than a human. It's a fascinating read."

Lisa shook her head in long, slow sweeps. "I don't care for fiction."

"Nonfiction only . . . At least you know what you like. So many people don't. I bet you'd tell your story like you dress, straightforward narrative nonfiction."

"Excuse me?"

"I'm sorry." Claire waved her hand to erase the question. "I didn't mean to say that. I mean, I love your boots, and we talk like that a lot in here, how we'd tell our stories. Maddie used it with the kids she tutored to get them to think about stories and new ways to write. With adults, she said it was an exercise in self-awareness."

She felt a blush crawl up her neck and scratched at it with her fingers. "I'd tell my story in third person with little self-awareness, or so Janet says." She clamped her lips shut and the heat bloomed. She'd said too much. She chastised herself—knowing about Lisa wasn't the same as knowing Lisa. She sounded silly and had unwittingly laid herself bare—again confirming Janet's comment on one of the first days Claire had worked at the shop.

It's like you live in those classics you love, in some odd third-person narration, as if you aren't in charge of your own story. Who is, if not you, for goodness' sake?

A blush had crawled up her neck then too. First, because Janet hadn't yelled "goodness" to eviscerate her; second, because Claire had no retort. She had stood silently, lips parted, humiliated. Only flashes of memory, glimpses of a brighter self long ago, made her feel Janet's indictment wasn't entirely true, or at least hadn't always been true.

Claire felt the hot wave anew and turned away to hide her neck. A blush was never a good thing, as it did not bring a second bloom of rosy, dewy youth. It brought splotches—pronounced freckles and an odd rash—that lingered for hours.

"I can imagine Maddie doing that, and Janet saying that." Lisa broke across Claire's thoughts and held out *The Extrovert Dilemma*. "Maddie tutored my own kids through honors English. In fact, one majored in English, he grew to love literature so much."

As Claire rang the sale, Lisa picked up a box of question cards called *One Hundred Starts to Great Conversations*. "Add one of these. This could be fun when the kids come home for Christmas." She held out another box wrapped in cellophane. "Forget that. Add this one." *Things Nice Women Don't Say*.

Claire reached for the box. "Janet purchased those."

Lisa laughed. "I suspected that. They aren't Maddie's style at all, but I bet they're hilarious."

Clair dropped the purchases into a bag as Lisa scanned the store again. "Thanks for dropping by today. Have a safe drive home."

Her words drew Lisa's attention back to her. "Yes. Thank you. Enjoy your quiet day too."

As the chime on the front door rang out behind Lisa, Janet materialized. "Thanks."

"For not searching for you? I did that once, remember."

Janet kept her eyes on the door. "I'm glad she still comes to the store, but . . . Awful things were said, Claire. Horrid things, mostly by me. There's no use going back." Janet busied herself by wiping down the sales counter of zero dust and straightening things already straight. She shuddered, as if resetting herself. "Want to see what I did after closing last night?"

"Sure," Claire acquiesced. There was no point in asking questions. Janet would only provide answers on her own schedule.

"Check this out. I added tiny lights all around the molding."

Beneath the hanging letters Claire found a thin strand of lights aligning perfectly with the groove in the wood.

"That must have taken you hours."

"I checked on Maddie's house, then . . . I had nothing else to do." Janet flipped the switch.

Claire shifted her gaze out into the store—and into darkness.

"Seriously? Again?" Janet grabbed her phone off the counter and pressed the flashlight. "I'll go flip the fuse."

Janet disappeared into the back as Claire stood in the dark. The sadness they had outrun last week made headway with the flip of the switch. She felt it seep across the room and pull the air from her lungs.

"It's all changing, isn't it?" Janet stepped beside her in the dark.

Claire didn't answer, and silence settled between them. It soon morphed into a wave louder than anything they'd experienced in that small bookshop. Louder than book launch parties, author signings, evening book clubs, employee silly sing-alongs, or the nights when the three of them had sat on the floor and laughed at all the oddities the bookshop's four walls witnessed on a daily basis, customers with their personalities, peculiarities, and all the books that spoke into those secret places.

The silence stole the last of Claire's breath. The Printed Letter had never been silent. The small shop had been filled with everything from exuberant laughter to sobby rages, but never silence. She couldn't speak it, but she agreed with Janet. It felt like the moment of release when she stopped pressing the tender spot on her knee on cold days. That moment when the comfort and the light compression lifted, and it was left aching, swollen, and always worse than before.

Some days, when the sun was bright, it was hard to tell if the Printed Letter's lights were on or off. The front bays let in so much light that the books often glowed like rainbows tossed about the shop. That was not the case today. It was all gray. It was all dark.

Janet flipped the switch. Nothing happened. "Go put out the Closed sign and I'll call the electrician. Maybe he's not busy this morning."

Claire wove her way around the gifts table, past the stationery display, Cooking, Politics, and Travel. So much life and literature packed into such a small space. A sanctuary. A haven. A bookshop.

And Janet was right. It was all changing.

Chapter 6

Claire

The store felt like a Christmas wonderland. Janet certainly had a gift for design and color, and the season burst from every corner. White lights, not colored, provided a glittering backdrop. Rich books with reds, greens, and white created the seasonal forefront in one window, while softer shades brought warmth to the other. The train made a soft whirling sound as it wove through the books and across the table she'd set near the window. Three hours to the store's annual Holiday Bazaar.

Claire reviewed her selections again. They needed to be perfect. The best books to give—to your sister, to your aunt, to your aging father and your surly neighbor down the street, to the party hostess, to the avid gardener, to your teenage daughter, to your aspiring young chef . . . Thirty-seven suggestions and over forty copies of each, stacked and ready for purchase.

She wiped her hand across an empty table. It sat waiting for the trays of meats, cheeses, and appetizers. The wine store had already delivered the night's choices: ten good Cabernets, five Pinots, six Chardonnays, and seven Proseccos. They would never go through it all, but it would be worse to run out of any choice, and once a trend started, the whole party could opt for one selection. She slid a macaroon from the box. The bakery on the corner had already made its delivery as well.

It felt good. It looked good. Every detail checked off. And no one had called to say the shop was up for sale. In fact, no one had called at all. Maybe, despite her fears, it could work out. The Printed Letter would remain the Printed Letter. Claire absorbed the look and tenor of the room, certain of one thing: she couldn't bear for this to slip away.

She cast back to before moving to Winsome. In Ohio they'd lived in a tight neighborhood—front doors unlocked; kids roaming between houses; friends ringing doorbells to borrow eggs, bacon, or a whole chicken; dropping by to decompress after work or to get a new idea or the ingredients for dinner. Weekends were spent enjoying barbecues and backyard games, with waved hellos at church and impromptu brunches following. She'd been at the center of it all. Yet in Winsome, she hadn't met her neighbors, only their dog through the fence. They had stopped by once and left cookies and a note by the front door, but she'd delayed returning the courtesy—and to do so now felt too late, too rude. But Maddie had seen her, welcomed her, and given her a place, right as she'd felt herself slipping into invisibility. She'd returned after reading *The Secret Garden*, eager for more, and walked away with not only a new book but a job and new friends.

Maddie's shop was worth a fight. Strong profits tonight, and the brother might not sell.

"I saw that." Janet poked her in the side.

"It's my last one."

"How many have you had?"

"Only three."

Janet laughed. "Eat one more and I'll slap you."

Claire covered her mouth to speak around the cookie. "Why does everything end in violence with you?" Her voice was teasing and light, but Janet's face fell.

"I was kidding. Is that what you think of me? Angry all the time?"

Claire shook her head.

"It's true, isn't it?" Janet narrowed her eyes. "Every little thing creates such havoc in me. It's like my reserves drained away and I can't fill them up."

Claire handed her a macaroon. "It'll get better."

They both chewed. The business of setting up was done and customers were few. Claire hoped most were waiting for the party.

Tippy Wilander approached. "I need to return this book."

Claire accepted the book and checked the spine. It was unbroken. "Did you decide not to read it?" She had personally recommended *All the Light We Cannot See*, but as this was the third return on her suggestions this month, perhaps she wasn't acquiring Maddie's gift of pairing people with books after all.

"My grandson found it cheaper online."

Claire walked to the register with Tippy three steps behind. "You'll find many books cheaper online, but we provide good recommendations and service, and the ability to come in, browse, and shop locally."

"True." Tippy tapped the book with one arthritic finger.

Claire rang up the return. "Here you go. We hope to see you tonight at our annual Holiday Bazaar. We'll be recommending books for everyone on your list this year."

"Maddie was so good at that. Are you offering a discount?"

"Absolutely. Tonight we're offering the party's usual 20 percent."

The older woman shoved her receipt deep into her handbag. "I'll be here then. I'll bring my grandson too."

"Please do."

Claire noted that as Tippy approached the front door, Janet opened it and sent her off with a cheery "See you tonight."

Door shut with a decisive click behind her, Janet and Claire locked eyes and stifled their laughter. Chuckling over Tippy's latest return with five other customers in the store would not do.

To resist temptation, and another macaroon, Claire waved to Janet. "I'm going to get a coffee. Would you like one?"

"Please." She sounded as exasperated as Claire felt.

But the coffee shop was no relief. Claire still found the atmosphere intimidating. It was always crowded and full of old ties, bonds between friends and patrons built over years, not months. She wondered if this was how Brittany felt each day at the high school—that you had to prove yourself, offer yourself up, and hope someone found you interesting enough to invite you in.

She joined the long line waiting to order and noticed Seth. She swiveled slightly to shift from his line of sight. She liked Seth but, irrational as it was, every conversation with him felt like a betrayal of Janet—as did keeping their chat outside the store window a couple weeks past a secret.

"I thought that was you." Seth closed the distance between them. "I saw Janet made more Christmas updates to the shop windows. It must bring in business; it's over the top."

"It is, isn't it? She's very gifted." Claire cringed. The one subject she didn't want to touch.

"She is." Seth smiled and stepped closer. He waited next to her, holding his own coffee. "I also saw the sign that the Holiday Bazaar is tonight. That was always Maddie's favorite event of the year."

"I started working in January this year, so this will be my first."

"The store was always packed. Maddie's two favorites, people and books, crammed into one evening. After Pete passed, I used to help her get the books out the door, carry them to the cars, and box up the orders to ship out the next day. I think I had almost as much fun as she did."

"From the accounts I knew it was a big night, but I hadn't really thought about the logistics."

"Have you got extra help?"

"I . . . We'll get it. Thank you." The barista waved her forward. "Oh . . . Two medium lattes. One with almond milk, one with coconut."

"Janet?" Seth nodded to the order. "Is she over the moon today?"

"She's excited about tonight, but I wouldn't say—"

"I meant Rosie."

"Rosie?" Claire felt a chill . . . She had a feeling she knew exactly who Rosie was. "Chase's wife had her baby." It wasn't a question.

"Last night. Two weeks early, but seven pounds six ounces, full head of hair, and plenty of fight. She's gorgeous . . . That's why I'm not downtown today. I'm driving to Indianapolis to see them." Seth caught Claire's expression and frowned. "Isn't Janet excited?"

"She doesn't know."

"Chase didn't call her?"

Claire shrugged. She was unsure, yet certain too . . . Janet would have shouted the news from the rooftops, and Claire could've eaten all the macaroons in the box and Janet wouldn't have threatened a slap.

Silence hovered between them. It grew into a living and awkward thing, only broken by the barista handing Claire her two lattes.

"I need to get back to the shop, but . . . Congratulations. I'm so happy for you. Someone should tell Janet. Please . . . This baby is everything to her."

Seth pulled out his phone. "Do you want to see a picture? Chase sent them and Laura also posted a few on Instagram."

"Please. No." Claire stepped back. "Janet hasn't seen a picture yet. I can't see one before her. I can't know this before her."

"But surely on Instagram?"

"Her kids have blocked her from their accounts." Claire blurted the words. "I—I shouldn't have said that."

Seth took a moment to absorb it. "I'll email them to her."

"Don't do that." Claire stepped forward. It felt too close, but necessary. "If you send her a picture, it means you're aware Chase didn't. It'll feel like salt grinding into her and, despite everything, I doubt that's your intention."

Seth's jaw flexed, and she wondered. Then his face softened. "That's not my intention. There's been enough of that for a lifetime." He slid his phone back into his coat pocket and gestured to the door. "I should go, and I expect you'll want to get those back before they get cold."

Outside the coffee shop door, he paused. "It was good to see you, Claire . . . And thank you."

He turned to the left, she to the right.

As she pushed open the shop's back alley door, a whirlwind struck her.

"I'm a grandmother!" Janet raced into the office and swallowed her in a hug, pressing the lattes between them.

"You are?" Claire set them on her desk and wiped off the foam that had escaped the lids and dotted her coat.

Janet bounced on the balls of her feet. "Chase sent this flurry of texts. See . . ." She tilted her phone to Claire. "Laura went into labor yesterday and I guess it was horrible and terribly long and they were so exhausted they're only now getting the word out. Rosemary Margaret Harrison. Or maybe she went into labor this morning. I'm not quite sure what he means right here." She pointed to a text with no caps or punctuation. "The poor boy clearly hasn't slept, but look . . . Look . . ." She scrolled through several pictures, each of a squishy red face wrapped tight in a hospital-issue pink-and-blue striped blanket.

"She's perfect," Claire offered.

"They're calling her Rosie."

"That's perfect too."

"Isn't it? I'm a grandmother! Isn't this the best day ever? And tonight? Tonight we're going to do this thing. I can feel it; it's all changing, but for good, Claire. Don't you feel it?"

Janet strode toward the front before she could answer, which was probably a good thing. Because if pressed, Claire, looking out into the now empty shop, would have told her the truth.

That while she wanted change, good, positive, beautiful change, she didn't feel it trended that direction—at all.

Janet

Claire rings up sales as I guide guests around the tables and shove books into eager hands as fast as I can. We chat through thirty-plus recommendations in an hour and a half, and shoppers are eager to finish off their Christmas lists. The wine still flows and the food is holding out—all except Claire's beloved macaroons. They were gone before we began.

In a day of great moments, this feels fantastic. Maddie would have loved witnessing the community she'd created. It's a packed house tonight—part party, part shopping spree, and part tribute to Maddie. Unlike her funeral service, this evening does her justice.

Most of the shoppers are our regulars, and a personal touch lands the sale every time. *Your husband will love this* or *Didn't you start a garden last spring?* or *Isn't this diet exactly what you mentioned last month?* I used to connect to people through Seth, and the two years alone have thrown me off, but tonight, unable to hide behind Maddie's love or cover, I sense I can connect through something new, through books. I can't give myself too much credit though. I busy myself with customers with whom I share no past; former friends I still avoid. Lisa Generis, my closest friend for almost twenty years, stops me by the wine table with a question and I panic—and lie.

"Claire is more the expert on the kids' section. Let me grab her for you."

I then spend the next half hour helping the high school volunteers ring orders—deep behind the counter and unreachable.

It's from this vantage point that I notice her. Maddie's niece. I refuse to let her presence bother me. She's taller than I remember, thinner too. Not fit thin, work thin. There's a difference. She looks tired, sustained by coffee and granola bars, a beige tired. Unlike at the funeral, her long brown hair is down and skimming her shoulders in a soft curl. She wanders around the shop, through the customers, talking to no one and touching the spines of books as if asking them to share their secrets. I suddenly feel possessive of the books, the shop, of Maddie herself.

I catch Claire's eye and throw my glance toward the niece. The shop begins to clear, but she lingers and I grow anxious. Time to find out what's up.

"You're the niece Maddie always talked about. I saw you at the funeral. You're called Maddie too, right?"

"Madeline."

Her tone implies that *Maddie* isn't good enough for her. I open my mouth to say who knows what when Claire steps between us.

"I'm so sorry for your loss. We hoped someone from Maddie's family might drop by."

Claire flutters at the end of her sentence. She wants answers, but is too polite to ask the questions.

I'm not. "We need clarity about the shop. Who owns the Printed Letter now?"

Claire glares at me. Madeline levels a gaze. I meant to throw a gauntlet and she knows it. I feel her sizing me up—just as I do the same to her.

"I do."

She offers nothing more and, oddly, I almost like her for it.

We three stand silent for a few beats. Claire speaks first. "We should talk. Give me five minutes to ring out Libby and Camille, and then we'll shut the shop."

Madeline and I are left staring at each other. But there's work to do so I walk away.

As Claire gently pushes octogenarian Libby through the door and tells Camille her orders will arrive soon, we turn to find Madeline assessing the shop. She stands arms crossed, and to me she looks like the vicar in that old novel Maddie read every year. He comes to the estate he's going to inherit on entail or something and starts examining every chair, every book, every dish, everything with a greedy eye. The daughters of the family laugh at him, but I don't find *Madeline* quite so funny.

Claire looks to me to lead the way. I shake my head. With a tiny Winnie-the-Pooh sigh, she concedes and approaches Madeline with an outstretched arm. I cluster three folding chairs together for our talk.

"Maddie left you the shop? All of it?" I blurt out. I meant to let Claire start, but as the Burns quote goes . . . *The best-laid schemes o' mice an' men gang aft a-gley . . .*

"Yes." Madeline again offers a short, aggressive reply.

Rather than add any softening details, she watches us. She's a lawyer; she's probably trying to figure out what we want and what grounds we may have to claim it. She makes some interior determination because she nods, to herself, not to us. "She left me the store, her house, her car, her debt. Everything."

Now I can't speak. How could Maddie do that? I didn't expect anything for myself, but to leave it all to this little ingrate in her designer boots, pencil skirt, and million-dollar attitude? Couldn't Maddie have been more discerning? And her *debt*? What does that mean?

"And what are your plans? For the shop? You live and work

downtown, right?" Claire's voice grates. It's curious and kind, as if we're sitting down for tea and this young ingénue is making her debut, not planning our demise.

"I . . . My plans have changed. Maddie's lawyer gave me a financial statement, and the store isn't faring as well as I'd hoped. It's not salable at the moment, at least not for a profit, and I don't . . . I can't afford to lose money on it. I have some time on my hands, so I thought I'd join you here and bring the store back up. In the spring I'll reassess and most likely list it for sale."

"As in three-months-from-now spring?" I almost lift off my seat.

"Yes."

"Let me get this straight—you're going to revive the shop during the quietest consumer quarter and position it for profitable sale in a matter of weeks? And you've run a bookshop before, so you know how it's to be done? And you're going to do all this from your downtown law firm?"

"Janet." Claire whispers my name.

Neither Madeline nor I spare her a glance.

"As I said, I'll be here. And it's that or I sell off the inventory at a discount and list the space separately. I googled it and—"

"You're getting business advice from Google?"

She reddens and I almost feel bad.

Claire cuts between us. "We have some ideas, and we can teach you anything you need to know."

Traitor. I glare at Claire, who widens her eyes back at me. I falter as I realize she is trying to protect me. We both know no one will pay me what Maddie did, and if we can get Madeline to honor it, even for a few months, it's a help.

I concede. "We're happy to stay on staff until the sale."

Madeline slumps as if from relief, then catches herself and sits straighter. "I would appreciate that, and I'm no longer at my firm so I'll work here with you in the store and learn what I can."

"What happened?" It was a burst of disbelief; I couldn't help myself. Claire glares at me. But there's no way *Madeline* gave up a six-figure salary for this. There's more going on.

"It was time for something new." She shrugs and suddenly looks so young. For all her sharp edges and stiff clothing, she is young—maybe only a year or two older than Alyssa.

"Janet, why don't we start to clean up?" Claire plucks at my sleeve before I can reply.

Madeline stands as well. "How can I help?"

Claire points to the farthest corner of the store where the drinks table sits. "Can you start over there?"

Madeline walks that way and Claire spins on me . . .

It's time for my lecture.

Madeline

I leaned back on the couch and scanned my apartment, seeing nothing. Instead I recalled my tour of Aunt Maddie's house hours before. My apartment and her house could not be more different—their structure, furnishings, smells, and fabrics. Yet they held similarities too. Without wandering through her house tonight, I never would have known we owned many of the same books. Not books you put on display, but books you keep on your bedside table. Books you read. Books you love.

I also noted we veered toward the same colors: reds, oranges, and yellows with only highlights of cool. And we both had a dish for keys by the front door. Tons of people probably do, but I smiled and decided to believe it was only the two of us. And I never would have guessed my favorite green couch, on which I now sat, was the exact color of the Printed Letter's sales counter.

Greg Frankel woke me this morning practically ordering me north to Winsome tonight. "It was your aunt's favorite night of the year, her literary showcase of sorts, where she helped customers find the perfect gift for practically anyone. It was also her best money-maker, so get up there and learn something. It's your store now."

I hadn't had the courage to tell him I was selling. I hadn't wanted to think about it myself. It felt wrong, almost dishonest, destroying her legacy like that. But it also made sense. It was the only logical solution—that came from another early-morning conversation, this one with Dad two days earlier.

"Real estate is not a bad investment, but the management will run you too thin. Sell it and get out. Use the money to diversify your portfolio into a real estate hedge fund. How are you invested now?"

I panicked—and lied. If I learned anything from the summer of 2000 and the crash that changed my world, it was that "portfolios" were ephemeral things that could hurt as much as help. I'd chosen to "invest" in things I could touch, feel, enjoy, then sell if needed. There was always a market for good physical objects that had already stood the test of time. None of this I shared with Dad.

"Dad, I've got an interview this morning and I need to prepare. Can we talk later?"

"Nothing to discuss. I wanted to advise a sale. Have a good interview."

Dad never liked to commit to future chats. I think they made him feel hemmed in. So my spendthrift ways and lack of a portfolio were still my secrets—for now.

But now that I'd seen the store, and met Claire and Janet, I wondered how I was going to get it ready for sale. I clearly walked into enemy-occupied territory tonight.

You're the niece Maddie always talked about. I saw you at the funeral. You're called Maddie too, right?

Janet was so abrupt, I could only stammer "Madeline" in reply.

She then sneered at me as if I wasn't worthy of Aunt Maddie's nickname, and I'm not. To have heard it all those years in adoration, then derision, made it powerful. I didn't know who Aunt Maddie was—new information conflicted with old assumptions—and all of it left me adrift. Yet the sense that she was worth knowing and understanding grew within me.

Neither Janet nor Claire paid too much attention to me at first. The store was packed and there were as many kids as there were adults. That surprised me. High school kids behind the counter. Young children spilling from the kids' section and clogging the aisles. They seemed as at home in the store as their parents and grandparents. It was light, lively, and everything Greg had hinted it would be. I heard Aunt Maddie's name again and again as if she were in the shop with us all, bolstering the mood and inspiring the sales.

Afterward I decided to dig for more answers and check out her house—my house now. The driveway was plowed, but the front walk remained pristine with new snow and glistened like the inside of a snow globe. The crunch sounded like I was crushing diamonds beneath my feet. I turned and looked both ways down Bunting Avenue. The street was resplendent with Christmas lights—all except Aunt Maddie's house. It stood cold and dark and empty. I'd never seen it near Christmas, but I would bet Aunt Maddie celebrated it well, with lots of lights.

I unlocked the door and pushed my way past an avalanche of catalogs. They spread across the hall under my feet. Stepping over them, I turned on the light. The small entrance hall was painted latte brown. I recalled it as off-white nineteen years ago, but the brown was better. It provided a good contrast with the white trim. It was fresh, modern.

I glanced into the living room. That was a new color too. Gone was the gray. Instead I found cream that showcased her art well.

She loved bright paintings, scenes and abstracts. Looking around, I began to wonder if I had copied her taste. There was a bold red elephant on the far wall, double matted in brown suede and red linen. I remembered Dad once commenting, *That crazy woman is dragging Pete off to Africa. Selfish, if you ask me. He's not well enough.*

Only after Uncle Pete died did Mom tell me it was *his* dream to go, and Aunt Maddie, unable to talk him out of it, had done everything she could to protect his health. There was no stopping his cancer though, and from what Mom relayed recently, there was no stopping Aunt Maddie's either.

I noted the small table to my right and the dish for keys. That's when my list of similarities began. But while we both had something practical on the front hall table, hers was a beautiful tightly woven little basket. I dropped in the house key and ventured deeper into her home.

The seagrass rug still covered the living room floor, but the sofa was now a soft beige with a bumpy texture that called for me to rub my hands over it. The two chairs were equally inviting, covered in a red, orange, and green floral. It was so warm and welcoming, I dropped into a chair before I could stop myself. It felt like home.

She had family photos lining the bookshelves. One of me at college graduation and another from law school. Yet she hadn't attended either event. *Mom.*

I walked into the kitchen. It was exactly what I remembered—white cabinets with white Corian countertops. We had white marble counters in our apartment growing up, and our housekeeper always got snippy with me when I spilled. But that summer, right after she'd redecorated her kitchen, Aunt Maddie had been the opposite. "That's why you buy this stuff. It's impervious. Try." She'd handed me a bottle of curry spice. "Go ahead. Rub it in."

I'd tapped out a small dot, then wiped it away.

"You can try a marker too. Everything. I sometimes leave notes for your uncle right here on the counter."

I wandered on. There was a small office off the kitchen, a powder room, and a back family room. This was where we watched old movies that summer. It had had a wood floor and a wonderful multicolored woven rug. That rug was gone now, replaced with another full of browns, creams, beiges, and yellows.

I walked up the stairs. The fifth one still creaked.

Four bedrooms.

Two bathrooms.

I tripped over the final step coming back down as a face filled the front door's glass window.

"Are you okay?" it called to me.

I caught myself with the banister and focused again, recognizing the guy from the park the day of the funeral. "What are you doing here?" I did not open the door.

"I saw lights. I thought you were Janet Harrison."

At Janet's name, I opened the door. "Why would Janet be here?"

He dipped his head as if I'd asked an unreasonable question. "She was here a lot, before, and has been keeping an eye on the house."

"Oh . . ." There was so much I trampled on with every person I met.

"Now that I know it's you, I'll go. If you're going to be here more or anything, you might want to take the key out from underneath the planter. It's right outside the back door." He turned to leave.

"Wait. Could . . . could I ask you some questions?"

He raised a brow. I chose to believe that meant yes.

"Janet and my aunt were close? I met her tonight and . . ." I let my question drift away, unsure how to end it. I only knew I was over my head, with no allies.

He chuckled, and that I understood. He surmised my meeting with Janet had not gone well, and he was right.

"She lived here Maddie's last couple months and took care of everything from food and thank-you notes to bills and nurses' schedules. It was a tough job—not that your aunt made it hard, but because Janet, in the end, lost her best friend. Go easy on her."

I almost retorted *Tell her to go easy on me*. Instead I pressed my lips shut.

He stepped away.

"You said Aunt Maddie brought you soup, but you knew her well too, better than soup and books, didn't you?"

He shoved his hands into his pockets and rocked back on his heels. "We became good friends. I think she enjoyed mothering me, and I found I wasn't too old for a mom's care."

"I expect we never are." I noticed his boots. Snow swirled around them. It had started coming down in earnest.

He followed my gaze. "If it gets above a couple inches, I'll plow Maddie's drive for you."

"Thank you . . . How much do I owe you? I see you've already done it at least once."

His eyes hardened. "Free of charge."

"Thank you."

"I'd do anything for Maddie."

With that he was gone. I turned back into the house and leaned against the door. Only when he pulled out of the drive did I grab the key from under the planter, lock up the house, and head home myself. Traffic would only build with snow falling.

Now I shut my laptop and looked around my own apartment. Despite all the work I'd put into it, it felt like the home of someone I expected to be rather than someone I was. Or maybe it reflected someone I'd never become. Aunt Maddie's home had been warm, inviting, and lovely—it wasn't the quality of the pieces within it, but how they reflected her, the *her* I remembered from my brief weeks visiting there, and the effect was beautiful.

My phone rang.

"Hey, Mom. What are you doing up so late?"

"Nothing. I couldn't sleep so I was up reading . . . How are you? What are you up to?" Her voice held her signature light, airy note. She was engaging in the prerequisite niceties before she hit her purpose.

"Nothing." I sank deeper into my couch and waited.

"Have you been up to Winsome? To check on Maddie's home and the store?"

"Mom?" I dragged the word out. "Why would you think that?"

Two could go fishing.

"Fine. I lost my iPhone."

"And?"

"Your phone was still logged in. Remember when you left it at Saks while we were shopping?"

"That was over a year ago. Have you been keeping tabs on me?"

"Not at all. As I said, I lost my phone this evening and yours popped up."

"Where'd you lose your phone?"

"I—"

She was a dreadful liar. She never reached for the first one, available and perhaps believable, but the best. Thinking up the best took time—and always killed her chances for something convincing.

"Mom? Where did you lose it? . . . Did you think about any privacy concerns here?"

"You're such a lawyer . . . I'm deleting your phone right now."

"Thank you."

"So how was Winsome?"

Now that the subterfuge had passed, her tone filled with gentle concern.

"Okay. Odd. I remembered so much of those weeks with her and Uncle Pete . . . And then she got mad and we left. But everything

I see and hear doesn't reconcile with what I experienced . . . I had thought she was wonderful, then horrible, and now tonight . . ."

"She was wonderful, Madeline."

Mom wasn't going to answer any of my questions, including those I couldn't ask. Her one sentence carried a finality I'd heard before. One that at work I'd used before. The topic was closed. The final word had been said.

I cast for a new topic. "One of the women who works at the store, Claire, gave me a flash drive of all the accounts as I left tonight. I believe she meant to help me, but after spending the last few hours reviewing the data, I suspect she meant to warn me. It's bad, Mom. Aunt Maddie's finances are in really bad shape."

"That's a shame. Will you lose the store? Maddie loved it."

"Dad said it'd be stupid to sell it without showing a profit, but it hasn't shown a profit in almost two years. It was draining her dry and her estate has other bills to pay too, and not nearly enough to cover any of it without some serious income."

"Do you want to sell it?"

"I have to sell something, Mom. Fast. And what else would I do with it? Moving up to Winsome and running a bookstore isn't exactly using my skills to their fullest potential."

Mom stayed silent a few beats. She'd heard Dad give the lecture enough times to know where it came from.

I opened my mouth to apologize for being rude, when she cut me off. "Who says?"

Two words, and it wasn't the bookstore that came to mind, or the house—it was a set of green eyes lit with disdain. I'd just undervalued Aunt Maddie's life and work, as clearly as I'd undervalued him.

I'd do anything for Maddie . . . And I didn't even know his name.

Chapter 7

Madeline

I drove my car out of the garage for the second time in two days. Living and working downtown, and working such long hours, I had hardly taken it out in the last two months, much less driven it back-to-back days. I had nowhere to go within my usual life that I couldn't walk.

All in all, a car hadn't been my wisest purchase, as Mom pointed out one visit, but it hadn't been my worst either. And now—according to Greg's asset list—I owned two cars. There was a late-model Volvo station wagon tucked in Aunt Maddie's detached garage.

As I followed Lake Shore Drive north to Edgewater, I noted the winter waves crashing the shore on my right and the Gold Coast buildings giving way to townhouses and parks on my left. The scene was magical—dusted with last night's snow, dotted with lights and quiet on the Saturday morning before Christmas. It felt like everything could be made new and all might end well.

But I couldn't see how. While part of me reveled in seeing this bright white beauty, another part of me knew I was only here witnessing it because I had failed. I had failed to accomplish the one thing I'd set my sights on since that day freshman year of college when I decided to drop finance as a major and pick up history instead. The day I decided to become a lawyer.

I passed through Loyola, Rogers Park, Evanston, Wilmette, Kenilworth, and drove farther north. I wove through Lake Forest with its large and graceful homes, where Chicago's nineteenth-century wealthy had once driven their carriages to "summer." That always cracked me up—a season becoming a verb.

A series of twists and turns then brought me to Winsome. Last night I'd driven straight to the store, picked my way by memory to Aunt Maddie's house, then bolted in a flurry of white to race the snow home. Today I wanted to see more. I drove around the neighborhoods flanking the lake, the small town center, and the tiny industrial area west of the highway. That stretch was packed with home goods signs—furniture, upholstery, metal fabrication, welding. I wondered if this was where those nineteenth-century wealthy came to hire builders and find materials for their Lake Forest summer homes.

Winsome felt the same as it had when I spent those three weeks here nineteen years ago. It was as if Chicago had forgotten about it—just north of wealth and just south of Wisconsin.

The parking space in front of the Printed Letter Bookshop only allowed for ninety minutes. I pulled back out and used the time searching for a more permanent spot to build up my nerve. I felt completely comfortable walking into a courtroom or telling a Fortune 500 CEO she'd violated numerous statutes, but the prospect of trying to run a bookstore scared me speechless. I knew nothing about it, and I've never liked surprises or the unknown. Yet despite what Janet said, if you knew how to search, you could find anything on the internet. Heck, you could learn all you needed on Pinterest alone. And I'd searched until the early hours of the morning, of every morning, since Greg dropped this into my lap.

I walked the several blocks, going over what I might say and how I should say it. Then I stopped outside the store, and all thoughts fled my brain. The window decorations were different from last night's party—and they were mesmerizing. Christmas was bold and glaring then, a celebration. Now the decorations exuded a softer, more inviting feel. In one window there was a Nativity scene and books highlighting multiple faiths and traditions. The covers in the background arrangement held tones of deeper reds, browns, and yellows—it gave me the feeling of sitting in front of a fire, enjoying the glow. The other window still boasted a winter wonderland complete with a real train trolling gifts through the book mountains, but new books had been added to the foreground.

I stepped inside, and both women stared at me.

Claire stayed behind the register. Janet continued straightening a table. It was decoratively crammed with what Aunt Maddie called her "bijoux"—little gifts like stationery, water bottles, notepads, readers, conversation cards, literary coasters . . .

I slowly made my way to the register at the back of the store, working my way around customers and taking in all the details with each step, and willing my stomach to settle.

"Hi."

"I wondered when you'd come back. We didn't expect you today." Claire's hand drifted to her neck.

"I thought it best to begin right away. I stayed up practically all night going through the store's accounts. And I have something for each of you."

"Something for us?" Janet crossed the store.

"These letters have your names on them." I handed each a thick ivory envelope.

There'd been one addressed to me as well, and I assumed, because their envelopes appeared identical, their missives might hold the same: a short note, a long list of books, and a quotation from the book of Proverbs in the Bible. I didn't understand why Aunt Maddie had included that last, but it was lovely. It began with a mother's advice to her son, and then it morphed into a description of a woman. At first I thought it described a good wife, and it chafed that Aunt Maddie thought I needed such advice. Everyone wanted to marry off the single woman. But it wasn't about a wife per se; it was about an industrious woman, a smart and savvy woman, a good woman. And that made me wonder more about the book list. So much so that I'd already downloaded the first three titles onto my phone.

"These are books." Claire had opened hers and was scanning down the page. "We sell some of them, but not all. I've only read one of them."

"I haven't read any on my list." Janet ran her finger across a title. "*A Christmas Carol*? Are we to order these to sell? By Christmas?"

"I don't think so . . . That one's not on my list," Claire said. "What else is on yours?" She stepped toward Janet, who pulled her letter close. "It's okay. I understand." Claire smiled and stepped back.

Janet tapped the letter against her chest. "If it's for me and not the shop . . . I'll share someday. Right now I want to sit with it."

I smiled too. "I remember Aunt Maddie saying you could lose yourself in a book and, paradoxically, find yourself as well."

I expected Janet to scoff, knowing how close she was to my aunt and sensing how much she disliked me, but she didn't. She examined her list, regarded me, then returned to the list. "She did say that . . . Thank you."

We had nothing more to say. I offered my next gesture. "My aunt left other lists. Tons of them actually. There are lots of notes and random thoughts in this file. I can leave it . . ." I waved my hand toward the office. I didn't want to trespass, but I hoped for an invitation.

"Come on." Claire led the way as Janet returned to the front and the customers. "I cleared out Maddie's things this morning. This will be your desk." She tapped the edge of a box sitting on the nearby bookshelf. "I left all the office stuff in the drawers, but there are some personal things in here you might want."

"Thank you." The desk was neatly laid out with pens, Post-it notes, and small dishes for paper clips and staples, all at ninety-degree angles. I also noticed a row of boxes on the floor with *Greg Frankel* written in bold letters. "What are those?"

"Maddie used to give her friend boxes of books for shelters, juvenile detention centers, and other groups he works with. I expected him to have picked these up by now, but . . . I should have asked you. It's your shop now."

I laughed. "No worries. I've met Greg . . . He can have all the books he wants." There was no way I was going to refuse Darth Vader anything.

"May I offer a suggestion?" Janet stepped into the office doorway. "It's three days before Christmas, and I think we should run a sale. Everyone loved last night and the sales were extraordinary. Can we offer 20 percent off for the next two days?"

She looked to Claire for an answer.

Claire looked to me.

I shrugged. "Can we?"

"January is slow on the floor, and a lot of the inventory won't move then. A sale right now will drive last-minute year-end traffic," Claire offered.

"That sounds good, right?" I nodded to Janet, and she dropped to her chair. Without speaking, Claire moved into the store to work. It was like watching a synchronized swimming team—each movement of one complemented the other.

I dropped into my new desk chair and absorbed it all.

The office wasn't a large room. Probably only fifteen by fifteen feet square, it held three desks, a worktable, and stacks of boxes along the walls—the two not covered by bookshelves. Janet's and Claire's desks fit what I'd seen of them so far. Both simple desks, but Claire's was precise. A stack of books. A wire file holder filled with multicolored files neatly tabbed. Two picture frames with smiling children and a handsome gray-haired man. A mug with *Let Other Pens Dwell on Misery* filled with black pens. Everything sat in the same precise order that graced my desk.

Janet's desk was a cacophony of color. Books, papers, markers, scissors, and glue . . . Elmer's glue? . . . lay scattered across the surface. A stack of books had swelled into a precarious leaning tower at the right edge. As she banged at her keyboard and the printer whirled next to her, I was sure it would topple.

I looked past all the activity into a small side room. It was filled with boxes and one high table in the center. It reminded me of an old drafting table, large, sturdy, and wooden, with big metal cylinders on one side to tilt it.

"What do you use that for?"

Janet followed my gaze's trail into the room. "Nothing since Pete died, but . . ." She hesitated, eyes fixed on it. "There's a skylight in there and the light is wonderful."

I stepped into the little room. She was right. Even on this gray day, the small skylight flooded the room with light. More bookshelves caught my eye, and I stepped to another tiny room beyond. Not bookshelves. Wallpaper. The bathroom was covered in wallpaper mimicking bookshelves, and someone had handwritten book titles over most of the book spines. *The Lion, the Witch and the Wardrobe*; *A Wrinkle in Time*; *The Catcher in the Rye*; *Anne of Green Gables*; *Gone Girl*; *1984*; *Fahrenheit 451*; *Pride and Prejudice*; *Inkheart*; *Cinder*; *Slaughterhouse-Five* . . . The writing went on and on.

"Maddie was sick in here a lot."

I spun to find Janet standing within the small space behind me.

"We thought she kept getting the flu, and then her doctor said it was ulcers. We used to write book titles on the spines to crack each other up, but when she started getting sick more and spending more time in here, I came in after work to add titles to make her smile. *A Wrinkle in Time*, the Lewis books as well as *Becoming Mrs. Lewis*, Tolkien, and so many others. You can see them all on these walls. She loved Agatha Christie, and all sixty-six of her mysteries cover the top of this wall. I first listed all her favorites. Then mine. That's how you get Hemingway and Vonnegut down here. And when she'd noted all those, I started putting up funny titles, *Diary of a Wimpy Kid*, and all the Magic Tree Houses. That was a trial. There are fifty-four of them. I particularly like number eighteen, *Buffalo Before Breakfast*."

"I loved those books. You wrote out all the titles in the series?"

She bent to the bottom row. "Along here . . . That was right before she quit coming to the store."

"I had no idea."

"Well—"

I turned to her, as I preferred to face an adversary head-on, and her voice told me I was about to get an earful. But she stopped. Her expression changed completely. It softened, and she wilted, as if worn out and lost—exactly how I felt.

"No one knew, not until it couldn't be hidden. She wanted it that way. For all her tremendous giving, she wasn't great at receiving. Maybe no one does that well." Janet backed out into the storage room. "I think this could be an amazing space."

"For what?"

She strode into the office and I got the feeling I'd be chasing her a lot. Rather than answer, she handed me a color printout announcing the Printed Letter's sale. It was charming.

"If that's good with you, I'll post some on the message board at the Daily Brew and put a couple in the window. Claire will send out an email."

I scanned it again. "Excellent. Put it on the store's social media sites too."

Another copy dangled from Janet's hand. "We don't have any."

"Nothing? The store's not on Facebook, Twitter, Instagram, Pinterest . . . Nowhere?"

"Should it be?"

"If you want to sell stuff."

Janet's eyes hardened. My tone was more incredulous than condemning, but it was deemed unacceptable regardless. How could a store not be on social media? How did anything survive without social media?

"Then you've got your first job. Take care of that and I'll go post these. The old-fashioned way." She grabbed a few more copies off the printer and left.

I walked to Aunt Maddie's desk—my desk—and sat down. As I pulled my laptop from my bag, Claire raced into the office. She pointed to a long row of boxes.

"About twenty of those arrive every day. They need to be unpacked, scanned, and put out on the floor. After you finish whatever you're doing, could you start that? I'll show you." She stopped herself. "I'm not trying to tell you what to do, simply what needs to be done. And we're crowded out here today, which is a good thing, and I want to get this email out real quick."

With that she headed to the front and I got busy.

Claire

The store was packed. A tight, loyal community, Winsome had quieted toward the bookshop in the past months, as if a collective pact had been made to give Maddie the peace and quiet she needed. But that time was over, and the store needed loyalty—storm-down-the-door-and-buy-the-books kind of loyalty—and Claire thought that Janet's graphic was the perfect call to action, a delightful mix of traditional Christmas charm and mercenary commercial flair. It invited the town to rally and celebrate the Printed Letter at a 20 percent discount on all purchases. Madeline also opened accounts across several social media platforms and followed every business in town. Reciprocity would be slow in coming, but the posts looked wonderful.

Tight, loyal community. The thought chased through Claire's head as she observed Janet ducking behind the calendars and adult coloring books. Aha. Lisa Generis was back. Claire shook her head. Janet avoided more friends than Claire had made in the year and a half she'd lived in town.

That was the downside of a tight, loyal community. Few people needed new friends. And some had so many they could afford to dispose of a few, apparently.

"Good morning."

Lisa smiled and pushed two books across the counter. "I'd like to purchase these." She slid *Magnolia Table* and *Eat to Live Cookbook* across the counter. "I heard you say last night that you liked this one. And I've heard good things about this." She tapped *Eat to Live.*

"They're both very popular right now. I've tried a few recipes from *Magnolia Table*, but not from the other."

"My aunt suffers from Crohn's disease, and I thought she might find the recipes helpful and the title bolstering. I . . ." Lisa stalled as if realizing she stood in Maddie's former shop. "But we don't really have final control, do we?"

"But we also can't deny that good food helps." Claire swept the book up as Lisa looked around. "Can I help you find something else?"

"That's the Harrisons' train in the window, right? I remember it from their annual Christmas parties. Is Janet here today?"

Claire focused on the sale. "She's somewhere. Would you like me to find her for you?"

"Not at all. I . . . It's nothing."

"Thank you for coming in today." Claire handed her the two books in a bag and moved on to another customer.

Several customers later, Claire noted certain sections near the front of the shop looking sparse. She signaled to Madeline to rearrange and restock as she could. And, contrary to Janet's diatribe against Millennials, Madeline got straight to work and didn't complain once. The young woman ran back and forth all day, hauling books and straightening shelves. Not to mention, she sneaked out at four o'clock to fetch coffees for the three of them. She helped in every way possible and was beginning—sort of—to laugh at her many mistakes.

Janet's voice carried across the shop. "Betty, this is perfect for Don. And, Carla, so good to see you again. How's Buddy? Is he still thinking of majoring in political science? . . . Come see what we've got for him."

The comment sent Claire double-time to the office. She needed to find those former-president memoirs and a copy of that NBA bestseller, fast. She knew that's where Janet was headed. Despite avoiding a friend here and there, Janet had a deep well of history and acquaintances in town. She remembered their interests and always had a book suggestion ready.

Trying not to feel jealous, and invisible, Claire grabbed several copies of the books she sought.

Madeline careening into her didn't help. "Sorry. I didn't see you there."

Claire set the books on the table just in time for Janet to pick up three and hand them to Carla Murchison.

Claire spun away and returned to the register, where a customer stood with his back to her, tapping his foot. "I'm sorry. We're so busy— Brian?"

"I came to see if you wanted to do a little shopping."

Claire looked from her husband to the full shop. "We're a little overwhelmed here."

"I brought you a replacement." He grinned and pointed to the magazine section. Their daughter was slumped against the wall leafing through *Harper's Bazaar.*

"She won't—"

Brian cut her off. "Brittany . . . Brittany, come on over."

The girl scowled, but obeyed.

"You can work the register, right?"

Brittany crossed her arms. "I worked here before she did."

"Excellent. I'd like to show your mom a coat I found. You can cover for her for a few minutes and do everything Mrs. Harrison says."

Father and daughter squared off.

"Will I get paid?"

"Depends on your attitude."

Brittany sighed, and Brian reached out for Claire's hand. "Excellent. We're off."

"But . . ." The words died as Janet smiled and waved good-bye.

They hit the sidewalk.

"This way."

Claire pointed the opposite direction. "Most of the stores the kids like are that way."

"You always say I'm impossible to shop for and I found an idea for me." He pulled her into a men's store and pointed to a deep-brown sports coat. "Mine's gone out of style and this is a slimmer cut, and I like this gold thread through here, don't you? What do you think?"

"I like it very much."

"Excellent. Then you can mark me off your list. And I picked up a few gifts for Matt this morning too." He turned to the salesman. "We'll take it."

As they waited for the coat to be put in a hanging bag, Claire pulled out her phone. "I have some ideas for Brittany on here."

"I'm sorry. I don't have a ton of time." He checked his watch. "What's on the list?"

"Do you have work? It's Saturday."

"Honey, I always have work. I've got a call in an hour. I really only wanted you to see the coat. I'll show you what I got Matt tonight."

"I should get back to the store anyway."

He kissed her as they hit the sidewalk once more. "Keep Brittany as long as you need help. The work will do her good."

And he was gone.

Claire walked back to the Printed Letter to find Brittany behind the register ringing sales, chatting with customers, bagging books—all with a smile Claire hadn't seen in months. Janet moved behind her and said something that made her laugh.

Then Claire stepped into her daughter's line of sight and the laughter stopped.

"Can I go now?" Brittany stepped away from the register as Claire circled the counter.

"There's only a couple hours until we close; why don't you stay?"

"This is not how I planned to spend my Saturday."

"We could use the help."

"Fine." She dragged the word so long it was clearly not fine. Brittany stepped away from the counter and followed Janet onto the floor.

Soon, it appeared to Claire, she forgot her anger. Brittany demonstrated finger puppets for a pair of five-year-olds, found *The Apothecary* for a middle schooler, and helped Mrs. Hale find books for all her sons.

Brittany startled when Janet tapped her on the shoulder with a "Well done today" as she was straightening the kids' section. She seemed shocked to find the store empty and already closed.

Claire was shutting down the register as Brittany shrugged on her coat.

"What's for dinner tonight?"

"Ugh . . . It was supposed to be chicken, but I forgot to take it out of the freezer this morning. What about . . . Salmon steaks will only take a few minutes to defrost."

"I. Hate. Fish."

"I don't want to go to the store. Let's head home and I'll figure something out. We can have pasta."

They drove home in silence, and as soon as they entered the house Brittany beelined to her room.

Claire heard Brian's office door open.

"Hey, hon . . . I didn't realize how late it had gotten. Have you been home long? What's the dinner plan?"

Claire dropped her bag on the counter and stretched her back. "Give me a few minutes."

Janet

Watching Brittany work the register is a revelation. Maybe it's all that time on their phones, but her generation sure understands technology. When she worked here a few times last year, I gave her a quick tutorial and she caught on like a house afire. I almost ask her why she quit coming—she's fantastic with the customers and is a wonder at piling on those little extras filling the counter—but I see her lock eyes on her mom across the store and I know the answer.

I remember those days.

Nothing I said to Alyssa was right. My very existence chafed. Part of me is pleased to see that my mother-daughter relationship wasn't the only one battered by the teenage years, and the other part of me wishes it were.

Poor Claire . . . I doubt she deserves this antipathy. If Brittany is anything like Alyssa, Claire has her hands full. And if Brittany is anything like Alyssa, this isn't a phase.

The first several times I called Alyssa after Seth left, she didn't answer. I left messages and she wouldn't call me back. Finally she did.

"You've got to stop calling, Mom. If I want you, I know where to find you."

"But we haven't talked. It's been three months since you moved, and I have no idea how the new job is or what your new apartment is like. Are you near the ocean? I was thinking I could come out next month and help you decorate."

"I'm fine, and I'm visiting Dad next month."

"You're coming home?" My voice was so desperate. One part elation, two parts devastation.

"I'm coming to Winsome, to visit Dad. I'll stay at his apartment."

"He hasn't got the space. Stay here. You can stay in your room."

"I don't think so, Mom. It doesn't work like that anymore." Her voice was all steel without any velvet wrapping.

"But—"

"I need to go." She hung up. No promise to call. No promise to drop by when she came to town.

I didn't call again—and she didn't drop by.

Things have thawed in two years, but not warmed. Yet I have a granddaughter now and that changes everything. Rosie gives me courage. Claire and Brittany have the store well in hand, with Madeline running around like a frantic chicken, so I slip out the back door into the alley.

"Shoo. Shoo." That darn cat is here again. It keeps coming back, though I can't figure out why. If it had any sense it would hang out behind the coffee shop or the deli—someplace with food.

It's too cold out here without a coat, so I return to the office and slip into the storage room with a brilliant idea. I pull my phone from my jeans pocket and tap the information icon next to Alyssa's beautiful, carefree face. The picture was taken eight years ago, right as she graduated college. She'd swung her arm around me, and Seth had captured her exaltation, my adoration, and the seemingly unbreakable bond between us. I click out the number on the store's landline.

She picks up. "Hello?"

"Alyssa?"

"Mom?" I imagine she's pulling the phone from her ear, wondering how she failed to notice my name on the screen. "I didn't recog— Where are you calling from?"

"The Printed Letter." I take a breath and dive in. "Could you please talk to Chase? I want to meet Rosie."

"Then call Chase or Laura. Why call me?"

"He sent me some texts yesterday, but he put me off about visiting. I think . . . I know if you talk to him, he'll invite me to come. I can't simply show up. Please. It doesn't have to be this way."

"What way?"

"Angry all the time. We have to move on."

"Really, Mom, that's what we should do? Move on? Call Chase yourself."

The line clicks dead and I am left holding the office phone in one hand and her smiling face, pressed cheek to cheek against mine, in the other.

I walk back outside. I need cold. I need air. I need this cat to leave.

"Get out of here. Shoo. You stupid animal!"

I'm not sure if I'm yelling at the cat, now long gone, or myself.

Chapter 8

Madeline

The New Year began with lunch.

It was a wonderful opening to a book and to my new year. I'd cracked the spine on the seventh book on Aunt Maddie's list first thing on January 1 and found this opening line. Since then I'd read books eight and nine too. Each book confirmed my suspicions—Aunt Maddie had a purpose.

Number seven, *A Year in Provence* by Peter Mayle, was an older book about a man who quits his corporate job and buys a house in France. Aunt Maddie followed it up with *Under the Tuscan Sun* as book number eight.

Part of me scoffed. *Real subtle, Aunt Maddie.* And another part was insulted by the implication that I needed two books' worth of "saving" from the life I had chosen. Yet the strongest part of me couldn't turn the pages of either of them fast enough. There was something so intriguing and compelling about seeing life from a new perspective, one that left me time and space to lift my head and wonder.

Today the sun was shining into the shop windows, books were selling, and I had slept better, and certainly more each night, in the three weeks since Christmas than I had in the entire past decade.

A noise caught my attention. Since I started at the store, I had learned a lot about the two full-time employees. Neither was very good at dissembling, especially Janet. Her eyes let you in, whether she wanted you there or not.

And right now, Janet overflowed. Her laugh drew my gaze to her, and I found her at the front of the store hugging the man from the park, the man from Aunt Maddie's house, he of the red Patagonia, green eyes, and snowplow.

Sitting on a stool behind the counter, I ducked my head and feigned deeper interest in my book—such deep interest a customer had to slide a book within my field of vision to get my attention.

"I'm sorry."

"No worries." She glanced behind her toward the door. "You were preoccupied."

She was close to my age, and I noted her wedding rings and her small curved smile.

I rang up her purchases, my face warming. It was true; the guy had entered my thoughts far too often. I blamed this semi–world of fiction I now lived within and the fact that I enjoyed so much free time—after all, a fifty-hour workweek left thirty whole hours I'd never had before for unbidden romantic scenarios.

I looked up as I handed the customer her purchases and felt my face grow hotter. She noted it too and glanced to the door again.

He had caught my stare—and worse, Janet caught him catching me. She followed his gaze, widened her eyes, then pulled him across the store toward me, pausing to squeeze the arm of the now grinning woman. "Did you get your new book club book? We got them in last week."

"I did, Janet, thank you. I adore a good love story."

With that, the woman threw me a last glance and was gone. I felt fifty shades of hot red as Janet, and the man, stood in front of me.

"Madeline, have you met Chris?"

"We spoke after Aunt Maddie's funeral, then again at her house, but not really . . . I'm Madeline." I stood and reached out my hand.

His hand was warm. He didn't let go. "Chris McCullough. It's nice to officially meet you."

"Nice to meet you too," I mumbled like a high schooler.

"Whatever you do, don't call her Maddie." Janet's dry delivery and wink returned me to the day we first met. I suspected she still misunderstood my confusion that day. I was working it out myself.

"I'll remember that."

Janet slid two books to me. "Will you ring these up for Chris? And use my credit card on file."

"You're not buying me books." He grabbed for them.

She pushed them out of his reach. "I am. I've asked you to read him; it's only fair. Besides, you'll love Powell. He's very Christie meets Silva. So read the Powell first, then your next Silva."

I peeked at the titles, *Redemption* and *House of Spies*, and rang the sale.

Janet continued talking as if I had disappeared. Yet it felt awkward and rude to walk away—and I was on the register—so I pretended to check the stock lists that lay on the counter, while still fully fixed on their conversation.

"So where have you been? You can't be too busy these days."

Chris chuckled, full of rich, rolling notes. "You'd be surprised at all the planning that goes on during winter. Mario's got me involved in some of the ordering and design work too. Not to mention the great demand for my mad snowplow skills."

He laughed again, at this or at himself, I wasn't sure.

He continued. "The other guys plowing this year tore up a few gravel drives, and I'm requested by name now. It seems I have a delicate touch."

"Surgeon's skill being put to good use?" Janet's voice lifted.

"Something like that."

"Speaking of that, how's Sonia?"

I watched Chris out of the corner of my eye. Something about Janet's tone cued me—this was important.

"She's busy. Still no date, but we're good." He peered at his watch as I handed him the books. "In fact, I'm meeting her at Bistro North for lunch."

"She came to Winsome?"

"Miracles happen and all that. Thanks for the books." He kissed Janet's cheek, murmured a "Thank you and good to meet you, Madeline" to me, and walked out of the store.

Janet stood watching him. I had so many questions. None of which I gave her the satisfaction of asking.

"So?" The one syllable tripped and dipped into at least three as she turned on me.

"So . . . I placed the order for this week. Will you check it and see if I missed something, and watch the counter for a few minutes?" I turned my laptop screen toward her and headed into the office. "Claire, will you look it over after Janet?"

"Where are you going?" Janet called after me.

"The deli to grab a sandwich."

"Oh . . . I want one. The number sixteen," Claire chirped from her desk.

"Me too, but number twelve. Go quick before the line grows." Janet shoved money at me and pushed me toward the door.

Three doors down, Chris exited the pharmacy ahead of me. I slowed my steps.

Janet . . . She guessed at my motivations before I recognized them myself. I stalled and almost turned around, certain my actions looked as high school as they felt.

"Hello again, Madeline." Chris's voice was strong and bright, and I liked how he said my name. It didn't carry Janet's occasional curdle or Claire's formality. It reminded me of one of my best high school friends. He always made my name sound like a song. I'd had a crush on him until we graduated. Now he was happily married with two kids and, according to Facebook, working as an insurance adjuster in Connecticut.

"Hi. I'm heading to the deli. You're going to Bistro North, right?"

"I am, but not for a few minutes. I got a text—my fiancée is running late."

"Your fiancée?" I tried, and failed, not to sputter on the words. "When's the wedding?"

He fell into step beside me. "Not sure. Almost two years and she hasn't set a date. Of course, I've only been stateside a little less than a year, but I'm beginning to think it's not a good sign."

His eyes told me he wasn't taking his doubts too seriously.

I laughed and, while I hoped it sounded light and genuine, I suspected it sounded as flat to his ears as it did to my own. "She probably wants it to be perfect. That takes planning."

"True. She is a planner."

We turned the corner. I counted three more storefronts before I would be free. I searched for a topic. "So you're a landscaper?"

"Yard worker more like. Vittigliano's hired me on as a favor to my brother, who happens to be the owner's parish priest. I'm trying to be the hardest-working guy on the payroll so as not to let anybody down. It's good work. I like helping things grow and, I have to say, there is a definite art to a well-plowed drive . . . And you? I didn't know you worked in Maddie's store."

"I don't. I mean I own it now, but it's not what I do. I'm a lawyer. This is just until it sells and I can get back to the real world." I expected him to laugh with me.

He didn't.

Instead he stopped and pointed above me to the red-and-green Winsome Deli sign. "Here's your stop. Have a nice day."

As he walked away, I looked up. The sun had vanished.

Twenty cloudy minutes later, sandwiches in hand, I pushed through the alley door into the office.

Claire greeted me in a voice laced with fear. "What have you done?"

She was hovering over my laptop, and I assumed she was checking my order.

"I figured I'd place the order for the whole quarter. We get a bigger discount for a larger order, so I ordered a sampling of the most recommended titles. Also there's a 50 percent discount option we weren't employing."

"That's because you can't return the books if you use that discount. And we never order that far out, and we never simply order what's recommended. The business changes, what's wanted changes, our customers, our store has its own personality. You've got titles here that we already have in stock, and we'll never sell many of these suggestions, and now we can't return them."

"Change the order then."

"I tried. You placed this yesterday."

"I forgot to tell you." I leaned over her. "It can't be too late."

"Twenty-four hours. No exceptions. It's like the airlines. What were you doing earlier? I thought this is what you were doing."

"I'd forgotten a few so I added on."

"Those we can cancel." A few clicks, then she pushed back from her desk and faced me. "The 42 percent discount lets us return books. And we do return books."

"You told me that, didn't you?" There was so much new information coming at me I'd forgotten. "I'm sorry."

I hated apologizing, and it felt like that's all I did these days. I had to apologize twice to Janet yesterday for freezing the register and for mis-entering the day's entire inventory. I had to apologize to Claire for stocking books on the wrong shelves. And I suspected I should apologize to Chris—I'd said something wrong, obviously, but I wasn't sure what.

"We can't cover this, Madeline. I showed you. The store account doesn't have this kind of cash on hand." Claire sighed and dropped back into her chair.

"It will." I blurted my answer without any idea how to make it true.

"How?"

Then the idea came to me. "It just will. Give me a few days."

Janet

"Who broke all your crayons?"

"What?" Madeline snaps at me. She's slamming books into the shelves. I follow behind her, pulling them out, then tapping them straight and into line.

"You've been growling since you got back from the deli. What gives?"

"You missed that I screwed up the ordering?"

I almost smile. Madeline does not like to be wrong—clearly. "You said you could cover it. No harm, no foul."

"Why are you being nice to me?" She stops and watches me, a small smile lifting half her mouth.

We've reached an interesting point, the two of us. Neither of us is sure of the other, but we both keep at it. On my side, it actually isn't because she's my boss and I want to keep my job, although both of those things are true. I see Maddie in her.

From what I gather, she and her aunt weren't close. To hear Maddie talk about her niece, I thought they were super tight. But Madeline? She's struggling with something, about her aunt, about her family. When she first entered the shop, I thought it was cut-and-dried. Maddie good. Madeline bad. Now I feel it's not so simple—and I'm beginning to like her.

I point to the shelves and she resumes her work more gently. I still follow and straighten what she leaves crooked. "So you've met Chris before? When?"

There's a hitch in her rhythm—a very telling hitch—and I know I'm right. I stifle a laugh because I know she'll think I'm laughing at her, and she won't appreciate it. But I remember those days. Those beautiful, trepidation-filled early days when you like someone. You can't explain how or why a single encounter ignites something in you, but it's intoxicating and you're hooked.

When I think of Seth now I feel it all over again—the lift, the lightness, the butterflies, the fear and the wonder. It's a lifetime too late, but I'm right back in those early fluttery moments when he'd grab lunch at the same New York deli I did. And one day he said hi. That's all it took. *Hi.*

"He dropped by Aunt Maddie's one night while I was there. He plows the drive."

Madeline's explanation cuts across my memories. As much as Maddie teased me that I live present tense with little reflection, some dips into yesteryear are warm enough to drown in. I pull myself back to now. "He and your aunt were tight. In her final weeks, he dropped by her house daily."

"Daily?"

Madeline stills like a tuning fork—contained vibration—and my heart hurts for her. Maddie always said her niece was a treasure, and loyal. And whenever I lambasted the little ingrate for never returning Maddie's calls or coming to visit, she cryptically remarked that I couldn't criticize the girl for her best qualities. And right now, Madeline's response has nothing to do with Chris and everything to do with her aunt.

"It's a shame you weren't able to know her better."

She looks at me sharp, then suspicious, then forlorn. But I'm not kicking her this time, I'm commiserating. I nod and grab a stack of books, then head to the front of the shop. The girl needs space.

The rest of the afternoon is too busy to wonder about Madeline. Customers fly in and out, and again and again I'm asked for suggestions. I find myself beginning, as Maddie did, with some questions. *What's your favorite movie? What's the last great book you read?* And her standby favorite: *What was your favorite book when you were sixteen?*

That last question surprises people the first time they're asked. Then their faces light and their eyes glance up as they drift back in time to that golden age and that one book that defined not only the adult they were becoming but the hidden expression of their inner world.

Then I reach for *Gone Girl*—because it's still super popular, though slightly disturbing as an expression of one's inner world—or *The Paris Architect* or *The Joy Luck Club*, a perennially great read, or a host of others that always hit the spot.

I am briefly stymied when a customer names *Little Dorrit* as her last great book and the one she read at age sixteen.

"Have you read anything more recent that excited you?"

Head shake.

My mind casts to Maddie's list for me and I feel a softness grow. I noticed it from the start. With every glance at the list, with every book read, words like *wait*, *rest*, and *ponder* come to mind. Foreign words. Intriguing words.

Claire, Madeline, and I haven't talked about those lists since the day we received them. I never saw their lists and mine sits on my dresser at home. Madeline saw me reading it once and I felt so vulnerable, as if my diary, and my heart, were open for anyone to dissect. So I took it home and there it stays.

But it wouldn't have exposed me. After all, it's merely a list of books. Yet I can't deny it feels personal, intimate, precious. I started reading them, but I get the books from the library. To pull them from the shelves here would capture Claire's attention. But I remember one now and offer it to the customer . . .

"Have you read *A Man Called Ove*? He's a well-drawn curmudgeon. Dickens had a few of those too. I think you might like dear Ove." I hand her a paperback copy. "Please try it and come back and tell me what you think."

Maddie always ended her suggestions with that line. Not because she wanted the customer to come buy again, though of course she did. She sincerely wanted to know what the customer thought, how she felt, and what might touch that deep place inside her next. That's what books do, Maddie used to say; they are a conversation, and introduce us to ourselves and to others.

Words flow from my lips easily today and, as that customer leaves, I find that I want to know what a young mom at the back of the shop thinks and needs. With her baby tucked close and with her limited reading time, rushed and scattered, I wonder what will reach her best. We talk and I sense I know her.

"Dana?"

"I wasn't sure you recognized me." She shifts her baby high on her shoulder.

"I didn't for a moment. You were blonder in high school."

She laughs and touches her long hair. She grimaces as if wondering when she last washed it. "We all were, but it got expensive and felt dated to me."

I hand her *Nine Women, One Dress*. "Try this. A little black dress is never dated, and it's written in vignettes. You can take your time with it."

She thanks me and walks to the counter. I smile. We women understand the transformative nature of "the little black dress" and dream of it, especially when a baby keeps us up all night and spits on our shoulders all day.

Late into the afternoon, customers disperse. Talk of snow quiets the town outside, and Claire and Madeline manage those remaining in the shop while I change the windows to over-the-top pink and red explosions for Valentine's Day. It's a month away and a stupid holiday if ever there was one, but it has to be done.

Again, this new feeling checks me . . . No, Valentine's Day is not all saccharine-sweet predatory consumerism. Seth bought me roses, two dozen red ones, every February 14, and they made me feel beautiful and cherished. Then there was always champagne. Always a bubble bath. And always a very good night.

With that thought, I staple pink crepe paper to my thumb.

Serves me right.

I shove my thumb into my mouth and roll from my crouch into a criss-cross-applesauce position in the bay window. That's when I notice the world outside growing white. "Hey . . . This is getting bad, everyone."

My announcement clears the shop and earns me a glare from Madeline. "You should head home then."

"Thanks, Boss. Don't mind if I do." I say it with sass, but in reality I'm scared of snow. Silly perhaps, but there is so much I can't do alone. At fifty-four, I have perhaps three full decades ahead of me of shoveling snow, changing tires, slipping on roads, salting my sidewalks. And according to *The View*, I'm losing a pound of muscle mass each year. I see it in my triceps and it's all very concerning.

So I dawdle. I don't want to go home. Not yet. I've set lights on timers at the house, not to fool a possible robber, but to fool me, and yet I'm never fooled. The house will be as cold, dark, impersonal, and quiet as it was when I left this morning and found it last night, and left it yesterday, and . . . It doesn't change and I doubt it ever will.

I finally give up and leave the store. I drive home slowly, hoping the snow will stop and I won't need to embarrass myself by calling

Chris for a favor. Not that he'll make me ask—I know he'll do the job. But for how long? The next three decades?

I walk in the door, drop my keys on the counter, and perch on a stool to make a whole list of to-dos to keep me busy this evening. I wipe down the fridge, vacuum the kitchen drawers of all those pesky crumbs, scrub the cabinet faces, and then move on to baseboards. That's when I stop. Enough. Enough cleaning. Enough hiding.

I decide to go for a walk.

I want to be courageous. I want to be strong. I am so tired of feeling scared. Besides, the wind has stopped, and although the snow keeps falling, the world looks new. I need new.

Without thinking about it, I walk . . . and four miles later find myself in front of Maddie's house. Her house is ablaze with light, and my heart jumps up, then sinks low and sits heavy on my hips as I remember *she* hasn't flipped all those switches, her music isn't playing from the speakers, and her cooking isn't making the air heavy and warm with garlic and tomatoes. I will myself to continue on.

I turn up the front walk.

I collect the newspapers and flyers off the porch and rap on the front door. The light above me flips on, blinding me for a moment as the door creaks and swings wide.

"Hello." Madeline sounds surprised but not annoyed.

Dressed in sweats, she seems more human, and younger. She reminds me of Alyssa at times. Both have armed themselves with an impressive professional persona, but as Madeline's cracks—as it did with the misordering today—I recall the fun I had with my kids.

A motion draws my gaze down. She curls her socked toes against the floorboards.

I'm intruding. I'm embarrassed.

"I was walking by and all the flyers and papers caught my attention. Here." I shove the bundle into her hands and turn to leave.

"Do you want to come in?"

I spin her direction, then away, back to the silent, snowy world. I feel like I'm five and my mom is offering me a cookie. She used to do that and when I reached for it, she'd pull it away with a "Not until you—" It was always something—clean my room, set the table, practice the piano. There was always a chore before the reward. To *be* was never enough.

Her quiet "Please" stops my vacillating and I step inside.

"Take off your shoes if you want, but feel free to leave them on too. I always think it's odd to be forced to take them off. I mean, I'm sure there's a vacuum around here somewhere, and isn't that what they're for?"

"There is. A good one too." I almost point to the closet, but stop myself. This is her house now. "I feel the same way."

With all her silk blouses, pencil skirts, and sleek pants, I expected fussiness. Instead I'm greeted with my kind of logic. Nevertheless, I slip off my boots and pad into the kitchen after her.

She flips through the flyers as she walks. "Seems I can get my . . ." She looks up as if the pronoun surprises her, then continues with a slight emphasis on the repeated word, "*my* house painted . . . new windows . . . siding . . . Oh, and I missed Christmas poinsettias from the high school hockey team."

"Maddie loved those boys. She always used to buy flowers from them."

Madeline dumps all the flyers into the recycling bin, except the one from the hockey team. I like that she saves it. No clue why, but it feels right.

I smell rosemary and chicken. I notice a head of broccoli on the counter. "Are you living here?"

Madeline blushes like Alyssa did when caught in a lie. "I'm not, not really. But it's snowing so hard I didn't want to drive downtown, and I need to start going through the house to clear it out."

She nods toward the counter. "One of the books on the list she left me got me thinking about food, and another was a cookbook. I've found Marcella Hazan and her *Essentials of Classic Italian Cooking* take time, but are worth it. Maddie clearly had a plan with that reading list."

She lifts the lid off Maddie's favorite bright-orange Le Creuset dish, and I peek inside. I'm impressed. The chicken is golden and the sauce thick. It took me years to get to that point with my cooking.

"It's almost done," I say.

She peers in beside me. "How can you tell?"

"Thirty years of cooking. There's a meat thermometer in that drawer. It should be 165 inside."

She reaches for the white thermometer, stabs the chicken, and smiles. "163. You *are* good . . . Do you want to stay for dinner? I can't possibly eat a whole chicken. Or . . . you probably have plans." She smiles, a small, enigmatic thing. "Or a date?"

I snort. "I haven't had a date in longer than I've been cooking. I'd love to stay."

The kitchen is full of silent busyness. She puts the chicken to the side to rest. I sauté the broccoli. She sets the small kitchen table. I pull out the plates. And throughout it all, I feel emptied with the gratitude that washes through me. It startles me at first, then rests comfortably inside my chest. I'm so tired of being a charity case or, worse, an object of passive scorn. At this moment, I feel like family.

"How'd you and Claire fill the hours after I left?"

Again, her half smile returns. "It was pretty quiet. We caught up on some computer work."

Claire

Janet futzed around a few minutes, then bolted out the back door. The snow was bad, but not that bad—yet.

"You can head home too if you want. I'll lock up." Claire joined Madeline at the front window. They watched the snow fall. All the customers had fled when Janet sounded the alarm.

"We've only got a couple hours till closing, and if this gets bad I'll crash at Aunt Maddie's house." Madeline quirked a smile. "Seems I own a house in town."

"Are you going to keep it?"

"Even if I wanted to, I can't afford it." The sentence accompanied a head shake that was long and, to Claire's mind, unconvincing. "I'll put it on the market in the spring, but I do like it. Aunt Maddie's personality is in every fiber of that house, and she had good taste too."

"She wasn't a shopper. I liked that about your aunt. She took her time, and when she found something she liked, you instantly saw the connection. I liked visiting there. It's a welcoming house."

Madeline tapped the window. "Why don't you go home? This will only get worse, and you've got a family waiting."

"I promise you Brian is tucked in his study and won't emerge until seven. He's a consultant, a fixer, and this latest company is in pretty bad shape." She paused as if a little jealous of the company. "And the kids are both out. Matt is at a friend's house for the night and Brittany texted that she's off to a friend's for dinner too."

"I'm sorry about the order. I thought I was helping."

Claire shifted to face her. "It's your store. I shouldn't have gotten so exasperated. Yet it has struggled for years, and keeping it afloat hasn't been easy." She pressed her lips together. She heard her tone, and hated it. It sounded as if she was trying to convince Madeline, anyone, maybe herself, of her competence—from a sideways angle.

Again she heard Janet's indictment as it floated through her memory. *It's like you live in those classics you love, in some odd third-person narration, as if you aren't in charge of your own story. Who is, if not you, for goodness' sake?*

If Madeline noticed, she didn't comment. Instead she continued. "I went back into the shop's spreadsheets after we talked, and I saw where you cut back on orders and switched the store to the returning discount. I should have done that sooner. I . . . I could've learned a lot by paying more attention."

"We have a good base of stock, and ordering the hot books, and almost only the hot books, keeps us relevant without too much waste. Beyond those must-haves, our customers buy along a few lines that I suspect are unique to the Printed Letter."

"And from what I discerned, you've tracked them." At Claire's nod, Madeline smiled again. "You did well by Aunt Maddie."

Claire faced the window. "Thank you. She did well by me too."

"I transferred some money into the store's account."

Claire turned with a raised brow. She had not expected that.

"It's enough for the next week, and I'll have more by then."

Claire asked nothing further. Madeline's tone didn't invite questions, and she suspected some hard choices had been made.

"Do you want to help me with something?" Claire tilted her head back to the store's counter. "I've been working on an online profile for Janet."

"A *dating* profile?"

Claire led the way to the back of the store. "She mentioned it a couple months ago, then dropped it. So I figured why not jump-start the process?"

"Because she'll kill you."

"Not if it works." Claire tapped her laptop on. "I researched a few sites and decided on OurTime and Elite Over 50. I stayed away from the larger free ones. They don't feel right."

"If you say so . . ." Madeline's eyes still bulged too large for Claire's comfort.

"What? What could possibly go wrong?"

Madeline raised one brow. Claire noted the effect—it was declarative and condescending all at once. She wondered if that's how Janet perceived her own raised brow.

Madeline shook her head. "Falsely impersonating someone online and setting up dates? Nothing could go wrong with that . . . Nothing at all."

Chapter 9

Madeline

Two weeks can change your world.

Just as Claire and I started to seek out dates for Janet, I found one for me—or rather, one returned to me.

Kayla and I met every few nights at a bar between our apartments whenever I returned downtown. She would text when she left the office, then we would grab one drink, have a quick chat, and both walk home again. I gave her insight into some of her work, unloaded the drama of my little world—and it felt good. I didn't feel like I'd fallen off the larger world outside sleepy Winsome, at least.

Then he walked in.

"Hey . . ." Drew dropped onto the stool beside me.

I pulled back and stared at him, noting Kayla held the same befuddled expression. As if nothing were at all out of the ordinary, he scooped a fistful of nuts and then grinned, trailing his gaze from my ankle boots to my jeans and up my dark-green sweater. "You look nice. I heard you're working in a bookstore?"

"I own a bookstore."

"We miss you at work." He nodded to Kayla, seeking confirmation. She nodded in agreement, then widened her eyes at me.

The three of us then held an awkward conversation until both Kayla and I pushed back and grabbed our coats.

"I've got an early morning. I'll see you in the office, Drew. And, Madeline . . ." She gave me a hug. "Call me."

A full eyes-only conversation revealed we both had questions, wanted answers, and needed to fully dissect what Drew was doing at our tête-à-tête.

She turned to go, but Drew pulled my hand back.

"Can you stay a little longer?"

And that's how it began. A slow conversation, full of starts and stops, and a hesitant ask for another. I had never known Drew to be hesitant. He wore it well.

One date . . . Two dates . . . And two weeks later, February arrived and I was sure I had a "boyfriend" again.

Hmm . . . That jump was too far too fast.

Drew was different from who I remembered. He was taking it, taking us, slow—really slow. We hadn't kissed, held hands, nothing. But each time we got together, he asked for another date. I could've seized the moment anytime I chose, but I wanted to watch it play out. The curiosity, the slow, almost courtship-like nature of our dates intrigued me as much as it confused me.

What's more, this new Drew wanted to know about my day; it was the first question he asked on each date. At the firm, our days often intertwined and he witnessed my daily happenings. Now he peppered me with questions about them and listened to my answers. I told him about Claire and Janet, the store, the customers, the ordering, the bookkeeping, and the window displays. I told him about Aunt Maddie's house and the garden I was beginning to imagine to the left of her back door, and then I stalled . . . *Chris*. My mind traveled there more often than I wished.

THEN TODAY CLAIRE AND I found someone we thought was a perfect match for Janet. I'd discovered a lot about her the night she stayed for dinner. I learned she had two kids, both only a few years younger than me, and an ex-husband who made her eyes shine despite divorcing a couple years ago. I learned she'd studied at the Rhode Island School of Design and was massively creative beyond the Printed Letter's window displays. She thought in shapes, colors, and textures in ways I couldn't fathom. I also learned that, while her delivery was horrid most days, her heart was kind. She had loved my aunt. I liked Janet more every day—and that changed the kind of man I let Claire "wink" at for her online.

Claire was frustrated with my response, just as she was when I caught her feeding the alley cat yesterday. "Why not? You object to my being kind to a kitten? I'm not bringing him into the store."

Now I got the same look with "Why not? You can't object to him too. He's a writer. Janet's a creative type."

I tapped the screen.

Claire wiped at the smudge and sighed. "Again, it's not a touch screen."

I ignored her. "Look at his word choice. He's got *precise*, *rigorous*, and *comprehensive* all in one sentence. That's a red flag if I've ever seen one. She needs more freedom and more support. What does he write?"

"Medical research." Claire straightened. "Fine. How do you know so much?"

"It's the way my generation dates."

She shook her head no.

"Oh, you mean about Janet? Easy. Look at her." My answer brought a flash of uncertainty to Claire's eyes, so I backpedaled. "I've been studying clients for years. It was part of my job. And since we started this, I've paid more attention to her too."

Claire nodded, as if satisfied, and wiped at the now invisible smudge again. She then scrolled down through the available men. "We need to pick one soon so they can have a first date this week, then if they hit it off they can have another next week. No one wants a first date on Valentine's Day."

"You're planning their dates too? There might be a limit to meddling."

"Please, I'm a mom. We know no limits."

"Fair enough." I laughed and batted her hand from the keyboard to read a profile scrolling by. "This one . . . He's an accountant. That might be a negative, but he coaches a rec center baseball team. That's good. Numbers, but also flexibility . . . Boys, chaos, and teamwork. He loves reading fiction too. His mind is malleable then . . . Pick him." I tapped at the screen.

I glanced up to find Claire staring at me.

"I'm serious . . . Pick him."

"Stop being so bossy. And stop touching the screen."

I almost apologized, for the third time already today, until she smiled. I sometimes forgot, despite the age difference, we were peers at the store—and becoming friends.

She wiped off the new smudge, then clicked the green button. "Now we wait."

"Wait? Why?" I reached out, then pulled back from touching the screen again.

"For him to reach out and ask for a date."

"What? That's how this site works? You're kidding."

Claire stretched her back. "This is what you'd call old-school. The man reaches out first and sets up the date; then we, I mean she, accepts."

"Why can't she message him?" It was my turn to stretch.

"Not here. Members are grouped locally so your first real communication is face-to-face. The man asks the woman on a date and there you go . . . It's an over-fifty site. I guess they—"

"They?" I raised a brow.

"I'm forty-six." Claire smirked. "So, yes, they . . . And *they* aren't as comfortable online. This site has really taken off because of its emphasis on IRL dates."

"IRL . . . And how do you know all this?" I mimicked her earlier tone.

"Brittany taught me that one. As for the site, you'd be surprised how many divorces happen in one's forties. You look up one day, after focusing on your careers and your kids, and you don't recognize the person across the table, or so I hear." She lifted her shoulders in a mini-shrug. "But I can tell you this, sometimes you don't recognize yourself."

"I wouldn't be. Surprised, that is. Our firm had five lawyers devoted exclusively to divorce cases. It's not easy work."

"Neither is marriage."

I opened my mouth to comment when Janet waved her hand from the front of the store. "Madeline . . . A customer to see you."

She discreetly pointed to a woman hovering near the door. She looked older than Janet and wore a faded full-length down coat. Feathers poked through small holes near the hem.

"May I help you?"

"I'm looking for Madeline Cullen."

"I'm Madeline."

She took a deep breath and gripped her scarf tighter around her neck. Whatever this woman needed, it was not a book.

"Mr. Frankel said to come see you. He said you'd help me."

"He did?" I kept my voice questioning, curious, but in my mind it arced up with sarcasm.

When Greg came to pick up his book boxes before Christmas, he'd wagged a finger at me and boomed, "I've got plans for you." Then he chuckled, carried out his boxes, and refused to say more. I was now getting an inkling of Greg Frankel's plans.

"I'm being evicted." The woman reached into a worn cloth bag, which reminded me of Mary Poppins's carpet bag. She pulled out an assortment of things to find her letter. A wallet, a book, glasses cases. A wad of receipts, Kleenex, a rosary. She dug deeper and brought out several papers folded together.

"Here. My landlord will evict me on the seventeenth. I did not pay my rent last month and I told him I will not this month. I have asked him to fix my toilet for four months and because he will not, I will not pay. My neighbor said she did that and her window was fixed within days. She says it is my right. But today he taped this to my door."

I scanned the letter. It was typical, and threatening. "Does this neighbor live in the same building?"

"Across the street. Does that matter?"

"It shouldn't, but I expect you have different landlords." Two women snaked around us. We were blocking the center aisle. "Come with me." I led her to the office.

Claire stood and excused herself as I cast around for a spare chair.

"Have a seat . . ." The only spare chair in the office was piled with books. I quickly cleared it. I read her name from the top of the letter. "Elena Hernandez?" At her nod, I continued. "Let's go over this whole situation."

An hour and a half later I printed off an intimidating letter to her landlord, written on newly developed letterhead Janet created on the fly between customers. The letter was full of my best legalese, including a promise to take matters to court.

Elena sat with both hands wrapped within her scarf the entire time. She released one only to accept the letter from me. After she read it, eyes wide, I pulled it back, folded it in thirds, and slid it into an envelope.

"I will not have to leave?"

"He's in the wrong and being predatory. I doubt he'll have the nerve to push any further. I'll mail this today, and if he doesn't fix your toilet immediately, I want to know."

"Thank you." She pressed her lips together and stood. "How much do I owe you?"

"I . . ." had no answer for that one.

"Mr. Frankel said lawyers as good as you can charge as much as one hundred dollars an hour."

I swallowed. "This didn't take very long, nor was it too difficult."

"I need to pay."

She pulled out a series of ones, tens, and a few twenties. She stretched to hand me the entire amount.

"That's too much. Let's say thirty dollars."

Her body shuddered visibly with relief. She pulled back everything but a twenty and a ten.

As soon as she walked out of the office I grabbed my phone.

"Greg Frankel."

"You're sending me clients?"

"Elena came to see you? Good. I wondered if she'd have the nerve. She lives up there, and I thought it'd be nice for you to work within your community."

"You did, did you? Good to know I'm worth a hundred an hour."

"Did you charge her the full price?"

I almost laughed at the concern in his voice.

"For ninety minutes and a letter, I accepted thirty."

"Well done, Cullen. I really appreciate that. Those are good people up there. Maddie used to send some my way, but to be honest, I'm swamped and not getting any younger." He paused. "If I hear of anything else, you game?"

Without thought I answered yes.

"Good to know. And I have a few books I want to order. I'll email you the list."

He hung up the phone without another word and I sank back into my chair. It bounced.

In over six weeks, I hadn't noticed it could do that.

Claire

Claire glanced back into the office. Madeline and the woman had been in close conversation for almost two hours. Up front, Janet was handling customers with an enthusiasm and warmth she hadn't seen in a long time. Claire suspected it was due to Chris. He had just left, after stopping by for another Silva book and a hug. He always left Janet brighter.

"I swear if I were twenty years younger. Mm-hmm . . . ," she had whispered as he left the store.

"Sure you don't want me to bring you a coffee?" He had ducked back inside.

"Why not? Thank you." Janet turned and winked at Claire. "Now he'll come back."

Claire laughed but didn't question. Rather, she returned to her computer at the sales counter to catch up on the accounting and stock lists.

Janet and Chris had become close at Maddie's house those last weeks, and now that the house no longer held them, he visited the store. He bought books, he helped with shelving, and he assisted customers when they were super busy. And the dynamic between Janet and him was . . . charming. There wasn't another word Claire could pin on it.

Rather than some warped May-December affair, their friendship reminded her of a much older sister finally getting to know her younger brother as an adult, as an equal. She could see mutual affection, loyalty, and the filial concern she'd read about in one of her books from Maddie's list: *The Four Loves* by C. S. Lewis. He wrote about loving puppies and poppies, brothers and sisters, lovers and spouses, and God. He talked about different kinds of love and the order in which these loves needed to be placed within human minds and human hearts. It was a tough concept, and it kept Claire chewing Lewis's words and thoughts late into the night.

Could one love a son, a daughter, a spouse too much or in a misplaced ordering? Could the love become enabling, unhelpful, and unhealthy?

Claire closed her laptop. She had stared at the same screen for ten minutes. The numbers were comforting—not improving, but no longer falling either. That was success. It was also a comfort to understand them and be able to effect change. While Maddie lived, Claire had been reticent to make changes. With Madeline, she had guided new procedures and new ideas with slow, measured steps. And the numbers brought solidity, answers, and definition when everything else brought confusion.

She thought of Brittany and their latest morning skirmish. Success in that quarter was not so easy to quantify, and the quarrel had left her unsettled. Maybe Lewis was right after all—love, and relationships, could be disordered.

The woman who had come to see Madeline walked past the counter lighter than she'd entered. On the way in, her shoulders were curled in, her hands clutched to her neck, her face pinched with fear. Now she walked with purpose. Without looking right or left, she headed to the front door.

Upon reaching it, she sank to the floor.

Claire leapt around the counter. "Janet!"

Janet turned and within a single step dropped next to the

unconscious woman and gently rolled her onto her back. She'd hit the side of her head on the wood floor and was bleeding.

"What happened?" Madeline ran from the back of the store. "Call 911."

Claire pulled out her cell phone. Janet, crouched low, reached for Madeline's hand. "Get Chris. He's at the coffee shop."

"Wh—"

Janet yanked her wrist toward the door. "Now."

Madeline ran out the door.

Claire connected to 911. ". . . We don't know. She passed out. She looks about sixty years old. We're at 413 Main Street. Winsome . . . Yes. She's breathing, but she hit her head on the floor. There's a lot of blood." She waved to the window. "A doctor is here now."

Chris barged through the door. Madeline, with a bewildered expression, stepped in behind him.

He crouched immediately and started pressing his hands on the woman. "What happened?" He pulled her sleeve back to feel her wrist. "Janet, undo her scarf. I can't get a pulse here . . . Did you lift her head?"

"What?"

"Did you lift her head at all?" He reached up and placed two fingers to her neck. With his other hand, he spread open one eye.

"Should I?" Janet moved to lift the woman's head.

"No." Chris pressed a gentle palm against Janet's shoulder. "I only wanted to know. There's no dilation of the pupils. She could have a head injury . . . Here." He reached into his pocket and pulled out a white handkerchief. "Press this very gently to her head to stop the bleeding." He surveyed the small crowd. "What's her name?"

Madeline answered from behind him. "It's Elena. Elena Hernandez."

He twisted to send her a quick smile, then bent over Elena again. "Elena, you need to wake up now. Elena? Open your eyes for me."

"That's bad, isn't it?" Janet inched closer.

"Not necessarily. She's breathing, and we don't know what happened." He returned his fingers to Elena's neck. "We wait."

"We wait?" This came from Madeline.

Chris shifted back to face her. "There's nothing more I can do. Her pulse is stable, albeit light. She'll need more of a workup than I can do on a bookshop floor, but she's not in danger."

Sirens wailed close as Elena's eyes fluttered.

Within seconds, paramedics strode through the door and everyone stepped away except Chris. He stayed close and with quiet work and confident gestures recounted all he knew and what further information he gathered as Elena gained consciousness. He then followed the paramedics out the door, only to duck back in once the ambulance drove away.

"I'm going to head over to the hospital. Luke is there today, so I'll touch base with him too, and I can let you know if I learn anything more about Elena." He directed his words to Madeline.

Claire observed her, and then him. The dynamic between them was . . . incandescent. She wondered if they felt it themselves.

Madeline smiled. "Thank you."

He left, and Madeline spun on Janet and Claire. "I thought he was a yard worker. He said he was, and he plows Aunt Maddie's driveway."

The two women burst out laughing. It was a full three minutes before either could reply.

"He's an ER doctor."

"Then why isn't he practicing?" Madeline asked. "That seems a waste."

Claire watched as color, humor, and goodwill drained from Janet's face. It took on all the hard lines of a mother defending her own. She stood and brushed her black pants free of dust.

"That's exactly what Sonia says."

Janet

After the morning's drama, I welcome a quiet afternoon. Customers come and go, no one asks for recommendations, and no one returns anything. I did see one woman taking pictures, knowing full well she was snapping shots to remind her as she built her online shopping cart, but I couldn't muster up the energy to ask if I could help her find something. That usually gets them to put away the phone and purchase at least one book. And it's not a disciplinary action, as Maddie often told me. It's a reminder that that's why we are here and this is what we love to do: connect readers with the story they didn't know they would adore.

I don't have the energy to address Madeline either, but her comment still bugs me. Right as I'm beginning to like her, it's obvious what she thinks of Chris. He's only as good as his job, and "yardman" may have been fine—I'll give her enough credit to believe that—but not now, not when doctor is on the table.

People do that all the time. Put others in boxes. Because I don't create art anymore, am I not an artist? Am I less than, because I work in a bookshop? Or was I less before, because I gave up my art and didn't work outside the home? Or am I still less because I can barely make ends meet now or before when I did sell my art? That's what it comes down to, and to nine out of ten people, nine out of ten Madelines, I am less.

Then I catch myself . . . I sound so angry and judgmental, even in my own head. Maddie warned me, and only now do I hear it.

Is this who I've become?

I wander around straightening things so as to appear busy, to give me time to work this out. I enjoy this work, and I love this shop. I love the community I found here. I love that it gave me a reason to get up every morning when all I wanted to do was roll over and never get up again. I do make enough to pay my bills and I am getting by, but . . .

I stand staring into the spare room. The sun came out for the first time in days about an hour ago, and it is lit with a gorgeous cold light. This room has been calling to me lately. I find myself here again and again, as if on the edge of something more.

As I walk back into the shop, Claire slams her laptop shut.

"Doing something naughty?" I tease. When she doesn't laugh, I stop. "What's up?"

"Nothing." She stares at me. She is lying.

I stare back, knowing if I give her ten seconds she'll crumble like a day-old cookie.

"We signed you up on a dating service."

All the blood puddles in my feet. "I don't want to date."

"You do. You said you did . . . Here, come see. Your profile is wonderful." She opens her laptop with one hand and pulls me closer with the other.

And there is my smiling face. It's a good picture actually. I remember that day. Chase had said something funny when he and his new wife, Laura, were visiting, and Seth caught the tail end of my laugh. That was over four years ago. "How'd you do this?"

"I pretended to be you. People make profiles for their friends in movies all the time."

I step back. "And nothing ever goes wrong in the movies."

Madeline joins us. I can tell she wants to smile but is trying to read the scene's tone. I look back to the screen. "You said I like cats. You can't say that." I tap the offending sentence.

Claire huffs and uses a tissue to de-smudge her screen. "You do like cats, just not that one in the alley. And you buy all those cat cards for the shop."

"Because they sell! But you can't say that. I'll come off like the crazy cat ladies in *Grey Gardens*."

"I'll remove it . . ." Claire flutters over the keyboard. "But he liked it." She clicks on a man's face. "He asked to meet. Tomorrow night." She takes a deep breath. "That's what we need to tell you."

"We? What?" Madeline's jaw drops faster than mine can. Her hands fly up. "I didn't know about that part."

"Ethan 22 wants to go out tomorrow, and I already clicked yes."

"Let me see this." I spin the computer to me and scroll through the entire situation. "What are these checks in the side column?"

Claire leans close. "That's for notes that only you can see. The men can't see what you write there. The checks are the ones Madeline approved."

I glare at Madeline. She raises her hands in surrender again. "I was trying to protect you. You should have seen some of the options. Here . . . I'll show you who Claire wanted."

Claire gasps and walks away. She wants us to think she's angry, but a few customers walk in and she's the most responsible this afternoon, or the least shredded. I notice Lisa Generis among them. While I never talk to her, I'm happy my presence hasn't kept her from the shop. She blew up when Seth and I divorced, or maybe I started it. It's hard to remember sometimes how things went down. I drop my eyes to the computer screen.

Madeline scrolls through men like a kid sorting Halloween candy. "Look . . . Oh . . . Read that one . . . Look here . . ." It's in these moments, when she forgets herself and tries to play grown-up, that I like her best.

"She put a lot of time into this, didn't she?"

Madeline grins. "It's a robust profile. They get the most hits. And here . . ." She points to the sidebar on the left. "Here are the details for tomorrow night's date."

"I haven't agreed."

"You did." She taps a bright-green check. "See?"

I smile at the smudged screen. Claire deserves it.

"You completely violated my privacy." I cross my arms. Part of me wants to only play at mad, and yet I do feel true anger, laced with fear, rise within me.

"We did," Madeline concedes. "And we impersonated you. You have legal grounds to press charges. Do you want me to tell you your options?"

She offers up the question with a straight face, and it dissipates all that's brewing within me. Then a tiny smile breaks out and I find myself smiling back.

"I'll get back to you on that. But I do say turnabout is fair play."

"What?" Madeline stiffens.

"Let's register you."

"I'm not over fifty." She points to the website's banner. "Besides, I'm seeing someone?" Her statement lifts in question or curiosity.

"Since when?"

"Since about two weeks ago . . ." She looks at the screen again, and I sense she's more comfortable looking at it than at me, but she doesn't stop talking. "We dated before, actually, about two years ago. We were both associates, and now . . . He's Duncan, Schwartz and Baring's new partner."

"You're dating the guy who stole your partnership?"

"I . . . I guess I am."

I can't explain it, but in this moment, I see myself in her. I see my daughter in her. And I feel sorry for us all. It's such a strange feeling, but I know with everything in me she's not happy and she's struggling to hide it.

We smell Claire's gardenia perfume before we hear her or feel her presence across the counter.

"So . . ."

I glance past her. More customers have entered the shop, but Lisa is gone. "I'll go, but I have nothing to wear."

"We can fix that." Claire grins. "I may not have many friends, but I know every shop owner in town."

Madeline looks to me.

"Claire claims everyone has lived here so long they've forgotten how to make new friends, but she's also the one who set up the quarterly coffees with all the local businesses. It's been an incredible boost that's helped everyone."

"That's brilliant."

Claire glows brighter at Madeline's compliment. "And very helpful right now." She passes us into the office and comes out with her coat and Madeline's. "Janet, I know your size, so you stay here and handle the shop. Madeline, you come with me."

I laugh as I see where she's headed.

Madeline does not. "Why am I coming?"

"Because you look like that almost every day." I twirl my finger up and down her crisp blouse and pencil skirt. "You've got one pair of jeans, which we're sick of seeing, and even if you sell the shop tomorrow, you can't keep dressing like that. It's horrid."

Madeline frowns.

"It's not horrid." Claire steps between us. "But it's not terribly welcoming for a small bookshop."

Claire pulls her away. Madeline is still frowning. I'm still chuckling.

It only takes thirty minutes to bring them back again. In that time I sold a copy of *Killers of the Flower Moon*, two copies of *Crazy Rich Asians*, and an English garden adult coloring book—I think the gray winter is getting to Beverly Parker.

Claire looks around the store upon entering and, noting it's empty, flips the Closed sign out.

I smile. "How is it that you're already back?"

She lifts four stuffed shopping bags. Madeline steps from behind her, equally laden.

"Because we brought everything here," Claire says. "All the stores let me take stuff so we can have a fashion show here. Then we'll go return what we don't want and purchase what we want to keep."

So that's what we do, and it's amazing fun. By the end I own a new navy silk blouse to pair with jeans and my good boots, and Madeline's got a whole new wardrobe.

"I can't buy all this." She pokes at her pile like it's a living thing. We voted she keep four sweaters, two blouses, two pairs of jeans, three fun necklaces, and a great black wool knit dress.

"It's not that much. That whole pile probably costs less than two of your stuffy blouses and less than that skirt."

She has the grace to blush, but there is doubt in her eyes. I'm not sure what's driving that and sense if I ask, she won't tell me—so I don't.

After we make the rounds to purchase or return the haul together, we part ways at our cars in the alley. I note the cat perched nearby, and I drop the remains of my morning muffin from its brown paper bag.

I drive home, and, oddly, the quiet house doesn't depress me tonight.

Chapter 10

Madeline

Four days until Valentine's Day.

Part of me sided with Janet and dubbed it a stupid-manufactured-pseudo-romantic day. But the other part of me wanted to be swept off my feet, go to a good party, see someone across a crowded room, and . . .

Most of me wanted Drew to step up to the plate. I'd laughed at Claire, so sure Janet shouldn't have to wait for Ethan 22 to ask her out, yet I was doing the same thing, waiting for Drew to make a move.

But it was undeniable—there was something lovely and right and pretty perfect when a guy orchestrated that first move, pursued you, and made you feel special.

Or maybe this was all Janet's fault . . . She'd sent me a Spotify playlist full of Van Morrison, Pink Martini, and a few other bands that made everything feel, as Claire would say, old-school romantic. And now I was standing outside in the freezing weather planting red flowers in the store's window boxes because . . . because I couldn't help myself.

"It's a little early for that."

I recognized his voice at the first word. We had met only a

handful of times, yet I knew his voice. That was not a good sign. *Sonia. Sonia. Sonia.* A firm mantra of his fiancée's name was bound to save me from whatever this was.

I replied without lifting my head. "Probably, but Valentine's Day is in four days, and they'll look pretty and roma— They were on sale. I checked the weather and it's supposed to reach the forties, maybe touch fifty this week. Won't they last a little?"

"Maybe the week." Chris stepped beside me. His hand brushed mine as he helped hold the flower within its small hole. I used my other hand, encased in my new gardening gloves, to dig deep in the store's window box and shift the soil.

"I haven't seen you lately." I focused on the flower.

"I've been busy, as odd as that sounds, considering it's winter and everything's frozen."

I glanced up. He wasn't looking at me. I followed his gaze. The streets were white with street salt—Chicagoland salts well in winter.

He turned back and stepped closer as I repositioned the drooping flower.

"Let me help." He nudged me away.

"You don't have gloves."

"Do you have a sink in the store?" He dug his hands into the soil.

"Of course."

"I'll wash my hands after. I'll live."

I stepped aside.

He made the hole I'd created deeper before he looked up again. "You need to go a couple inches deeper. If you get all the roots under, they'll stay warmer. Maybe you can get a week before the freeze kills them."

I pushed potting soil into the hole. The flower no longer drooped.

"How do you like it here?" he asked, his face inches from mine.

"I like it." I gazed into the window. I could barely see past Janet's pink and red window extravaganza, but what I could see made me smile. The store was busy this morning. I didn't know all the customers' names yet, but I recognized many. The elderly man who bought romances for his housebound wife, laughing at the heaving bodices on the covers as he paid for them. The high school kids who came in and bought gifts for each other's birthdays when together, or books for themselves when they were alone. A few, probably Aunt Maddie's former tutees, occasionally staying an hour or two longer to help shelve or check out customers.

"It suits you." Chris swatted the furry pom on top of my hat with the back of his hand.

I grimaced. "They made me buy it." I unzipped my coat. "This too." I revealed a purple chunky wool sweater. I complained about it to Claire and Janet—despite what they said, it had cost a fortune—but I also loved it. It was soft and flattering and fun. And I actually smiled now while dressing each morning.

"The pom and the store suit you." Chris's tone dropped. I felt myself tipping forward to catch every syllable.

"It's different from everything I've known, anything I ever anticipated for myself. And working with those two is different too."

"Good different?"

"Yeah . . . But the store is still struggling, and that's a concern."

He followed my gaze into the store as he straightened away from the window box. "I didn't catch it. I've wanted to tell you that. Not that I necessarily would have, but I wonder sometimes if I should have."

Before I asked what he meant, he continued. "When I arrived I was pretty low. I came to visit Luke, got sick, and that's when I met Maddie. They were great friends. Then when I decided to stay, she kinda took me on as a charity project. It was the best thing that ever happened to me. Your aunt knew how to love well . . . Anyway, looking back, I realize she was sick then. That was January a year ago, and when she finally got diagnosed in July, the game was up. I believed her when she said she had a sensitive stomach, was sore from lifting book boxes, had never had much of an appetite . . . I didn't pay enough attention."

"It's not your fault."

"Maybe." He wanted to argue. Instead he swallowed, his Adam's apple lifting and falling with the motion. "Thank you."

We moved back to the flowers. He made a hole. I lifted in the red poppy.

"I didn't know you were a doctor."

"I'm not much of one lately." He shrugged.

"Elena Hernandez would disagree."

"How's she doing?"

"She's fine. In fact, she was here yesterday to help us out. She said it was dehydration, and they sent her home after two IV bags of saline. She also said that within minutes of the mail arriving, her landlord was up in her apartment fixing the toilet. So she paid the rent and all is well."

"That's fantastic." He shoulder-bumped me and it felt like a hug.

I couldn't help but think of the night before when I'd said almost the same words to Drew. His response had been different. "That's all she got? It took him four months. You should have pushed for equal terms on a release of rent."

I felt myself lean into Chris. I liked his response much better. Drew's was probably in the best interest of my client, but it was clinical. This felt emotional. Working with Elena had felt that way too. She was pleased. I had no sense that she wanted better terms or a fight. She wanted a working toilet.

I pulled back. *Sonia.* I yanked the last flower from its plastic container.

Chris scooped another hole with his fingers. "You're inspiring, you know that? You're doing work you love and work you're trained for, in a place totally new."

"Not like you, huh? Thinking it's time to join the real world again?"

The words escaped me before I could stop them. I didn't mean them and certainly not in the tone I said them. I was nervous. I was always nervous when he was near. Every time he walked into the store I felt my throat close. Yet I'd ordered every book Alex Powell and Daniel Silva wrote, to make sure he had a reason to keep stopping by.

And Janet had said Sonia wanted Chris to practice medicine again, and I figured if he did, when he did, she would set a date. It sounded logical—manipulative—but logical. That made me nervous too. He would get married. It felt like I was promoting the one thing I was dreading.

The second the words registered, which was a half second after they left my mouth, I felt their unintended cruelty. "I—"

Chris cut off my apology, pulling his hands from the soil and brushing them against each other to rid them of the loose dirt. "I didn't think I had left the real world . . . I gotta go. You can manage that last one."

He shoved his hands in his jeans pockets and, with straight arms, shoulders practically touching his ears, he walked away.

The last flower tipped over.

Janet

I'm a voyeur. I admit it. Yes, I do my job—I help Betsy find a new diet book, Mrs. Jennings a book on old English silver, the Winsome

Women's Club next month's mystery selection, and Ted Billings something he hasn't yet read about Cold War spycraft—but I'm also completely attuned to the red poppies being planted outside and the two star-crossed lovers planting them.

That's what I call them now—in my head. Neither has recognized it yet, though I suspect Madeline has an inkling. I give her credit, she's reining it in. There was a tiny lean a moment ago. A drift that she righted at the last moment . . .

Chris? He has no clue. The poor man thinks he's coming around offering help and friendship. He's also reading at a lightning pace. He thinks it's good literature driving him into the shop, but he lights up like Seth did when we first met, every time he walks in the door—and he's not looking for me as he cranes his neck above all the customers and scans the shop. What a heady feeling that was . . . I remember it well. Seth shone whenever I came near, and the adoration made me glow too.

The memory brings one of Maddie's book list titles to mind. There was a line that still haunts me although that book was number three on the list and I'm at number ten now. *An ever increasing craving for an ever diminishing pleasure* . . . It haunts me because I understand it. When did feeling that glow, chasing that adoration, become more than loving that man?

I'm still watching them when Chris beats a hasty retreat. *Madeline, what have you done?* I take a step toward the door when a woman enters my field of vision. I almost step around her when I realize she's talking to me. I shift my focus. I recognize her but I can't place her.

"I'm looking for Maddie Carter."

"She's . . . Do you mean the owner?" Flustered, I point out the window. Madeline sees me, dusts off her hands, looks in the direction Chris walked, and comes into the store.

"Do you need me?"

I gesture to the woman.

"I'm Madeline. Can I help you?"

The woman rushes forward, all energetic enthusiasm. "I'm Carlotta Antonelli. I'm giving the book talk and demonstration next month."

"The chef? *The Pressure Cooker Made Easy*? Wonderful . . . I didn't expect to meet you before the event."

"I was up at Boswell Book Company in Milwaukee for a lunch demonstration today and was driving back downtown and thought I'd stop by. They did something really interesting up there, and I thought we could do it here too."

Claire pulls up beside me.

"They procured all the ingredients, and the owner and her assistant brought in the pressure cookers. We cooked two dishes. It's a lot of food, but it made for a more exciting demonstration and, I think, more sales."

Claire raises her hand like a schoolgirl. "It's a great idea. I'll bring my pressure cooker."

"Me too. Happy to," I chirp.

Madeline waves her hand between us all. "I'm the owner. I'll bring mine."

"You have one?" I ask.

She looks lost, and I almost bet money she has no idea what a pressure cooker is.

"Didn't Aunt Maddie own one?" She nods between Claire and me in hopes we'll throw her a bone.

We don't, and I again marvel at the dynamic between us. In less than two months, we get each other, we enjoy each other, and we're not above leaving one of us hanging on a ledge for a moment.

Carlotta looks flustered. She lost control of her own idea as soon as it was out of her mouth. "I . . . Three might be too much with all the chopping . . . But maybe if one of you could act as sous chef . . ."

"Madeline will do it," I offer.

"I can't cook." Her voice wavers.

"Can't *yet*. You have a cookbook on your list from Maddie. Remember?" I smile sweetly as her eyes widen. I don't think she remembers telling me that; I can tell she's terrified I've seen her list. I don't remind her of our dinner together. "And besides, you are the owner," I add with a syrupy grin.

Carlotta jumps at the chance to disengage from us. "Perfect. If you email me the three recipes you choose from the book, I'll work out any changes in proportions so you can get the right amounts and we'll be set."

"Wonderful. I'll pull it together and we'll see you next month." I grin to Carlotta, then to Madeline. I'm so helpful today.

I wave, Carlotta flees, and Madeline glares at me.

"Don't worry, I'll show you where to find Maddie's pressure cooker." I wave my hand to the window. "Don't you have some flowers to finish planting?"

She glares again and heads out front. Feeling buoyant and optimistic, I head the opposite direction. I tap a text to Alyssa.

I sent you chocolates for Valentine's Day. They should arrive by the 14th.

My phone beeps immediately and my heart jumps. I love Valentine's Day.

Arrived yesterday. Put them in the office kitchen. Gone in minutes.

I hate Valentine's Day.

Claire

"We need to talk." Claire twisted in her seat. She peered out the office door into the shop. Janet stood near the front chatting with David Drummond. He rarely bought a book, but came in at least twice a week for a long talk. They used to trade off who would talk with him, but since his wife died, Janet stepped up every time. Despite all her bravado, Janet understood loss.

Madeline pushed back from her desk. "About?"

"The accounts are too low. We've dipped into the store's reserves or Maddie's personal account every month for the past year, and they can't cover this month. We've recovered a little, but not enough. Your deposit bolstered us to see us through the monthly bills, and that check last week took care of the ordering snafu, but . . . we're in trouble."

"And I thought this would be so easy." Madeline slumped so her forehead met her desk.

"What do you want me to do?" Claire asked.

Madeline sat straight. "I hoped it wouldn't come to this, but I already headed it off." She reached into her bag and slid a check across Claire's desk.

"Sid McKenna Interiors? What is this?"

"The mortgage, this month's stock orders, salaries . . ."

"What'd you do? Rob a design shop?"

"Sold another piece of furniture."

Claire waved the check. "Some piece of furniture." The check was large enough to buy a car—not a new luxury one, but still a car.

Madeline blushed. "Sid has a policy that he'll take anything back for a full refund within the first year of purchase. I've never taken him up on it before. From his surprise, I doubt anyone has."

"What was it?"

"A breakfront bookcase. Eighteenth-century French. You should have seen it. It was gorgeous. I . . . I haven't been a spendthrift and I thought it was an investment, and technically it was . . . I don't know. I guess I always thought there was time and . . . It doesn't matter now."

"Is everything okay?" Claire asked.

Madeline shrugged and spun to face her desk again. "The store needs the money. Go ahead and deposit it."

Claire photographed the check, deposited it online, checked the previous week's sales numbers, then spun to face Madeline again, glancing once more toward the front of the shop. Mr. Drummond was gone, but a host of new customers kept Janet occupied. "Are you still planning to sell?"

"I can't keep it going. You must see that? Anything unexpected happens and we're done. A flu virus that keeps customers away or tons of snow that makes people shop online more . . . Anything, and any progress we've made is gone. And regardless, it's still not enough to touch the debt Maddie accrued. Any—"

"Whoa . . ." Claire raised a hand. "I see how hard you're working. No one can blame you. I'm not sure Maddie knew how bad things were."

"You did."

"But I also couldn't make changes, not to Maddie's shop, not at the end. I couldn't do that to her, so . . ."

Madeline took a deep breath. "The Realtor said winter is tough, and the trend now is to drop the price every couple months to bolster interest. So there's no point in listing during a dead time only to drop the price when things pick up in spring. I'll list the store then. I'm sorry." Madeline cast a glance out the office door. "Don't tell Janet . . . Not yet."

"You can't keep it from her. She needs to find work. That can take time."

"Not yet, please."

Claire nodded and the conversation died. She remembered the summer before she married Brian. She and a few friends saved a business by creating their own weekend consulting group. The five of them revamped their favorite cafe's business plan, marketing, accounting, ordering—everything in a month—so they could enjoy the best eggs Benedict in the world every Saturday morning after a Friday night out. Everything had felt so simple, clean, and possible then.

Madeline walked past her into the storage room and shut the door.

Alone in the office, Claire dug into the White Box from the Midwest Independent Booksellers Association. It arrived quarterly and was packed with ARCs soon to release. Janet usually got to it first, but today it was hers. She ripped it open, expecting the smell of new books to clear away the gloom. It didn't. The box was filled with books the Printed Letter would never buy. Books set to release late summer and early fall, and by then the shop might be a Bluemercury or that "stripey one" as Janet called Sephora. She closed the box and placed it on Janet's desk.

Hours later, Claire pulled into her driveway and watched her house with the same sinking feeling that had swamped her looking within the book box. She searched for lights, movement, life, and found none. She pulled into the garage, opened the back door, and determined to get a dog.

Brittany surprised her a few minutes later. "What are you doing?"

Claire slid her iPad across the counter. "I'm looking up dog breeds. I'm thinking a King Charles Cavalier. Not too big. Not too small. What do you think?"

"You need another hobby?" There was a bite to Brittany's question.

"That's not fair." Claire pulled the iPad back. "And it's rude."

"You've already got the Printed Letter."

"Which is a job."

Brittany shrugged and walked away. Minutes later she was back. "By the way, I got called out today in practice for wearing the wrong uniform. Do you have any idea how humiliating that is? I had to sit out the entire first half of the match."

"Did you forget it?"

"It wasn't clean." Brittany took a deep breath, and Claire felt the momentum build like water getting pulled back before the tidal wave hits. Any second she'd be under it.

"I told you we were wearing the yellow today and you said you'd have it ready. I grabbed the stack this morning and no yellow. It's not in my room either."

"It must still be in the basement."

Brittany stared at her.

"You could learn to do your own laundry."

"When you say you're going to do it, I don't need to. But if you're too busy, with your store and your dogs, let me know and I'll handle it."

"It was a mistake, Brittany. I'm not sure why you think—"

"You don't get it, do you, Mom?" Brittany's lip quivered. She caught it between her teeth.

Claire wondered if the flash of vulnerability was real or manufactured. Lately Brittany pushed at every button, with tears and temper tantrums, but quivering lips were new—and they washed Claire with guilt rather than anger.

When you're new, you don't want to stand out.

The words floated between them as if Brittany had just said them—again.

Claire sighed. "I'm sorry. I'll go check the basement." In six months Brittany would be off to college, and these were not the last emotions, the last season at home, she wanted her daughter to remember. This wasn't a season Claire wanted to remember either.

Brittany's eyes flashed confusion. Claire knew she'd been expecting a different response, aching for it. There was something so indulgent, freeing, about a good yelling match—and they'd had plenty of them. Claire's acquiescence clearly disarmed and confused her.

"When's dinner?"

"One hour. I'm making shrimp linguini in pesto."

"That's one of your best." Brittany's face lit with a smile and she looked six again. She walked away, but this time there was a bounce to her step. The kind of bounce only kids and dancers achieve without effort.

Claire was left wondering why life couldn't always be so easy—to fix a wound, emotional or otherwise, one only needed pasta, shrimp, basil, pine nuts, and parmesan.

She pushed away from the counter and her iPad of puppies and headed to the basement. There were two basketfuls she'd left on the dryer the night before. She carried the laundry upstairs, and when a loud rap didn't bring Brittany to the door, Claire entered her room.

Clothes, art supplies, notebooks, Spanish flash cards, and general clutter lay everywhere. She stepped through the mess as if trying to avoid land mines. She could hear the music and the shower. She paused and noted there was no new artwork on the bulletin board. For years, Brittany had created at least a few pieces each week. It was how she relaxed. Art had gotten her through three moves.

She walked over to Brittany's desk, the massive oak desk Brian had used for years. He gave it to her when his own father died and he inherited that monstrous partner's desk that took up their entire study. The desk was piled with textbooks, pens, paper clips, chapstick, lip gloss . . . She had four different containers, three mason jars, and a mug all full of different pens and randomness. Post-its were scattered about with chemical formulas and math equations. Brittany worked hard. It was easy to forget that.

Claire touched objects, letting a physical connection soothe the missing emotional one. She'd lost touch with her daughter's internal life; it was always so rich. There was so much going on with art, math, science—she was a thinker, a ponderer, more likely to spend hours drawing and designing than on Snapchat. Yet the walls remained unchanged and a fine layer of dust marred an open palette of watercolors.

Claire heard her own whispered words before she recognized the prayer. She thought of the books she'd read from Maddie's list. A common theme came to life as she scanned through her daughter's world, worried at the stagnation she detected. It was not that putting others first wasn't good and shouldn't come before self, but Claire now saw that in each book, every character—real or fictional—had to learn the balance, that line not to cross. There was an order to love and to life, and the sacrifice of self needed to be coupled with the courage of conviction.

She looked across the room again. Was that what she lacked? The courage to reach her daughter? The courage to defy her when necessary? Yet she felt tired and worn, guilt eclipsing all else as Brittany struggled.

Claire opened the drawer and heard a roll, felt the shift in weight. She pushed the sweaters aside as her world turned red.

"What are you doing?"

"Putting away your laundry."

"I didn't ask you to do that. Don't you knock?" Brittany stood in the open bathroom doorway wrapped in a towel. Her wet hair created a puddle on the wood floor.

"I did knock." Claire held up a half-empty Smirnoff bottle. "Explain this."

"It's not mine."

"Whose is it?" She shook the bottle. "Do you drink?"

They faced off, and the pause grew.

"It's Tracy's." Brittany reached for the bottle. Claire pulled it back.

"Who's Tracy?"

"You haven't met her."

"I haven't met any of your friends. Why don't they ever come here?"

Brittany dropped her hand. "They have their own routines, Mom. I can't change where they hang out."

"Well . . . wherever that is, you won't be there. You're grounded. For a month. And if Tracy wants her vodka back, her parents can talk to me. She's a minor and this is illegal."

"You can't do that."

"Watch me." Claire walked out of the room and shut the door behind her. Brittany was yelling, screaming something at her, but she didn't open the door. With a shaky breath, Claire walked down the stairs and let the distance dim the diatribe.

She poured the vodka down the sink and threw the bottle in the recycling bin, certain Tracy's parents would never call.

Chapter 11

Janet

"Happy Valentine's Day."

I push open the alley door and call out nice and loud into the shop. It feels as if I'm setting the tone for the day, and I want it to be a good one—unlike the last few days, in which I've felt scattered and distant from Claire and Madeline.

We've come to know each other well, packed in here so tight, and we work with a certain energy. But I can sense it's not right at the moment. We're not right.

Madeline has been at Maddie's house more, made more visits to the bank, and cleared out the small storage closet with an almost frightening amount of determination—then locked herself in it, repeatedly, with her cell phone. She's also developed those worrying vertical lines between her brows. But she's lucky—her muscles seem to pull into two smaller lines rather than my singular deep channel.

Claire's distracted too. She sits staring at her computer, shelves books in the wrong sections, and looks horrible. Her normally neat, sleek bob is frizzy on top with little wisps of hair standing straight. And she's not sleeping—that's obvious, especially as she's wearing less than her picture-perfect makeup. She's basically forgotten about under-eye concealer. Looking at her makes me ashamed of myself because rather than console her, I console myself with the thought that even in my worst moments, I doubt I look so lonely. I feel it, but always work to hide it.

"You're in a good mood. It must have been some date." Madeline emerges from the storage room.

Date?

"Ah . . . Yes . . ." I busy myself with my coat, my bag, and my memory. "That was a few nights ago, but yes, it was good."

Claire materializes as well. "It sounded great to me. Tell her . . . Don't you want to relive it?"

We congregate behind the counter. There are plenty of places to sit in this store, chairs in the office, a little corner with three seats in the back near the classics, and tiny chairs in the kids' section, but we stand behind the counter like the booksellers we are—and the Printed Letter is not open yet. Claire flicks her fingers at a paper coffee cup sitting in front of me. I nod my thanks and take a sip.

"We met at the Capstone Grill in Evanston. He lives and works downtown, so we met halfway. And—"

Madeline jumps in. "What does he do? It said insurance, but what type?"

"He's a salesman."

Madeline's face pinches like lemon is on offer rather than a romantic story. I almost laugh.

"We met at seven and . . ." I go through the evening moment by moment, working hard to remember what I told Claire and how I told it.

"Tell about the kiss." Claire pokes Madeline in anticipation.

"He already kissed you?" Again the lemon face.

"It's not high school," I quip and continue. "Besides, it was a completely appropriate and romantic brush across my lips, right at my car. That perfect lean, pause, and linger." I press my lips together in memory, and that really sells it.

"That's fantastic. I knew it would work." Madeline morphs from sour to smug.

"You did not." Claire thwaps her this time. "It was my idea."

"True, but I selected the guy . . . When are you seeing him again? Tonight?"

"No way." I jump at the thought. "He asked, but it's too soon. It's Valentine's Day. That's too much pressure for a new relationship, and I told him I had plans."

"Look at you." Madeline arcs a brow. Clearly she's been watching Claire. "So smart."

"*Do* you have plans?" Claire asks.

"No."

"Me neither," they both say simultaneously.

"How can you not have plans? You've got a boyfriend, and you a husband." I point to each.

Madeline shrugs. "He's got a case to close and will work late. He said he'd drop by, but I wouldn't expect him before eleven at the earliest, and that's hardly Valentine's Day anymore."

"And Brian's in San Diego. He left this morning. But I did get roses."

"We'll be each other's dates," I offer. "Dinner at Mirabella's? One of Alyssa's best friends, Lexi Pappas, is the hostess. I bet she can get us in."

I suggest the connection so easily and without thought, as I've done a hundred times before. Only then I remember . . . along with losing friends in the divorce, I lost the kids and their friends too. For years our house was the gathering place. While I didn't allow drinking, I always stocked the best snacks, and I listened—never advised, only listened—and kids responded to that. Beyond all that, they also understood that whatever went down, Mrs. Harrison would get them home safe, no questions asked. That crew felt like my own—and now they act like my own, politely nodding a stiff hello if we happen to pass on the street.

Claire heads to the office to print out the promotional material I designed for the pressure cooking demonstration. Madeline heads to the front of the shop to check inventory. She's obsessed with the gifts table stock and her little bijoux. She's like Maddie that way—she, too, thought all those little baubles revealed the life and personality of our shop. If they sold, we thrived. Considering their robust margins, she was probably right.

When Madeline first arrived, she changed the composition of the bijoux collection. I noted *Intelligentsia Conversation Starters* and serious notepads trimmed in gold with embossed typewriters and tiny quill pens. Yet now the more colorful notes with pineapples, penguins, and hot air balloons are back. She even added a line of cards with catchy little messages. My favorite is *Dear World, This may sound slutty, but I want to be used. Love, Grammar.* It makes me laugh every time I pass by.

They go to work and I sink onto the stool behind the counter to recall the actual date of a few nights past. Ethan 22 drank too much. He talked about his ex-wife, no, two ex-wives. He tried to order for me. He called me Jan. And when we reached my car and he leaned in for that kiss—which was never going to be a delicate brush of the lips—I used his pause to duck away and speed off.

Claire is right. I do want to relive the date—each and every moment, again and again.

So I'll never forget and go on another.

Claire

The day flew by. Customers came and went. Small gifts were purchased—the little red notebooks, pens, tiny coin pouches with appliquéd hearts, and everything on the dedicated "Hearts" table sold faster than Claire could ring the sales.

Though busy, she watched Janet out of the corner of her eye. There was something forced about her jocularity upon entering that morning. It took hours, but by lunch she'd relaxed. Her smile appeared genuine, her face less pinched, and her eyes opened wider. Claire noticed around three a peace she hadn't seen before crept into them.

"What's up? I see that little smile."

Janet startled at the register. "Nothing."

"Spill."

"I've made a decision, that's all. About dating."

She refused to say more, and Claire backed away. Any decision that brought that flush of pink and an enigmatic smile was a good one.

"Oh . . . I got the reservation for tonight. It was a very formal 'Yes, Mrs. Harrison, I'll take care of it,' which was a little hard to hear, but we're in."

"I'm sorry."

"Can't say I don't deserve it." Janet shrugged in an it-is-what-it-is manner rather than an I'll-never-make-it-out-of-this-hole manner. That was a good sign too.

Madeline joined them from the back office. "We can put the sign out now, can't we?"

Janet followed the last few customers to the door, and with a cheery "Good to see you. Enjoy your evening," she shut the door and turned the sign. *Closed for the day. Thank you. We'll see you tomorrow.*

"Come on, grab your coat. I need out of here." Madeline turned back to the office without waiting for answers.

"What's up?"

"The bank wants to meet again about Aunt Maddie's loans. She took out two loans, in effect second mortgages, on the store and her house last year. I wouldn't be surprised if they call them both. Neither was listed in the balance sheet Greg gave me, because she did it in October and had already signed everything with him in September. She did not have good legal counsel, didn't ask Greg about them at all, and—"

"How is that possible? She was bedridden by November. I was with her every day—"

Claire spoke over Janet. "But you've been making the payments?"

"They're billed in one sum. I didn't realize there were two different loans, putting both the house and the store in jeopardy. I even asked about options for the house . . . Now I get the banker's reaction. It was complete disbelief, verging on rude. He must have thought I was an idiot."

"How could he not say anything?"

Madeline sighed and pulled on her coat. "He had to assume I knew."

They plopped into Claire's car. She looked beside her; Janet's face was drawn tight. She peeked into the rearview mirror; Madeline stared out the window.

"I've never been to Mirabella's. I hear it's fantastic."

No one answered her. And no one spoke again for the ten-minute drive.

They were assailed with scents of truffles, olive oil, stew, wine, and spices upon pushing through Mirabella's revolving door. Claire felt everything tight within her unwind. Janet's and Madeline's expressions implied the same was happening for them.

The floor was covered in small white tiles with a black octagon accent every foot or so. The place had the feel of an authentic Art Deco French bistro with black, white, touches of red, and the light notes of French gypsy jazz playing over the sound system.

They found a tiny spot to rest and ordered the special of the evening, champagne and truffle fries. Claire and Janet perched on two stools at the corner of the bar. Madeline stood wedged between them.

"We've got about fifteen minutes until the table is ready." Janet took a sip of her champagne and noted Madeline's shoes. "Here. Sit. You're like a tree. How can you stand in those?"

Madeline twisted one ankle to examine her four-inch block heel. "Most of what I own are heels. These aren't my highest."

Janet nodded to Claire. "That's what we'll shop for next. Shoes."

"Not on my budget."

"Forget I said anything then. We'd rather have you and the shop than new shoes." Janet raised her glass. "Cheers. To the three of—"

She stopped, and all the color drained from her face. Against the white tiles, the noise, and the warmth, she turned puce.

"Janet?" Claire stood and followed Janet's line of sight over the low wall separating the bar from the restaurant. Three tables away sat Seth. With a woman. Her hair was dark, shoulder length, deep and rich, with hints of red as it lay over a fitted ruby-red sweater. She was all the warmth that Janet lost.

"Oh . . . Sit. Now." She pushed Janet back onto the stool.

"It's Valentine's Day. I mean, you don't go on a first date, right? Not even a second, you don't—"

"Stop." Claire stood in front of her, blocking any view. "It absolutely could be a first date, or they could be friends, both feeling lonely tonight. You can't let this derail you."

"He doesn't look lonely."

"Come on, Janet. Don't do this." Claire turned and peeked again. Janet was right. Seth seemed animated, and happy.

"Do you want to leave?" Madeline asked the question.

"No." Janet threw back her last sips of champagne. "I thought it would get better. Today . . . I thought it could all be okay. Forget it. I want this not to hurt so much. I want this to be over."

"It will be." Madeline gestured to the wall. "They're leaving."

Janet's eyes shot to the door, then widened in horror. There was only one obstacle between Seth and the exit—their corner of the bar.

"Janet?"

His voice froze the three women.

Time stopped for a beat. Then picked up at double pace.

"Seth? How are you?" Janet's face flooded with blood and brought her color close to normal.

"I'm—"

"Happy Valentine's Day." Janet cut him off with a cheery exclamation.

"Yes, I got your text this afternoon. It was . . . unnecessary, but thank you. This is Lana."

"Nice to meet you, Lana. I'm Janet."

"It's lovely to meet you." Lana studied Seth, then Janet.

Claire realized she had no clue who Janet was—which meant Seth had never mentioned his ex-wife, at least not by name. What that meant, she wasn't sure, but she was sure Janet would not take it as a good sign. Not to mention Janet would feel, to her, like one step closer to denying her existence.

"We should go," Seth offered. He tapped Lana's back and turned to the door.

His manner clearly cued Lana to the moment's significance. Her open expression clouded.

Janet smiled and reached out a tentative hand, only to drop it midair. "It was good to see you, Seth, and you, Lana."

Seth ushered his date into the revolving door without a look back.

As the door spun him away, Janet slumped.

Claire wrapped an arm around her. "You were so calm. You handled that beautifully."

"You really did," Madeline agreed. "Very impressive."

"I texted him today. What a fool. I actually texted him Happy Valentine's Day. I'm going to be sick."

"What were you thinking?" Claire pushed the silver bowl of fries toward Janet.

"I was thinking maybe he was lonely. I was thinking I don't want to go on any more dates. I have no clue what I was thinking. Please. I'm going to be sick. Can we go? I need to go."

Claire pulled back and grabbed her coat. "Then we go. Madeline, I'll get the car, you get the bill."

"Wait." Janet clutched at her arm. "Give him two minutes to get out of here."

"We'll be fine. If he sees me, I'll tell him I forgot my purse." Claire pulled out her keys and shoved the bag to Madeline. "By the time I get back, he'll be long gone."

She wove through the waiting throng and out the door. Madeline waved to the bartender.

"Mrs. Harrison? Your table is ready."

Janet tugged Madeline's sleeve rather than turn to Lexi, the hostess. Madeline spoke, "I'm sorry. We need to leave. Can you give our table away?"

"Of course." The young woman didn't look at Janet again. She spun on her booted heel and disappeared.

No one spoke until they reached the small lot behind the shop.

Claire twisted in the driver's seat. Janet was now the expressionless one in the back. "Are you going to be okay?"

"I'll be fine." Janet pulled herself up and out of the car. She pointed to the shop and spoke to Madeline, who had climbed out of the passenger seat. "Do you mind if I go in and pick out a book? A nice romance?"

"Take anything you want."

"Do you want me to stay with you?" Claire called.

Janet shook her head. "Go home. Hug your kids and call your husband. Remind him what he's missing."

"They're probably out."

Janet shook her head again. "You told me Brittany's grounded."

"True . . . I'll go. See you tomorrow?"

"See you tomorrow. I'm going to grab something horrifically steamy and head home too."

Madeline clicked the keys to her small car. "And I'm going to drive an hour south to an empty apartment and wait for a lawyer who may or may not show up."

"Sure you both don't want books too?" Janet put her key into the lock.

"I'll pass. If Drew doesn't show, I'll work on some of the cases Greg sent me. Happy Valentine's Day."

"I'll see what the kids are doing and then find a movie on demand."

"Such romantics." Janet sighed and pushed her way into the shop. She leaned out with a final wave. "Good night, ladies."

CLAIRE PULLED INTO HER driveway. Tonight the house was lit. Her mood lifted as she walked in to find Matt sitting at the counter eating a bowl of cereal.

"I left pot roast."

"I ate it already."

She glimpsed the television in the family room, which could be seen from the kitchen island. "What are you watching?"

He shrugged. "Some movie I found."

The commercial ended. "That's not some movie, that's *The Breakfast Club*—a pivotal moment of my youth. Bring the bowl into the family room and I'll watch with you . . . I love this movie . . . Wait until you see how they change. They—"

"I'm not allowed to eat in the family room."

"Who says?" Claire winked. Matt grinned and followed. "Where's your sister?"

"Dunno." He flopped onto the couch, and milk sloshed onto his T-shirt.

"Isn't she here?"

"I haven't seen her."

Claire pulled out her phone and texted Brittany.

Call and get home right now.

No reply.

She pulled up Find My iPhone. Brittany's phone was offline.

Claire sank into the couch, laughed in all the right places, answered Matt's questions—yes, people really did dress like Molly Ringwald and Judd Nelson back then—and hoped she convinced him that all was right in the world, at least within their home.

But the second he left to play video games, she felt her facade crumble. Her phone screen was dark. No call. No text. No Brittany.

She dragged a throw blanket over her legs and readied herself for a long night.

Chapter 12

Madeline

As I drove downtown, my thoughts turned to Chris rather than Drew. When he stopped by the store this morning, everything within me said *He's engaged. Stay at your desk*. After all, I was in the back and he wouldn't ask for me. He never did. I hadn't seen him since my nervous foot-in-mouth moment at the flower box and wondered how he'd look at me now. Probably as he always did—I was the only one hyper-aware whenever he came near. He didn't seem to notice me, when I wasn't trampling on his dignity.

Stay at your—

Midmantra, I'd pushed back and headed toward the store front.

"Hey, Janet, have you seen— Hello." I hoped my voice sounded far more surprised and genuine to him than it did to me.

But Janet wasn't fooled. She banked a smile and innocently asked, "Yes?"

"I . . ." I stalled. I hadn't gotten that far with my fake question. "Never mind. Doesn't matter."

"Hello there," Chris chirped. "Happy Valentine's Day." He then turned back to Janet. "I brought you flowers." He pulled a tight mixed bouquet from behind his back.

"Sonia is a lucky woman."

"Aww . . . I was only thinking of you."

She swatted his shoulder.

"Don't worry. I got her flowers." He winked. "Bigger ones."

"As you should. Thank you."

"You're welcome." His voice carried a sweet solemnity.

I drifted away as they talked. There were customers—the store was overflowing with last-minute Valentine's Day shoppers, so it was a good time to leave the office work behind and get out on the floor.

I'd found I liked working the floor. Even more than I had enjoyed client work at the firm. There I helped clients with important stuff, but we rarely laughed or smiled, and we never joked. Contracts, estate planning, and tax codes didn't lead to a lot of jocularity. But now I connected people with books, gifts, puzzles, and fun stuff.

It was the best of both worlds most days, as I got to play with that other stuff too, in the side storage room I'd cleared. Aunt Maddie's old tutoring room fit a desk and three chairs, one behind it and two in front of it, quite comfortably. It fit me and my new clients perfectly.

Because Greg kept sending me cases. They were only little things that people needed help with, but they all mattered. Elena's landlord fixed her toilet, another woman finally secured a restraining order against her abusive husband, a suit got filed against another predatory landlord in Elena's neighborhood, and a kid got out of foster care and back with his mom. And as payment, the mom worked in the store three evenings a week. In fact, last night she brought two friends along, and I cleaned with them. I wasn't sure who enjoyed it more. She loved the books and sharing them with her friends, and I loved hearing about their lives and their children.

"How is your Valentine's Day going?"

I'd turned and found Chris standing across the gifts table, Janet nowhere in sight.

"I've always laughed that it's a Hallmark holiday, but it's helping our bottom line so much I can't complain."

"Excellent. It's good to see the store thriving. Maddie would be pleased."

Loans and debt aside, it looked thriving. Janet's displays were opulent and gorgeous, but if you mentally took them apart piece by piece, they weren't expensive. She did a lot with little money. And Claire had rearranged some of the shelves so that we featured more rather than stocked less. She had taught me a lot about the character of our shop and our customers, and I'd begun to understand the unique mix of people and purchases. She'd made other changes too, including placing orders with more selectivity. Costs were down and sales were up, foot traffic too.

But it wasn't enough . . .

"What? Your face fell." Chris stepped around the table.

I wanted it to be enough. On some level, at some point, maybe at that moment, I began to see myself staying. It became a shop rather than a store and I was emotionally invested. I belonged—and I wanted Aunt Maddie to be pleased with it, and with me. Greg had been right that first day. Aunt Maddie had trusted me with her legacy; I couldn't take that lightly. I no longer wanted to take that lightly.

And yet . . .

"Can I ask you something?" I tilted my head to the corner of the shop and walked that direction. Chris followed, so I assumed that meant yes. "When we met, after Aunt Maddie's funeral at the park, I told you she was my aunt, and you . . . I sensed you knew about me and didn't like me."

"Is that a question?" He stood so close I could see the flecks in his eyes and smell his cologne, or soap, I wasn't sure which.

"Yes."

"I may have misjudged you."

I kept quiet. He rubbed his chin. That clean-cut straight chin from the day at the park carried a five o'clock shadow today. It looked good.

He took a breath and started talking on the exhale. "I loved your aunt. I met her during a rough time, and besides Luke, who's my older brother and has always gotten me out of jams, she's the one who showed up, and listened, and loved me. My mom's been gone a while, so your aunt became pretty special to me. And when she was dying, she talked about you a lot. You were so close, only forty miles away, but you never came. You should have heard her go on about you. You could do no wrong. Some brilliant hotshot lawyer . . ." He dropped his voice and his green eyes bored into mine. "But for me, you were the woman who never showed up to see her dying aunt."

"Okay then."

"No explanation?" He straightened—and that's when I realized how close we'd come together over my question. "Why'd you ask?"

"I could tell you I didn't know she was sick, which is true, but it goes deeper than that. And I still don't know the whole story. I thought I did, but nothing fits like I thought . . . Did Janet and Claire feel the same about me?"

"We never talked about it, but why wouldn't they?"

"Because until you know the truth, you shouldn't judge people." I blurted out the words and felt five years old again.

He smiled, as if placating a child, and that made it worse. "You are right. None of us should have judged you."

All afternoon I busied myself with customers as I played his words over and over in my head. During our short moment at Mirabella's they still dwelt in the background. Now as I drove south to my apartment after leaving Janet in search of her romance novel, I acted. I tapped my steering wheel to bring up my phone and tapped again on *Mom*.

"Happy Valentine's Day, darling. Do you have fun plans tonight?"

"Not really. I had fries with Claire and Janet from the bookshop, but Drew won't drop by till late if he does at all."

"Fries?"

"Never mind. It's a long story . . . Do you have a sec?"

I heard her shift and suspected she was easing deeper into her favorite brown velvet armchair. "Sure. We just got back from Eleven Madison Park."

"Are you kidding? Go Dad."

"It was the most opulent and longest dinner I've ever had, and every bite was perfection. It was incredibly romantic. Now your father has fallen asleep in front of the TV. What's up?"

I heard the affection and adoration in Mom's voice and wondered when that happened. I remember when it left. Summer of 2000. That summer affected far more than stocks. But its return . . . I hadn't registered it until now.

"I need to know what happened between Dad and Aunt Maddie. I know his fund lost most of her and Uncle Pete's retirement, but why didn't she ever forgive him?"

"What?" I heard shuffling and surmised Mom was now climbing out of the brown velvet chair and crossing to her office or to the kitchen—somewhere out of Dad's earshot. "What made you think of that?"

"I'm here, Mom, in Winsome every day, and she's all around me and she seems pretty great. That's how I remember her too. Those few weeks here were the best of my life, then Dad hauled me home and . . . It was horrible, if you want to know the truth. We never talked about it, but nothing was the same after that. The girls at school, some never forgave me that their families lost money with Dad, and we weren't the same either. You two never laughed. We were barely ever in the same room. It was like the crash ruined us all, and it never got better; at least I didn't feel it did before I left for college."

"Is that why you never came home for a summer?"

"Yes."

"I wondered. You always had some school program or internship. I thought it was us, that you were bored with us."

"Not you, not exactly, but New York. High school was tough, Mom."

"New York can be a tough place." A softness to her voice told me she understood.

I didn't speak into the pause. Eventually she did.

"It wasn't the fund, Madeline, ever. Maddie never cared about the money, and your father is and always has been a responsible manager. It was about a woman. Your father had an affair."

My breath hitched.

"It had been going on for about a year by that trip, and if it hadn't been for you, I believe he would have left. I'd known from day one; your father is horrible about keeping secrets. He thought he was clever, but . . . You know him."

A small laugh escaped because it was true. Dad lived in the world of high finance and he had mastered it. We lived in the real world, and that was a place he knew very little about.

"She was in San Francisco, and when he decided to take you with him, I suspected it was the beginning of the end. He was taking you to meet her. Then he left you in Chicago and that, oddly, made it worse. I called Maddie and I vented . . . Oh, the things I told your aunt." Mom paused. "And that was my mistake. Whatever was between me and your father should have stayed between us, but I hadn't talked to anyone in a year and I was drowning. New York is a very small town about these things, and you're right that spring had already worn me down and . . . Well, your aunt always was a good listener." Mom drifted away.

I assumed she was reliving the day or the years that followed. "Then what happened?"

"Whatever she hit him with when he came back to Winsome got him on a plane home and ended the affair."

"What did she say?"

"She never told me and I never asked. Part of me was ashamed I'd told her at all, and another part of me was embarrassed that his big sister could send him home while I could only whine and cry. I was so humiliated about all I'd told, all that she might have repeated, that I didn't confront your father either."

"You talked about the affair. You confronted him about that at least." They were statements; the answers were too obvious. No one could keep silent.

"I didn't say a word. You both came home and I thought I could forget. But I was so angry. I tried to work through it, but I couldn't get there. I couldn't forgive him . . . That's what made life so rough, not the tech crash. I'm sorry about the kids at school, but no adult blamed your dad. I had no idea you were feeling all that."

"I thought that's what made life tough for you too." I felt a tear run down my cheek. I swiped it away.

"It was never that. I'm so sorry I didn't confront him or forgive him. I let my anger taint everything . . . Finally, a few days after you left for Cornell, I started to move out. It was like we had this demon living with us, and once you were out from under it, I wanted out too. Have you ever read the book *Rebecca*?"

"No."

"When you do, you'll understand. Even dead and gone, a person or an event can affect lives, for good or for bad . . . Anyway, your father caught me. He was supposed to be on a trip, but instead he walked in right amidst all the boxes and the moving men, and we had it out. Not much was salvageable in the living room after that fight."

"That's why you redecorated." It felt as if a lightbulb switched on. I always thought that was a cliché, but when it happened, light flooded the dark places within me. My teenage years twisted as if in a kaleidoscope and began to make sense.

"I had to. I threw most of it."

That was something I never expected. Mom didn't throw an insult, much less a chair. The image of her pitching books and lamps and glass figurines was almost comical—if not so sad.

"But you didn't leave." I dropped the next bread crumb for her.

"No . . . I scared your father. I scared me. By the end, we were heaped together on the living room floor sobbing. We started counseling that very afternoon."

"But what about Aunt Maddie?" I took the Ohio Street exit off I-94 and headed east.

"Oh . . . honey . . . He was so ashamed. Pride is a terrible thing, and, despite everything, it still has a good grasp on your dad in some respects. That's what it comes down to. Something broke within him when she confronted him. He adored her and felt exposed more than he could handle. Nothing she said or I said could change that. She tried for a while, and then she told me she needed to respect his decision. She didn't reach out again until last November."

"And now?"

"And now his ulcers are back . . . Her call changed everything. He talked about going to see her, flying out to Chicago to see you, then driving north, and then—" She stopped. Our connection was so clear I could almost see the tears. I could certainly hear them. I felt my own eyes fill, then spill.

"She died." I supplied the answer and turned down my street. "But all those years, Mom, I thought I was being loyal to him. I thought she blamed him and had cut him off. Do you know how many times I hurt her feelings? I didn't want to betray Dad . . . and I had it wrong. All of it."

"Why didn't you say anything?"

"I'm the kid, Mom. I didn't know I had to say anything. And I thought I understood." Nineteen years vanished and it was eighth grade all over again, and I was young, confused, and angry.

"You're right. You're right and I'm sorry."

A deep breath pulled me back together as I turned into my building's parking garage. It was over now. Yelling at Mom wouldn't turn back the clock and couldn't change how I had treated my aunt. "How is Dad doing?"

"Dinner tonight was fun. He's beginning to smile again. This has been really hard on him. He's carrying some very heavy regrets right now, and in this life he can't make them right. Neither of us can."

"I'm right there with you." I turned off my car and leaned back against the headrest. "I'm home now . . . Thanks for being honest, Mom."

"I'm sorry I wasn't sooner."

I pressed my palms against my eyes. "Can we talk more later?" My head pounded.

"Anytime. And if you want to ask your father about it, you may. I know he'll talk to you."

Her voice held such confidence, such surety, I believed her. For the first time I understood the two Moms in my memory. The first was kind and loving and attentive, then silent and sad, but the second held a determination and definition I admired. She had come on the scene during college, but I hadn't recognized it. I had always viewed my world as pivoting around the spring and summer of my eighth-grade year. I missed the more seismic shifts during college.

"I might, someday." I offered the words, but knew I would never follow through. The thought of chatting with my dad about his affair was horrific.

"It's up to you. But you and me? We can talk anytime, about anything."

"Thanks, Mom. I love you." I reached to my steering wheel to click off. "Wait. What changed, Mom? I mean, you did—I see it now and wonder how I never did before—but what did it?"

I felt change happening within myself and wanted a road map, needed one, if such a thing existed.

"God, forgiveness, and a good therapist. I also made the decision to trust your dad again. It makes you vulnerable, without a doubt, but every relationship has to have it."

"Thanks for the honesty, Mom. I love you."

"I love you too. Why don't I fly out and we spend a few days together?"

I felt my head shake before I replied. I didn't want her to see the shop. I didn't want her to see the mess I'd made of Aunt Maddie's legacy, my empty apartment, and the tenuous hold I had on my world.

"I'm pretty busy right now. Can we schedule something later?"

"Of course. We'll talk soon."

I tapped off as guilt rushed over me. For years I had pushed her away. I didn't mean to, but I hadn't understood our family. I'd misunderstood and misjudged so much in my world and hurt my aunt and my parents in the process. I'd just done it again.

I opened my apartment door as a text from Drew pinged my phone.

> Still working. Won't make it by tonight. Hope you had a good day. Talk soon.

I dropped my keys and phone into the china bowl by the door. "Happy Valentine's Day."

Chapter 13

Janet

"Happy Valentine's Day. Is it wonderful with Rosie? Did you buy her something girly and pink? I remember—"

"Mom, it's late. They've gone to bed."

"It's not that late." I hear the desperation in my voice. No one likes desperation, so I try again. "I just wanted to say hi and hear how you all are doing."

"We're good, but tired. She's growing a lot. We had her six-week checkup last week and she's in the ninety-fifth percentile for height and weight. Laura's beat with all the feedings."

"Have you tried formula?"

His pause feels heavy. He clears his throat. I've heard that before. He is trying to be diplomatic—with me. My son is trying to be diplomatic with me.

"Laura would like to breastfeed for the first six months. We got a pump. She may give that a try next week, but these are the early days, Mom. She's loving being with Rosie."

"Of course . . . It's a beautiful time, and I don't mean to bother her. Or you. I just . . . I'd love to see Rosie."

Indianapolis is so close I can almost smell my granddaughter's downy hair. But to drive down and arrive unannounced, to be coldly invited in and asked *How long do you plan to stay?* . . . Call it pride. Call it self-preservation. I won't do it. I need an invitation.

"When things calm down we'll work something out."

An invitation is not on offer.

"Of course." I repeat the words again like a parrot. "I understand. Give her a kiss for me."

"Will do . . . Thanks for calling, Mom."

"Sure. I love—" He taps off. ". . . You."

I drop my phone back into my bag and wander into the shop. There is no one left to call. No one left at all. And the rhyme only makes it worse.

The clouds above and snow below send a soft purplish light through the windows. It's enough light for me to find a romance I haven't read and enough light for me to find that bottle of wine in the office fridge no one has drunk.

I uncork an indifferent Pinot, look for a glass, and, finding only a stainless steel water bottle, decide drinking from the bottle is good enough for me.

Good enough for me.

What an interesting phrase . . . And what a fool I've been . . .

Seth was good enough for me.

Alyssa and Chase were good enough for me.

Our life together was good enough for me.

And in one night I threw it all away—and with it the life I'd known and all the friendships we'd constructed together. After almost thirty years living in one town, I belonged. I was part of the town's fiber as it was a part of me—only fibers can break.

He'd been so encouraging and attentive. Men have no idea how seductive those two things are. I wanted to believe I still had it. I wanted to believe I was still an artist and more than a middle-aged wife, mom, and sometime volunteer, that I could still feel those same highs and lows and bring them to life on canvas. He said I could. He said such talent rarely came through the community center's adult classes. He said that some of his students down at the Art Institute didn't display my innate understanding of form and texture on their best days.

It started with the art. One class. Then another. Seth wondered. I balked. *I gave up a lot to be a mom. You never had to make those sacrifices and now I want to do this for me.* My self-righteous indignation filled me, satisfied me—and I believed it too.

It started with the art, but it was fed by a touch on my shoulder, a finger trailing down my arm to the brush in my hand. He guided my fingers, gliding the brush along the line of cheek on the canvas. *Press here for more definition. Create shadow. Create play between the darkness and the light.*

And it moved fast. *Stay for a drink tonight . . .* And then . . . *Must you rush home?* The two of us perched on stools drinking good Cabernet. He brought the bottles from his private collection and they were always rich, heady, full of dirt, earth, and life. His knees touched mine when he swung them side to side getting lost in his descriptions of life, travel, and art—his world, his passions. Our knees intertwined as he locked eyes on me and listened. He listened to stories of my world, my passions—my hopes and dreams.

It's all in front of you. Art is never lost. A finger trailed up my cheek and created shadow. Dark played against light. *You're exquisite . . .*

And then there was Seth's face the moment I walked in the door, that very night. He'd waited up, which was unusual, as if he, too, felt the shift in our world. Anger didn't fill his eyes. Anger came later. That night he was empty, disoriented, as if everything he'd held to be true had flipped so fast he'd missed the motion and was left unbalanced, unable to stand.

In my mind I see him dropping limp into a chair, but I wonder now if I've created that image and rewritten that scene.

I do remember that his resignation ignited my anger. Anger

always comes first for me. Anger keeps embarrassment, humiliation, shame, all manner of painful emotions at bay—for a time. But it requires so much fuel. And while it burned hot that night, and for a couple weeks after, it soon flickered out. Shame replaced it, and shame doesn't need much fuel to thrive. It can live on tiny nibbles for years, possibly for a lifetime.

I didn't apologize that night. I had quipped for years that I never apologize. It had become our joke. We played with that light so often we long ignored the darker aspect of this trait. Only now do I see the truth of it. Back then, not to apologize was a weapon. Why capitulate when a good dinner, a gentle joke, a back rub, tears, or sex always worked?

I did try crying. I recall that. The tears were real—and ineffective. I never got close enough to try the back rub or the sex. Seth packed a bag and left that first night.

And when the tears failed to bring him home, I tried yelling—in the lawyers' offices, in the house when he first came to pack his things, in the parking lot of the grocery store. I yelled and I yelled and I yelled—until there was no one left to listen.

And that's how I landed here . . .

Maddie—Seth's friend first, and my last friend—gave me a job and a reason to climb out of bed each day.

I tap my fingers along the book spines. I need something scintillating and scandalous tonight. I need to forget today and remember what it was like to be touched and loved. Isn't that what Maddie always said—good, fully dimensional characters let us live their lives vicariously, and bad ones tell us about the authors? I could use a good character right now. I need someone else to become. I need another life to live. I need people to put these books back straight. Why can no one do that? This entire section is askew . . .

The messy shelves require concentration so, bottle empty, I bend to rest it on the floor. It tips and rolls. As I watch it stop in a patch of moonlight, a shadow covers it. It's so dark no light penetrates the shadow, and I wonder if the bottle is still there. I look up as a man passes by on the sidewalk and the light returns.

Seth?

I'm not angry anymore. And he's not on his date. He's alone. I know that walk, that lope to his stride. I walked beside it for almost thirty years, and this afternoon I had hoped—

"Seth, come back!" I dash to the door, kicking the bottle in my path. The door is locked and my fingers bungle over the deadbolt, then the lock in the knob. Why haven't we fixed these? They don't move.

"Wait," I call again as I wrench the door open and stumble onto the sidewalk, weight and momentum carrying me faster than my legs can move.

It's empty. A few parked cars. A few streetlights. But no man. In fact, no one.

But . . . I wonder as I look to the corner. The lock took time—perhaps enough that he may have just turned the corner.

"Seth!" I call his name again and follow.

I round the corner and head behind the shop to the alley. One more corner and there he is, crossing through the alley toward the town's public lot. People are spilling out of Bistro North and more from the bar down the street.

I don't care who hears. "Seth!"

He turns.

I step back. "I—I thought you were someone else."

The man, shorter than Seth, broader than Seth, younger than Seth, calls "No problem" and resumes his walk.

The air leaves me, wilts me, and that darn cat is blocking the Printed Letter's alley door.

"Don't you ever learn? Can't you see nobody wants you!"

My yell sends it scurrying away and I'm left alone.

Chapter 14

Claire

Claire pushed up from the sofa, blinking at the sunlight coming through the living room window. She had fallen asleep in a half-sitting pose, and her back felt stiff and her neck was cricked on one side. She rubbed it as she slid her phone from the coffee table. No texts from Brittany. But a missed call and three texts from Brian.

I tried to call. Are you awake?
I'm sorry I missed tonight.
I love you. Sleep well.

She smiled. It was easy to blame him—the easiest thing in the world really. But it wasn't right. Brian worked hard and he loved her and the kids, and he never missed texting every night he was away. Wait, that was new . . . They used to *talk* every night. They'd recount their days, his work, her work, and all that the kids had going on. When had that changed? Claire laid down the phone. It changed when she quit having things to say.

She tossed the throw blanket back onto the sofa and headed to the stairs as Brittany raced down. Claire stepped back in time not to be squished.

"You were grounded last night, yet you weren't here when I got home. Where were you? What time did you get in?" She followed Brittany into the kitchen.

"You were asleep on the couch. I didn't want to wake you." Brittany shrugged and grabbed a Kombucha from the fridge and popped the top. "I didn't think studying violated my jail sentence, but we can talk about it later. I've got a physics study lab starting early this morning." She walked back to the stairs and called up. "Your ride is leaving."

The house shook as Matt pounded across the upstairs hall, then down the stairs.

"Lunch?" he called as he passed.

"I . . . I just woke up."

"I'll buy today. Bye, Mom." He waved and flew out the door.

Brittany offered nothing other than one last look and shut the door behind them both.

Claire stood there dazed but also aware—Brittany hadn't answered her questions. She had stepped around them. How many times had Brian warned her? *You're not her friend. You're her mom.* And how many times had she replied, so certain? *I am both. She doesn't need me hovering.*

At one point perhaps that had been true. Or maybe it was the impossible dream moms wanted to believe. But Brittany had seemed so lost for so long, Claire was sure her daughter needed a friend to listen far more than she needed a mom to chide. Only now—no longer trusted like a friend nor respected like a mom—did Claire question her motivation and her actions.

The evening, the grounding, and Brittany's evasion picked at her for the three-mile drive to work. Brian had come down hard about the vodka bottle, but then he went out of town and all the punishments he laid down, Claire couldn't enforce. She'd lost that thread of authority and it couldn't be woven back again—at least she didn't see how.

She played it over and over, fantasizing what she should have said, could have said, to make her daughter answer, obey, and come back to the relationship they'd once shared. That's what she missed most—the Brittany who was—the girl who stayed up late to draw and create, the girl who made homemade cards for every occasion, the girl who came home crying in the fifth grade because the teacher asked for her best handwriting and that would take too long.

Claire could almost feel Brittany's lanky limbs drape across her lap as they had that day when she pulled her close. She remembered the feel of her, the smell of her, as she pushed Brittany's hair back and kissed her brow. *Sweetheart, she doesn't understand. You give her your third best handwriting. That's what she expects. No one has handwriting like yours.*

But this morning was different. The tone and tenor had changed yet again. Claire felt it. It wasn't avoidance or disrespect. Enmity charged the air. It was tangible, but not something she could articulate to Brian two thousand miles away. It would have to wait until he got home—in three days.

As she pushed open the Printed Letter's alley door, she saw the cat creep into view.

"You need a home, sweet thing. Wait here. I'll get you milk."

It hit her the second she stepped inside. Ice. Her first thought was that the furnace had finally died. Her second was that broken heaters don't generate a breeze. She rushed from the office into the store front and faced disaster . . .

All the paper in the world had been scattered. She looked to the open front door, wondering how wind could do so much damage. Then a torn cover, half of Martha Stewart smiling from her *Homekeeping Handbook*, shifted in the breeze. No wind had torn Martha from her 752 pages of sage advice.

Claire stepped through the debris to shut the door. With gloved fingers, she pushed it closed, avoiding the knob or anything else the police might want to see.

She then dialed the police's nonemergency number. "I need to report a break-in." As she described the scene and gave the address, she noted several Sharpies scattered amidst the pages. She let her gaze drift up. "Sharpie . . . They took the Sharpies we use for authors to sign books and drew all over the shelves. It's unbelie— I *can't* wait in my car. I'm already in the building."

Claire tiptoed her way back to the office, the storage room, the side room, and the restroom. "No one's here . . . Yes, I'll stay still." She stood at the counter surveying the damage. Books torn, scattered, shelves drawn on as if they were coloring books, smashed picture frames, a tossed wine bottle, and . . . She sniffed. *Did someone pee in here?*

Two police officers soon arrived. They entered through the front door and treaded lightly through the mess to Claire.

One of the officers whistled as he scanned the scene. "This sure is something. Don't see much of this around here."

"I don't think anything was taken. The register is untouched, and I forgot to make the bank deposit yesterday. It's still in my desk."

"That's lucky."

"This doesn't look like luck." Claire noted the Hemingway note smashed on the counter.

"No, it doesn't," the other officer replied.

Claire felt a presence to her left. Madeline stood in the doorway to the office, jaw dropped. Her eyes flew to the ceiling moldings. Claire's gaze followed, though she knew what she'd see. Nothing. Most of Maddie's beloved letters had been smashed and lay in twisted piles of wood, glass, and paper on the floor amidst all the other wood, glass, and paper.

"We hung those together. Uncle Pete did that for her."

"I'm so sorry, Madeline."

The officer stepped forward, and Claire watched Madeline's eyes focus and harden. "How did this happen?"

"We don't know yet. I'm hoping you can help us."

Claire couldn't hear what they said as they moved forward toward the evidence technician, who was photographing every inch of the store.

After a few moments Madeline waved Claire to them. "Did you get to the bank yesterday?"

"I forgot, but the deposit is still there. The register wasn't touched either."

"Then this is vandalism and not burglary?" She turned back to the officer, whom Claire now knew was named Brennan.

"It appears to be, but we'll cover all the bases to make certain." Officer Brennan then asked both women a series of questions, all of which had the same answer:

Does anyone hold a grudge against either of you? No.

Did you terminate anyone recently? No.

Do your neighbors or any local businesses have complaints against you? No.

Does anyone wish you harm? No.

Officer Brennan nodded and returned to the technician.

Madeline lifted her hands in a gesture of defeat. "This is Class 2 felony kind of destruction."

"What does that mean?" Claire whispered.

"It means we lost a whole lot more than ten thousand in property damages, but probably less than a hundred thousand." Madeline pointed to the center wood columns running the length of the store. Three of the four were buckled.

Claire stared at them. "Those are support beams. We need to bolster those. Do you think the ceiling will hold?"

"I have no idea."

Three hours later the officers left, and Claire and Madeline stood alone in the chaos and the cold.

Claire buttoned her coat's top button. "I'm going to turn up the heat. It'll take forever to warm this place up."

Madeline spun around as if remembering something. She touched a fresh indentation on the wall, the blue paint torn from the drywall. The Hemingway note lay beneath it on the counter, ripped by the shattered glass.

"I saw that earlier. The glass cut it to shreds." Claire reached for it.

"Don't. You'll get hurt. It's ruined anyway."

"Let's leave it and start cleaning."

"I told you . . ." Madeline drew a deep breath. "One thing and we were done for." She looked at Claire. "This is a little worse than a hard snow or the flu."

"Don't say that. We can fix this." Claire heard the desperation in her voice. She needed those words to be true. "I'll get a broom. You call the insurance company, and a contractor."

Madeline

Insurance.

I meant to call. It was on my list . . . Who doesn't handle that first? The safety net, the backup, the protection. But first the partnership loss, then I planned to sell, and it was only going to take days, a week at most . . .

Excuses.

Every single one of them.

Bottom line: I forgot about the insurance.

End result: I was sunk.

The Printed Letter's policy, as any business insurance policy, was tied to the entity's owner—be it an LLC, a corporation, or an aunt. The Printed Letter's policy ended with Aunt Maddie's death.

None of this was insured. And the money had run out. Her money. My money. All of it.

Not that her policy would have helped anyway—she cut her contents clause when the shop stopped making money, and she scaled back her general liability into legally dangerous ground three months before her death. She was lucky no one slipped on an errant book or her uneven floors and took it all from her. Instead, they'd now take it from me.

Aunt Maddie's insurance coverage had been laughable.

Mine brought me to tears.

"It's not that bad." Claire touched my arm.

Her consoling gesture made me feel like a jerk. I wasn't the only one who'd pay for this. She and Janet would too. And Aunt Maddie's beautiful shop . . . I needed to throw up.

"It is that bad. We have no insurance."

Her touch turned to a tap. "I've got the policy in the file. Give me a sec."

I shook my head and explained. How any lawyer could forget that detail was a little harder to articulate.

Claire absorbed the mess. "But this is probably thirty thousand dollars of damage in stock alone, maybe more. There's structural damage too. We need a contractor."

"I'm aware of that."

She sighed, an audible, heart-worn sound.

"Exactly."

"If they find who did this, you could win damages in court, right? The officer said they might get something off the bank's surveillance cameras next door." Claire wasn't giving up.

"If they came from that direction. But even then we can't count on any compensation. It rarely works the way you might think."

I stepped away. I needed to do something, some form of forward motion to stem the drowning feeling that swamped me. Nothing in my life had prepared me for this. Nothing in my life had prepared me for the past three months . . . College, law school, clerkship, associate, partner. That was the path. Bankrupt bookshop owner who had no idea what she was doing on a daily basis, much less the next day, was not part of my plan. Ha. *My plan.*

When had my plans ever worked out?

Claire picked her way to the front of the shop as if she were playing hopscotch, stepping around scattered books and debris. Plaster dust sprinkled her hair as she passed beneath a hole in the ceiling. A gaping wound existed where yesterday a charming drop chandelier had hung. She returned with more purpose and headed to the office. I suspected she was searching for the defunct insurance policy—the mom in her needed to fix this.

I pulled out my phone to take pictures. The police had theirs, but perhaps I could capture something new, something different—maybe something that would help us in court, assuming we found the vandals.

As I walked around snapping photos, I was again horrified by the crime. It was senseless. It felt as if someone had enjoyed this—torn books, thrown them in the air, and laughed as pages fell like snowflakes to cover almost every square inch of floor. Two small wooden chairs from the kids' section had been destroyed—not picked up and slammed against the wall or the floor, but tossed. They had smashed upon landing fifteen, twenty feet from their points of origin. One must have taken out the chandelier as it sailed by.

I then photographed the three central beams and the damaged walls. Someone had wielded the baseball bat, now lying under Spirituality, with a vengeance. And Claire was right, someone had used World Travel as a latrine. Definitely a man, as the urine started at waist level in Monaco and traveled south through Zimbabwe.

After pictures, I began to clear the floor. I picked up any salvageable books. Greg would help me place them. We couldn't sell them, but they couldn't and wouldn't go to waste. They could still benefit someone . . .

Greg. I had to call Greg and tell him I'd lost Aunt Maddie's beloved shop.

And it was beloved. I suspected she put God and Uncle Pete above the shop, but it might have been close running. I imagined her indomitable spirit digging in to clean up with the cheery statement that the new stock would be even better. She was the one who saw the vision and led the charge all those summers ago when I only saw books and work ahead of me. But she'd been right. She'd created magic and something significant. If she saw it now . . .

I only saw my aunt cry once. Granted, I hadn't known her well, but I hadn't forgotten it. I had just landed in Chicago for law school when my mom called.

"Uncle Pete died on Tuesday. Your father refuses to go to the funeral. Will you go? Family should be there."

I remembered feeling hot with fury, no matter what she'd done. "What is wrong with him?"

"He's having a hard time with forgiveness, my darling." Mom gave a small, self-deprecating laugh I didn't understand.

Now, a decade later, I read so much more into that moment. Dad wasn't trying to forgive Aunt Maddie. He was trying to forgive himself. I lived under the lie that Aunt Maddie had betrayed him. But Mom didn't know that—she had thought she was sending me as a family emissary, whereas I had thought she was offering me a "hall pass," an appropriate way to see my aunt without being disloyal to my father.

I'd stood in the back of the church for Uncle Pete's funeral, full of wonder at the beauty of it. So many friends stood and spoke of his kindness and generosity, his faith and his sense of humor. We should have allowed such a moment for Aunt Maddie. Dad had directed the funeral details. *Short and simple* had been his dictum.

At Uncle Pete's service I watched Aunt Maddie thank everyone for coming to honor her husband, thank everyone for their years of friendship and support, and thank everyone for showing such love—that's when she saw me. She pulled in the corner of her lower lip, and tears flooded her eyes. She faltered a heartbeat, unable to speak. Eyes locked on mine, she finally added, "God is good," and sat down.

On her walk up the aisle, she stopped, hugged me long and hard, and said, "I understand how hard all this is. It means everything to me you came today. I love you, Madeline."

Today. That word stayed with me. The way she said it made it feel final, as if she, too, had understood—a hall pass was only valid for a short time. She had known her brother much better than I knew my father.

So many secrets, and they damaged us all. And now *today* the last bit of her, my beautiful—and "crazy" in all the best ways—aunt, was beyond repair.

Claire materialized with a broom and brought me back to the present. "You okay?"

"No." I grabbed a tissue and blew my nose. "Put anything that can still be read over here, and we'll give it all to Greg Frankel."

Claire helped with the stacking, then used the broom to start pushing loose papers, smashed crystals, and debris into a far corner. We both cast nervous glances at the center beams.

I was still sorting books when she emerged from the back office wearing rubber gloves and a stern expression.

"I'll tackle World Travel," I said. "You shouldn't have to do that." I straightened and put out a hand for the gloves.

"I don't mind, and I need it done. The smell is disgusting." She started in Zimbabwe and stood and stretched her back when she reached Scotland. "Where's Janet?"

"It's only eleven—she has at least another hour before she'll call herself officially late." As I dropped my wrist, I caught sight of a wine bottle. "I thought you said no one entered the office."

"No one did that I can tell."

I held up the bottle. "But isn't this what we bought for the Lillian Vance signing?"

Claire bit her lip. I could tell both our minds traveled the same direction—and to the same person.

Who, at that moment, pushed open the front door.

"What happened?" Janet threw her arms wide. "Are we redecorating?"

"Hardly." I held up the bottle. "Do you know anything about this?"

My question was answered without any words. Her eyes widened in confusion, then narrowed in memory. She looked around the shop and her face greened, which made her blond highlights look harsh against her skin and the shop's floodlights. The softer light emitted by the chandelier was gone.

"You did this?" Claire's voice was barely a whisper.

"No. No! How could you think that? I didn't do any of this. I left the store exactly as we left it to go to Mirabella's last night." She pushed the door shut behind her and leaned against it. "When we got back, I did come in and . . . I did drink the wine, but . . ." She stopped, then started up in a rush. "But I left the shop exactly as I found it. In perfect shape."

I narrowed my eyes.

"Don't look at me like that. How can you not believe me? I'd never do this." She shifted her gaze between us, too fast, too frantic. "Why would you think the worst of me? What do you expect? That seeing Seth on a date would send me into a drunken destructive frenzy? Nice . . . You set me up on a date . . . I'm moving on. He is too . . . It was bound to happen."

"It was a hard night," Claire offered.

"Please." Janet sneered. "If that's your logic, you could've done this. Your husband's never home and your kids use you like live-in help. How is your life any better than what I've got?" She turned back to me before Claire could reply. Not that she would, or could. Her lips dropped open and didn't shut.

Janet stepped toward me. "And you're no better. How dare you accuse me." Glass ground beneath her foot. "You want out. What better way to break even than file a massive insurance claim?" She stepped through the debris and stood near one of the center beams. Her gaze trailed up it. "This was a nice touch. If that last one had been smashed you could've brought the whole ceiling in."

"Get out."

"What? You accused me. A little turnabout is only fair play."

"We're just confused." Claire stepped forward to keep the peace. "You were the last one here, and the police said there was no forced entry."

"How is that possible? The alley door locks automatically." She stepped over a pile and almost slipped on the shifting paper. Her eyes shot to the ceiling. "The chandelier. The letters." Her bravado faltered. Maybe she, too, understood what those letters meant to Uncle Pete, to Aunt Maddie, even to me.

"The vandals came through the front door."

In that moment, Janet aged. Not as if time took a toll, but as if she took her own measure and exacted a toll on herself. All her bravado evaporated. Her eyes moved back and forth as if watching a movie only she could see.

"I walked out the front door. I saw Seth. At least I thought I did, and I followed him around to the back. It wasn't him . . . I must have left the door open when I ran out."

"You did what?" Claire's voice inched up a few notches.

"I didn't mean to. I ran out the front and . . ." Janet's eyes filled with tears. She waved her hand back and forth, possibly in hopes that quick movement would reveal another scenario, another movie that let her off the hook. "I came back in through the alley. I had my keys in my coat pocket, so I grabbed my bag and went home."

"You drove home like that? Drunk?" Claire was yelling now.

"I—I— No . . . I must have. But I didn't do the damage. I left the door open, that's all. I'm not responsible for this. I—" Janet covered her mouth with her hand as if trying to stop the words from spilling out. She lowered it. "This is bad. How can we fix it?"

"Stop." Claire opened her mouth again, but I cut her off with an outstretched hand, fingers splayed. "There is no insurance, Janet. We can't fix this. Collect your stuff and get out."

Janet

"No . . . I can fix this." I shake my head back and forth. It's useless, but it feels like if I shake hard enough a new picture will emerge. I'll be different and I won't have destroyed the one happy thing I had left.

She sees me. In that moment, when I realize what I did, Madeline sees all of me. The awareness hits her eyes so fast I can't breathe. She understands what a shell, what a fake I am.

I feel it too . . . All the warmth falls from my face, and the color—you can feel color drain. It starts with the oranges and yellows, the warm colors full of hope. Then the greens, the kind I'd once seen in Seth's eyes, and other shades brightened and made strong by the sun. The bridge colors fall next—those connecting colors that smooth the way from light to dark. I once used them to portray dawn and dusk. Now I slide right past them into darkness, and puce. Puce is the color when you've got nothing left to throw up, but you keep at it, clinging to that toilet seat or that thread of hope, praying it won't snap. That's the color Madeline sees. And by witnessing it, she ushers in a new one. A green-black I've never felt before—the color of certainty, finality, complete aloneness.

Yet it's not as harsh and rigid as some might think. Rather, it's a negative space that leaves you very cold.

Claire stands there staring at me as Madeline issues the order to get out, drops her broom, and bolts to the office.

"I can't believe this happened."

Claire doesn't reply.

"Someone came in and did all this? They walked through the front door?"

"Not hard to do when it's wide open." Claire has one hand on a hip.

I stare at her. For such innocuous words they're choreographed to pack a punch. "I didn't mean to do it."

"And yet . . . it happened."

"Stop already. I get it. I'm a horrible person. But I didn't do this, and it's a *book*shop." My voice pitches high. "Who does this to a bookshop? People love bookshops. We—"

"We lost our jobs, and the Printed Letter. You understand that, right? Whatever this meant to you, it's gone—and for me too."

Her statement stops all motion, then releases a surge of fight. The kind I haven't felt in years. But it's always there. It was there the night Seth left and it's back now. When pushed into a corner—I fight.

"What do you mean? The shop is doing better. We've worked our butts off here and she knows it." I point after Madeline, who, I gather by the slamming of the alley door, is now gone. "She loves it here. This won't change anything. It's a hiccup. She's completely forgotten about selling."

"She also forgot about the insurance, and without it there's no money to restock or rebuild. Including structural stuff, she could be looking at sixty to seventy thousand dollars here. There's no way to keep the doors open, Janet."

"There's no insurance? . . . But she's got money. She paid us in full last month."

"She's been emptying her apartment to pay for all this and to satisfy the bank's request for a cash balance in our accounts. Haven't you been paying attention? Maddie left the store in debt, double mortgaged it and her house. She struggled since Pete died, and Madeline can't cover it."

"Madeline made a fortune. Believe me, I know what those firms charge and what they pay."

"She didn't save. She says she invested it in furniture. It doesn't matter. She's thirty-three. Who cares what she did with it? She didn't expect her salary to dry up, and she didn't ask for all this. That girl's been breaking herself in two trying to keep this afloat."

"To sell it for a profit," I counter.

"At first, yes, and then because she had to, but . . ." Claire lifts her hand toward the office. "I get the feeling she doesn't want to anymore. At least she didn't."

"I didn't know." I see something hard in Claire's eyes.

"It wasn't hard to see."

We stand facing each other. It feels like that day at Maddie's funeral. Our eyes clash but we aren't arguing. I've cost us another lifeline, and it's my last.

"What can I do?"

"Help me clean."

"She fired me."

"You owe her more than leaving now. You owe Maddie more than that too."

She's right. I owe Maddie much more and, truth be told, I owe her niece more too.

Claire works the whole afternoon in silence. I do the same, but I keep looking at her, wanting to talk. She's not ready and I can't blame her. I love this place and, as much as I dismiss Claire's attachment, I know she loves it too. The woman I see out and about in town is not the woman I see in here.

Outside the Printed Letter, Claire is contained, silent, worried she'll say the wrong thing, wear the wrong thing, do the wrong thing. Everything about her is fashioned not to be noticed—her makeup just right, not too much to be beautiful and striking, only enough to create a blank palette. Her hair is the same, brown bob, with flyaways normally tamed by a little hair spray. If you don't notice something or someone, you can't reject it—or her.

But inside these walls Claire keeps the books, handles the ordering, arranges the events . . . In here, she's the most capable woman I've ever met, with all her right angles and spreadsheets. And I've taken this from her. I've taken it from us all.

I didn't think it possible, but for five and a half hours, Claire says nothing and avoids all eye contact. I've been cut off—again.

Madeline never returns. Part of me won't be surprised if I show up tomorrow morning to find the locks changed and the windows covered in For Sale signs. Part of me won't blame her. But I will show up.

We keep the door locked all day. A few customers knock, we open, they ask, and we tell them the story—only it's a break-in now. Claire leaves out my involvement. I want to hug her for that, especially when she tells the story to nosy Harriet Smoot from my block.

I call a contractor friend of Seth's, who, to my surprise, arrives after lunch and sets up three temporary supports next to the smashed beams. He says no problem and the supports are ample to keep things safe. He also says he'll put together a proposal for the repairs and bill us later for the beams. I smile and thank him. Maybe by then we'll have some way to pay him.

I spend the afternoon with Mr. Clean Magic Eraser sponges scrubbing Sharpie from all the shelving. The marks are faint now, but everything should be repainted. If there's time . . . I'll repaint it all myself.

I almost make the offer to Claire, but she's still cleaning the floor. Her head is down and she looks broken. Clean shelving isn't going to help.

The sun sets, the store is dark and clean, and we're still not talking. My hands are chapped and raw and the pain feels right. I climb off the stool and head to the storage closet to put it away. It's only five thirty. A half hour until closing and, even though we never opened, neither of us will leave early. Claire won't on principle. And I can't—what if the door locks do change? What if this really is the end?

I slip out the back door, hoping Claire won't notice, and return with two decaf lattes from the Daily Brew.

I raise a cup toward her. "I splurged and put vanilla syrup in yours. Figured you deserved the treat."

She accepts the offering.

We sit side by side on the stools behind the counter.

"I screwed up, Claire. The one thing I didn't want to happen has, again."

She sighs. I suspect boosting me up is the last thing she wants to do, but that's exactly what I've requested.

"You have to stop thinking that way. Doesn't it become a self-fulfilling prophecy? Isn't that kind of the definition of self-sabotage?" Her voice is so tired. Worn away. Beyond what cleaning a shop should do to a soul.

"I shouldn't have said what I did today. It was cruel and I didn't mean it." I rub her back. "Are you okay?"

"No." She takes a long sip and looks straight ahead. "I loved it here. It's the one place I felt like I was contributing."

"What about your home? You've got Brian and two great kids. I was a jerk this morning. You should never listen to me."

"What did you say that wasn't true? I'm irrelevant there. Matt only needs to be fed. Brittany wants nothing to do with me. And Brian's gone so much . . . he doesn't notice. So I guess I know something about self-sabotage, because I probably did that to myself too."

"What do you mean?"

"I'm exactly where I asked to be." She pushes off the stool. "But I did love this place. Even Madeline. Hasn't it been fun? Some of it? All of it?"

"Stop . . . Stop . . ."

She worries me. For once someone else is worrying me more than myself. I stand and grip her by both shoulders. "I see you, Claire. You're relevant to me, and I'm going to fix this."

I have no idea how, but I will.

Chapter 15

Madeline

I hadn't seen Chris in two weeks, not since the horrible day-after-Valentine's when I fired Janet and walked out of the trashed bookshop. I'd stumbled into the Daily Brew and chosen a small table in the corner, actively avoiding eye contact with the few people I recognized.

"May I join you?"

"No." I recognized his voice and answered without looking up.

There was no equivocating with my *no.* It was beyond firm. Then I glanced up. First he looked surprised, then hurt.

I almost backed down, but something stopped me. Anger? Fear? I have no idea. But I added nothing to soften my single word.

"Sorry I bothered you."

I nodded. He left.

But now here he was downtown in Chicago, in my neighborhood, sitting near the table the hostess was indicating for Drew and me. He sat with a woman, Sonia I assumed.

She wasn't conventionally pretty. She had wide-set eyes and a broad mouth. Her jaw was perfectly square and offset by long dark hair that cut in below her chin and fell straight beyond her shoulders. She appeared serious in the moment we made eye contact, but I suspected she knew how to laugh.

Chris needed someone who could laugh. He seemed disposed to it, though I sensed it had been a long time since he'd laughed well.

And that was my problem. I hadn't seen Chris in two weeks, but I'd been thinking, and was still thinking, far too much about him.

Drew pulled out my chair right as Chris's eyes followed Sonia's and hit us.

"Madeline?"

"Hi . . . How are you here? Volare is kind of a neighborhood spot." I wanted to add *My neighborhood spot*, but stopped just in time.

He unnerved me. It was apparent he didn't like me, and that bothered me. Most people liked me. Sure, I could be uptight—Janet used to point that out daily—but I also knew how to have fun, as Kayla and a bunch of friends would attest to. But Chris . . . He tolerated me. That was the best I could say for his attitude.

I still hadn't told him why I'd been such a horrible niece—in his eyes, a horrible human—and that bothered me every moment my thoughts drifted his direction. It bothered me all the time.

"I live a few blocks east of here, in the Sienna Building," the woman offered.

"Me too." I waved my hand in the general direction of our buildings. "Not in the Sienna, but I'm practically across the street at 420 East."

She smiled, and I was right. She had an amazing smile. It spread across her face and up into her eyes.

"How do you two know each other?" she asked Chris.

He did not smile. "Winsome."

The woman rolled her eyes. She was making fun of him, and that bothered me too. I turned away, ready to be done with the whole confusing meet-and-greet.

She called after us. "Come. Come join us. We're bored with our conversation."

"No, we—" I moved to sit.

"Sure." Drew stepped toward them. "You live in the Sienna? I toured that when I first graduated law school."

He pulled up next to her—he didn't even know her name—and I dropped into the only seat left, next to Chris.

"Sorry about this," I murmured.

"No biggie . . . Sonia," he interrupted them, "this is Madeline Cullen. She took over the Printed Letter in Winsome."

"That little store you always talk about? The one that closed down?"

"It didn't close down. We had to close for a week for some cleanup and repairs, but—" I pressed my lips shut. I had no idea why I was defending my "little store," especially as she didn't care. She had already turned back to Drew.

Chris continued. "Sonia works at Fidelity."

Drew handled his own introduction, to Sonia alone. "Drew Setaro. I'm not up in Winsome either. I'm a partner at Duncan, Schwartz and Baring."

It was my turn to roll my eyes.

Chris caught it and sent me a ghost of a smile.

A waiter took our orders, and we batted conversation around the table like a badminton shuttlecock. A hit started us off, but it landed soft and fizzled out, to start again with a new serve. It only got rolling when Sonia and Drew cut Chris and me out completely.

We both heard Sonia offer up Chris's occupation, past and present, but he still didn't engage.

"Reading and gardening is about all he does, but he'll go back to medicine soon." Sonia laid a hand on his arm. "Right?"

"Perhaps." Chris's ravioli fascinated him.

As it should have . . . He'd ordered my favorite, a pork belly and ricotta ravioli, forcing me to order the Bolognese so as not to copy him.

He offered Sonia nothing more, so she returned to greener conversational pastures.

I stepped into the silence. "Do you find it fulfilling? Working in landscaping?"

Chris found something in my voice. By his narrowed gaze, I assumed it tasted condescending and bitter.

I opened my mouth to refute his assumption, but stopped. Rather than annoy me, it created a flutter in my gut. His not liking me physically hurt.

I tried a new tack. "Like me, you're trained to do more."

As soon as it was out of my mouth, I regretted it. I had meant "something else." I meant to show commonality between our situations, and us, but nothing was coming out right. And what was worse, Sonia heard me.

"That's what I've been saying." She pulled Chris by the arm again. "See, hon, I'm not the only one who feels that way."

Chris didn't reply to me nor did he look at her.

I scooped up the last of my pasta and tried to dig myself out of the hole another way. "I owe you an apology for the coffee shop a couple weeks ago. I was beyond rude. It was a bad day."

It took him a second to shift gears. He'd been someplace else. "No worries. When I saw you I hadn't heard about the vandalism. I'm sorry about all that."

"It wasn't your fault." I offered my first true smile of the evening. It felt like he'd waved a white flag between us.

"It wasn't Janet's either."

My smile and his flag evaporated.

"Debatable." I shoved in a massive bite to stop myself from saying more.

The last two weeks at the shop had been chilly and painful, and not because of the broken heating system. Janet had shown up the next day, and the one after that, and the one after that. I never reminded her I'd fired her because I couldn't . . . I couldn't be that person. She was hurting. Claire was hurting. And, on some level, I was broken and couldn't put my pieces back together. Even Greg Frankel sensed it, and rather than going in for the kill when I told him about Aunt Maddie's shop, he consoled me.

"Maddie would tell you to give up the shop in a heartbeat if she ever thought it caused you concern or pain. It was only to bring you and anyone else who entered those doors joy. Let it go. You did well, Cullen."

I sat for an hour at Aunt Maddie's kitchen table after that call and sobbed.

Not that Chris would believe that, or anything good about me, for one second. He probably envisioned me stalking Janet each day, trying to shove her out the door.

I hadn't. Instead we had worked side by side, in silence, both licking our wounds and trying to figure out what to do next. And, to be completely honest, I couldn't have made it to that point without her. Living in Winsome for so long, Janet was the one who knew whom to call and how to get a good deal from the contractors for repairs. She had two bids by the next morning to fix the structural damage and she then negotiated an amazing price and had been honest with them too—she told both companies we could only pay once the shop sold. Her statement didn't faze them; it devastated me. But as hard as that was to hear, it was also true. I was out of furniture—and options. Both contractors agreed, and while the chosen one took a week to make the shop safe, I used the time to hire a Realtor. By last week, the Printed Letter was open for business and on the market for sale, along with Aunt Maddie's house.

"She feels terrible," Chris whispered. "You must know that, because she shows up every day and you haven't kicked her out. And yes, she left the door open, but vandals did the damage. They are responsible for their choices, not her."

"I get that, and the law is on your side. She's clear in that regard.

But from my perspective, despite all her help, I'm finding it hard to forgive her. Is that what you wanted to hear?"

"Who said forgiveness was supposed to be easy?"

He followed his perfectly delivered—and I assumed, by his tone, rhetorical—question with one for Drew.

The lift in one corner of his mouth created a tiny comma inside his check. It told me it was deliberate. He had turned to Drew to leave me no quarter to question or protest his challenge—only time to ponder it.

And after I did that, I still sat cut from the conversation, marveling. The man should've been a lawyer, not a yardman or a doctor or whatever he was. I finished my dinner in silence.

"Are you walking east or Ubering?" Drew asked Sonia as we gathered our coats.

She stretched to look out the window. She had a long neck, an Audrey Hepburn neck. I liked her less.

"It's not that cold tonight. Shall we all walk?"

Outside, Drew and Sonia stepped ahead of Chris and me, full of conversation and laughter. Chris and I remained silent.

At the Sienna, Chris took a step back rather than a step forward. "Sonia, I'm going to head to the Metra. I've got an early start tomorrow."

"Snow coming in?" Her voice bit.

He looked to the sky. "It's supposed to stay above freezing. Now that it's March, I doubt I'll plow much more this spring. I'm working on some garden designs and have an early meeting."

"Fine. Call me later." She gave a collective wave good-bye.

Chris faced us. "Thanks for joining us tonight. It was nice to meet you, Drew." He motioned to me while backing away. "Madeline."

"Wait." The word was out before a plan was formed. I looked between him and Drew. "I'm heading back tonight too. Let me grab a bag and I'll drive you north."

Drew lifted a brow. I had surprised him.

"I'm meeting with the Realtor at eight and the bank at ten . . . You have no idea how much I have going on."

He chuckled. "I like how your definition of *a lot* has changed."

I wasn't sure if he was being sincere or sarcastic. "I guess it has." I twisted to Chris. "Are you waiting or going?"

Our eyes met. I sent him a challenge this time—of what I wasn't sure—but he locked eyes on me and I knew he was in.

"Waiting."

"Good. Come up. I'll only be five minutes. Drew?"

"Nah . . . I'll head home. I've got a big day tomorrow too." He kissed my cheek. "I'll see you soon. Later, Chris."

Chris followed me into my building.

Again, no words.

It took me five minutes to pack a bag. He spent the time standing in my dark living room looking across the few blocks to the darker lake.

"I'm ready if you are." I grabbed my keys and headed out the door.

"Hmm . . ."

I turned to find him still examining my apartment. I stalled and tried to see it from his perspective. It had become bare over the past two months, not that it was ever crowded. The breakfront was the first to go. Two eighteenth-century end tables had been next. I hadn't had the nerve to go back to Sid McKenna Interiors to sell those, so I sold them, and a lovely set of chairs, to a high-end consignment store—sold it all cheap and only kept 50 percent. It was not a smart move, but pride got in my way.

Until I couldn't afford pride. When I sold a small dresser and a pair of sconces, I tried another shop. But when I sold the Henry Moore—last week—I took it back to McKenna. He graciously took it on commission, sold it high immediately, and gave me 80 percent. Sid McKenna was my hero.

That's where I got the money to pay my mortgage, Aunt Maddie's mortgages on both her house and the shop, and the interest on her additional loans. I also paid the premiums on new insurance policies, complete with contents coverage, one for the shop and one for her house. Not only was it unwise not to carry it—I jumped every time someone tripped in the shop while I was searching out the best policy—but the real estate agent commented that no one would list either property without it.

The money also paid Claire's salary, and Janet's. Chris was right—I had fired her, but she came back every day and she worked hard. I told Claire to cut her a check too. There was nothing left for the contractor. I simply had to hope he was sincere when he said he could wait. A lawsuit was the last thing I needed.

In that moment I saw my apartment with new eyes. It was sterile. Despite having nothing of any value left to sell, had it always felt that way? I shrugged and swung the door closed behind us.

"I used to love that place." My verb pulled at me. When had my feelings changed? If Chris noticed my confusion, he didn't comment. In fact, he said nothing at all.

We got in my car and headed east. Turning left off East Chicago Avenue and heading north on Lake Shore Drive always made me think of an old movie Aunt Maddie and I had watched that summer. She loved *When Harry Met Sally* and enjoyed pointing to all the Chicago spots of old in it, especially the scene in which Harry and Sally drive the wrong way to head to New York from the University of Chicago. Aunt Maddie yelled at the screen, as I'm sure she'd done countless times before, with laughter in her voice, "You're headed to Wisconsin. Turn around."

I felt laughter bubble with the memory and, on the inhale, I caught Chris's cologne or aftershave, or whatever it was. He filled my car with a mixture of citrus, soap, and something richer . . . I wanted to say bergamot. It smelled amazing, and I caught myself leaning closer to catch more of it. I righted myself and tried to redirect his questioning look with the memory. "My aunt used to yell at that movie— What?"

"Nothing."

Chris was so close I could feel his tension. It occurred the second I mentioned my aunt.

"Not nothing. Can we just lay it out? You don't like me and it's painfully obvious."

"Painfully?"

"Well . . . it's uncomfortable, and I'm not evil."

"I barely know you, Madeline."

A line from my current read from Aunt Maddie's book list came to mind. *Elinor agreed to it all, for she did not think he deserved the compliment of rational opposition.*

I loved that line. I'd laughed out loud when I stumbled across it and read it at least five times to commit it to memory. It was so true. It applied to work and it applied to life. So much did not call for rational opposition.

I clamped my lips shut. Chris had leveled a charge at me—horrid human—and he didn't deserve my confidence or my defense.

I let the silence grow.

He squirmed.

I remained quiet.

He grew fidgety and spread his fingers wide across his knees, compressed them into fists, then went through the motion again, and again.

Finally he broke. "Your aunt was an amazing woman. And at the end Janet moved in with her so she wouldn't be alone. There were nurses there and hospice came, but Janet never left her side. To have someone you love near you matters."

"So this is about Janet. You're mad because I'm hurting her."

"It's about them both."

We drove a few beats more before I added, "You were there too, weren't you?"

He focused straight ahead. "I would stop by to explain in layman's terms what was happening. Doctors and nurses can forget that, how scared people get and how little they understand. But not Maddie . . ."

He filled the car with a deep, resonant chuckle. It wasn't derisive or tinged with sorrow; it was joyful.

"She wasn't scared at all. I think she listened to me to make *me* feel better, like I needed something to do. She'd reach over and touch my hand and say I was really good at all that, but not to worry so much, that I wasn't responsible for carrying the weight of the world . . . She liked my name."

I wasn't sure what he meant, but I didn't interrupt. He was lost in the memory.

"Like I said before, she talked about you a lot." I kept my eyes on the road, but I felt him staring at me. "Downtown to Winsome isn't that far, but you never came . . . Once when I got ticked and threatened to call you myself, she said I couldn't blame you for your best quality."

Best quality.

I turned onto Sheridan Road and let the words sink in, wondering. "Loyalty. She meant loyalty."

"How do you figure that?" His voice swam in sarcasm.

And while that should have bothered me, it didn't. I was swamped by Aunt Maddie's grace. She had understood on a deeper level what my own mother had failed to see. Somehow Aunt Maddie had known all along.

I gave Chris my explanation, not because he deserved it, but because it hit me so powerfully I needed to articulate it.

"I was being loyal to my dad, her brother. No one ever explained what had gone wrong between them, at least not until recently. I simply knew it was big and ugly and changed everything. But she knew. I suspect she knew what I thought had happened, and she let it alone to be good to my dad, to not lessen him in my eyes. She took the hit so he didn't have to." I peeked at Chris again. "I can't say I'd go back and behave differently, because I don't know how I could. I was a kid when it started and . . . Can we just say . . . Never mind . . . Thank you."

"Why are you thanking me?" His sarcasm morphed to curiosity.

"Because what I thought was true all along was true. She was kind and wonderful and she understood me and she forgave me and she never forgot me." I felt tears pool but refused to let them drop.

Only brief directions to his house broke the silence as we drove north. I pulled into his driveway. His home was similar to Aunt Maddie's—small and cottage-like with a front porch.

"Thanks for the ride." He climbed out and held the door. I thought he might say more.

When he didn't, I whispered a "You're welcome" as the door shut, then reversed out of the driveway.

He didn't walk inside. Instead he stood on the porch, lit by a single bulb, and waited as I drove away.

I glanced back through the rearview mirror and mentally let him go. I smiled, feeling lighter than I had in months, maybe years—it didn't matter anymore that he didn't like me.

Aunt Maddie had loved me.

Janet

Toughest two weeks of my life.

I laugh to myself. Seriously? Did I really just think that? I'm standing here in line at the Daily Brew telling myself that working unasked and uninvited at the Printed Letter has constituted the toughest two weeks I've ever lived.

Clearly, I'm getting soft.

But that isn't all of it. To be fair, in those two weeks I also contacted former friends, asked favors, and imposed on old ties that had long been broken. Only they didn't feel long broken. Both contractors, Lewis and Anthony, had been polite, kind, even warm. And generous—to do the work without pay, until the shop sold? That generosity, I suspect, was not based on our past friendship but rather sprang from a love and respect for Maddie and for the Printed Letter. Yet I was the one who brokered the deal.

After Lewis finished the work, we reopened to a flood of customers. Word had gotten out that the shop was going on the market, and the entire town came in to either buy books or protest Madeline's decision. She looks close to tears most days. Only Elena and the cleaning crew can make her laugh in the evenings. I try to stay up front to take some of the load from her, but dealing with the questions, the concerns, the loss, each and every day, from that many customers is hard.

But the toughest two weeks of my life? Please . . .

I glance at my phone to bring up Apple Pay and see my granddaughter's smiling face. Two and a half months old and smiling—and I haven't held her yet. Forget the past two weeks—*that's* the hardest thing in my life right now.

I pay, grab my three lattes, and return to the shop. I hand one to Claire and place one on Madeline's desk. She's in the storage closet. She spends a lot of her time there now. It's got a desk and three chairs in it, and Maddie's attorney friend, Greg Frankel, sends Madeline cases—so many she's practically running a tiny law firm. The day she put the shop on the market, she didn't come out of the room at all.

Her clients are wonderful, though. Elena brings us sopaipilla, Ana Paula helps us clean the store, and Bernard is a wonder with all the odd jobs no one has addressed since Pete passed away a decade ago.

Madeline emerges with a broad smile. "Not to worry, Mrs. Lutz, I've had tremendous success with a single letter. If we have to take it further we will, but I doubt it will be necessary."

An older woman follows her out, grips both her hands in thanks, and shuffles out our front door.

"Landlord again?"

Madeline nods to Claire. "What's with these people? She has no heat." She then notices the Daily Brew cup on her desk and looks to me. "Thank you."

"You're welcome." I say nothing more. I still don't have the words for her, so I walk out of the office and into the shop.

March means spring, and that means a new window display. I've worked out the design over the last several days—I've worked through several designs. They've felt magical—my art coming to life in my head, along with all these thoughts, feelings, and promptings I've never experienced before. Part of me wants to hold this tight and savor it. It's like an awakening, and I want it to unfold slowly and take my time, but another part knows it's to share. I've learned the cost of secrets in any and all forms.

THIS FEELING, AWAKENING, WHATEVER I call it, this chase for light, started the day after we found the vandalism. February 16th. I showed up for work because I couldn't risk it. I couldn't risk Madeline changing the locks or shutting me out. It would have been the end of me. It sounds so dark and dramatic now, but two weeks ago it felt very real. It prompted a late-night call to Chris.

"I need to talk—I need to talk to your brother. Can you set that up?"

I'd woken him up. His "Janet?" had been groggy, but his "What's going on?" was clear and urgent.

"Nothing. Nothing that serious, I shouldn't have woken you, but . . . I need help, Chris."

"We'll be right over."

"No, I—" I stopped midprotest. He'd hung up. And while I hated that I'd woken him and knew he would now wake his brother, I was also thankful. I was so terribly thankful not to be alone.

Within a half hour, tea was made and Chris and Luke sat with me at my kitchen table. I told them what happened at the shop and what led to it, and how I felt. To hear the words tumble from my mouth startled me. I said things that were true, but also things I hadn't known were inside me—anger, yes, but also pain, regret, fear, longing, and shame. The shame was deeper than I fathomed. It felt endless. I concentrated on Chris. I trusted him. To tell all this to a priest was too intimidating. At least that's what I told myself until halfway through when I realized it wasn't.

Father Luke drew out my story and my feelings with no judgment. He led me to my own conclusions and to my own heart with such care, I went deeper and allowed myself to admit more than I ever had before. It was like falling backward into a pool. I kept falling and falling, but there was no fear, only warmth as I was drawn deeper.

He shared two verses with me. The first made me feel safe and the second startled me: *You hem me in, behind and before, and lay your hand upon me.* I felt the powerful, soothing truth of the words and I rested there.

The second verse I recognized from Maddie's letter to me. On the second page, she'd transcribed a chapter from the book of Proverbs. I'd read it all winter, but rather than bringing me comfort, it had pricked me—and here it rose again, on this night. I pulled her letter from my book and slid the pages across the table.

Luke broke it down for me. Maybe Maddie knew I wasn't ready, maybe she understood I'd need time with it. But now it opened like the flowers Madeline had planted in the window box outside the store. They'd unfurled in the morning sun. Yet they also withered with the frost five days later. I didn't want to wither. I fired questions at Luke almost faster than he could answer.

He talked of a woman who *plants a vineyard* and *dresses herself with strength and makes her arms strong*; a woman who *opens her hand to the poor and reaches out her hands to the needy*; a woman who *makes herself coverings* and is clothed in *strength and dignity*; a woman who *laughs at the time to come*. I wanted every aspect of that woman to be within me.

Even now, two weeks later, imagining the ability to laugh at the time to come fills me with wonder. Is such a thing possible?

The description went on . . . This woman *opens her mouth with wisdom, and the teaching of kindness is on her tongue*. I memorized it all—especially the last part. *Her children rise up and call her blessed; her husband also, and he praises her.*

When Luke finished reciting the verses that night, I laid my head on the table. "It's about a wife. I already threw that away." I hadn't realized that's where it was all headed, and the hope I'd felt vanished away.

But then that touch . . . *lay your hand upon me.* It was Luke's hand on top of my head, the way my father used to do when I was very young, and again I felt safe and warm. I felt loved.

Luke spoke softly, as if addressing that young child. "It's about a woman, who may be a wife. But it's first and foremost about a woman, and it's not an unattainable description of an idealized woman. She's born of experience and, I like to believe, knows her worth because she knows who created her. One of my favorite things John Paul II ever said was 'Woman transcends all expectations when her heart is faithful to God.' All expectations. And I've seen it too. My mom was amazing. My sisters are strong women—two are unmarried, by the way, and this is who they are. They don't need a husband to be this woman. I believe God can do tremendous things through you—once you stop trying to wield all the power yourself."

Luke ended our time in prayer and offered to visit again—and we did. The next time, two days later, I was brave enough to meet with him alone. Chris had work and I needed to take my own steps, in courage and, as Luke advised, in faith.

We've met every day since for coffee or tea or a cookie, and I've read and prayed . . .

And I still don't have the courage to talk to Madeline, or to Seth.

"THIS IS TREMENDOUS." CLAIRE'S voice draws me back to my work.

I step back to stand beside her. The window is green now, and I've filled it with books forming bouquets of bright spring colors and stories. Publishers have defied winter's gloom, the nation's gloom, and showered the public with colorful covers that promise fresh starts and new beginnings. The spring offerings provide a chaotic mix of genres and colors and artwork, and it looks glorious.

Claire drapes an arm over my shoulder and pulls me close. "This is your best work."

"Thank you." I sink into her embrace. "Any movement on the shop?"

"Interest, but nothing definitive." She glances back to the office. "She won't talk to me about it. Go easy on her. She's lost weight. I don't think she's eating."

I nod in understanding and commiseration, but mostly because I'm unable to speak.

Claire

Claire left Janet to her work and returned to the office, puzzling over the conundrum that was her friend. Janet had been more distracted at times in the past two weeks than she'd ever seen her, and yet she had never been so present either. Which, like everything with Janet, made no sense. She would check out with a smile across her face, but then Claire would turn around and find some annoyance put away, a coffee on her desk, a troublesome customer soothed, or, like now, a window display that rendered her speechless. What would it be like to carry such creativity and talent within?

Claire bounced back in her seat and tapped closed an Excel file.

What would it be like?

The question lingered. She thought of Brittany. Though untrained, she possessed talent like Janet's. Her art—impromptu sketches of pencil and pen, watercolors, pastels, oils—covered her walls and they were extraordinary. But there was nothing new. Claire had noted again yesterday when putting away the laundry that it had been weeks, maybe months, since anything new was pinned on the walls. She had walked over to the desk and noted that a fine layer of dust now stretched beyond the watercolor palette to the sketch pad and the metal boxes of art supplies. Something intrinsic to her daughter had been lost and she didn't know how to recapture it.

"She doesn't draw anymore." Claire had curled into bed next to Brian last night.

He kissed her head, pulled her close, and dismissed her concerns.

"But it's part of her and she won't talk about it."

"Then make her."

Claire had rolled back to see his eyes. He wasn't being cavalier.

He was serious, and Claire found the statement wasn't as shocking as was his complete confidence that it could work.

When she didn't reply, he continued. "Don't worry. She's a teenager. She'll come back to it. Besides, when does she have time? Between school and whatever it is on that phone that's so exciting, she's pretty booked."

"I'm still concerned."

"She's almost eighteen and heading off to college. I think you can take a breath now."

Claire hadn't felt sure, but as Brian rolled closer, she forgot to dwell on it further. She'd remembered it again that morning, but came no closer to any answers.

"What are you doing up so early?"

Matt had wandered into the kitchen a full half hour before the kids usually left for school.

"I asked Brittany to leave early. I need help from my math teacher, and if I'm not ready Brit won't be happy."

Claire set her coffee down on the counter and perched next to her son. "She doesn't seem happy regardless. Has she said anything?"

"She never talks to me."

Matt shrugged, but it didn't hide the truth. He was hurt. He and Brittany had been close once, wrestling, fighting, warring as kids do, but always with an element of fun behind it. That was gone too.

"What's the trouble in math? I'm good at math." Claire laughed at Matt's expression—it was a better option than tears at his incredulity. "I was a math major in college."

"You were?"

"How do you not know this?"

Matt shrugged again. "You're Mom." He opened his backpack and pulled out a sheet of double variable algebra problems.

"Well, your mom can do this . . . Let me show you how." Tutoring was a mix of learning algebra and learning Mom. "I was state math champion senior year in high school, did you know that? And after college, I worked at Price Waterhouse, right before it became PwC, and friends and I started a consulting group on Saturdays to do pro bono work, mostly for businesses we liked so that they wouldn't close, but it was fun. We got free drinks, free breakfasts, and one clothing store outfitted me for a couple years in thanks for the help we gave them. And—"

"Why'd you stop?"

Claire put down the pencil. "We got busy and Brittany was born and we started moving and . . . Those were good reasons then, but we're in a different place now, aren't we?"

"I guess . . . Is this the right answer?"

It was. Claire hugged her son as her daughter entered the kitchen with a scowl.

"Let's go."

"I don't need to go early. Mom helped me."

Brittany looked from Matt to her mom, then to the door. "Well, I do, so grab your stuff."

She was out the door with Matt trailing.

Claire sat at her desk and let it all shift before her. Like Matt's math problems, there was an answer. If she could shift the variables she might see it clearly. She might see Brittany clearly.

The truculence of January and February had morphed into invisibility. Now Brittany ate in silence, went to her room and worked in silence, slept, then went to school and returned again. There was no chatter, none of those ever-important friends lighting up her phone, and no study dates.

She didn't even question the grounding, which had expired—unnoticed—last weekend.

Chapter 16

Janet

Dr. Oz says we emit electrical signals, that attraction to someone else is not only a mix of pheromones, but a result of the electrical signals our bodies send. He also claims that you can feel them, and not only in romantic situations. They generate within us during any emotional situation like a non-shocking static cling thing, I guess. I doubted him. But I was wrong and he is right—I feel them. Right. Now.

I enter the shop a full two hours before opening, because today I want to talk to Madeline and Claire. I rehearsed it all night. Words I've never said. Words I am late in saying. The shop has been busy lately, giving me no time and no privacy. Which is a good thing—Claire actually smiled as she paid the bills a couple days ago.

"We've got money in the account. Real book-sales money that puts us ahead this month."

I thought she might cry.

Now I'm the one who feels like crying, I'm so nervous. I look to Madeline and I pray she won't fire me—again.

Pray. Another word I'd never said, an action I'd never done. Until now. In the past month, I've felt called to it, wooed toward it—it feels like bread and wine and chocolate, all in one.

"Can I talk to you both?"

Madeline's head lifts and without a word she spins in her chair to face me.

Claire bounces back in hers. "What's up?"

Clearly the signals are real. They feel them too.

"I've been studying, reading, and praying a lot this last month, and I need to . . . I need to apologize and ask for your forgiveness."

I pause a beat to let my words sink in, and begin again before either can reply. Waiting is too stressful, and going off script is not an option.

"I've been a mess, and that's not an excuse, it's a fact. But I let that mess consume me. I fed it and it spilled into everything and I'm responsible for that. I'm sorry for everything I've done that put me and my mess ahead of you and ahead of my job here. And . . ." I take a deep breath. "I ask you to forgive me for leaving the shop open that night. I will try to repay the lost stock and the repair bills, but as you know, that could take time, lots and lots of time, but if you'll let me, I'll stay, I'll 'work with willing hands' and bring you 'good, and not harm.' And after the shop sells, I'll still work to make this right between us."

"What did you just quote?" Madeline speaks first. Her eyes narrow.

"Proverbs 31. I memorized it this month."

"It was in your letter from Maddie." Claire speaks this time.

"On the second page. Yours too?"

She nods and waves her hand at me to continue. "You memorized it?"

I spread my hands apart. "Yes, but that's not the point, or maybe it's another point. The real point is . . ." I look to Madeline. "I am truly sorry."

Madeline stares at me. I expected it would be tough, but Luke didn't warn me about how vulnerable you feel when apologizing. It's a standing-naked-before-a-judge kind of vulnerable. I look down. I'm kneading my knuckles into swollen red balls.

"What does it mean to you? The proverb, I mean. Do you know why she put it in your letter?"

I almost hug Claire for breaking the moment and changing the subject.

"It's advice to a son about a good wife, but it's also what we women can be, married or not." I look to Madeline. "It must have been a favorite of Maddie's. And it's who she was, who I can be, and who I want to be. It can't be too late, not for me, because I don't believe Maddie would tell me about it if it were. But to get there, to be that person, I have to start by saying I'm sorry. I destroyed what we had, and the three of us did have something special, for however long it was going to last. I'm so sorry I caused such harm to it and to us—and to Maddie. I ruined what she built here, and it's not just this physical place. I know that too."

Claire glances to Madeline. She wants Madeline to speak. It's not going to happen.

"That's all I want to say . . . Oh, and thank you. I want to thank you for letting me work here this past month. It was very generous of you." I turn to walk into the shop and begin my first-of-the-morning ritual—tidying that darn kids' section.

"How do you know it's not too late?"

Claire's question surprises me. Her tone shocks me, especially the break at the end, right before the lift. It is soft, curious, and exposed. I look to Madeline first and suspect she agrees with me, for she is staring at Claire too.

"For the shop?"

Claire shakes her head, and it is the saddest, slowest motion I've ever seen.

I have no pride left, so I plunk into my desk chair and wheel it toward her like a crab. I press my hand to my heart. "Because I keep reading and feeling this *yes*, right here, again and again, and it's not that I'm agreeing with anything—it feels like the opposite, that I've gotten so much wrong, but yet I'm loved and, if I ask for forgiveness, I can be forgiven and it can be spring. And that compels me to change. All the grace and mercy and love that's there for the asking, for the receiving, is not a fairy tale."

"I like fairy tales." Claire's smile is again so sad I reach for her hand.

"I do too, especially true ones."

It feels like it's only the two of us in the office.

"Tell me the whole thing."

As I recite what I've memorized, I pull out my sketch pad. I glance to Madeline. Her jaw hangs open, that inch of disbelief, as she pushes from her chair to hover above us. It's only a drawing, but they seem to like it. I took all the strong words, the action verbs, from the verse and interwove them in a word cloud. The cloud forms the long silhouette shape of a woman standing, and the words are a mixture of block letters and script, inks and colors, tone and texture. I used some wonderful light water-based pens and overlaid them with thicker inks to create motion—as the woman in the verse clearly is not standing still.

"It's gorgeous." Madeline stares at me.

"Thank you." She's talking about my picture, but I feel like she's accepting my apology too. They are the first words she has spoken *to* me and not *at* me in a month. And truth be told, this is the first morning I have given her the same courtesy.

I tear the page from the pad. "You may have it."

She jumps back. Her hands fly up. "I can't take that."

"I can make another. You should see what—" I stop. Madeline is not interested in what I'm doing.

But Claire is. "We should see what?"

"I've been working a lot lately, and I've got some things I really want to sell. My dream would be to host a show at that new gallery on Chestnut Street, but it'll take years to build up inventory for something like that. Also, I put my house on the market again, at a lower price. It'll all take time, but I will pay for the damages, Madeline."

Claire smiles. "That's amazing, Janet."

"It's time to move on, and it's not so amazing."

"Work here, between customers, at least for now." Madeline's voice shocks us both. Claire's jaw drops and I resist using my pointer finger to lift it shut.

"I don't understand."

Madeline points to the small room with the skylight. Even on this cloudy day, it's flooded with beautiful light bathing a ton of boxes and debris. "Let's clear that out, and you can work there. You wouldn't need a lot for a show here. We could pair your works with books and make an evening of it."

I almost laugh. She sounds like Maddie—like a true bookseller.

"But there may not be time." I don't say it with venom and she doesn't take it that way.

She pulls her chair over. "True. Or we may have just enough. Bottom line is I forgave you a couple weeks ago, Janet, and I'm sorry I didn't say it. I wasn't sure how. This . . ." She circles her hand between the three of us. "This is not something I've had before, or at least not in a really long time. I'm sorry too."

"Then don't sell the shop. We can make this work." I have all the energy and the hope in the world now.

Madeline shakes her head. "I've been sending out résumés to law firms. I need to go back to what I know and what will pay the bills. I haven't been a good 'life manager,' as my dad would say, and I'm out of options."

"You were handed a pretty big job to manage." Claire pushes out of her chair and walks into the storage room. Without saying anything more, she starts tossing out empty boxes.

Madeline takes them one by one and flattens them with a box cutter.

The electricity shifts and the tension breaks. I feel it shatter and rain around me. Silence turns to talking, giggles turn to chortles, and chortles make Claire choke on her own breath, which only starts the cycle over again.

Within an hour the storage room is cleared and Madeline hangs my first piece of art using a small paneling nail and a binder clip. She calls her simply *The Woman*.

Claire claps, fingers to palm, like any good art snob. "What's next?"

Madeline looks at her watch. "It's almost time to unlock the door."

But I take a different tack. I know exactly what's next for me—but it'll take some time and a whole lot of courage. "I have to apologize. To Seth."

Again both women's jaws drop.

Chapter 17

Madeline

The Ides of March. The day of settling accounts. I remembered it from college, first as the Roman deadline for settling one's debts, then as the date given to Julius Caesar's assassination. A settling of debts as well, I supposed.

Either way, it certainly lived up to its reputation this morning. Nothing could have shocked me more than what Janet laid out before the shop opened. I felt it like an electric shock that flashed, then lingered as we cleared out her new "studio." Maybe it was her talk, maybe it was the change in her, maybe it was because she had actually apologized for something, for everything, but whatever it was, the energy in our little office shifted and it now glowed.

I had noticed something different about her since the vandalism, but I hadn't wanted to see. I pushed it away, convincing myself she felt guilty, not sorry; that she wanted to keep her job, not offer true help; that she was a good actress, not a good person. I misjudged her. Which shouldn't have surprised me; I've misjudged a lot over the years.

But what shocked me more was our brief conversation right before I ran to grab our sandwiches from Winsome Deli.

"Why don't I run an art studio out of the spare room and you run a law office out of that closet?" Janet pointed to the storage closet I had cleared to handle Greg's cases. "We'll work the front, of course, but Claire can handle the shop's backroom work."

"That's only for the few cases Greg Frankel sends me."

"It's not real law?"

"It's definitely real law, but it's not—" And that's where I stopped. The words *what I'm trained to do* were about to launch next and they were wrong.

She tilted her head as if examining deep inside me rather than seeing the surface of me. It gave me the strangest feeling of transparency. I almost looked down to make sure I was still material.

"You're a good lawyer. Here. Doing this."

On that note, I grabbed the sheet on which we'd scribbled our lunch orders and fled out the back of the shop.

You're a good lawyer. Here. Doing this. The statement soaked into me and filled every cell. It wasn't what I had imagined for myself. It wasn't part of the dream, the vision, or the plan. Yet stuck in that dark, windowless room, I'd experienced some of my best law moments—some of my best any kind of moments—in almost a decade.

True, there was no view, no suede chairs fashioned at different heights, no expense accounts—no accounts at all—but the work was some of the most creative and meaningful I'd ever done. Fifteen, no, over twenty people had walked through that back room and been helped by me for a price they could pay—some working in the shop to pay in kind or bringing baked goods because we became friends.

Greg was right to laugh last week. I was as shocked by my enjoyment as he was shocked by my eagerness for more. "You've surprised me, Cullen, and I love surprises."

My elation at his comment surprised me as well. Admiration, maybe grudgingly given, from an unexpected source—a source I'd come to admire and respect over these past months—was a beautiful thing. Maybe one never grows out of delight in approval. And now I sat, grinning that I had surprised Darth Vader when really I had surprised myself.

Sandwiches devoured and the shop relatively quiet, I gazed around our office and marveled. It wasn't all good, not yet, but it was getting better. With each sale of furniture, sacrificed for this place, something had cracked inside me. I thought, at first, it was the end—my security wrenched away piece by piece. But rather than break me, the cracks opened spaces that had never existed before.

I decided to trust. That's what Mom had said. That was, among other things, what had changed her life—not in things, not in her abilities or what she could do or hold, but in people. For her, one person in particular. For me, perhaps I needed a few more.

I walked the floor, trailing my finger along the books, offering to assist customers as I roamed. Mrs. Neuland had lost another pair of her plus-five readers, so I ordered her a new pair and a spare to keep in the shop for her next visit. Janet was in her "studio," so I chatted with David Drummond and helped him find a new book. And two middle schoolers walked away with a childhood favorite of mine, *Number the Stars*.

Claire reconciled the books and reported that since we reopened after the vandalism, sales and traffic were up, and the woman who habitually returned books she found cheaper online had actually kept four purchases in the past two weeks. Not only that—Claire had heard about a new book club starting and offered them 10 percent off their selections. Within hours the word had spread and two more clubs called to place orders.

A line from Janet's morning recitation came to mind. I didn't tell the others Aunt Maddie had transcribed it in my letter too. At the time I figured it was a mistake or that it meant something for her and not for me. But now I wasn't so sure . . .

She looks well to the ways of her household and does not eat the bread of idleness.

It was Janet and Claire who had households. They were the ones with families who relied upon them. But me?

I stalled at the front window, ablaze with color. I did have a household. My concerns involved a family of sorts—Aunt Maddie's legacy had come with more than a shop, a house, a car, a storage unit in Waukegan, and debt. It came with family and a community, who had, in some ways, become my own. And I had worked hard to keep them—to keep us—together. Without understanding it or meaning to, I had looked well to the ways of my household—yet I'd failed.

I LEFT WORK EARLY to drive to Chicago and wander the beachfront before meeting Drew for dinner. It was a brutal walk, but the biting wind felt appropriate, a challenge—if I could withstand that, I could endure anything.

"Sorry I'm late." He dropped into the seat across from me.

I lifted my head and found that in my fifteen minutes of waiting, Girl & the Goat had completely filled. Upon entering there were at least a few other tables still available, but now every table was taken and a crowd filled the small waiting area.

"Thanks for getting here early. If we relied on my schedule, we'd never get into the good restaurants. I can't imagine keeping up this pace another decade." He tapped the menu against the table and called the waiter over. "I'll start with a glass of Mount Veeder Cabernet. Madeline?"

I glanced down, but all the words swam before me. "The same."

Alone again, Drew leaned forward. "How's the store going?"

"It's hard to say. Great and terrible both fit. Along with the breakfront, coffee tables, and that statue I told you about, I sold my car a couple days ago . . . And that's the end of it. Despite the fact the shop's operating expenses are now in the black, the bank will take it, and Aunt Maddie's house. Without one or both selling, I'm done for."

"I can't imagine what you've been through. You should come back to the firm."

"I've sent out résumés, but not there. I can't do that."

"Are you okay?" He reached for my hand.

I shook my head as my future played out before me. I'd sent out a dozen resumes, but I didn't want to return to a law firm at all. I wanted Aunt Maddie's legacy, Aunt Maddie's community, and all that came with it—good and bad.

"I need to go. I'm not where I'm supposed to be, even if it's only for right now."

"I figured that a while ago." Drew pulled away. "I also figured we're never going to be friends, are we?"

I blinked. I was not expecting that. "Is that what you've wanted?"

"I hoped. Maybe I hoped for more, but I was fairly sure on that one early on. You're different. You're lighter and happier, except tonight." He tried to smile, but it fell flat. "And never with me."

"I'm sorry. I'm not sure who I am most days right now."

"Quit worrying about who you are. What do you want to do?"

"Keep that silly bookshop. Run a law practice out of a storage closet. A few neighbors have come in for advice and somehow it got out that I'm a lawyer, a good one, who charges only a hundred dollars an hour."

No offense, but you're trained to do a lot more.

The criticism I had floated to Chris bit at me. Drew was right. He and I couldn't be friends, let alone more than that. Right or wrong, he was somehow mixed up in the way I judged myself and the scales I used to judge others. It wasn't his fault, but it was true. He was part of a life, of a me, I no longer wanted.

"Then chase that. It's a whole lot better than applying for jobs you don't want." He sat back and sighed. "Look, I work over ninety hours a week, the same as when we were associates. The 'big dream' doesn't come with time off. In fact, I'll be on my computer again tonight. But I thrive on it. I'm not sure you ever did. Why would you sign up for more?"

I watched him and it felt as if I saw him for the first time. He did love the work, and always had. What I saw as a challenge to meet, a ladder to climb, he saw as a puzzle to solve. The law was his bay window to explore within, to create art within. That's what Duncan, Schwartz and Baring saw in him—and they'd been right to reward it.

"Why did you break up with me?"

My non sequitur widened his eyes for a beat. "Everything was a competition. I love the law. I loved you. One had nothing to do with the other, but it wasn't like that for you, and it was obvious."

"But you said 'I need more.' You implied it was me, that I wasn't enough."

"If you remember, I said I needed more of you, but you couldn't hear me." He held eye contact. "With you moving on, I thought . . ."

"What?"

"Maybe we could try again. Maybe our worlds were enough apart. But we can't. I can't. Something about me, the firm, who knows what . . ."

He was right, and I had no desire to convince him otherwise—there were no butterflies, no eagerness to get closer, no fear I might hurt him—no desire to trust him with the most vulnerable parts of me. "I'm sorry."

"Don't be." He smiled, and it wasn't the tight smile I'd seen over the past several weeks or the flat one from moments earlier. This one reached his eyes. It crinkled their corners and it reminded me of . . . It reminded me of Chris. "But call Kayla off, please. She hates me. Undeserved, I think."

"It is, and I'll let her know." I laid down my napkin. "This is rude, but I need to go. Do you mind?"

"There it is."

I tilted my head in question.

"That enigmatic smile of yours. It's a new expression you've developed, and something tells me you have better plans now." He nodded toward the door. "See you later, Cullen."

"Thank you and good luck, Setaro."

I fled the restaurant feeling lighter than when I'd entered it. The Ides of March—a good day to settle accounts.

And there was one left.

I COULD'VE WON AN Olympic medal for the two miles of speed walking back to my apartment. I didn't want to Uber. I wanted nothing hemming me in. I wanted to feel space. I wanted to see green. There was none in this part of the city, but I knew where to find it.

Aunt Maddie and her book list. Every title led me here . . . How had she known? And had she meant for me to read them in order? If she had, if she'd thought that far ahead and listed them with purpose, she could not have chosen better. Each story gently propelled me to question my own. To say I'd experienced an awakening as real and significant as my current read would be an understatement. Natalia Fenollera's Miss Prim had nothing on me. I could feel it. I could taste it. I was ready.

I took the elevator up to my apartment and stood exactly where Chris had stood. I tried to see it anew, but all I sensed was that no part of me lived there anymore. I had stayed at Aunt Maddie's house two or three, sometimes four nights a week for the past six weeks. I claimed it was because I needed to sort the house, but I had finished that over a month ago. The truth was I liked it there. I liked me there.

I liked bundling up and sitting on the porch as the sun set. I liked curling into the wicker chair with a bunch of blankets and reading the books from Aunt Maddie's list. I liked walking to the end of the drive to pick up the paper I'd never canceled. I liked looking at those flower boxes and wondering what I might plant there or in the small patch to the left of her garage. And I liked wondering where I got the desire to plant anything, anywhere, at all.

I grabbed a suitcase from my closet—no overnight bag this time—and threw in as much as it could hold. I grabbed two laundry baskets and filled them too. I cleaned the kitchen, the bathroom, left it all spotless, and then headed to Aunt Maddie's Volvo parked in the underground garage.

Within four hours, I physically and emotionally left a place I'd called home for eight years.

TRAFFIC WAS LIGHT, AND I was on his doorstep before I'd fully worked out what I needed to stay. But I pressed ahead and rang the doorbell. I stood beneath the porch's one light. Too bright. I stepped back. Too dark. I stepped to the side. Maybe this wasn't such a good idea. What time—

"Madeline?"

"Hi . . . You're home."

"It's one a.m. Why aren't *you* home?"

"It—it is? Were you asleep? Of course you were. I woke you up. I'll call you tomorrow." I backed away.

"Madeline."

I stopped. There was a striking quality to his voice, not unkind, but it didn't leave any wiggle room. He stood under the porch light dressed in a plain gray T-shirt and striped pajama pants. His feet were bare and his face stubbly.

"I'm sorry."

"For what?" He ran his hand over his face as if realizing what he must look like. The grimace led me to think he was embarrassed.

I thought he looked wonderful. But I was here for a purpose . . .

"For implying that you were any less for what you did. For not seeing you for who you are. For not being super grateful for all you did for my aunt and all you've done for me . . . For not seeing you."

"You said that already."

"It deserved repeating." I stepped back again. "I'm sorry . . . That deserved repeating too."

"Do you want to come in?"

I waved him back into his house. "It's one a.m. You should sleep."

"Stay." He pointed to a swing at the end of his porch. "Go sit there, and don't leave."

He disappeared and I sat. The night felt still, and late, and the wait stretched too long. I grew embarrassed and I gathered my nerves to leave.

Chris intercepted me at the door draped in blankets. "I told you to stay." He stretched a mug my direction and crossed back to the swing. "I asked you to stay."

I took it, sniffed it, and sank onto the swinging bench next to him. "You made me hot chocolate."

He placed his mug on a side table, wrapped a blanket around me, and tucked it beneath my chin, leaving one arm out for the cocoa. After sitting down, he set the swing rocking with his now wool-slippered foot.

"Start all this from the beginning."

I laughed. "Where to begin."

I meant it rhetorically, but one glance at Chris and I knew he was serious. So I began at the beginning, the summer of 2000, and I told him everything—from my point of view, which, as I have learned, was highly subjective.

Cocoa gone, but wrapped warm and tight, I finished my story and found myself curled into him. He didn't have his arm around me; it lay across the swing's back, but he hadn't pushed me away either.

I pushed myself away. "I . . . I think I'm tired. I didn't mean to do that."

He shrugged. "You did nothing wrong."

Facing each other now, I asked a question of my own. "Why aren't you practicing medicine right now? I'm not judging. I'm asking. Like me, I bet you have a story."

"Don't we all?" He offered the same rhetorical tone I had offered a solid hour or two before. And like him, I held my gaze steady.

"My last assignment was working triage and emergency surgery in Kandahar, Afghanistan, and it was hard, beyond hard."

"You're military?"

"I was. Army. I worked overseas in various capacities for six years, and it felt more like fighting against death than fighting for life. Objectively one could call them the same, but they don't feel the same. I was worn out when I arrived in Kandahar and wrecked when I left and . . . I wanted to help things grow. Luke found me a job. It's as simple, or as complex, as that."

"How did you meet my aunt?"

"I told you about the soup."

When I said nothing he conceded and backed up further.

"As soon as I hit stateside, I came to visit Luke and Sonia, and I got sick. Doctors couldn't figure out what it was; I certainly didn't know. Luke thought it was more psychological and spiritual than physical, and he might be right. But your aunt came over and she listened to me. She brought me soup and books and she shared her life with me. And when I was strong enough to move out of Luke's place, she brought food every night for a week as I settled in here. Then she got sick and I did the same for her. That's what was the worst over there. Those young men and women died and their loved ones weren't near. There was no one to hear their stories, hold their hands, and tell them not to be scared, at least not someone they might believe. So when you didn't come—"

"I get it. I truly do."

"I should have listened to Maddie. She said you were loyal, and wonderful. She never faulted you for a second."

My heart soared, and I almost tipped into him again. One word kept me straight. *Sonia.*

There was no denying it, and I hadn't been doing a very good job with denial anyway, but I liked Chris. I really liked Chris. And I wanted to ask . . . I couldn't help myself. I needed him to tell me something glorious about Sonia so I could walk away and feel no regret, so I could hop in my car and say *The best woman won* and believe it.

"Will Sonia be okay if you don't practice again? I mean—" I could not finish with *She was dreadful at dinner*, so I left it hanging between us.

Chris sent me a wry look, as if I'd said the words aloud. "She wanted what I was, or what she thought I was. We got engaged soon after we met a couple years ago. I was only stateside six months that year, and while I thought letters and emails were good for getting to know each other, they don't beat face time. Working stuff out side by side matters more than either of us realized. I guess I put on a facade over there and she did the same here . . . We weren't what either expected when I arrived last year."

"But . . ." *Wanted. Thought. Weren't.* Past tense. I was so tired I wasn't hearing correctly. "But you are fine now?"

"We will be." He scrubbed his hands across his eyes. "We called off the engagement a couple weeks ago."

"I'm sorry."

"You are?"

I stared at him.

He blinked, and I got the impression his question surprised him. "You didn't seem to like her much at dinner."

"That's not fair. You have to admit, your date and mine had a much better time together that night than either had with us."

His eyes shadowed as if he was parsing my words. I wondered if I'd upset him, but I had only pointed out the obvious, and he had broken up with her—or she with him. Still, it had been his fiancée at the table that night. As I now understood, I hadn't really been on a date. I had no claim to hurt feelings.

I touched his arm, then withdrew my hand. It felt too intimate. Somehow the air charged whenever Chris was near. "Do I need to apologize again?"

"For what?"

"I upset you, saying Drew and Sonia had more fun together. I figured you'd noticed."

"One would have to be blind to have missed that." He chuckled, a short exhale laced with relief. "They did have more fun, and that was one of the reasons we ended it. Not because it upset me, but because it should have. And it didn't bother her either. Did it bother you about Drew?"

"Not at all." I couldn't get into Drew. Not tonight.

Chris pushed off with his foot. We started swinging again. The gentle motion rocked me back into his shoulder. Without looking at me, he dropped his arm around me. Soon the electricity I'd felt softened and, tucked warm and tight under the blankets and under his arm, my eyes drifted shut.

Chapter 18

Claire

To Claire it seemed Madeline was swept away by Janet's fantastic drawing. And why not? All those words, those beautiful words formed into a lithe woman, strong and completely feminine in shape. Madeline was quiet, contemplative the rest of the morning; she'd even left early, saying she needed to take a walk on the beach—a beach walk in icy March winds.

Claire could tell that she saw hope in Janet's drawing. The hope that Janet must surely have felt as she created it. They both saw a promise for good things ahead.

Her children rise up and call her blessed.

Janet had recited the words twice, adding a significant glance, as if Claire would rejoice in them and savor each one. Instead she had pushed her chair away. Claire saw only failure, and what lay lost behind.

As she pulled into her garage, she wondered if her children would notice she was home, much less rise up to welcome her. The kitchen was dark except for a single light above the small built-in desk in the corner. She laid her bag on the counter and opened the fridge.

"How was work?"

Claire spun. "I didn't see you. What are you doing studying here?"

Brittany pushed back from the desk. "I wanted to see you when you came home. You don't call upstairs anymore."

"It bothered you."

Brittany nodded slowly as if remembering saying something like that.

"Did you ask me something?" Claire cringed. Her voice sounded like she was addressing a stranger and not her daughter.

"I asked how work's going."

Claire grabbed ingredients for dinner from the fridge. "Good. Better, actually. We look better for a prospective buyer, at least. The shop has loyalty and it's back to making money, which is unbelievable considering where we were, so perhaps someone will keep it as a bookshop. It'd be a loss if it goes."

"And you'll lose your job."

"You don't need to worry about that. I'm hardly the one keeping us solvent." Claire stopped and turned. "That kind of lessened it, didn't it?" She waved a carrot at her daughter. "Don't ever do that. Don't diminish what you do. Yes, I will lose a job I love—or, as you called it, a hobby."

She narrowed her eyes. At herself, not at her daughter, who wouldn't see her expression in the dim light anyway. The barb was unnecessary, but she still hurt. It hurt that her daughter had diminished her that way, and that she let her.

Claire pulled out a cutting board, half expecting Brittany to decamp. When she didn't, but instead rose to stand near her, Claire pushed the cutting board, knife, and carrots her daughter's direction.

Brittany picked up the knife and starting cutting.

Claire opened her mouth, and shut it right before *Cut them longer and thinner* escaped. She sighed instead. "I shouldn't have said that. I know you think working at the bookshop is silly, and someday you'll have this great career and perhaps not understand that I chose to stay home with you and Matt, but I did, and it was a good decision. It was the right choice for me and for all of us. But you two are more independent now, and I . . . I loved that job."

"I'm sorry." Brittany laid down the knife. "I'm sorry I said that."

"Don't worry about it." Claire pulled her into a hug and smelled lavender in her daughter's hair. She kissed her forehead, noting she could barely see across the top of Brittany's head.

"Did the police ever catch the vandals?" Brittany focused on the cutting board.

"They won't. Whoever trashed the store came from the opposite direction of the bank. The cameras only caught shadow, and canvassing the surrounding shops yielded nothing. I doubt they'll keep searching much longer."

"No fingerprints?"

"That was never an option. Too many people come and go, and the vandals left nothing behind other than that bat. I gather the grip on it didn't keep prints or something. The police also found a lip gloss none of us owned, but it was generic and could've been from anyone at any time."

Brittany picked up the knife as if to resume chopping. She held it loosely in her hand. "So it's all over?"

"Not over . . . Unfortunately Madeline has to pay for it, though Janet announced today she's going to try to as well."

Claire stopped. Brittany never needed to know of Janet's involvement. No one did.

She rushed on. "Madeline had no insurance for the shop, so she has to cover the loss personally. And she can't until it sells."

Claire began scrubbing potatoes. She thought back to the laughter and lightness before Valentine's Day, to the tension and chill afterward. The atmosphere had warmed today; it felt new. But that was merely the thaw before the end, not the change toward a new beginning.

Brittany stopped slicing the carrot and studied the counter once again. "You were happy there."

"I'm happy here too, and—" She took in Brittany's slumped figure. "What is it? What's going on? You used to talk to me."

Brittany laid down the knife. "I've got a lot of homework."

Yet half an hour later, she was back. Claire was perched on a stool sorting the mail as Brittany passed in front of her. She pulled down a glass and filled it with water, then circled the kitchen again.

"Have a seat." Claire kept her eyes trained on the mail. The side-by-side approach hadn't worked, and Brian's *Then make her* idea wasn't so laughable anymore.

"Why?"

"Something's up, and if you share it I suspect you'll feel better."

"How do you know something's up?"

"I'm your mom." Claire straightened. "Okay . . . You haven't been eating; you're quieter than usual, which was already very quiet; you haven't been sleeping, though I commend your expertise with concealer; and now you're circling the kitchen. And you have a small bald spot on top of your head."

Brittany gasped. Her hand flew to the top of her head. "Is it bad?"

"About the size of a nickel, so whatever it is that has you stress-pulling out your hair is significant."

"I didn't realize." She rubbed the top of her head as if trying to regrow hair.

"Stop and talk to me." Claire captured Brittany's hands with her own. "Now."

Brittany's eyes widened at the command. Claire was a little surprised to hear it herself. It was the most forceful single word she'd said—ever. It didn't hold the almost imperceptible question mark that gave her an emotional out when her children disregarded her requests and orders. It gave Brittany no out—and they both felt it.

She watched her daughter and saw fear. The word floated before

Claire as real and tangible as if it had been written within Janet's word cloud.

Brittany regarded her without protest or complaint. Then she burst into tears. "I didn't mean to. I didn't mean for it to happen, but it was my fault. I saw the door and—"

"You saw what door?" As Claire asked the question, the entire scene materialized before her. "Brittany?"

"We were driving around when I pointed out the door. I laughed about it. Someone said they wanted to get a book so we went in. It was fine at first, but it got out of control. I tried to stop them." She wiped the back of her hand across her nose and eyes. She was soaked.

Claire pushed off her stool and grabbed a box of Kleenex. She placed it in front of Brittany and pulled one out for herself. Brittany blew her nose.

"I'm sorry, Mom."

"Who is 'them'?"

She shook her head. "I can't. I'll take the blame. But I can't say names. They'll kill me."

"Are you scared of your friends?"

Brittany shook her head again.

"You're not scared?"

"They're not my friends. I can't . . . I didn't know anyone, and . . . Oh, Mom, it's been so hard, and no one would talk to me and I . . . I just wanted to be liked."

Claire sat again and pulled Brittany close. "It's okay. We'll figure this out. Tell me the story from the top."

Through tissues and tears Brittany replayed the night, starting with skipping last period, driving around, and ending up at the bookshop. Claire suspected a few things had been left out, but what happened from the time Brittany spotted the open door fit with everything the police had found.

"Were you all drinking?"

Brittany remained silent.

"Was the driver drinking?"

Brittany shook her head.

"How many were in the car?"

"There were six of us." She blew her nose again. "Are you going to tell Dad?"

Claire stifled a laugh. *Are you going to tell Dad?* It was every child's greatest worry.

Unbidden, a line floated to Claire. *How often it is a small, almost unconscious event that marks a turning point.* Claire let the sentence fill her. It had come from a book on Maddie's list. She had devoured it, page after page, letting Corrie ten Boom's life and experience fill her senses and imagination. She marveled at how Corrie's strength grew as her faith and love grew ahead of it, ahead of her.

But could Claire do it? Could she take that next step? It was her daughter, her beloved baby girl.

Claire closed her eyes and leapt.

"I won't tell your dad. You will. And then you will tell the police."

NOTHING MORE WAS SAID. If Matt noticed that there was even less conversation at the table than usual, he didn't comment.

Claire suspected Brittany was in shock. Claire was in shock. She also suspected Brittany thought if she said nothing more Claire wouldn't make good on her threat. It wasn't an unreasonable thought; it had happened plenty of times before.

But at midnight Claire couldn't take it anymore. The house felt stifling and sleep distant. She knocked on Brittany's door. "I'm going to take a walk. Maybe down to the beach."

Brittany closed her science book. "That's over a mile away. It's late."

"It's a safe neighborhood, and I need to get out. You finish your homework and get to bed. I'll be back within an hour." She turned without waiting for a reply, grabbed her coat, and walked out the door.

Part of her expected the heaviness to lift as the front door closed. Without clouds, without wind, the sky felt vast and wide, magnifying her smallness. She stared at the stars in search of perspective and found none.

She walked the mile to the bluff overlooking the beach and still felt no relief. In the moonlight she could see the waves pounding the shore and hear them dashing across the breaker rocks piled at each end of the beach. They created an endless rhythm that pulled at her as she envisioned what lay ahead of her daughter.

It's like you live in those classics you love, in some odd third-person narration, as if you aren't in charge of your own story. Who is, if not you, for goodness' sake?

Janet's words flooded back. When would they leave? Why couldn't they be replaced with other words and other thoughts? And how much was she herself to blame?

It started with a tear, nothing so dramatic as a sob. That would take energy, and she didn't have any left. She felt her nose stuff and her cheeks freeze with the tears, then like the waves, the crash came. She felt the rip deep within her as she heard a footfall behind her.

"Are you all right?"

She spun, both hands out.

"I'm not going to hurt you." The man pointed to the house across the street behind her. "I live there. I don't sleep much and I saw you. I—I wanted to make sure you were okay."

He stepped into the light.

"Mr. Drummond?"

Only a couple feet from her now, his face creased in a smile. Slightly bald and slightly stooped, David Drummond stepped closer. "You're from the Printed Letter."

"I am." Claire rubbed her nose across her wool coat sleeve before she could stop herself. "I'm sorry I bothered you. I should go."

"I think you should stay. Would you like to come sit on my porch?"

"I'm keeping you up."

"At my age I rarely sleep." He turned and walked to the porch.

Unable to muster an independent thought, Claire followed.

"Please give me a moment." Mr. Drummond went into his house to return a moment later engulfed in a down parka. "We used to have tissues. I think I've let some things go, but it's clean. I promise." He held out a dishcloth.

"Thank you." Claire hiccupped and rubbed the towel across her entire face.

"What has you out here at this time of night?"

Claire faced the lake. "Failure."

Claire wasn't sure what she expected, but his silence surprised her. She swiped the towel across her eyes again and faced him. "I've failed at the one thing I had to do because I was too scared to do it."

"What was that?"

"Be a mom. My daughter—" She couldn't say it. "She's in trouble and I don't know how she got to that place, but she did and it's my fault. I wasn't there, not really, not how it mattered. And I hate this. I hate that this has happened and that I didn't see it coming and I hate that I stood aside when I knew she was in trouble. I knew and I did nothing. I hate that I have no control over any of this now and I hate who I've become. I hate—" Claire gasped, frightened at the dam that had broken within her. "I'm sorry. I didn't— You didn't need to hear all that."

"Betty and I raised five children. I expect we've been where you are. She was, a few times, for certain."

"What did you do?"

"The best we could, within each moment we had. Isn't that all we can? I don't say this to make you feel better. I have been in the hard places too. We had one son in rehab three times. That's a dark place and a helpless feeling for any parent."

"How is he now?"

Mr. Drummond brushed a hand slowly between them. He had long fingers that trailed behind his palm. "We can discuss him another day."

Claire stilled. "I'm sorry."

"Thank you."

They sat in silence for a long time listening to the waves. Claire didn't need to speak anymore. She was unsure what she could or would say if pressed, and Mr. Drummond didn't demand it. He simply listened with her. Eventually Claire felt the tension within her dissipate, and she found it. Perspective.

She stood, which prompted him to stand too. The chair scraped the porch floor as he pushed against it for support.

Claire reached for his hand. It was cool, too cool. "I kept you out here too long, but you helped me. More than you can know. Thank you."

"I am glad I was here. You ladies let me come talk. It was nice to return the favor, and you got me through the darkest part of the night. I may sleep now after all."

Claire nodded. "Me too."

As she stepped down the stairs, he called after her. "You and I haven't visited in the shop often, but you should call me David."

"I'd like that, David, and I'm Claire." She waved from the sidewalk. "Thank you again."

Claire turned, and with each step the sound of the waves retreated and her conviction grew. Another line from one of Maddie's books came to her—from the only book she'd read before Maddie's list suggested it. Dostoyevsky's *The Brothers Karamazov.*

Love in action is a hard and dreadful thing compared to love in dreams.

The line had not struck her before. But it did now, as clearly as if the printed page sat before her. David was right—the darkest part was over.

It was time to wake up.

Chapter 19

Janet

I love hugging Chris. He probably lets me because I don't get to hug my own kids. I'm grateful for that.

"I'm sorry I'm late."

I sit back down and he slides into the booth across from me. We've been doing this every Wednesday for the past five weeks, every Wednesday since Valentine's Day, getting together for a burger. I suspect he feels the need to check up on me—or maybe Luke told him to do it. Luke is a wonderful man, but a typical older brother. And Chris is a typical younger brother; he can't say yes to Luke fast enough.

"I thought you were coming by the shop today." I slide a book across the table.

"*Church of Spies: The Pope's Secret War Against Hitler*. Luke will be so jealous." He turns it over in his hands.

"You finished all the Silvas. I think you'll love this one. I've been listening to the audiobook while I paint. But you didn't answer my question."

"You didn't ask one."

Chris stares at me. No blinking. He knows what I'm after. He's messing with me.

"Fine. *Why* didn't you come to the shop? You rarely come in anymore."

"It's spring. We're starting prep work for spring plantings, and besides, pressure cooking isn't my thing."

"That's not the point. It was a lot of fun and there were a number of young women there, single young women." He gives me no reaction so I continue. "At the very least you could've walked away with some of the food. Madeline, Claire, and I all brought in pressure cookers, but Claire called and said she wasn't coming in for the demonstration so we got her share too. And the author was great. She chopped like lightning, drew in the audience, everyone bought her book, and Madeline and I left with tons of food. Two single women can't freeze that much, much less eat it all. And a baby. She brought her baby."

"Who brought a baby?"

"The author. Her babysitter canceled so she had to bring this gorgeous little baby in and we got to hold her. You should've seen Madeline; she was so stiff I wondered if she'd ever held a baby, but she got the hang of it and by the end she didn't want to give her back. Wouldn't you have wanted to see that?"

"Madeline stealing a baby? No."

I stop. He's not giving me anything to work with. But he glows. And that tells me all I need to know.

For two weeks after he and Sonia split he was dour and grumpy and dull. For all her prickly parts, I was sorry they broke up. Sure, Sonia was a little squeamish around Maddie and death, but who wouldn't be? And I couldn't blame her for reacting poorly when everything she'd expected or dreamed about her life with Chris veered off course. No one should be judged by her first reactions, and she would have come around. After all, she loved Chris, at least the man she knew from his letters.

But maybe that's what went wrong. Maybe Chris was right when he told me they hadn't had enough "time served" before their engagement, that they hardly understood each other. Maybe you can't simply trust that marriage will sort all that out. Yet if it was right to call it off, it shouldn't have made the man so grumpy.

Then last week, this happens . . . I have no idea what it is, but he twinkles. It's a distinctly unmanly word, but it fits. It's in his eyes, his cheeks; even his hair seems to stand on end like it's electrified. He won't say who or what is responsible. He won't say anything—and he's not coming by the shop, so my opportunities to snoop are limited. But I have my suspicions.

"Come by my house at least. My freezer is packed and the food smelled amazing at the shop. Or drop by Madeline's. I gave her more than I took, since I can cook. That woman . . . You should have heard the questions she asked the author. You'd think she doesn't know a carrot from a cucumber."

"I doubt she's done much cooking. Her apartment is down near Sonia's, and I gather her hours used to be as crazy. You can't blame her."

"Then you haven't heard."

"Heard what?"

"Well, if you came by the shop like you used to, then you'd know that Madeline doesn't live downtown anymore. She put her condo on the market. Maddie's house is still on too, but she's living in it now."

"Since when?" He looks stunned.

Bingo.

"Last week. She said it was an Ides of March thing, a settling of accounts or something about trust and letting go. I'm not sure exactly. She talks really fast when she's excited. Anyway, she was downtown having dinner, decided it on a walk, and moved that night, like at midnight. She left her key with the doorman and called the Realtor the next morning. Something's up with her. She's like a whirling dervish around the shop, a perpetual caffeine high."

"What does Drew say about it?"

"I doubt he cares."

He picks up his menu, despite the fact that he orders the same Swiss olive cheeseburger every Wednesday.

"When are you going to tell her?"

"Tell who what?" He feigns nonchalance—poorly—and keeps his eyes fixed on the menu.

"Tell Madeline you're interested in her."

He shakes his head but doesn't raise his eyes. It must be a fascinating menu.

"You're not going to?"

"Sonia and I just called things off. There has to be time here. Not everything is some great rush."

"Yes, it is. And you don't need any time. You and Sonia knew it was over the moment you hit US soil. I commend you for trying, her too, don't get me wrong, but even Maddie knew."

This gets his eyes up and the menu down. "She never told me that."

"She trusted your judgment."

He sits back and watches me. "You talked about this? About me? What else did you discuss?"

"We were a couple women together for hours on end and she was dying. Of course we talked about you. We discussed everything. Mostly she talked and I listened, then at the end I did the talking and she smiled or tried to frown depending on whether I got stuff right or not . . . You can hardly blame us. She always had your best interests at heart, we both did, and she loved you like a son."

With that, his face lights again as only Maddie could light up a soul. His eyes soften with the memory of her. "I know."

"But back to you and Madeline."

"There is no me and Madeline."

"She broke up with Drew that night too, or they didn't break up because they never were. That was a little confusing too. But either way, there is no Drew."

Chris actually blushes. I've never seen it before and probably won't again, but when a military man blushes it's adorable. It started in his cheeks and spread to the tips of his ears. He looks slightly sunburned.

"When? Before or after the key with the doorman and moving north?"

"You *were* paying attention," I tease. "And before. At dinner. Before the doorman, the key, and the drive north. Why?"

He doesn't answer. He sits back as if remembering something, something long and enjoyable like a movie or a book. I watch his expressions change with what I assume are the scenes in his head. They are very good scenes.

"What? You have to tell me." I rap the table to cut short his stroll down Memory Lane.

"I didn't know any of this." A slow grin grows all the way to his eyes and crinkles the little wrinkles in their corners. He still sports faint tan lines from his time overseas and only in crinkle and release can I see them.

"But you're happy about it?"

"I'm not unhappy about it."

I swat his hand as the waiter arrives for our orders. "But you'll come by the shop?"

"I'll be there tomorrow."

Claire

"How can you still be pushing this? You can't take our daughter to the police. She's about to hear from colleges. What if it's a felony? . . . We can punish her here, ground her, institute consequences, make her pay the store back, but we are not doing this. It'll ruin her."

"I don't want to do this without you, but I will. I am doing this."

Brian sits on the edge of the bed. In four days, he has aged. We have both aged.

And we argued all night. The first night he got home, we fell into bed together and I sobbed into his chest. The second night we whispered in hushed voices about what had happened to our daughter and wondered how we got to where we are now. The third night I told him my plan. He didn't believe me. The fourth night I made it clear, and we never slept.

Brian circled back again and again to what could be done at home. He fixes problems for a living, and with companies he is formidable. With our daughter, he was inexhaustible. He approached the situation, and me, from every angle. At some points I felt so boxed in I almost caved. But one deep breath at a time bolstered the conviction that I was present, and my dogged refusal not to step away again, from my daughter or from my life, got me there. If ever I thought Janet might be right, that I did live in some strange third-person unaccountability—no more. That is not going to be my story, nor the one I pass on to my kids.

"We don't need to go today," he offers.

I sink to the foot of the bed. "We do. Canvassing it again will not change the outcome. I won't dwell in the past, and I refuse to be scared of the future. We need to move forward, and that is Brittany's next step. She'll carry it for the rest of her life if we cover this up."

He stands, arms crossed, legs wide, in front of me. "She'll *pay* for it for the rest of her life. Everything she's worked for will be over. She'll be through."

"That's not true. She pays now, yes, and then it's over. She'll have the rest of her life ahead of her and this can be a memory, not a cancer."

"You're naive." Brian spits the words.

I have never heard such derision, or such pain, from him before. He is a calm man, slow to anger, quick to forgive—under normal circumstances.

I stand and face him. "You're the one acting naive."

Rather than circle each other again and come to no better conclusion, I leave the room. In my periphery I see him drop onto the bed, his head in his hands. I can't blame him for his point of view. He wants to protect our daughter. I want the same—which is why I fought him. He didn't come to my crossroads. He hasn't read a list of books full of people experiencing far worse and yet understanding that there is more that matters in a life than what happens in a moment, or on this earth; that it often isn't the events that haunt us, though those hold power and can harm us, it is the choices we make within those events we carry all our days.

As much as I tried, I haven't been able to articulate that. Probably because I don't have the language yet. Maddie's books provided a trail, like bread crumbs, leading me to who I want to be or maybe back to who I once set out to be, but they didn't give me the language with which to share the journey. I have to appropriate the stories, make them my own, find my own voice, and learn—there is so much to learn.

All Brian can see is that his beloved little girl might go to jail, get a "record," be cut from college, and lose every hope and dream we collectively share for her. And none of those dreams is bad. I still want every good thing for Brittany. I kept saying that over and over last night, but he couldn't hear me; he wouldn't believe me. He also can't accept that none of those dreams can be real, valid, or possible with this standing in her way.

I cross the hall to Brittany's bedroom. The door is open and music warbles through the door from her bathroom. Coldplay. I haven't heard Brittany listen to them in months. Maybe since we moved to Winsome. It has all been angrier music, with words I could hear but not understand and with a sensibility that left me cold. She has changed so much in the past year and a half—I realize how desperately I have missed her and how much I have failed her.

I let her slip through my fingers, so afraid to throw up obstacles or roadblocks that I failed to provide a trail to follow. Maddie did more for me with a list of books than I did in countless dinners and loads of laundry for my own daughter.

Speaking of which . . . Laundry is scattered around the room. As I pick up each piece, I remember. I remember when Brittany wore it and how she did her hair that morning. And rather than get angry that it is all on the floor wrinkled, clean mixed with dirty, I find myself smiling at each memory. Brittany's delight with this new green shirt, how she pulls on these sweatpants the moment she walks in the door each day after school, how she wears this black sweater for luck when she has a super-hard test, how her eyes look almost tawny against this fawn-colored sweater.

I gather each piece and either fold it and lay it on the bed or drop it in the bin. The sweater still carries a hint of her perfume, Clinique's Happy. Will she ever feel that way again? Will any of us? I hold the sweater tight and waver—until Brittany opens the bathroom door.

"I'm ready."

She doesn't say another word as I follow her out of the bedroom and down the hall. Brian catches sight of us as we pass and trails behind.

Brittany leads the way down the stairs and through the kitchen. I called into work, so no one expects me there, and I secured a ride to school for Matt so he is long gone, completely oblivious of what lies ahead for his sister. I found it hard to believe he hadn't heard Brian and me arguing early into this morning, but his open expression and bright eyes at breakfast confirmed he caught none of it.

"So we're ready?" Brian crosses in front of us to open the back door. He holds his car keys loosely in his fingers.

"You're coming with us?" I assumed, since I forced this choice, I would do it alone.

"If you can't beat 'em, join 'em." He quirks a lopsided smile as he opens the door, then freezes as he absorbs his words. "That's not right, is it? You should always stop something bad. I mean—"

"It's okay, Dad. I get it."

"I'm sorry. I'm nervous."

"Me too." Brittany steps into the open doorway, but gets pulled back and swallowed within a hug.

Brian bends into her, whispering in her ear loudly enough to bring tears to my eyes. "I love you. No matter what you did, no matter what happens this morning or for every morning of your life after this one, never forget for one moment you're my daughter and I love you. If I could take this on myself, I would."

He catches my eye above Brittany's head, and I understand. We are both powerless to do the one thing we want—absorb the punishment and the pain, the entire cost, so she doesn't have to.

We drive to the station in silence.

I've never been to the Winsome police station before. I've never been inside any police station before. It is a brown brick building, nondescript and uninviting. Brittany looks so small and young to me as we enter.

I realize that someday she won't be able to say to her kids at forty-six what I just thought: *I've never been to a police station before.* Stupid as it is, it almost makes me cry. I press a finger to the corner of each eye and take a deep breath. The air is cold—ideal for clearing the eyes and the heart.

"May I help you?" an officer asks, scanning across mom, child, and dad.

Brittany takes control. "I need to talk to someone about the vandalism at the Printed Letter Bookshop on February 14th."

"We can't talk about the specifics of an open investigation."

Brittany nods. The yellow lighting washes the color from her face and with each head bob I see the small bald spot on top. She twists to look at Brian, then to me. It is Brian who puts a reassuring hand on her shoulder and presses her forward.

"I need to talk to someone because I know who—I did it."

"Excuse me?" The officer's gaze bounces between the three of us again.

Brittany doesn't look right or left this time; she simply offers her statement again. "I vandalized the Printed Letter on February 14th."

I wonder if she has been awake all night rehearsing that one line.

The officer flicks her hand toward three beige chairs. "Wait over there and I'll get someone for you."

Brittany turns and lowers herself into a chair. She doesn't sink. She sits upright. Alert. Brian and I, again, flank her. I look over her head to Brian and falter because what sounded like the right idea in the safety of our bedroom, what I'd been so sure of when arguing, suddenly feels very real, very scary, and very permanent.

And there is no turning back. *I vandalized the Printed Letter on February 14th.* I sit, certain those words and their staccato delivery will live with me forever.

"I hear you have information about the Printed Letter case." An older officer stands before us. He is dressed in blue with a badge and no gun. I'm thankful. I can't handle a gun right now.

"Yes, sir." Brittany stands.

"Come with me." The officer turns to go.

"Can we— Can we come with her?" I swallow and hope my next sentence won't crack like that one.

"How old are you?" He lifts his head to assess Brittany.

"Seventeen."

"You must come." He throws the words to us and continues down the hallway.

He leads us to a small anteroom. It has a window that looks out on the parking lot, and it is nothing like the cinder block interrogation rooms I see on TV. It is carpeted and holds a laminated table and four blue fabric chairs.

"Now, why don't you tell me why you're here." The officer sits on one side. Brittany and I sit on the other as Brian pulls the fourth chair from the officer's side of the table to again flank his daughter. Useless as it is, we are certainly trying to protect her.

Brittany tells the story as she had told it to me, and as she told it to Brian. No details vary. No details go missing. A group got together, no studying; they drove around; yes, some were drinking; she saw the open door, and she drew their attention to it; yes, she went inside, participated in pulling out some books, but tried to stop them when things got more destructive; yes, someone found Sharpies and drew on the bookshelves; yes, two boys wielded a bat the driver had in his trunk; they drove off; she walked home.

"It was a cold night. You left your friends and walked home around one a.m.?"

"I told them I was leaving earlier, while they were still inside. I thought, since they knew my mom worked there, that they were making it worse to get to me, and if I left they'd stop. So I crossed the street and stood in Home Slice's doorway to watch. I couldn't leave them there. I needed to make sure they didn't do something really bad."

I straighten. This is new.

"What did you think might happen?" The officer doesn't lift his head from his notes.

"I wasn't sure."

"What happened after you crossed the street to watch?"

"They were inside about twenty minutes more, then they drove away and I walked back to the store." Brittany looks at me for the first time. "It was so much worse than I thought. I thought I was preventing the worst, but they did it anyway. I'm so sorry."

The officer glances up with a look of surprise, not realizing the apology is directed to me.

She faces him again. "Then I walked home. I remember tapping my phone to turn on the light to go up the stairs. It was 1:24."

"And, again, who was with you?"

"I can't say."

"You can't?" His voice remains steady.

"I won't say." Brittany stiffens as if prepping for battle. I recognize her stance and her expression and realize my own mom had been right. You are who you are at two, at seventeen, and maybe even at forty-six. You can just forget or get lost for a time.

Brittany continues. "School can be a tough place, and if I give names . . ." Her voice drifts off. I am not sure if it is because she doesn't know the consequences or, worse, she does. "Besides, it won't change anything. My punishment will be the same, right? I was there. I did it. I started the whole thing."

The officer watches her for so long she gives up the fight and slumps in her seat—maybe that was all she needed it for, that last question and that last stand.

"Okay." The officer flips his notebook shut. "This is what's going to happen. You're going to get photographed and fingerprinted, then—"

"Is she going to jail?" Brian blurts out the question.

"Then . . ." Eyes on Brian, he repeats the word as a ghost of a smile plays on his lips. "She's going home with you." He then addresses Brittany alone. "You're a minor, and you'll most likely be charged with a municipal ordinance violation, and a court date will be set."

"But no jail?" Brian needs clarity.

"I highly doubt she'll see the inside of a jail. With no previous record and at her age, this is a misdemeanor. I can't tell you what the sentencing will be, and you will need a lawyer to advise you, but . . . being seventeen makes this a whole different ball game."

He stands. We stand.

"You two may come out here while we take care of processing, then you all may go."

The officer leads Brittany from the room. Brian steps back for me to follow first, and as I pass he covers my hand with his and squeezes.

Chapter 20

Madeline

Claire looked frazzled, acted jumpy and on edge, and was easily startled.

"Did someone get you this morning?" I finally asked.

"What?"

"You're not yourself and your desk is a mess." I pointed to the chaos. There wasn't a single right angle, and papers littered the surface. "Did someone get you this morning?"

"Get me?"

"April Fool's Day. Did your kids play a prank on you?"

"That's today?" At my nod, she wilted. "That's not funny. I didn't realize . . . I need to talk to you."

She glanced toward the office door. There were only a few customers scattered throughout the shop and Janet was handling them all. Janet handled a lot lately, despite putting in hours upon hours in the back storage room. We couldn't call it that anymore for it was truly an art studio now.

We helped her construct shelving units from IKEA to hold her supplies; Chris sanded and refinished the old drafting table so it was completely smooth; and she covered the walls in sketches and drafts, while her larger pieces stood propped against the wall next to the bathroom. It was an inspiring space. I often found myself wandering into it simply to see what was new.

Claire stood and closed the door between the office and the shop. We never did that. I sank into my chair but didn't relax.

"Brittany is planning to come in after school today to talk to you." Claire stalled and I waited. "Two weeks ago she confessed that she and a group of classmates were responsible for the vandalism."

"The vandalism here?"

"Yes." Claire offered nothing more. It felt like she was giving me a moment to rant and rave. When I did neither, she continued. "We went to the police ten days ago, on March 20th."

My eyes widened at that. Working in law, I had seen plenty of parents try to hide their kids' actions, ultimately making the legal, moral, and emotional ramifications far worse.

Claire twisted her hands together. "She made a full confession and wanted to come to you right away too, but Brian and I wanted to wait until we could offer something."

A change came over me. I felt it. The friend, the bookshop owner, the youngest of our tribe of three, became first and foremost a lawyer once again—and I held my tongue.

"We'd like to offer you payment for all the damages and repairs. I know you've asked the bank for an extension, but the numbers won't work for them. And when the shop does sell, you shouldn't still have to pay. We'll deal with Brittany repaying us somehow, in some way. Unless you plan to sue, and I don't know how that works."

"When is her court date and what is the charge?"

Claire had not expected these to be my first questions. She cast about for an answer. "Um . . . June 12th and it's called a municipal ordinance violation."

"I see. Can I get back to you on your offer? I need to consider this."

This surprised her as well. We both knew the bank wasn't going to extend time or credit. I had only asked to stall foreclosure while they processed the paperwork, in hopes my condo might sell and save the shop.

Claire stood to leave, then turned back at the doorway. "Do you mind if she comes in? She needs to talk to you and apologize. Brian and I feel that's very important. She does too."

"I agree. May I speak to her in private? She's a minor, but I figure this is not between a lawyer and a client or, worse, adversaries, but, shall we say, something between friends?"

"I like that—us being friends."

I laughed then and felt the tension in the room lessen. "We'll be fine, Claire. Thanks for telling me."

She visibly calmed for the rest of the day. She remained quiet but was far less jumpy. I didn't ask if she had told Janet, but I suspected she hadn't for two reasons. One, Janet was incapable of keeping a secret. And two, I doubt Janet would've pulled an April Fool prank about harm to the shop had she known Claire carried the burden for just that scenario.

At four o'clock, Claire lifted her phone. "Brittany texted. She's on her way."

"Brittany?" Janet called out from the customer desk. "I love that girl. I haven't seen her in weeks."

Claire's face paled.

I rolled my chair to hers and whispered, "Bring her back here and shut the door. Tell Janet whatever you want."

She left me to meet her daughter at the front door. Soon I heard the chime, the footsteps, and the small knock on the doorjamb.

Brittany was not what I expected. I'd seen her working in the shop once before but hadn't caught her name. I thought she was simply another high schooler Janet had wrangled into helping out before Christmas.

While Claire was lovely, in a nondescript brown-bobbed-conservative-mom way, her daughter was a blond, blue-eyed, bright, almost kinetic kind of girl. It was clear she was nervous; it was clear she'd been through the wringer. But it was also clear that all those bright qualities would bloom again soon.

"Come in. I'm Madeline." I stood and stretched out my hand. "You must be Brittany."

Claire shut the door behind her daughter. Brittany maintained steady eye contact with me, and I respected her for that. To stand square in front of an older adult, one you've wronged, and a lawyer besides, was tough at any age—at seventeen, almost impossible.

"Please sit."

"May I stand?"

"Of course." I couldn't resist a smile. At Duncan, Schwartz and Baring, I always stood too.

"My mom said that she told you this morning. I'm sorry it's taken me so long to come apologize in person . . . There were things that— I'm so sorry." She took a deep breath that shuddered on the exhale. It felt as if whatever she'd prepared fled her and she was trying to summon it back. "I . . . I shouldn't have done it. I absolutely know that and I can't explain why I did, why I was here that night. I've gone back over it again and again, and . . ."

"Things went wrong long before that, didn't they?"

Her nod was almost imperceptible. "How did you know?"

"They always do. There's an old saying about boiling a frog in water. You start slow, with cool water, and the frog won't jump out. You start with little lies, little compromises, and little angers that you let grow, and soon your judgment is compromised. You don't see danger coming, so you don't jump out of the way."

"No one has said it like that, but that's how it felt."

"Your parents are concerned with the boiling water right now. They'll get to the source of the heat later. Or, at seventeen, you might want to spend some time digging out that one on your own."

She sighed a *Will I ever be done with this?* kind of sigh while I almost keeled over. Where did *I* get such wisdom?

Wisdom I hadn't applied to myself. But wasn't that what I'd been doing these past few months? Taking myself back to the beginning—as I saw it—and trying to work through, understand, and surrender all those hard places that had bruised me along the way? I wasn't so different from Brittany. She was actually sixteen years ahead of my curve.

"Do you know what your parents have offered me?"

"To pay you for the damages. We haven't figured out how I'll pay them back, but I will. I know it's a lot."

"It is." I nodded. "And how do you feel about the charges?"

"Lucky. It's a misdemeanor, and the police said it won't go on my permanent record. The officer said judges often give community service as punishment."

"True. Do you know what the charges could be if you were eighteen?" At her head shake, I laid it out. "The amount of damage would make it a Class 2 felony, and it could carry two to five years in jail and a twenty-five-thousand-dollar fine. That's not to say it would, only that it could."

"I'll be eighteen next month."

"Then it's good we're not having this conversation a couple months from now."

She smiled, then banked it in remorse. "But just because the penalty isn't all that doesn't mean I'm not sorry. I hope—I hope you'll forgive me someday."

"Brittany, I'm glad you're seventeen too. You have a lot to be thankful for here, and it's okay to smile." I stepped toward her. "And I forgive you now. The fact that you are here and willing to talk to me alone speaks volumes, especially as I know you couldn't have done all that damage alone. However you and your parents proceed is between you three. As far as I'm concerned, you and I are good. Thank you for coming in today."

I offered my hand. Hers was hot, as if the boiling water had not been merely a metaphor.

"Thank you." She opened the door and returned to the shop.

Moments later the chime rang and rapid heel clicks preceded a now rosy-toned Claire. "Was it okay? Did she apologize well?"

"She apologized great."

"Will you accept the money?"

She wanted this settled, and I couldn't blame her. "Give me time?"

"Of course." Claire stepped backward. "Sorry. I shouldn't push you. This is all new for you. I've been thinking about this, and we've talked about nothing else for two weeks, but of course you just found out. You need time. I—"

"Claire." I raised a hand. "How could you hide this from us, Janet and me, for two weeks? We're here together every day."

"I— You must feel so betrayed."

"Betrayed? Not at all. I meant you shouldn't have carried this alone. You've dug into all the finances of this place with me, you've streamlined everything in this shop. In many ways you've given more to what my aunt left to me than I have. This place is clearly important to you, and . . . I thought we were friends. How could you not let us help you?"

"I was embarrassed. I had one job and I failed."

"What was that?"

She raised her one brow. Clearly I had missed the obvious. "Mom."

"I disagree, but I'm not a mom so I can't weigh in too heavily on that one. But consider this: the girl who left here moments ago did an incredibly courageous thing, and she did it well."

Tears filled Claire's eyes. They did not spill over. "Thank you."

"Who is Brittany's lawyer?"

"We haven't gotten there yet. I know we should, but she's not contesting anything, and Brian— It's hard to think about asking any of our friends. Once we do, it'll be all over town."

"I'll do it."

"You will?"

"She needs a lawyer and, although she's not contesting the charge, a good lawyer can make a world of difference when it comes to sentencing, and a good lawyer can make sure it stays off her record. Some counties aren't as thorough at expunging those charges as they should be. And . . ." I smiled. "A good lawyer who is also the victim can probably do more than all that."

"You'd do that for her? For us?"

"I will have to charge you the full one hundred an hour." I delivered the line with a straight face.

"A deal at four times the price." And there was Claire's first genuine smile.

It matched my own.

Janet

"What are you up to?"

The shop has long since closed, but Madeline and I are still here. Claire went home, but as the two of us have nowhere to go, we plop onto the stools side by side.

It took a while, but I adore this girl. She's a couple years older than Alyssa, and there is some of that I'm-so-sure-of-myself that her whole generation carries, but there's no push and pull like there was for so many years with my own daughter or that existed when Madeline first started working at the Printed Letter.

Maybe it's because I never struck the balance between mom

and friend with Alyssa. But with Madeline, I get to be friend. As my boss, technically she's the one with the power—and after the Valentine's Day Shop Massacre, I give it to her. But more than that, I see in her all the qualities Maddie raved about for so long.

Madeline and I often find ourselves sitting behind the counter, as if monitoring the bookshop, despite its locked doors and the Closed sign on display. We laugh, we chat, and we share far too many Skittles.

Rather than answer my question, she tosses me a pack of Tic Tacs and begins to straighten the bijoux around me. "I bought you those. Didn't you say they were your favorites?"

I shake the container. "Are they real or is this an April Fool's prank?"

"Real."

I pop one in my mouth and open up my computer. "Thank you. In return, I started a profile on Match, also real."

"Claire passed on that site. Said it wasn't right for you."

"Not for me. I closed all my accounts. That date was a disaster."

"It was?" She faces me. She studies me. She is such a lawyer. "You little liar. You said it was great, but I knew it. I knew you were lying. You were all . . ." She scrunches her face like she's eating something disgusting.

"I didn't want to hurt your feelings. And what if that type of guy was my only option?"

"*Was* connotes it's not your only option anymore." She lifts a brow.

"I'm opting for celibacy." I press my lips shut.

She doesn't believe me, but she smiles and leaves it there. She won't press me. I've noticed that about her. We may think of each other as friends, but she doesn't press like a girlfriend usually does. I often wonder if it's because she's wired like that or because I'm basically her mother's age. I suspect it's the former. I've noted she's careful around friends, the few new ones she's made working in the shop, and even Kayla, who has come up from the city to visit. She treats them gingerly, as if afraid they'll decamp. Or maybe she keeps them at a distance so she can decamp first—I haven't figured that one out yet.

Either way, I appreciate her discretion right now, and when I'm ready to share my heart's desire, she'll probably be the first—no, the second to know.

"This profile is for you."

"No way." Madeline bumps me from the computer.

I've worked on the profile for a couple days, so it takes her a minute to digest it all. Her eyes bug wide.

"You can't say this stuff about me. I don't like long walks. I can't stand the opera and—"

"You walked the beach that evening."

"I needed to think. And you can't—"

A knock at the door silences her.

"My date is here. Clean up the profile yourself then." I toss out the challenge as I head to the front and unlock the door.

Chris enters, eyes trained on me. I almost laugh. Kids these days!

Instead I offer a calm "Give me a sec. I've been trying to set up a profile for Madeline on Match, but she's resisting. In fact, she's behaving very badly."

Madeline blushes. Chris turns beet red. I walk back to Madeline's side and flip open the laptop she slammed shut. "Chris, come look at this. What do you think?"

"I'm no use. I've never been on those sites."

Madeline's blush deepens, and now I feel horrid, certain I've crossed that line. It's such a thin one, how does one not trip over it? Every moment of every day? I've humiliated her. Chris doesn't see it; he's too busy managing his own embarrassment, but I do. In trying to fan a spark and have some fun, I've embarrassed her—the last thing I meant to do. If I've learned anything in the past six weeks, it's that simply not looking to the past is not the same as living in the present. I need not dwell there, but I do need to learn from it. And here, again, I have trampled another's feelings to satisfy myself. My stomach clenches and I suddenly feel very, very old.

"Chris, do you mind if we skip dinner tonight?"

"It's Wednesday." He looks shocked. He sounds shocked.

"I . . . I'm not up for it." I shut the laptop and gently tug it from Madeline. She stands mute next to me. "I thought I was, but let's skip this week. I'm sorry." I circle the counter, turn him by the shoulder, and press my palm against his back. I want him out of here as fast as possible. I need to apologize to Madeline. I can apologize to him later.

It's funny, but it feels like since I offered up my first apology a couple weeks ago, I've done nothing but apologize since. *I'm sorry; the cat is scared of me, not you. I've yelled at it a few times, but I've quit . . . I'm sorry, that wasn't a kind thing to say . . . I'm sorry I'm a few minutes late today . . . I'm sorry I cut you off . . .*

I've said that last one several times, a few here in the shop when I cut off someone who was speaking too long and another couple times to slow cars on the highway. The latter never hear me, of course, but it still needs saying. I keep needing to say it. I wonder when that will stop, and if I want it to—and when I will get the courage to give the only apology that truly matters.

Chris resists my push, but I keep at it. Finally at the door, he turns and speaks over my head. "Janet and I get burgers on Wednesday nights. She's bailing. Do you want to grab dinner?"

He then lowers his eyes to mine. I can best describe the look as a "glower." I found that word in one of the books Maddie suggested for me. It's a look of sullen dislike, discontent, or anger, and it fits. I can't blame him. My plan has gone horribly wrong and my solution is equally clumsy. I almost want to yell—*I'm new at this being a nice human stuff, but I'm trying! Can't I get a do-over?* But I keep my mouth shut, doubting they'll appreciate my sense of humor.

"No . . . I . . ." Madeline trails out words. She so clearly wants to go and is so clearly going to refuse.

I double down on all my mistakes. "Please. Go. I've screwed everything up tonight. I'm sorry I got involved in any of this. I should have gone straight home at six o'clock and called the day done. Madeline, get your coat and go get a burger. I'll lock up. Chris, stop glowering at me. I'll head home, drink tea, and watch a movie, after I take down my horrid efforts at that profile I was setting up. Madeline didn't know about it, so let's all forget the last ten minutes ever happened and you go to dinner and have a nice time."

"I—"

One syllable from Madeline and I moan because she's going to double down on her mistake too. But Chris cuts her off with a "Please" and she stops.

The glower is gone and his eyes are on her, with an endearing warbly smile accompanying them. I want to hug him. I don't.

"Sure."

I spin to face her. Eyes locked on Chris, she's caught the look too and is sporting her own matching smile and her own answering blush.

I return to the counter with my mouth clamped shut, willing myself not to say another word.

Madeline passes me, shrugging on her coat as she heads to the front door. "You'll be sure to lock up?" She throws out the question before thinking, then her lips part in an adorable little guppy motion.

"No matter what happens, I will be sure to lock up." I wave. "Now you two kids go have fun."

Both send me a sharp look in reply. Nevertheless, they walk out the door, together.

And now Chris is the one with a hand on someone's back, gently leading her away.

Claire

Brittany is working on homework at the kitchen island when I walk in the back door. She used to do that in Delaware, in Missouri, and in Ohio, but never in Illinois.

"Was it okay? After I left, how did it go?"

I pull her into a hug. "It went fine. You did a wonderful job and I'm proud of you, sweetheart. You've taken on all the responsibility and you're doing great."

She grips me tight. That is new too. I haven't gotten a hug, a real hug, in Illinois either.

"Do you mind if I go up and finish my homework? The light is better up there."

"Not at all. Thanks for waiting for me."

"No problem." She tosses the words over her shoulder as if it is the most natural action in the world, and maybe it will become so again.

I pull the ingredients for dinner out of the refrigerator, the spices from the cupboard, and lay them on the counter. Spicy curry shrimp. My favorite dish because tonight feels like a celebration.

As I sauté the shrimp, I hear the garage door open, then the back door. Brian lays down his briefcase and faces me before greeting me. "How'd it go?"

"Hello."

"Hello. How'd it go?"

"It went well. She spoke to Brittany alone so I don't know what was said, but Brittany came out looking much better than she went in."

"You didn't ask? What about paying her?"

"I didn't. She treated Brittany like an adult and, I gather, Brittany behaved like one. I offered our payment plan beforehand and again after Brittany talked to her, and both times she said she'd think about it."

"I knew it. She's going to sue us. She's a lawyer. Big law does not leave money on the table, and she has a case. No judge, jury, or anyone could deny her that."

"She will not sue us and she's not 'big law.' She's back-of-a-bookshop-stuck-in-a-storage-closet law, and I think she's considering not accepting anything rather than going for more. And . . ." I wait until I have his full attention. "She offered to represent Brittany in court."

"She did?" Brian's face falls, his eyes fill. His entire body slumps as he reaches one hand out to the counter. "She's going to be okay, isn't she? Our baby is going to be okay."

"She already is. She's a new kid." I rewind that in my head. "She's back to being the old kid."

And that's how I feel too. Something within me, that had given up or gotten displaced, is back and alive. And rather than an end, and a slow-fizzling-out one at that, I am at the beginning.

I turn back to the shrimp.

Strong arms circle my waist. "I owe you an apology, and more. I wanted the easy way out; I wanted the wrong way out. If not for you, we wouldn't be here. And every time I say I'll never take you for granted again, I do. I love you more than you know, but less than you deserve."

"This is a problem." I flip off the burner as that new beginning sparks to life. "You can make up for it though."

"My pleasure."

At first touch, I wonder how long it has been since Brian kissed me, really kissed me beyond the quick brush of coming and going, or a peck before we turn out the lights too exhausted to say or do more. There is something so decadent about kissing; kissing for itself, not as foreplay or a gateway to anything else. Kissing like it is the first time, the last time, and the only connection we'll ever have—that kind of kissing. Soon the thought drifts away. All thoughts drift away.

My husband is still kissing me.

Chapter 21

Janet

This is extraordinary." Madeline walks into my studio. We call it that now, just as we call her storage closet The Firm.

"It's not too raw?" I step back to see the painting in its fullness. It's the largest piece I've attempted and the most ambitious. It almost looks like a city map crunched together. Buildings lie on top of each other in different gradations of color and shadow rather than spread out properly on streets. I attempted to convey an image across time rather than one across distance. But that's only on the surface.

If one looks closely one sees they aren't buildings at all. Some are, but others are people, events, recognizable milestones in a life, some good, some bad, some glorious, some devastating. This painting isn't to sell. It's for me, and the devastating, right now, far outweighs the glorious.

But I started at the end and am working my way back. In many ways, the painting is linear, and on the far right, it opens in broad streaks to the blank canvas. I may fill it in someday, but I need the blank space right now. It represents my new beginning. My new spring. That's what I'm chasing.

"It's raw." Madeline perches on the room's single stool. "But not overly dark; it's exactly how I feel today."

"That's not good. What's up?" I lay down my brush. She's been carrying around the letter Maddie left her today. At least I think that's what it is. In the past two weeks, I noted hers tucked in a book on her desk, resting beside her hand while she looked checked out and dreamy, sticking out of her handbag, or held loosely between her fingers as it is right now. I've also noted scribbles on it, probably notes on the books she's read.

I do the same. I've scribbled a little word picture next to each book. They've changed me and I still have five left to read. I wonder how many she has left and what they've meant to her. It's too private to discuss though. Maybe someday . . .

Madeline shakes her head and stands to leave. "Keep painting. I didn't mean to disturb you. I wanted—to see what you were up to."

I get this girl. *A connection* is what she was going to say. She wanted a connection with someone, at that moment, but she pulled back before committing. The word floats between us; we feel it. But we both have our armor, and time, expectation, and fear have made that armor very strong, so she doesn't ask and I don't push.

"I'm here when you're ready to talk," I say.

She flaps the folded letter in her hand, and I doubt it is Maddie's letter after all. It's crisp white rather than ivory and she looks as if she doesn't want to touch it, but also can't let it go. She taps it against her thigh. "Thank you for that."

I return to my painting to give her privacy to leave. Instead, I feel her drop onto the stool again. She sits in silence.

It feels like eternity, but it's probably only five minutes before she speaks again.

"What inspired it?"

"I've come to believe that until I really examine my life I won't be able to accept it, and either apologize or be grateful for everything in it . . . And I'm trying to work through that—especially how to apologize to Seth."

"Divorce takes two people, Janet." Madeline's voice is flat. The lawyer sits with me now.

"Yes, but in our case it was the wrong two people." I wave a paintbrush at her. "I get what you're saying, but I carried a New York–size chip on my shoulder the day we moved out of the city, and I made him pay. Never overtly, and for the most part I wasn't aware of it, but I'm aware of it now." I twist back to the painting. "So I've been digging in, trying to understand and confess it, apologize for it, then let it go. Without all that, I can't move forward."

"Making art is a vulnerable thing, isn't it?"

"Sometimes it feels like I'm bleeding onto the canvas and if I don't paint I'll die. I need this . . . And that's another thing. I say I need it so much, and I do, yet I put my brushes down almost thirty years ago. Who was I punishing? Seth? Or me?"

"Probably both . . . Have you talked to him yet?"

I bite my lip. I recall how shocked Claire and Madeline looked when I admitted to them that I'd never told Seth I was sorry.

"I don't understand," Claire had said. "You had an affair, you wanted him back, but you never told him you were sorry? Never asked him to forgive you?"

"I felt cornered," I told them. "I'd felt like that for years. At the time I thought everything I'd done and given up had been for him, and I resented it. I understand now that I made those choices, each and every one. But it was easier to play the victim, and much easier to attack."

Articulating it to them that morning made it clear to me. Since then, I've thought it through a thousand times and backed away a thousand times. It is time.

"Seth takes the 7:25 train into the city every day. I'm going to meet him at the station tomorrow morning." I face Madeline. "I'm telling you that to be accountable. If I walk in here tomorrow not having done it, don't be nice to me."

She quirks a sideways smile. "Me? Not nice?"

"You can manage it."

She waves her letter at the painting. "You can't say all that in public."

"There is no private anymore. I can't go to his apartment. He's never once asked me there or shared the address. I know it, but only from the divorce papers. And I can't say this over the phone. It needs to be face-to-face, so it'll have to be public." I grimace as all my inglorious public moments play before me. "I'll be super quiet."

Madeline pushes off the stool. "Are you staying late tonight?"

"I told Claire I'd take over Thursday evenings. Home is quiet." I look around. "Here gets quiet too, but it doesn't feel like it. All this has sound as well as color. As usual, I'll stay a couple hours after closing to read and paint, then I'll lock up."

"How many books left on your list?"

"Five out of nineteen. We should talk about them someday."

She looks at me, and I wonder if I've crossed a line. As though I've asked to read her diary.

She finally nods and I finally breathe. "I'd like that. I have only three left. Three of seventeen. Each has been a revelation . . . And you don't need to say that anymore."

I raise a brow. I've almost appropriated Claire's signature move.

"About locking up. I know you'll do it. I trust you."

Madeline wanders back into the office. And despite the short distance, it is a wander. She walks slowly, shifting from side to side as if her mind is miles away. She worries me.

For the past two weeks she's been walking on air, humming, working, making business cards for her one-woman law firm. She's moved full steam ahead—toward what, I'm not sure, but with it has also come an openness I appreciate. She's more trusting now. Maybe it only extends to our circle of three, but Madeline has let us in. Maybe it extends further . . .

Chris has pretty much been the same since our talk last month too. Now he drops by for lunch, sitting with the three of us but only looking at her. He switches out the flowers in the store's window boxes every few days as new varieties come into bloom. They burst with color. And I had to give up my Wednesday dinner date yesterday because Madeline had some charity event downtown and Chris joined her, looking dashing in a tuxedo.

But today, all that light and life are gone.

"Whatever it is . . . it'll all work out," I call after her.

"Mick Jagger would disagree."

I can't decide if I'm more impressed with her wisdom or her music. Either way, she's right. You can't always get what you want.

Madeline

"What are you doing out here?"

I leaned back and noticed the change in light. It felt like I'd just sat down and opened the envelope, but the evening light told me otherwise. It shot pink and orange across the sky to the west. The east had already darkened. The air still held that scent of earth and spring from this morning's rain, and the redbud trees at the edge of Aunt Maddie's front yard were covered in flowers. The beauty only made the loss hurt more.

Chris leapt up the stairs and plopped next to me on the top one. He leaned over and kissed my cheek. He'd done that for the first time a couple nights ago after we'd brought blankets down to the beach and sat huddled in the sand, watching the moon rise. When he drove me home and came inside for a defrosted dinner from our pressure cooking demonstration, he kissed me on the cheek. I kept my face still and straight—noting that he lingered along my jawline—and hoped.

It was hard not to turn into it and kiss him, really kiss him, but I forced myself not to move. He was the one who'd ended an engagement, and I wasn't sure . . . Did he still carry her in his heart? Are there rules for that kind of thing? Is there a set amount of time that ensures you aren't a rebound? I wasn't interested in being that.

It was hard not to turn my head now too. I glanced at him and felt that punch in my gut, again. I wanted more—a lot more—from Chris. Drew had been right to break up with me, both times. I never saw *him*. I only saw what he meant for me, personally and professionally. With Chris, one look and I was terrified to lose something beloved. So much had already been lost, and according to this letter, more was about to go.

I handed it to him. "Who sends this on tax day? Do banks find this funny?"

I'd come home, depressed from the shop, grabbed the mail, and found more depressing news in my mailbox. Rather than extend the loan or threaten me with future action, or even give me a few weeks' reprieve while they investigated my request, the bank had sent loan call notices for both the shop and Aunt Maddie's house. The letters arrived on the same day, and on the very day Uncle Sam would deposit the last of the proceeds from my car to cover owed taxes.

"Why are they calling them?" Chris's eyes ran up and down the page.

"Because they can. If I'd been Aunt Maddie's lawyer I'd never have let her sign those terms, but she did and they're valid. The loans can be called at any time for any reason."

"But why now?"

"I expect they're deemed more risky. You can be sure the bank manager noted our damage at the shop, especially as the police canvassed his employees and requisitioned his surveillance data, and Aunt Maddie had been transferring money for months before she died—all from her accounts at the same bank. They knew. And I've been doing the same, really, just selling off stuff to keep them afloat. Anyone looking at the accounts could tell that too."

"I thought the shop was doing better."

"The shop is doing great. Once given free rein, Claire's been brilliant. But it's not enough to fill the hole Aunt Maddie's estate was already in."

"How can I help?" He wrapped an arm around me.

I tipped into him. "Tell me it's going to be okay. You don't have to know it or believe it, but I'd love to hear it."

He tightened his grip and dropped a kiss on the top of my head. "It's going to be okay."

Tucked under his arm and against his chest, I almost believed it. "How'd I get here? I played by all the rules, checked the boxes, did what I was told and did it well. I'm supposed to be a lawyer with job security, not a bankrupt bookshop owner overrun with debt and three properties she should never own and can't pay for . . . Yet here I am." I pushed off him. "The day I quit, one of the partners at my firm remarked that because I didn't get a trophy I was giving up. Everyone says that about our generation. Is it cliché because it's true? Isn't that what I did? If I'd stayed, I could pay for all this."

"What's the good in asking that now?"

"Because if it's true, then none of this was done for the right reasons."

"Maybe it didn't start out that way, but you stayed for the right reasons."

"You're giving me more credit than I deserve."

He leaned back and watched the sunset with me. "You could say the same thing about me."

I threw him a *nice try* glance.

"I'm serious. Reality trashed my idealized version of saving the world, and I caved. I came back to the States, lay on my brother's couch for six months, physically sick with nothing anyone could name, and then got a job I have no skills for, a job my brother got me because no one says no to their priest. If that's not an 'I'm picking up my ball and going home' scenario, I'm not sure what is."

"You were—you *are* healing."

"Then why aren't you? Thinking of your life and your work in a new way is hard. And just because no one was shooting at you doesn't mean you didn't need to heal, and that you didn't land here for good and legitimate reasons, and not because of some Millennial temper tantrum."

I chuckled at the image, but not because he was right. As much as I wanted to believe him, there was a thread of truth to my version as well. My arrogance, my hubris thinking that I could step in, bend things to my will, and leave again was now going to destroy Aunt Maddie's legacy—and everyone would lose by it.

"What do I do now?" I tipped back into him.

"I'm the wrong one to ask." His kissed the top of my head again. "Luke always tells me that eternity only reaches us in the present. We can't revisit the past and we can't assume a future, so I guess I'd say don't dwell on what's done and don't try to answer tomorrow's questions. Deal with today."

"Then today I'm hungry. Can you stay for dinner?"

"Yes, but I'm cooking." He pushed off the steps, returned to his truck, and pulled out two bags of groceries.

"You went shopping." My voice cracked. After all that happened today, two bags of groceries—the care behind two bags of groceries—almost brought tears.

"I have a confession." He stood in front of me. "Janet told me you'd had a rough day."

"I love her." I heard my words and chuckled again. "I never thought I'd say that. I didn't tell her about the bank's letter."

"She watched you all day and knew something was wrong. She's got a soft spot for you too." He winked and led the way into the house.

Three hours and a glorious chicken parmesan later, we were back on my front porch. His hand wove through mine as he stepped down the first stair and we stood eye to eye. He lifted his other hand and twirled a loose curl forward onto my shoulder.

"Don't give up."

"I don't have anything left to give. Until that stupid condo sells. And now, unless a miracle happens in fifteen days, the bank takes this and the shop and I'm back downtown."

"You'll move back?"

"I have to until the condo sells and I can find something cheaper. I got a call from a firm too. I have an interview next Thursday." I shrugged. "Funny thing is, everything points me back downtown, right as I felt this is where I'm supposed to be."

"As I said, don't give up." Chris brushed my cheek with his fingers. "Let's simply trust we're where we need to be."

I nodded.

With that he closed the distance between us. His movement wasn't hesitant or questioning; it was bold, consuming, and confident. His kiss was a declaration. This was no rebound. This was no fleeting affair. This was real, and meaningful, and now—and nothing from yesterday or tomorrow mattered.

After a few seconds, he pulled back and searched my eyes. His didn't ask the questions one might expect after a first kiss. Was that okay? Was that too much?

Are you with me? was the question I saw in his eyes.

My lengthy reply filled our second kiss, third, and countless more, until he gently pulled away.

My answer still played in my head as I stood until his truck's taillights rounded the corner.

I am.

Claire

Brittany passes me on the stairs. "Did you go in my room?"

Out of instinct, I brace myself. We had come to blows countless times over this issue in the past year—violating her privacy, encroaching upon her freedom, whatever she called it. I was always the bad guy, and she had created countless teenage ways to tell me to get out and leave her alone.

"Laundry. I put your whites and T-shirts on your bed."

"Did you see the drawing of Yellow Bear?"

I blink. "Yellow Bear?"

"Come see." She races up the stairs ahead of me. "I drew it last night."

I follow her into her room. There is a new watercolor pinned above her desk. In fact, there are several new drawings since the last time I looked. A large yellow Labrador sits staring out at me. He has a certain tubby Winnie-the-Pooh quality that makes you want to throw your arms around his neck, squeeze, and say "Silly old dog," which was why Matt named him Yellow Bear.

I run my finger down the edge of the paper. "That's how I remember him. Did you draw it from a picture?"

"The one I took the afternoon he wouldn't come in because of the butterflies. Remember how he sat there and watched them? . . . Do you think we'll get another?"

"A dog? I stopped researching them . . . We're busy right now."

"And you work."

When I took the job at the Printed Letter—when Maddie foisted it on me—I felt useless at home and lost in Winsome. Only recently, on that afternoon when Brian forced Brittany to work at the shop, did I realize my daughter thought I had stolen it from her. I can give it up now—if I need to.

"We can consider a dog."

Brittany spins on me. "What do you mean?"

"Nothing to worry about. Nothing that involves you." I busy myself with collecting odds and ends to take to the kitchen—two empty glasses, a dirty plate and a bowl.

Brittany steps in front of me. "That's not true. Almost everything about the Printed Letter involves me."

I sink onto her bed and she plops next to me. "If I'd been here more, if I'd been here to listen, to notice, then maybe . . ."

I let the words trail away. I am not trying to pass on my sense of guilt. She carries enough already. Again, I wonder if I am trying to be mom or friend. Drat, that line is so thin.

"I'm not two."

Her reply jolts me.

"I'll be eighteen in two weeks, Mom. I knew what I was doing. I didn't stop myself. That was a choice, my choice, and you being here wouldn't have changed anything. And you are here. You are here practically each and every day when we get home. You can't keep me safe, not like you could when I *was* two. That's becoming my job now."

"When did you get so wise?"

"Since I got charged with a municipal ordinance violation."

I sputter out a soppy laugh and pull her close. "I love you."

"I love you too. So don't quit the Printed Letter. Please. I loved working in that place when we first moved here because it felt good. It's a good shop. Your friend . . ."

"Maddie?"

"She was a very special lady, and that shop matters."

I sit back and straighten her hair. My hug pushed one side up and untangled it from her ponytail. "It does matter, but it also may not be my choice. Madeline got a letter from the bank today calling the store's loan. Maddie had a lot leveraged, personally and professionally. Madeline's been working to negotiate the debt, but there still aren't sufficient funds. The shop will go."

"Why don't you buy it?"

"She turned down our offer to pay for the damages. I think she feels it's one thing to be awarded damages in a settlement and another to extract them from a friend. I couldn't change her mind, and she won't file suit against us either. I actually asked her to do that."

"But what if you, with that money, offered to buy some of the store or pay it toward the loan? Wouldn't that make the bank happy? You could secure the loan."

"How do you know about securing loans?"

"Please, Mom. I got an A in Consumer Economics."

"Maybe." I kiss the top of her head. "That's not a bad idea, Brit." Balancing all the dishware, I head out of the room and down the stairs. *Why don't you buy it?*

Why don't we buy it?

Brian is watching baseball in the family room. I sit on the ottoman in front of him and rest the dishes in my lap. He stretches up to look around me, fully notices me, and, bless him, drops back into his chair and turns off the television.

"I've seen that look. What's up?"

"The money we were going to pay Madeline? Why don't we invest it in the shop? Buy a percentage of it? She can draft the LLC or partnership papers or whatever they are, but the Printed Letter is in trouble, and we could help by buying part of it, at least until her condo sells."

"Is it a good investment?"

"Does it matter?"

We stare at each other in a silent conversation, one born of twenty years of marriage.

His face softens. "You can make a go of it, can't you?"

"I can, especially with Janet and Madeline. The three of us . . .

We can do it. It's an amazing place, Brian, and this community needs it. I need it. And it's different now. With all the social media Madeline's added, it's younger, without losing all that was good before. We've brought in a whole new clientele base, and her law work has done that too. People who never stepped foot in the shop are coming in, asking for recommendations, buying books, and joining book clubs. It was always important to Winsome, but it's changing Winsome now . . . It's changing me."

Brian doesn't speak for so long I think he is going to say no. It isn't like we have a ton of money, and it isn't like putting money into the bookshop is a sound and secure move. But it is the right move. I know it.

He rubs the top of his head, and for the first time I link it to Brittany's hair pulling. Like father like daughter.

I stand. "I didn't mean to upset you."

"Wait a minute." He gently pulls at my elbow so as not to disturb my tower of dishes. "Don't rush away. I was going to say part of me feels guilty about this. This money was earmarked for Madeline, and now it'll be used to take her store from her."

"It's not like that."

"She might think it is."

"I'll tell her that's not what we mean, but I don't want to lose it either, Brian, so it's worth the risk. We have fun there. We're sharing stories, sharing our lives, and . . . Nobody saw me." I feel the horrid pressure of tears fill my sinuses and will them not to come out, not to crack my voice. "I got lost and I'm getting found."

His face falls. I set the dishes on the floor and pull it close to mine.

"It's not your fault, don't look like that. It was mine. But Maddie saw me and she offered me a job, and Janet, for all her flaws, saw me, and Madeline too."

"I see you."

"We both got busy. It's hard moving. Everyone has to find their place and . . . Don't. You're a good man and I love you, but you have to admit we've been going through the motions. This thing with Brittany . . . I go over it day and night, and you do the same. I'm not sleeping and you're certainly not. Who knows if we could've prevented it, but it was the culmination of time, of slipping apart, and me not . . . I was the one who chose to be home, and yet I can't say I held them accountable enough or that I was present enough. And I'll never answer those questions because I can't go back, but I am waking up from wherever or whatever I let happen to me."

"I didn't know."

"Because I didn't tell you."

And as much as I want to share everything with him, there are places he still can't go. I have no way to tell him of the cacophonous emotions jangling within me—to feel wired for others yet irrelevant; to need community but equally to be unable to find one; that cleaning, cooking, and caring for my family is a pleasure and a blessing, but it isn't the same as feeling connected to them; to do things for others isn't the same as being with them; that watching television side by side isn't always "spending an evening together." And that each year I feel gravity pull at my face, my breasts, my soul, and I wonder . . . I wonder what within me is compelling enough that anyone would stay with me. God, Brian, my kids, even friends. But I say none of this and maybe I don't need to. I offer it up in prayer.

"Let's do it."

"Really?" The first tear falls.

"Yes."

One word. Brian says nothing more. He doesn't lay out a plan or terms or do anything I suspect he itches to do. This is what he does for a living, after all. He takes over businesses and turns them around. Yet by saying only that one word, we both understand the Printed Letter lies in my hands. This is my venture, and however I fashion it and whatever plans I make for it, he supports me.

The second tear falls as I recognize the blessing of twenty years of marriage and I realize the skills for this next step have been within me all along . . .

"Madeline mentioned the other day that she'd let Brittany work there, pay off her debt in kind. And we're going to expand our community outreach. Madeline and Greg Frankel have established really great relationships across Winsome. We have tremendous support from a whole area of the community that never entered the shop before. We need to build on that, perhaps with in-shop book clubs. And the cat. I'm going to bring in that cat that lives outside the back door, once I bathe it. What's more welcoming than a bookshop cat? And Janet is starting up her art again. She already sold two pieces we displayed in the window, and she's there at all hours, asked if she could have the late Thursday shift. She could be ready for a hosted event at the end of the summer . . . And I know . . . I know what to do about Maddie's smashed letters."

"What?"

"It's a surprise."

Brian laughs at my enthusiasm.

"And let's make that date night again we used to do years ago, and maybe we can get the kids to play a game on Sundays like we used to. Brittany will be gone to college in four months, and Matt is three years from walking out the door too . . . And it's spring. Let's take a weekend and go somewhere. Take a vacation with me, Brian, the two of us, and let's make love more, and go to the movies more. Remember when we used to do that?"

"Slow down." His eyes dance. "Yes. Yes, to all of it."

I feel a smile bloom—something lovely and true that age and gravity can't touch. "I should let you get back to your baseball."

"After all that? I don't think so." He hooks a hand around my neck and pulls me close.

Chapter 22

Janet

I barely sleep all night. I finally fall into a deep, dreamless slumber well after four a.m. My alarm chirps at six. I almost roll over, then I remember the day. There is no way I'm missing Seth at the train today and there is no way I'm not looking my best.

It takes time on a normal day to tame my hair. Today I want soft, silky perfection, and after thirty minutes with the dryer and a round brush, I'm almost ready to take scissors to every defiant curl. But not quite . . . A thin green sweater, capri pants, and a pair of ballet flats Seth and I bought downtown one day are laid out at the foot of my bed. I dress and head to the Daily Brew.

With two lattes in hand, I wait.

Seth's car pulls into the lot, and I watch as he walks toward the station. His hair is almost fully gray now. The last time I looked, really absorbed his presence, probably in his lawyer's office, it was a salt-and-pepper affair. The gray suits him. He looks distinguished. I glance down to my now shaking fingers. I feel old and brittle. Tired and scared in a way I haven't felt before—or haven't let myself admit to before.

I catch the instant he notices me. His step hitches then swings through, as if willpower alone drives him. I intercept him at the edge of the parking lot. We are close to the platform, but out of earshot of all the passengers waiting there.

I stretch one latte his direction. Our fingers interlace for the briefest touch before he pulls the cup away. He shifts it to his other hand and straightens the hand that collided with mine stiff and firm, ridding it of softness. I watch and feel certain it's an involuntary gesture. He's not a cruel man. He's a hurt man.

He stands there looking at the cup. He looks young, unsure, and it reminds me of when we first met. Twenty-two, both straight out of college, and living in crowded apartments in New York. We thought we were living the dream—maybe we were. He worked a hundred hours a week at an investment firm and I worked installations for an art buyer. And from the day we met, every moment was spent tangled up with each other. Then fall came and with it a transfer to the Chicago office. Only a month in, we thought the other was oxygen itself. Proposal. Marriage. Move. All before the leaves changed color.

"I'm sorry."

He tries to step past me. I shift in front of him.

"I'm not in the mood today, Janet. Is this something that would be best said through your lawyer?"

I cringe. He hasn't heard me. I feel it. He can only see what I was, or at least what I became in those last days.

"I don't need a lawyer for this." I take a breath and step inches closer. "I came to say I am sorry. I am sorry for my betrayal. I'm sorry I broke our vows, Seth."

His eyes flicker in question. He wants to scoff. He wants to ask *Is this a joke?* I stand still and I don't add or retract a single word. And I don't step away.

His confusion is palpable now as he clearly digs back into his memory. I'm not sure he knows about his eyes, but I do, and they give me hope. They soften from emerald to moss as he digs into our almost thirty years of marriage. He can't find it. He can't find a single time I apologized. I'd pout, leave the room, or play the victim until I was forgiven. But I never said I was sorry. I never felt I needed to.

He quits his search but stands on shaky ground. Seth, until those final days, was rarely unsure of himself. Finally he nods and takes a sip of coffee. "Thank you for this."

The train whistles as it approaches the station.

He steps around me and, without a look back, he's gone.

DAY TWO IS BRIGHTER. The sun rises earlier and earlier each day, and today I not only have sun, I have new flowers opening along my front walk. The tulips and daffodils are joined by bluebells, and I can tell my bearded iris isn't far behind.

I hop in my car, lattes already in hand. I made the coffee at home today and put his in his favorite to-go cup. He left it behind. He left everything behind.

Again I spot him before he spots me. His shoulders slump as if he's exhausted, and I almost turn away. I'm not trying to add to his burden. I'm trying to relieve it. A questioning voice pricks at me . . . *Are you trying to relieve his or yours?* The answer is both. I'm now honest enough to admit that.

I step toward him and hold out the dark-blue tumbler. He grasps it in his hand as if trying to determine its weight, its significance, and if it's something he wants to hold on to.

I talk before he can choose to let it go. "The Daily Brew is going to get expensive, so I'll bring you coffee from home." I throw out *home* carelessly and try not to flinch. I'm not trying to manipulate him either.

Nevertheless, he stiffens. "How many times are you planning to do this?"

"As many as it takes."

He takes a sip, watching me over the top of the cup, but he says nothing. When he lowers it, I begin.

"I'm sorry I didn't listen."

"What?" His brows join over his nose in confusion.

"I was more interested in what I had to say than in truly understanding what you felt. Again and again, I put my needs and my need to express them above yours."

He stares at me, and I figure it's a good time to go.

Without thinking, I lift onto my toes and kiss his cheek. Then I walk away and don't look back, berating myself the whole way. That kiss was *not* part of the plan.

DAY THREE IS WARM. Spring is truly in the air—and it's early. It usually envelops Chicago in late May or June, but color is bursting forth this last week in April with all the attending smells. The bearded iris opened this morning, and right next to it, the fritillary too. It's my favorite and I feel so thankful it's here and blooming today.

I lay awake again all night, questioning my motives and that impetuous kiss. I almost decide to end the apologies, but one look out my window and the fritillary changes my mind. Seth planted those for me. *It's a strong flower, an unusual flower. It reminds me of you.*

I hadn't appreciated those words years ago; I'd have rather been a beautiful, delicate flower than a "strong and unusual" one. But fritillary *is* unusual. It seems to grow upside down, with the delicate blooms facing down and the pointy leaves sticking up like the hair on Beaker, the Muppet lab assistant.

I watch the flower and soon my thankfulness is replaced with a new understanding. Life is so terribly subjective. I defined myself and never wondered how Seth viewed me or how that could change my world. Fritillary *is* strong, but it's actually quite beautiful too. And those blooms? Extremely delicate.

I fill my cup with coffee and grab another travel mug for Seth. His reaction has surprised me. I expected wary, but I also expected his eyes to remain hard and unyielding. Yet on day one they softened. But to be fair, we didn't divorce because he hated me. We divorced because I broke his heart. And, if I had to guess, he believed I hated him or had stopped loving him in some way. After all, why else would one ever have an affair?

But it was never so simple. I wanted him, but couldn't figure out how to reach him. I wanted something of myself back, but couldn't lay the responsibility of finding it upon myself. I also had no idea that the answers, the joy, and the assurances I required could never be found in Seth at all.

Father Luke is right. It takes three, the right three, to make a marriage work. But Madeline is still wrong. It doesn't always take two to blow a marriage up—one can do it quite thoroughly on her own.

"Good morning." Seth sees me first. I look down for a moment, and when I glance back up he is heading, with purpose, straight to me. "You don't need to keep meeting me here. What do you want, Janet? What do you expect to happen?"

"Nothing. I expect nothing from you." I hand him the cup. "I hope you'll listen, but I don't expect that. I simply hope you will."

With that, I begin. "I resented your success. I resented that I had to give everything up so you could achieve it."

He opens his mouth to speak, and I cut him off with a raised hand.

"I get the irony of cutting you off after yesterday when I said I need to listen more, but . . . I need to explain before you speak. I need to say that what I just said was wrong. It's the lie I chose to believe. You never asked me to give up anything. Every time I wanted to pursue art again, you encouraged me. It . . ." I took a deep breath. "It was easier to blame you than face the possibility that I might not have what it takes to make it. I'm sorry for that. I'm sorry I made you carry that for me."

"Janet . . ."

"Have a good day."

As I ran away I again berated myself. I had come for three days, and had a few more ahead of me, yet I didn't have the courage to hear what he might say in response. I didn't want his anger, but I also didn't want his pity, and I didn't want him to let me off the hook and end this work right as I was beginning it.

If I didn't see this through now, something told me I never would. And that might be the worst loss of all . . .

DAY FOUR IS POURING. An optimist might say Winsome is being made new by the rain. We're in the last days of April, and "April showers bring May flowers." But to me, the day feels dark and scary.

Seth finds me beneath the platform's awning.

"You should've stayed home on a day like this."

I smile and hand him the coffee. "I'm sorry for making you feel that what you did was never enough."

He opens his mouth to speak as the train's whistle blows.

People jostle around us and our moment is gone. He nods and lets the throng push him toward the waiting train.

I'M ALREADY TIRED OF the rain. I yearn for warm May days. I juggle the coffee and the umbrella and head to the parking lot. I'm late today, feeling old and worn, and he's already there.

My heart skips a beat. He's watching for me.

I step to him and hand him the coffee first, as I've done each morning. "I'm sorry I never played with you. You asked me over and over again to golf, run, walk, ski, fish, countless things we could do together, and then you stopped asking. I'm sorry I led you there."

"This is not necessary, Janet."

I can't interpret his words or his tone. His voice is soft and, to me, that means pity. I simply reply, "It is necessary." And I walk away.

Pity is more painful than anger.

Over the next several days, after buying a pack of paper to-go cups at the grocery, I meet him with an apology each morning. It feels like I'm coming through a valley. The first day felt so good. I felt strong. Then I went down a steep slope, and carrying this burden got heavy and it felt never-ending. The rain didn't help. Those days felt hard and oppressive. And I was affecting Seth—not in a good way. Circles darkened under his eyes, and his smooth gray hair of day one appeared tousled for many days afterward, as if he, too, was having trouble sleeping and couldn't sort himself out each morning.

But around day eight, the burden lifted. I was so grateful to feel the sun again on day ten, and to see Seth looking brighter on day eleven.

I apologized first for using the kids as weapons in fights; the next day for cutting him out of my emotional world and leaning on friends rather than on him. The great irony of those two is that, in the divorce, the kids and the friends all sided with him. The next days covered some instances of passive-aggressive behavior, which, by his expression, he remembered too.

And finally, today, I return to the affair. Yes, a lot led to it, but in that final moment, I could've stopped, run home, and changed our lives—for the better. I chose not to.

"I was a fool, Seth. I probably still am, but I'm learning. I'm learning about wisdom and faith and love, real love, and the proper ordering of love. I'm learning about humility and forgiveness. I'm learning about all the gifts I've been given and all the fruits I have failed to produce—one being patience."

He chuckles and I laugh with him. Patience has never been my strong suit.

"I won't bother you any more now. There's more to apologize for, and that's one thing I'm learning about this journey; there's a lot of grace, but only if you offer up the sins. But I won't burden you any more with them. All you need to know is that, without qualification, I am sorry."

I scrunch my face because this vulnerability isn't comfortable, and right now I'm close to tears. I don't want Seth to see me cry. That's all I did those last days before we signed the papers. I sobbed and behaved horribly, all to manipulate him into feeling guilty. To cry now feels no less manipulative. Maybe I'm being hard on myself, but I'm not sure. I'm not sure of anything anymore—but I am learning.

I reach up and kiss his cheek. I have ended the last three mornings with such a kiss and he hasn't stopped me. It feels right, like another aspect of vulnerability I need to endure and even welcome. This time I linger and breathe in the scent of him. He's still sandalwood, musk, and mint. I close my eyes to carry it with me.

I turn to walk away and feel a light, tentative touch on my arm. Had it been winter and I'd dressed in a wool sweater and a down coat, I never would have felt it. But I do and I turn.

"I wasn't perfect, J."

I close my eyes again. *J*. A very intimate nickname, only ever used by him, and one I always cherished because J meant "jewel" and only we two knew it.

"But you *were* a good husband. I didn't do this to make you feel guilty."

"I don't think that. Part of me has no idea what to think . . . I need more time."

"I understand." I turn away. I'm not forgiven—maybe I never will be.

"If I stop at Patisserie Amélie on my way home tonight, do you think I could bring a couple almond croissants to the house tomorrow morning? You have the espresso machine."

"Yes. I do. And yes."

I burst out the words so fast and loud two women stare.

Seth chuckles. I blush.

"What time?"

"Anytime you want." I rise up on my tiptoes and lower slowly in hopes he hasn't noticed I almost bounced like a kid.

"You like to sleep late on Saturdays." He smiles and I can barely breathe.

"You wake early."

"Compromise? I'll be there at eight thirty?"

I can only nod.

With that he walks toward the platform. This time . . .

He looks back.

TWO DAYS AFTER PASTRIES, I receive a text.

Three days after pastries, I receive an invitation.

Five days after pastries, I am holding Rosie in my arms. She is more beautiful, more perfect, than anything I could have imagined.

Two weeks after pastries, I face the most terrifying moment of my life: Seth arrives unannounced at my front door.

"Do you want to come in?"

"No."

"Then . . ." I stall, unsure what's happening. His face is tight, intense, and I fear I've hurt him again in some way.

He steps toward me and lifts his hands. I see them coming to my face as if they're moving through water. Time slows and crystallizes. I hear myself whisper "Don't" without thinking the word first.

"Don't kiss you?"

I nod. I shake my head.

His hands reach my face and hold me. "Which is it?"

"I only wanted you to forgive me if you could. I . . . It's not an exaggeration, Seth, when I say I won't want to survive you leaving again. And if you kiss me, I might start to believe that—"

"There you have it."

"Have what?"

"I forgive you. And this . . ."

He pulls me close and covers my lips with his. I feel myself resist and pull away. It feels like a wave receding from the shore, smooth and low.

Then I feel it. The instant I stop resisting and the wave stops receding. The momentum builds and rushes forward and, as I tip toward him, I am filled with light. It shoots out of me, consumes me. He forgives me. And right here, right now, is the perfect moment to be lost within.

Chapter 23

MADELINE

Eternity only reaches us in the present.

The more I think about it, the more I believe Luke is right. Janet too. I look back, and I cannot dwell in past mistakes. Maybe Aunt Maddie knew I would start there, but as I work through the last few books on her list, I will not dwell there. That is not how I tell my story.

I glance across the kitchen and watch as Janet struggles to open the wine, Claire sautés the asparagus, and my mom tosses the salad. I pull the chicken parmesan from the oven.

"When did you learn to cook that?" My mom closes her eyes and inhales. "It smells wonderful."

I blush, wondering if I should confess. Instead I take in her smile and again feel so glad I called her a few days ago . . .

"Please come visit. I'm sorry I've put you off for so long."

"That's all right, dear."

She wouldn't hear any more about it, though we both know I have pushed away for years, from her, from everyone.

So Mom arrived yesterday morning, and we enjoyed the first few hours of her visit together before I took her to the shop. We talked about everything—my ups and downs, the offer on my condo that arrived moments before her flight, my fears of losing everything to find none of it mattered, my fear of chasing something new and how scary yet exciting that felt—and there were some vague references about this new man who filled every heartbeat, but only tangentially. I still wasn't ready to verbalize Chris.

But, of course, the moment Mom walked into the Printed Letter and introduced herself, Claire and Janet spilled every detail.

I returned from buying our sandwiches to find Mom perched on my stool behind the customer service counter as if she'd been there all along. For a second, I felt out of place. Looking at the three of them, so near in age and experience, I felt like an outsider. I heard words like *daughters*, *parenting*, and *collagen*, and stepped away.

Janet noticed me and called out, "Get over here before Claire and I share all our secrets."

Gratitude, friendship, and something more ephemeral but real swept over me. *Love.*

Then Janet handed me a wrapped gift. "We've been waiting to give this to you. It was Claire's idea. Open it."

I pulled back the blue paper. Inside was a painting of the letter *A* framed in black wood matching the frames of Aunt Maddie's smashed letters. But it wasn't simply a letter *A*. The *A* was centered and bold, in beautiful sapphire ink, while words floated through it in an intricate design.

Anne of Green Gables, *Animal Farm*, *Alice in Wonderland*, *Atonement*, *All Quiet on the Western Front*, *And Then There Were None*, *Antony and Cleopatra* . . . The titles went on and on, crisscrossing and overlapping, in different sizes, shapes, and inks. It was stunning.

"We hoped these could replace the smashed letters. We can hang all twenty-six letters of the alphabet along the molding."

"I love it. I can't believe you're doing this."

"We can hang letters from your clients too, like your aunt had. You already have a few wonderful ones," Claire offered.

"No. This isn't my shop." At her expression, I changed my phrasing. "This isn't *only* my shop, and these are perfect. Thank you. Aunt Maddie would have loved them too."

They nodded their agreement, and the rest of the afternoon was spent introducing Mom to customers, new friends, and my life in Winsome. Mom even took over for Janet at the register when she stepped away to talk to Lisa Generis. We all held our breaths, watching. When the two women hugged, we collectively sighed—including Mom—and then they left together to grab a coffee.

JANET'S TSK-TSK PULLS ME from yesterday and confronts me with the chicken parmesan I just laid to rest on the stovetop.

"Are you really going to keep silent? Because I know this dish."

My blush grows hotter. "Okay, Chris made it, but I helped. While you were on the porch, he came in from the back." I look between three perfectly still women with their six unblinking eyes. "What? He offered."

"At least we know it will taste good." Janet winks and hands each of us a glass of wine. "To us."

Tonight we celebrate our new venture, and I'm so glad Mom is here to share in it.

Claire is the first to raise her glass, which feels right as she now owns 51 percent of the Printed Letter and manages it. Janet and I work full days, but we also do our own things right there during business hours, out of the shop's "Firm" and its "Studio." She has also hired some of my clients to work more regular hours. They are thrilled—we all are thrilled.

Janet raises her glass next to toast another new employee, though she wasn't invited tonight, and will not be legal to drink for another three years.

A couple weeks ago, Brittany started working with us three

afternoons a week, and she's thriving. New friends, different friends, drop by to say hi during her shifts, and often they purchase a water bottle, a tumbler, a card, or some cute trinket from Aunt Maddie's beloved bijoux selection. They leave a fun, positive energy behind them when they walk back out the front door. We feel it. The entire shop feels it. In fact, Mr. Drummond switched from visiting us in the mornings to coming late in the afternoons to be a part of it all. His long chats with Janet are over, as he now shows up and is equally likely to seek out Claire or simply enjoy the girls' banter as he helps some of our older customers find good books. "Gentle books," he calls them.

"*The Tower, the Zoo, and the Tortoise*? *Major Pettigrew's Last Stand*? *A Man Called Ove*?" Claire questioned his definition of gentle a couple days ago.

"Yes. Yes. And maybe. *Ove* is only for those in the right frame of mind," he told her.

"I agree, David, and I appreciate your sensitivity."

Looking around tonight, I realize our little family has grown. *Our little family. Our household.* It comes unbidden, and it feels right.

We put down our glasses after the third toast, this one to Janet and her slow steps toward Seth, and the fact that she's visited and held Rosie two times already this month and will again over a long Memorial Day weekend starting next Friday. I pick up the platter with the chicken and lead our small band into the dining room.

Something catches Janet's eye, and she walks across the living room to the bay window overlooking the porch and into the front yard.

"What is he still doing here?" She points to Chris digging along the driveway.

"He wants to finish the flower border before he starts at the hospital next week. That's why he was in the backyard earlier. He's helping me build a raised garden."

"What's this?" Mom follows us.

Janet doesn't miss a beat. "Madeline forced Chris back into medicine, so he's finishing up some planting while he still can." She tilts her head to the window.

Mom gets a gleam in her eye. Only two days and she has Janet's measure. Claire steps beside her. Her gaze follows and she isn't so sure; two lines form between her brows.

I feel the need to defend myself. "I did not do any of that."

Claire raises that one brow. And like Janet, I wonder how much time and money she spends perfecting that thing. Maybe someday I'll ask.

I point to it. "Put that down. I did no such thing. We've been talking about it, and he's ready. He was never going to stay out forever. He loves medicine; he only needed time. Does no one in your generation ever take a breather?"

"A time-out, you mean?" Claire lets one corner of her mouth tip up.

Not for the first time, I realize I underestimate her. Her sense of humor is dryer and often sharper than Janet's. She wields her humor and personality with more subtlety, and that makes them more powerful.

Janet reacts too. "No, we were too busy working to make sure your generation felt all self-assured and validated."

"Ha-ha."

Claire shakes her head and flicks a finger back to the table. "Let's eat. Chris's chicken is getting cold."

Janet doesn't move. Mom doesn't move. Both stare out the window. Janet has a soft, beautiful look on her face. Mom's look is filled with more wonder than certainty. I don't understand her expression, either of their expressions, and I find myself watching them rather than Chris. When no one follows Claire, she returns to us as well.

"What are you staring at?" I finally ask them both. I whisper it because only a whisper feels light enough not to destroy this moment.

"He adores you." Mom keeps her eyes on Chris.

I look out at him. He's so hard at work in the orange and purple evening light he has no idea four women are standing mesmerized by him.

"I adore him too," I answer.

Claire sighs. "He'll ask you to marry him."

"Don't you see?" Janet glances to the three of us, then back out the window. "That's what he's doing right now."

Janet loops an arm around me and squeezes—and we head to the table.

For the love of books . . .

(A note from the author)

Maddie's list to each woman was a love letter—so I'll let Janet, Claire, and Madeline keep them private. On the other hand, I can't help giving a peek behind the curtain . . .

If you wondered about some of the books referenced but not named in *The Printed Letter Bookshop*, here is a list of every book alluded to within these pages, though some only in a whisper. This accounting isn't an endorsement—I'll confess there are a couple I have not read. But if you choose to reach for one or two, or twenty . . . Enjoy!

In the Midst of Winter
Harry Potter
Anna Karenina
War and Peace
Dr. Zhivago
The Secret Garden
Flowers in the Attic
The Giver
Gathering Blue
The Hunger Games
The Lion, the Witch and the Wardrobe

The Lord of the Rings
The Girl on the Train
The Further Adventures of Ebenezer Scrooge
The Catcher in the Rye
The Outsiders
Lord of the Flies
Fahrenheit 451
The Brothers Karamazov
The Horse and His Boy
Unbroken
Seabiscuit
The Life of Pi
Persuasion
All the Light We Cannot See
Pride and Prejudice
The World of Winnie-the-Pooh
"To a Mouse"
A Christmas Carol
A Wrinkle in Time
Anne of Green Gables
Gone Girl
1984
Inkheart
Cinder
Slaughterhouse-Five
Becoming Mrs. Lewis
Diary of a Wimpy Kid
Buffalo Before Breakfast (Magic Tree House #18)
Magnolia Table
The Apothecary
A Year in Provence

Under the Tuscan Sun
House of Spies
The Paris Architect
The Joy Luck Club
Little Dorrit
A Man Called Ove
Nine Women, One Dress
Essentials of Classic Italian Cooking
The Four Loves
Killers of the Flower Moon
Crazy Rich Asians
The Screwtape Letters
Rebecca
Martha Stewart's Homekeeping Handbook
Sense and Sensibility
Number the Stars
The Awakening of Miss Prim
The Hiding Place
Church of Spies: The Pope's Secret War Against Hitler
Animal Farm
Alice in Wonderland
All Quiet on the Western Front
And Then There Were None
Antony and Cleopatra
The Tower, the Zoo, and the Tortoise
Major Pettigrew's Last Stand

Acknowledgments

I had so much fun with this story. It felt as if, in writing about friends, I got to spend time with friends. Unfortunately, while writing, I'll admit that most of that was in my head, and I now owe many of you long-overdue phone calls and lazy lunches.

But for now, here are my thanks! Elizabeth, I'm forever grateful for your insight into the world of books, bookstores, and book buying and, of course, for being my first reader. Thanks also to the incomparable women at the Lake Forest Book Store, who not only let me into the back room but who set a high standard for Madeline, Claire, and Janet. You all always know the perfect book and share it with a smile. Kristy and Sarah, I'm not sure I'd get through a writing day without your prayers and your texts. Becky and Suzanne, you're in that camp too. Thank you so much for your daily support in all my writing endeavors.

Endless gratitude also goes to my agent, Claudia Cross, and to Amanda Bostic, Jocelyn Bailey, LB Norton, and Jodi Hughes for . . . well, everything; Kristen Ingebretson and HCCP's design team; Paul Fisher, Allison Carter, and Matt Bray for all your marketing support; Becky Monds, Laura Wheeler, Kim Carlton, and Savannah Summers; and the sales team for championing my stories.

Mason, Matthew, Elizabeth, and Mary Margaret always deserve

my endless thanks. Thanks for picking up so much that I drop and encouraging me at every step, even when I forget dinner.

Last, but never least . . . Thank *you*. Thank you to the readers, bloggers, reviewers, and now friends who generously read my stories, trust me with your hearts and time, and share me with your friends! Thank you for joining me and reaching out and meeting me on social media or in person.

I'm beyond grateful to welcome you to Winsome and hope we'll meet there again.

Discussion Questions

1. The author begins the story with three different verb tenses. What did she intend to convey with each choice? Did each character fit this portrayal for her voice and her story?
2. Janet contends, "The past holds no hope," and chooses not to dwell there. How do her feelings change? Later she states, "Not looking to the past is not the same as living in the present." What does she mean?
3. Aunt Maddie and her letters exert an influence on the three women. The author calls out another character who also exerts power over this story despite not being in a single scene. Contrast Aunt Maddie's influence with Rebecca's from Daphne du Maurier's *Rebecca*. Is it true, as Madeline's mother states, that "even dead and gone, a person or an event can affect lives for good or for bad"?
4. Perspective is an important theme in *The Printed Letter Bookshop*. How does Madeline's perspective change? Janet's? Claire's? How much does each misjudge in the beginning? How clearly does each see in the end?
5. "For the present is the point at which time touches eternity." This quote by C. S. Lewis precedes the story and is alluded to by Chris and Madeline. What does it mean? How is it revealed within the story?

6. Janet asks at one point, "What is a heroine?" What are your thoughts about characters, and what constitutes a hero or heroine?
7. How did you feel about Claire switching from third person to first? What drove her to reclaim her voice? How easy it is for someone to lose his or her voice?
8. Awakening is another theme within each woman's story. Discuss the "trail of bread crumbs" Maddie left for each.
9. Janet confesses that she has never told Seth she was sorry. Do you know people like that? How easy or hard would it be to live by that rule? How easy or difficult is it to say you're sorry to someone you've hurt?
10. Claire says she has to "appropriate the stories, make them my own, find my own voice, and learn." Greg Frankel lists a series of books to help teenagers at risk. What have fiction stories taught you? Do they hold as much power as Claire and Greg believe? Can fiction truly affect change in our lives?
11. Claire talks about the order of love. Do you agree or disagree that love can be "wrongly ordered" or cause harm rather than bring life? Do you think she was too hard on herself regarding Brittany's attitude and actions?
12. Madeline tells Chris, "Until you know the truth, you shouldn't judge people." Does she follow her own edict? If she does at the end, when did she begin? Who helped her along the way?
13. Would you like to visit the women of Winsome again?

Visit Katherine's website for more questions and information for book clubs.
KatherineReay.com

Don't miss these other stories from Katherine Reay!

"Katherine Reay is a remarkable author who has created her own sub-genre, wrapping classic fiction around contemporary stories. Her writing is flawless and smooth, her storytelling meaningful and poignant."

—Debbie Macomber, #1 *New York Times* bestselling author

Thomas Nelson
Since 1798

Available in print, e-book, and audio!

About the Author

Katherine Reay is a national bestselling and award-winning author who has enjoyed a lifelong affair with books. She publishes both fiction and nonfiction, and her writing can also be found in magazines and blogs. Katherine holds a BA and MS from Northwestern University. She currently writes full-time and lives outside Chicago, Illinois, with her husband and three children.

KatherineReay.com
Instagram: katherinereay
Facebook: katherinereaybooks
Twitter: @Katherine_Reay